GEORGE SIROIS

EVER
UPWARD

⚔ PART TWO IN THE EXCELSIOR JOURNEY ⚔

The characters and events portrayed in this book are products of the author's imagination and are used fictitiously. Any similarity to real persons, living or dead, is coincidental and not intended by the author.

Printed by Aelurus Publishing, June 2018

Cover design by Molly Phipps

ISBN 13: 978-1-912775-01-9

www.aeluruspublishing.com

To Cheryl, who gave the two of us
more than I could ever imagine

And

To Scarlett Grace,
more than I could ever imagine

"Jesus went out as usual to the Mount of Olives, knelt down and prayed, 'Father, if you are willing, take this cup from me; yet not my will, but yours be done.' An angel from heaven appeared to him and strengthened him. And being in anguish, he prayed more earnestly, and his sweat was like drops of blood falling to the ground..."

-- Luke 22:39, 41-44

"Why did I have to be the Chosen One?"

-- Rodimus Prime

CHAPTER ONE

In the beginning, there was only an idea. That idea became a reality. And then, from that reality, came the planet Denab IV. It wasn't perfect, but it was good, and it was worth fighting for, as were those who called it home.

Excelsior recalled this mantra while stumbling through the dimly-lit Caverns of Yelsew. He started speaking it out loud, but stopped after the first line and coughed on the stifling hot air in his lungs. The cold dust crunched under his boots. He couldn't believe this was his people's home for so long. Now, that was no longer the case. The eternal guardian of Denab IV accomplished his mission. His beloved Denarians were free, and they left this underground labyrinth behind. Excelsior smiled when he recalled their victory over the oppressive Krunation Empire.

The smile dropped when he heard the voices filled with fear and panic from outside.

"Help us! Please help us!"

He broke into a run and his pulse quickened as he emerged from the caverns. He expected sunlight awaiting him, but instead, thick black clouds covered the horizon.

Black ash filled the air and blew across the scorched ground. Where there were once trees, now there were collapsing hunks of burning wood. A ball of pure white energy hung over the majestic mountain known as Klierra Peak.

Excelsior gasped at the agony-filled moans of Denarian men and women. Tears filled his eyes and dripped down his face while he looked at the people he swore to protect laying at his feet. He squeezed his sword, looking for a Krunation—any Krunation—to tear apart.

How dare they do this to his people.

How dare they do this to Denab IV.

How dare they do this to him.

"Ex...cel...sior..."

He followed the weak voice and saw someone leaning back against a large rock slab. It was an old white-haired man wearing a white and gold ceremonial robe. Along the fabric were ancient Denarian hieroglyphics meaning "Ever Upward." He struggled to breathe while thick red blood leaked from the corner of his mouth.

Excelsior forced the name from his mouth. "Acerus?"

It was him, the High Elder. The same man who first encountered Excelsior when he was still in his ethereal form. The same man who kept his beloved Denarians from succumbing to the will of the Krunation Empire. He was a living pillar of strength, and here he was, toppled, defeated, dying.

Acerus looked up at Excelsior and pointed a trembling finger at him. "You did this."

"No," Excelsior said, shaking his head.

Acerus continued to point at him, his voice as unstable as his hand. "You... did... this... Matthew."

And from the ball of energy above Klierra Peak came the humming noise once again. Excelsior grabbed his head and squeezed his eyes shut. "No!" he yelled.

After a long moment, the humming subsided, but another noise took its place.

A voice.

A hiss.

"Yesssssss."

"No!"

Excelsior's eyes snapped open, and he fought to catch his breath. He looked up, expecting to see the suffocating gray clouds from his dreams. But instead, there was a clear black sky with the stars surrounding him. The stillness was soothing, almost rejuvenating, and Excelsior's breathing slowed and stabilized.

It took the demigod several seconds to remember he wasn't lying down on the ground. He was standing up, his arms outstretched. He flexed his feet, expecting to feel some kind of surface beneath them, but he felt nothing. He looked down and realized he was floating in the stratosphere of the planet Denab IV.

"Whoa," was the only thing escaping his lips, while one question after another flooded his mind. How did he get up here? Why was he so far away from his fellow Denarians? What was he supposed to do while he was here? Despite being such a safe distance from the carnage he saw in his head, Excelsior still couldn't shake it. The scent of his Denarians' ashy remains hung in his nose.

"That didn't happen, did it?" he whispered.

Excelsior expected an answer from within confirming it was a dream. It had to be one, not another flashback like the ones he experienced on Earth. There, he was Matthew Peters, a high school student who overachieved at underachieving. He devoted all his time to a webcomic instead of his studies, a webcomic about a certain character from a certain faraway planet. He had no idea the stories were a manifestation of Excelsior's memories.

But that was another time, in a far different place. Excelsior was no longer a figment of Matthew's imagination. Once again, he was a god made human through a worthy host. And after returning home, Excelsior and his Denarians defeated Emperor Nocterar and the Krunation Empire.

But he still felt incomplete, as though he needed to reconnect with this planet he created so long ago. After several days of celebration, Excelsior left his people and walked to Klierra Peak. He relaxed his mind and allowed the living force within to control him like a puppet on strings. He floated past the mountaintop, stretched out his arms, closed his eyes… and passed out from the altitude.

Excelsior asked himself, "How long have I been up here?" Did it work to be this high up? Could he feel a difference? He felt the wind whipping around him and it prompted another question: shouldn't he be cold? He looked down at his flexible and durable suit of armor—metallic-colored shirt and pants, silver and blue breastplate, black gloves, matching boots—and concluded it wasn't just comfortable; it did a great job trapping heat.

The demigod took one more deep breath and closed his eyes again. He purged himself of any negative thoughts, especially the nightmare that almost shattered his concentration. The darkness lifted, and he felt himself plummeting, then twisting and turning like he was on the universe's largest roller coaster. The different land masses so far away from Edenaria came into focus, and Excelsior realized he already knew them all.

There was Axsella, one large steel military stronghold stretching across the entire land. A long runway led to a hangar, which kept hundreds of small single-manned planes. An adjacent opening led to a beach where over a dozen boats of various shapes and sizes were at the ready. An open common area was in the middle of the complex. In its center was a large statue of two Denarians standing back-to-back.

Excelsior identified one of the two as Elder Klierra—known on Earth as Dr. Katherine Sierra. The other subject was one Excelsior never saw in person, but he knew without a doubt who it was. Valertus. Klierra's son, the first Denarian to join with Excelsior's lifeforce.

His heart soaring with pride, Excelsior moved on and followed his nose to Collagra. Lush multi-colored plant life dominated more than half of the land. Beyond that were four various fields separated by a large processing center.

"This must have been Grannik's tribe," he deduced, remembering the large Denarian telling him of the skilled hunters and farmers on his land. Excelsior inhaled the aromas of the grown and prepared foods, and his mouth watered. He tried some of the native Denarian food at the celebration in Edenaria, and it was the best he ever tasted. He couldn't imagine how amazing it must taste when it was fresh.

Before he could get any closer, Excelsior shot back into the sky. He zoomed past Collagra and floated over Nelleram. He gasped when he saw so many eclectic-looking homes of various shapes, sizes, and colors. They were beautiful, so unlike anything Matthew Peters ever saw on Earth. This was the exact opposite of the cookie-cutter houses of suburbia. Creativity was everywhere, so tangible Excelsior could reach out and touch it.

He also noticed the villages weren't well populated. Maybe some Denarians were still hiding. Maybe they were still celebrating on Edenaria. Or…

He choked back the feeling of dread. Maybe there weren't many from Nelleram left alive to come home. Were they slaughtered, like the mother and father of his friend Zorribis?

Excelsior passed over a flat clearing of land, watching a Denarian man and woman kneel and run their hands on the thin green grass. He flew past them, leaving a faint gust of wind left in his wake. He felt like an intruder on a deep conversation because the woman was crying and yelling something indecipherable. He flew past them, leaving a faint gust of wind in his wake.

Who were those Denarians? Why was that woman crying? Excelsior pushed past those questions and continued on with his journey. He swept past the smaller land mass he knew was Krephthera. He knew of this land's turbulent history and decided not to focus on it now. Besides, a much more inviting land was waiting for him with open arms.

Rellata. Excelsior passed over lush, soft green grass surrounding large columned structures. It all looked so inviting, he wanted to drop to the ground, lie on his back, and read a book. Denarian men, women, and children were sitting in the grass in various conversations. None of them seemed like they had a care in the world.

Again, he had to ask, how long was he up there?

Excelsior saw a giant outdoors amphitheatre where thousands of Denarians sat and listened. An older man was addressing them while giving broad gestures with his arms to the sky. He smiled when he identified the man as one of the Elders.

"Quinterus," he exclaimed. He didn't know him very well, but felt great affection for his son, Radifen. In both life and death, they made their species proud, as did Grannik, Karini, and Zorribis, the lone survivor of the group sent to Earth.

Maybe that was the story Quinterus told the crowd, how Radifen fought and gave his life so Denab IV's savior could return. Yes, of course, Excelsior convinced himself, since he couldn't hear what the Elder was saying. He felt another whooshing sensation, as though he were on another roller coaster. Only this one wasn't dropping; it was going up and up and up…

….Excelsior's eyes snapped open, and his consciousness rejoined his body in Denab IV's stratosphere.

"I did it!" he yelled out to the heavens. In a matter of seconds, Excelsior not only saw each land mass of

Denab IV; he could identify them and provide a detailed description. He was positive Valertus and Semminex never felt this connected.

Man, if only he was able to do this while he was still working on the webcomic.

His mind flooded with infinite possibilities, Excelsior descended from the stratosphere. His feet touched the rocky surface of Klierra Peak. He looked out at Edenaria with a new clarity he never thought possible. The village. The Leap of Faith. The rocky terrains. The soft fields. The rivers and surrounding oceans.

"So beautiful," he said as the wind blew in his face. He could see everything in a whole new light, and he could hear something just as new. A soft chorus of voices filled his ears—men, women, and children—but he couldn't decipher what they were saying.

Excelsior squeezed his eyes shut and concentrated harder. It was a chore to keep himself relaxed, but after several minutes, he could hear them all loud and clear. All at once.

And they were screaming.

The sudden burst startled Excelsior. The piercing noise intensified, and once it found his ears, it wasn't letting go. Excelsior removed his helmet and dropped it at his feet, revealing the short brown hair and youthful face of Matthew Peters. He slapped his hands over his ears and whispered, "Please stop." But it only grew louder. Excelsior felt his head tighten, his lungs collapse, his joints stiffen.

He stumbled around the top of Klierra Peak, and one last combined burst of physical and auditory agony made his knees buckle.

He fell, leaving his helmet behind.

The screaming finally faded, but not for the reason Excelsior preferred. He was falling from the highest point on Denab IV, and the unforgiving ground was getting closer.

Excelsior knew only one course of action. Once again, despite the pain he felt earlier, he closed his eyes and let go. This time, he wasn't greeted with pain, but peace. One image of Denab IV after another flashed before his eyes. The mountains. The valleys. The caverns. The bodies of water. The Leap of Faith. The various Denarian clans. The Elders watching over them.

And then, a new image entered his mind, one that made him smile while he kept his eyes shut. The image came into focus and smiled back at Excelsior. It was an older man with dark hair threaded with gray and brown eyes sporting crow's feet. He was standing in the middle of a bedroom and giving an enthusiastic fist pump.

"I think we're on to something, Matty!" the man yelled.

Jason. Jason Peters. Matthew's uncle.

Excelsior opened his eyes. He was still in the air, but everything was slowing down and he wasn't in freefall anymore. He looked at himself, at his hands and arms, and saw he had the same glow covering his body as when he levitated to Klierra Peak. Did thinking of Jason provide some missing piece he needed to defy the planet's gravity? Whatever it was, it worked, and Excelsior didn't bother to question it. He tilted his body upwards and, as though he were held in the palm of a giant hand, pushed himself up and out, flying over the land of Edenaria.

Despite the distance from the land below, he never felt closer to it. He flew toward the river and, rejoicing in the serenity he now felt, dipped his hand into the cool and clear water. He cupped his hand, allowing water to fill it, drank from it, and smiled.

He was home.

He drifted above a forest near the river when one particular tree caught his eye. It was larger than the others surrounding it, but darker. He flew closer to examine it and gasped.

This tree was dead. It remained upright, but its trunk was burnt black and its branches were little more than twigs flapping in the breeze. Excelsior flew closer, and suddenly he could hear traces of the screaming he heard while standing on the top of Klierra Peak. But instead of what seemed like hundreds of voices crying out as one, there were only two coming from this tree. Two children. Denarian children. Excelsior's eyes filled with tears. He lowered himself to the ground and walked toward the trunk of the destroyed tree. "What happened to you?" he asked out loud while pressing his hand against the blackened trunk.

Suddenly, a bright burst of light illuminated the darkness in Excelsior's mind. He squeezed his eyes shut and saw three Denarian children, two girls and one boy, running from a small pack of soldiers. Excelsior recognized the bald heads, scaly skin, and black body armor of the Krunations.

Excelsior watched the children reach the tree, grab hold of the closest branch, and begin to climb. The

Krunations taunted them, yelling, "There is nowhere for you to go, you little Denarian scum!"

"You killed our mother!" the younger of the two girls yelled back.

"And you are about to join her," one of the soldiers replied. He aimed his blaster and fired, but the laser bolt bounced off the tree and struck the soldier in the chest. He collapsed in a heap, smoke rising from his wound.

"How many times must you keep making the same mistake?"

A female Krunation strode toward the tree. She wore tight, black leather-like material, complete with an open full-length coat and boots with thick soles. A thin layer of black hair was on her head, and her scaly face carried a look of utter contempt. Instead of carrying a blaster rifle, she held a small canister filled with a thick orange liquid. She shook it and scolded her soldiers while walking around the tree.

"The Sancterrum trees are protected," she said. "They have always been, so their life cycles can complete without interruption."

"We apologize, General Hodera," one soldier said with his head lowered.

"And now, to you three." Hodera turned her attention back to the children in the tree.

"We know you will need nourishment soon, and this particular tree you climbed does not supply any. So you will have to come down from there, and we will be waiting. But if only the older girl surrenders herself to us, then we will leave."

"No, Arinna," the boy cried out.

"Yes, Arinna," Hodera yelled back. "You can end their suffering by giving yourself to us right now."

Arinna looked to be no more than twelve Earth years in age. Her long black hair hung over her bare shoulders. Her blue shirt had several small tears, and her pants were covered with dirt. She looked up at her brother and sister, then back down at Hodera and the Krunations, and started to climb down.

"No! Stay here. Not with them," the other girl called out to her.

"I will be fine," Arinna said. "Get to safety as soon as they leave."

"Wise choice, my dear," Hodera said. Once the girl was close enough, a soldier quickly grabbed Arinna and hoisted her over his shoulder.

Hodera stared into Arinna's eyes. "You have a magnificent gift, young one. And we look forward to serving our master with this gift." Hodera continued shaking the container in her hand while speaking, the top of it aimed at the tree. The liquid began to bubble.

"What is that?" Arinna asked.

"Something we need to test." Hodera opened the canister. The liquid splattered all over the trunk, and a Krunation soldier fired a blast from his rifle. The liquid ignited, setting the tree ablaze.

"No!" Arinna yelled. "You said you would leave them alone."

"I said we would leave," Hodera replied. "And now we are leaving."

The Krunations hurried away and Arinna cried out to her brother and sister, who screamed as the fire approached them.

Excelsior jerked his hand away from the tree, trembling, tears rolled down his face. Those children. That girl.

He looked down at his hand, which was covered in black soot. This poor tree.

He continued to look down at his hand. There was nothing he could do for the children, and he had no idea of the girl's fate, but maybe...

Excelsior pressed his hand back on the trunk and closed his eyes. A great gust of cooling wind surrounded him, and where his fingers felt soft decay, they now felt thick bark that once covered this Sancterrum tree. He heard the weak branches growing and snapping into place.

The wind encircling Excelsior died down. He opened his eyes and took several steps back. The Sancterrum tree was now completely reformed, standing tall and proud as though it were never harmed.

He struggled to come up with the right words to perfectly capture what he was feeling, but could only run his fingers through his hair in disbelief as he said, "Wow."

But the sudden burst of satisfaction gave way to sadness as the children's screams echoed in his mind. His shoulders slumped, his arms dropped to his sides. "I'm so sorry. I'm sorry I wasn't here."

"But now you are here, Matthew."

Excelsior gasped and quickly turned around, looking for the female voice he heard. He knew that voice. Could it really be her?

"Klierra?" Excelsior called out. "Elder Klierra? Where are you?"

"I will always be with you, Matthew," Klierra's voice echoed in his head. "I always will be, just as you and Excelsior will always be one. And it is your responsibility to complete his mission."

Mission? What else was there? Did she see what he did with the tree? Valertus never did anything like that, at least as far as he could remember.

"What else is there, Elder Klierra?" Excelsior asked. No response. Once again, he was alone. But if one Elder won't answer his questions, maybe another will.

"Acerus."

Excelsior touched the bark of the reinvigorated tree one more time. He relaxed his mind and his feet left the ground, his body angling toward the main village of Edenaria. The gust of wind accompanying him whipped through the branches of the tree, and one large, dry leaf snapped off the branch and fell to the ground. Then another. And another.

CHAPTER TWO

"**G**eneral?"

The intrusive voice of the Krunation escort interrupted Hodera's restful sleep. Until now, the waves crashing against the small silver boat carrying her and two escorts were soothing enough to lull her into a state of relaxation. She did not know how much time had passed, nor did she care. She opened her eyes, looked around, and saw they were not yet at their destination. Her stare at the Krunation carried with it a look of pure contempt.

"We are approaching Krephthera," the escort said.

Hodera could have grabbed him by the throat and demanded not to be spoken to until after they reached land. But she surprised even herself when she replied in a calm and even tone. "Thank you." She turned her head to her right, her cue of dismissal to the Krunation.

The soft tone must have surprised the Krunation as well, because after several seconds, Hodera turned back and saw he was still standing there. Maybe he wasn't hearing properly.

"Thank you," she said again, not bothering to add his name since she didn't know it, nor the name of the other Krunation accompanying him. But the escort must have absorbed her words this time, because he gave a soft exhale, returned to the front of the boat, and sat down beside his fellow Krunation soldier.

Behind the hood covering her head, General Hodera's eyes narrowed and her jaw clenched. Krephthera. Hearing the name of this place set her on edge, but her escorts seemed to be much more enthusiastic to be there. Both volunteered for this voyage to the homeland of the Krunation Empire. Where a golden palace was built with the blood and sweat of Denarian slaves for the benefit of all who called this island home. Where they were nurtured, toughened up, properly educated, and then prepared to complete the unfinished goals of their god at any cost.

"By Tornatrax, where is it? No sign of it at all!"

The shocked cry from one of Hodera's escorts brought her back to the present. When the island drifted into view, she stifled a laugh. The golden palace was completely gone, replaced by the flat swamplands occupying nearly all of Krephthera.

So the rumors were true. How wonderful, she thought. She couldn't wait to see the faces of the Matera now that their precious extravagance was taken from them.

The boat touched land, and two Krunation females smaller in size and build than the average warriors stood at the edge of the land, each holding a plank the size and width matching the boat. Beside them was a small, gray hovercraft with two seats, one behind the other. Two females positioned the plank on the edge of the arriving boat, and Hodera's two escorts leapt from their seats and stepped into the water. They connected two strong black tethers to each side of it, keeping it in place. The Krunations in charge of the plank stepped away from the boat. Their boots made loud squishing noises on the wet land as they dropped to one knee.

The little one on the left of the plank said in a voice matching her muscle tone, "Right this way, Gener—" Hodera stood and the female's voice changed, now dripping with contempt. "Oh. You."

The two Krunations immediately stood and, without saying another word, walked to their vehicle. It hovered above the ground and raced back into the swamp.

Servants. The lowest of the lows. So low, they might as well trade in their scales for smooth skin and swear their allegiance to the Denarians. Especially considering their disrespect toward her, but then again, this was Krephthera. Disrespecting General Hodera may as well be the law of the land.

The sound of Hodera's thick black boots striking the plank echoed through the sticky, humid air. She stepped off the boat, her shoulders back and her face still covered by the hood. The water-logged ground felt soft under her boots, but it was hard enough to allow her to walk with a quick pace. Her escorts did their best to keep up with a half-jog, half-walk.

The air grew thicker with each passing step and Hodera took a deep breath, filling her lungs with humidity. She heard the shuffling of feet to her left and turned toward the noise. Three Krunation females with the same scrawny build and size as the two who met their boat stood by a series of gray objects resembling long, pointed rocks coming up to their knees

Hodera gritted her teeth when a Krunation glanced at her. She knew what the waste of evolution was doing, what they were all doing. These females were there to ensure what was inside those objects was getting the proper amount of light and water to become the next breed of Krunation warriors. They were keeping their temperatures regulated and providing the only consistent cool air on the island. They offered protection, maybe even love.

Hodera knew nothing of protection or love. Heat and isolation were the only memories from her first years of life. The only cries heard when she hatched were her own. Whatever lives were incubating in there, they would have so many opportunities, and it sickened her to see those casings getting fawned over like they were the riches upon which this planet was founded.

She looked over her shoulder at the servants. "What happened to your precious palace?" The servants bared their teeth at her in anger.

Hodera's walk evolved into a strut, and her escorts increased their pace so they were now several steps ahead. She heard one ask, "Do you think this will ever again look like it did when we were hatchlings?"

"I wish I could say," the other answered.

Hodera smirked under her hood. They couldn't possibly be sad about the current state of Krephthera, could they?

"What is that?"

One of her escorts pointed to the sky. A sudden whooshing sound from a distance prompted both Hodera and the other escort to look up. Something was descending from above the stratosphere.

"Do you think it is—"

"Excelsior," Hodera said. "So he has been watching over us all this time. Just as he said."

"He?"

"Never mind," Hodera said, walking on through the swamps.

Each step prompted more scornful looks from Krunation servants doing their assigned duties, but Hodera stopped paying attention to them. Her gaze alternated between what lay ahead of them and the Denarian savior flying above them. Where could he be going next?

The three arrived at a patch of dry land surrounded by deep waters. Hodera let out a quiet chuckle, and the two escorts gasped at what was in front of them. Sitting on top of the land was a tall, unstable, and completely unimpressive-looking metallic structure, made of four tall steel beams connected to each corner of a thick orange glass. Sunlight shone through the glass, giving a colorful glow in the central area, but it would have been more spectacular if anyone bothered to clean the accumulating algae.

One of the escorts pointed at the pathetic attempt at a structure and said to his partner, "This is why the Denarians do this kind of work."

The sudden sound of splashing caught Hodera's attention, and she looked down to see small, gray fish below the surface. They were swimming so violently, they seemed to be fleeing from something. But what?

Hodera's eyes widened when she saw the answer to her question. The fish trying to escape were no larger than her fist, but the amphibious creature revealing itself as their pursuer was the size of the rest of her arm and chest. She smiled as the creature launched itself from below, causing water to spray everywhere. It opened its wide mouth and chewed into the fleeing fish, taking a moment to revel in catching and destroying its preys before sinking back into the water.

"Perhaps the wrong creatures were given the gift of evolution," Hodera said to her escorts.

Another creature popped out of the water, baring its teeth for all to see. But it was met with a harpoon penetrating its body and pulling it from the water. Hodera watched in horror as one of the smaller servants reeled in the creature, then used her free hand to squeeze the top of its head until it crunched.

"How dare you," Hodera shouted to the servant. "Something as beautiful as this deserves more than attention for sport!"

"That is not meant for sport." An older Krunation female with flaking, scaly skin walked to Hodera. She had an elongated neck, narrow eyes, and a tiny pointed nose. The sunlight reflected off the silver dress draping over her skeletal frame. "Our food production is at an all-time low. That will provide meals for the beloved Matera."

"Beloved Matera," Hodera scoffed. "Those words could never sound natural together. Not even when coming from the mouth of a Kitera."

"Not natural to you," the Kitera said. "But we forgive you for your ignorance."

"'We?'" Hodera asked. "You speak for the Matera as though you are their equal. They are responsible for the Krunations' continued existence on this planet," she said while pointing to the raised area ahead. "You are responsible for--"

"You know nothing of what I do," the Kitera cut her off. "Now state your business."

"My business is none of yours," Hodera spit back. "I wish to address the Matera themselves, not the hangers-on waiting for them to die so they can succeed them."

The Kitera held up a bony finger. "You watch your ungrateful tone, General."

"I should be grateful?" Hodera laughed. "For being left to die as a hatchling? They have only made me who I am, which is the extent of my gratitude to them." She surveyed the flat swamplands for a moment. "Although maybe I should be grateful to Excelsior for wiping your 'glorious' palace from existence. I only wish I was here to see your reaction."

The Kitera clutched the collar of her silver gown and said, "Even without the palace, I have more than you will ever know."

Hodera stepped up to the Kitera and hissed, "Do you? Then tell me your name."

The long silence hung in the air with the humidity. Hodera motioned to her escorts to follow her and pushed past the useless Kitera. She heard the soft voice of a young Krunation female behind her. "Is that General Hodera?"

"She is undeserving of such a title, little one," the Kitera answered. "Now rejoin your fellow Mynera students... and tell me where that casing has gone!"

Hodera turned around and followed where the Kitera was pointing. To her right, where there were normally two casings being cared for, there was only one. To the left of the space was a Krunation female attendant rotating a casing, her hands shaking so hard, the hatchling-to-be vibrated on its platform. There was little room in the space for the female's feet as they were almost on top of each other.

"Sivtra!"

The Kitera's sudden shout caused the nervous female to slip on the platform. She let out a panicked scream as her left leg flailed, and her hands reached for the casing. Suddenly, the light next to the young female began to bend, and a Krunation casing appeared, as did a diminutive Krunation male with a slim build. His left hand pressed against the casing tall enough to reach his puny chest. His right hand reached toward the female Krunation, and he grabbed her arm before she could fall. Assisted by the Krunation male keeping her in place, the female steadied the casing on the platform and turned to her colleague. "Thank you," she said. He nodded.

"Sivtra, where were you?" the Kitera said.

"I was... I was right here," Sivtra said, his voice as timid as his appearance.

The Kitera pointed to an empty space on the opposite wall. "Take that casing over there. Now."

Sivtra released his grip on the female Krunation, picked up the casing from the platform, and walked into the water. He and the casing faded from sight.

The Kitera shook her head as Sivtra emerged from the opposite side. "Useless," she said, then shooed the Mynera student away.

Once the Kitera and Mynera were out of sight, Hodera turned her attention back toward the small Krunation setting the casing in place on the opposite wall as instructed. He turned toward the general, stood up straight, and held up his right fist. His face held deadly sincerity.

"Not as useless as you may think, Kitera," Hodera whispered to herself as she nodded to Sivtra, then walked on with her two escorts.

The General stopped in front of a patch of dry land separated from the walkway. Four slim-figured Krunations sat in silver chairs positioned in a circle. They wore matching flowing red and gold gowns covering their entire bodies except for their scaly arms and bald heads. Hodera could see their gowns were wrinkled and faded. Their seats were arranged in a pentagonal shape, with the Krunation sitting at the tip keeping her back to Hodera.

The seat in the back left position was empty.

Hodera studied the faces and saw there may have been some attempt in the past to make them look beautiful and youthful, but that was a long time ago. Now, they wore visible frown lines and bags under their eyes. Their scaly skin was flaking, and Hodera saw flecks of it strewn on the ground.

"General Hodera is requesting permission to address the Matera," one of Hodera's escorts announced. Hodera scowled at him for mentioning her by name.

"The Matera do not wish to be disturbed," the four Krunations answered as one.

"Your general does not care," Hodera said. "I request an update on the latest potential warriors."

"You have no place here," they called back, still keeping their eyes on each other. "You have others under your command more than adequate to request the update."

"You mean, others that are not deformed freaks?" Hodera asked, anger lacing her voice. She reached for the hood over her face.

The collective voice of the Matera spoke with a hint of panic. "Do not remove your hood!"

Hodera saw all four remaining members of the Matera recoil as she revealed her head and smiled with satisfaction. "Why are you all so afraid of your fellow Krunation?" she asked, her voice mocking. "Do I remind you of something in particular? Something from your past, perhaps? A mistake?"

"The Matera do not make mistakes," they answered as one.

"Of course," Hodera said. "Which explains what happened to me!" Her voice grew louder, but not loud enough to drown out the voice inside her own head, the hatchling crying inside her broken casing with no one around to comfort her.

The Matera with her back to Hodera turned to face the general, and Hodera scoffed at the sight of the gaudy red jewel embedded in the golden crown on her head. For a moment, there was nothing but hate-filled silence, and Hodera yearned to snatch that crown and toss it away, claiming the jewel for herself.

"What happened to you has made you who you are," came the collective Matera's cold response. "Our decisions are for the greater good of the Krunation Empire."

"Which is why I am here," Hodera said. "The empire is now in ruins. Our master Nocterar is gone. Our offensive forces have defected from my authority and joined Connoram's defensive squadron. Surely you are aware of this, since Excelsior dared to take your palace away from you, as his people took away Nocterar's fortress." She smiled before adding, "Excelsior has been floating above the planet, mocking us with his rediscovered power and likely inspiring Denarians from neighboring lands to come out of hiding. I am in need of new warriors to match those rising forces and fulfill the wishes of our master Tornatrax."

"We are fulfilling the wishes of our master Tornatrax," the Matera said. "Hatchlings are being prepared in the timeframe he has given us. Their process shall not be circumvented for the agendas of his underlings. Especially those who share the genetic material of his enemy."

Hodera's face twisted as if she'd swallowed something vile, and she ran her hand over her head. "Ahh, yes. The source of your contempt." She nodded toward the empty seat in the pentagon. "Or should I say, the product of the source of your contempt. You already dealt with the source itself in the manner you saw fit, and you tried to rid yourselves of me as well. But Tornatrax blessed me with a task as he blessed you with yours. I am the future of the Krunation Empire! Without me, the Denarians would have overrun this planet a long time ago, and none of you will admit it was a half-breed who ensured your safety."

The Matera spoke again, voices dripping with derision. "And yet, with all of your arrogance and self-congratulatory speeches, you fail to realize no Krunation soldier can save us from what has already been inflicted upon us."

"What are you talking about?" Hodera's eyes narrowed with suspicion.

"You are still young," the Matera answered, "You do not feel it yet, but you will. And you will be notified of your soldiers' readiness in due time. Not a moment before. Now, return to Nocteris. We find your presence disturbing."

"You will be more disturbed in due time. And you, the one with your back to me..." The one in the front center looked up to show she was listening. "You will never forget me!" She left them, walking toward the transport, her escorts keeping pace with her.

"Some chose not to stand by Connoram, General," one of the escorts said.

She nodded. "If we do not have a replenished offensive squadron soon, the Denarians will overpower us by numbers alone. We must strike against their leaders as soon as possible."

"But how?" the escort dared to ask. "The Matera said—"

"Yes, yes, I know," Hodera said, growing impatient. She looked to the sky. "There are more options than just the Matera. We can no longer rely on these relics."

"Not all are relics, General," said a shaky voice from behind them.

Hodera and her escorts turned as one and saw nothing but empty space. And then Sivtra emerged from out of nowhere, trembling, his arms at his side.

One of the escorts held up his blaster rifle and pointed it at the scrawny Krunation. "Stand back!"

"Put down your weapon," Hodera said. "He means us no harm. Sivtra, is it?"

Sivtra nodded and held up his hands. "I am not armed."

"On the contrary," Hodera replied with a smile. "Quite the gift you have. What brings you to us?"

"I wish to serve my general," he said, growing confidence buoying his voice. "The Matera have enough servants. They do not need me. I wish to do my part to ensure the end of Excelsior's reign."

Hodera's smile widened as she placed a hand on Sivtra's puny shoulder. "I may have a very special mission for you."

"Anything," Sivtra said. "Anything, General. Anything to get me to Nocteris where I belong. Where I can proudly wear the uniform of the Krunation Empire."

"We may not have one in your size," the escort still holding his blaster rifle said, sneering at Sivtra, who narrowed his eyes and tightened his fists.

"The gift you have," Hodera said. "You can make anything you touch invisible?" When Sivtra nodded, she said, "And I assume you know how to operate the vehicles here?"

"Yes, General," the boy answered.

"Excellent." Hodera moved behind Sivtra and placed her hands on both of his shoulders. "So much loyalty in this small frame. Loyalty, not height, will lead you to Nocteris."

"Only Krunation soldiers belong on Nocteris," said the other escort.

"If he succeeds in his mission," Hodera said, "then he will be a Krunation soldier."

CHAPTER THREE

"Matty! So good to see you!"

The sun shining over Denab IV began its descent as Excelsior touched down outside the main village of Edenaria, and gave his friend Zorribis a tight embrace. The darker-skinned Denarian wore a smile on his face that made Excelsior believe he was hiding something.

"How long have I been up there?" Excelsior asked, pointing to the sky. "It looks like you guys have been busy getting the main village back in shape."

"We have been, yes," Zorribis answered. "We can accomplish a lot in six months."

The subtle response blew Excelsior's mind, and he went from shock to anger. "Six months? I've been floating over the planet for six months? And you didn't check in to see if I was okay?"

"I told you, if we needed you, I would contact you," Zorribis answered. "And besides, we knew you were not in danger. The longer you stayed up there, the more we could sense your presence. It was very soothing. And, as you can see, very inspiring."

Excelsior and Zorribis walked side-by-side along a cool marble-like path into the main village, and Excelsior let out a low whistle at what he could only describe as the biggest suburban subdivision he had ever seen. Rows upon rows of completed houses were in a circular configuration, each house about thirty feet apart from the next. He could see at least fifty houses in front of him, with many more in the distance in all directions, and each had a yellow glow within shining from their windows.

"Are those—?" Excelsior began to ask.

"Iridinsects, yes," Zorribis answered. "They are plentiful here in Edenaria, and they also detect any Krunation activity."

"Makes sense. Just because Nocterar's gone, doesn't mean the whole species is gone."

"Correct. Some of our younger men and women are training under Nosgood in Axsella. Once they are ready, they will come back and patrol for us."

There was a buzz of excitement as Denarian men, women, and children were walking around, running, working on their homes, or engaging in conversation. They stopped at various times to wave to Excelsior or hold up their fists and call out, "Ever Upward!" Excelsior smiled and returned the gestures, but when they reached the center of the village, he looked down and whispered, "Wow!"

In the very center was a large circle cut into the marble-like substance, the same emblem Excelsior wore on his uniform. Within the circle was a deep purple shimmering with a silver shape in the bottom center, the tip of a sword. Three black lines protruded from the tip, signifying the three elements of Excelsior: Strength, Leadership, and Innovation. Below the seal were the words etched into the smooth surface: He Has Returned.

"Edenaria is truly a microcosm of the whole planet," Zorribis said. "People from all clans working together to create something wonderful. Beyond the village, you will see crops tended to by Collagran representatives. The Child Development Center is next to it so nutrition is funneled directly into the children's growth pods."

"Development center?" Excelsior asked.

"Valertus' idea," Zorribis said. "You do not know it?"

Excelsior shook his head. "Can't remember very much from his time."

"Ahhh. I will have to show you how it works. It is quite fascinating, and the growth pods survived the transition from the caverns."

Excelsior felt as though Zorribis was about to tell him about "the Denarian birds and bees," and quickly changed the subject. "Where's your home?" he asked.

"Along the outer rim. Elder Ducera was a guest before Niterra took her to the Regeneration Chambers."

"She needs to go there already?" Excelsior asked, recalling how the Elder cared for Zorribis' clan. "I would've thought Acerus would go there before her."

Zorribis shook his head, and Excelsior could see his friend's shoulders were slumped. "She was the oldest of all Elders. Acerus is actually one of the younger ones."

"Guess being the High Elder put some extra wrinkles on him," Excelsior said, remembering how quickly US

Presidents seem to age during their years in office. "Why aren't you with Niterra and Ducera?"

"The aircraft Nosgood gave us only has two seats. And Niterra wanted so badly to take her there, I could not refuse."

"Get used to it," Excelsior said. "My dad used to joke about how he couldn't say no to my mom."

"And I could never say no to Niterra," Zorribis said with a smile. "Besides, I wanted to be here when you returned so I would invite you to stay with us while your house is built."

"My house?" Excelsior asked. "I get a house too?"

"Of course. You carry the spirit of our creator. We would not expect you to live in the streets."

Zorribis had a point. Excelsior looked around and imagined the possibilities of how he would like his own house to look. Nothing too flashy, maybe something similar to the house Matthew and his uncle Jason shared. "You did all this while I was gone?"

"More repairs than anything," Zorribis said. "So many homes were abandoned when the Krunations took Edenaria. Fortunately, Connoram was given authority over the initial imprisoning and destroying property was not a high priority for him."

"Connoram," Excelsior nodded. "The Krunation who let you go, right?"

"Yes. And I hear he is still alive and still a high-ranked officer within what's left of their empire." He gave Excelsior the same sly smile from before. "We almost extended an invitation to him."

"Invitation? What else did I miss?"

"Niterra and I will be bonded in three days."

Excelsior's eyes widened, as did his smile. He gave Zorribis another embrace as he yelled, "Congratulations! Now I'm really glad I showed up when I did."

"I would have contacted you. We need you to stand with the other Elders for the ceremony."

"Ahh, yes. How are the…" His voice suddenly trailed off, and Excelsior looked past Zorribis toward one of the homes behind him.

"Are you okay?" Zorribis asked.

"Yeah, I thought I saw something moving over there."

Zorribis turned, his hand on the blaster pistol in his holster. "Where?"

Excelsior took a few steps toward the home and looked around. After a moment of non-activity, he shook his head. "I don't know. Must not have been anything. Anyway, where was I?"

"The Elders," Zorribis answered.

"Right. How are the rest of them doing? I saw Quinterus was on Rellata."

"Did you hear what he was saying?" Zorribis asked.

"No. Why?"

Zorribis paused for a moment, then answered with, "Curiosity."

"Oh-kay," Excelsior said with more than a hint of suspicion in his voice. He gave one last look back at the home where he thought something was moving, then asked Zorribis, "But how is everyone else? You mentioned Acerus before."

"Acerus…" Zorribis' voice trailed off for a moment. "High Elder Acerus has been in his home for the past two months. Very unlike him."

"No one checked on him?" Excelsior asked.

"The other Elders have been, conveying information. They only say he is doing well, but will not say anything more."

Excelsior gave Zorribis a pat on his shoulder. "Where's Acerus living these days?"

Zorribis pointed toward a home to their right in the center of the village. A light blue and white colored cottage, it looked like the exact opposite of what someone carrying the title "High Elder" would want for themselves. Two windows were on either side of the door, as well as one on the roof, allowing plenty of natural light. It reminded Excelsior of the type of quaint and simple assisted living home Matthew Peters' grandparents moved to in California.

"Stay here," Excelsior said. "And keep an eye out for anything. I'll be a few minutes." He walked with urgency toward the High Elder's home and knocked on the door.

"Yes?"

Excelsior pushed open the door when he heard the warm voice of the High Elder. Acerus's home looked as cozy on the inside as it did on the outside. A twin-sized bed was hidden in the corner and away from any of the natural light coming in from the front windows and skylight. A round table was in the center of the main living space with seven chairs positioned around it. Six of those chairs were reserved for Acerus and the other five Elders charged with supervision over Denab IV— Ducera, Tricerus, Klierra, Quinterus, and Sestera. The last was reserved for Excelsior, where he sat several times when he was in Semminex's body.

Above the table was a large eight-legged insect the size of Excelsior's hand. Its gray body emitted a yellow glow shining down on the six chairs, and its stick-like legs were firmly planted in the ceiling. Excelsior smiled when he saw the insect, the yellow glow giving him a sense of peace.

Then his gaze fell on to Klierra's empty chair. If only she were still here, he thought. He would have loved it if she saw her wishes fully realized; Excelsior's lifeforce fully integrated with Matthew, the two sharing the same body and working together to bring Denab IV to its fullest potential.

"Acerus?" Excelsior called out.

Acerus sat up in his bed, then swung his legs out with a painful lurch and rested his feet on the floor. He groaned as he pushed himself up. "Is that you, my friend? You have returned already?"

Already? Excelsior thought. Did the High Elder know how long he was gone? "Yes. I'm here, High Elder." Worry gnawed at him when he saw how slowly Acerus moved.

"Oh, forgive me," Acerus said as he stepped from the shadows and into the light cast by the insect above the table. Excelsior gasped when he saw the wrinkles on the

High Elder's face. They appeared to have doubled since the first night of celebration.

"Are you all right, sir?"

"Please, Excelsior," Acerus waved his arm. "How many times have I told you? There is no need to call me 'sir.' No need to genuflect to me. If anything, I must be genuflecting to you. You are responsible for me being here, not the other way around."

"I'm sorry. I keep forgetting. But are you all right?"

"I look terrible, do I not?" he said with a warm smile while pointing up at the insect on the ceiling. "Even in this calming light cast by the Iridinesect. Yes, it feels as though I am aging almost as quickly as the Sancterrum Trees. Is this the same fate awaiting me, Excelsior? Is this why you have come here? To watch me breathe my final breath?"

Excelsior contemplated Acerus's words. He didn't know about the dream he had while floating above the planet, did he?

"We would get you to a regeneration chamber," Excelsior said. "We need you with us."

Acerus shook his head. "No, my friend. When it is my time to expire from this plane of existence, I must be allowed to do so. We are simply entering a new age on this planet. The Empire which held us under their boot is in pieces. Our savior and creator has returned to us, in the body of a strong and good-hearted young man. The kind of man who would not only fight for the lives of his people, but also use his powers to restore the life of someone he never met. You have proven to us and yourself, you are fit to take the Denarian race into that era."

Excelsior's smile was sheepish as he looked back at the Elders' table. "How's Lokris?"

"Fully recovered, and we have offered her the seat of her fallen sister, Elder Klierra."

"Wonderful news. So she will be Elder Lokris, then?"

"She will be, yes."

"Where is she? I'd love to congratulate her."

"Resting for now. She will go to the Leap of Faith at sunrise to welcome our Denarian ambassador home."

"Denarian ambassador?" This was news to Excelsior. He never considered Denab IV would have an ambassador.

"Oh yes," Acerus said. "Arinna. She has been traveling to several different star systems, befriending so many species."

"Wow. You know, on Earth, we have people convinced we didn't land on the Moon. Some even think the Earth is flat."

Acerus gave an amused chuckle. "As your people would be fascinated by what we can do, I have always been fascinated with what they refuse to do."

Excelsior gave a look of embarrassment. "I wouldn't necessarily call them 'my people.'"

"Quite the contrary," Acerus said. "There is still the family of your current host. This may be your home now, but you will always have a connection with Earth. You do know you can always use the Leap of Faith to visit your loved ones, yes?"

Excelsior thought of his uncle Jason – hopefully still working on the webcomic they agreed he would carry on for Matthew – and smiled. "I know." The smile faded as a wave of guilt washed over him for even considering it.

"But I remember what happened the last time I used the Leap of Faith to go there. Can't take any chances with the Krunations still a threat."

"Of course," Acerus said.

Excelsior changed the subject. "So, you said Elder Lokris will be at the Leap of Faith?"

"Yes, and she will also speak at the Bonding Ceremony, since Elder Ducera is unable to do so. Unless you have any reason why this should not happen."

"Absolutely not." Excelsior still needed to get used to the idea of his opinions mattering. "And please, don't think these kinds of decisions need my approval. We're all in this together."

"Yes, of course. Our will be done." Acerus' body slumped over for a moment, and Excelsior lunged forward to put his hand on his shoulder.

Acerus waved him off. "Do not worry about me. Time appears to be accelerating, my friend. The days are getting shorter. The air is growing heavier. Tell me, how do you feel?"

"As strong as I've ever felt, and I feel more connected with the planet than I have in… well, a long time." Excelsior kept the moment on top of Klierra Peak, when he heard all those painful screams, to himself.

Acerus smiled. "I am confident this planet is in more than capable hands. And I know the rest of our people felt the same when they saw you floating above, watching over us."

Excelsior fought off the urge to wince. Once again, he didn't have the heart to say he wasn't watching over anyone, having fainted as soon as he reached Denab IV's stratosphere. He turned his head away from Acerus and his eyes locked on a colorful panoramic image that looked like it was painted directly on the wall. More than half of the image was a dark gray with a bright yellow beam of light cutting through the gloom and crashing to the green grass. Two figures were on opposite sides of the blast, one with a white face ducking away from the energy, the other with a dark green face reaching out toward it.

"Is this new, Elder?"

Acerus nodded. "Yes. It is still drying, but it is finally completed. I felt the urge to begin after you left. Apparently, your abilities as a storyteller have inspired me. Do you recognize it?"

Excelsior nodded. "The story of Candassus and Abrattus, right? Candassus was a Krunation and Abrattus was a Denarian."

"Yes. One of the oldest legends in our species. When the corrupted power Excelsior expelled came to our planet in the form of a sword."

"Candassus is the one reaching toward it, right? Just as the story said?"

"As the story said, yes," Acerus said. "To this day, it is our greatest cautionary tale."

Excelsior laughed. "'Cautionary tale.' You just reminded me of something my father once told me."

"Your father?"

"Matthew Peters's father," Excelsior corrected himself. His thoughts drifted back to a much simpler time, back when he was a ten-year-old kid living in New York City, and when he visited the Metropolitan Museum of Art and saw a special sword on display in the Arms and Armory section. This was a sword unlike any other on Earth. It was estimated to have been there since prehistoric times when the closest thing to a weapon was a bone. While Matthew was at the museum, he heard a deep humming from the sword, calling to him. Once he snuck under the ropes and his fingers grazed it, he received a powerful shock and drew the attention of the museum security guards.

Matthew was quickly pulled from the group and brought to the security offices where he had to wait until his father came to take him home. Fortunately, Matthew's father wasn't as angry with him as the security guards thought he should be. Disappointed, yes, since the guides instructed the students numerous times not to touch anything. But he placed a comforting hand on his son's shoulder and said, "Matthew, there are certain times in life that define all of us, whether we're the most powerful person in the world or the least powerful. And when we're gone, there are only two ways we're remembered: as an inspiration or as a cautionary tale. I expect great things from you, and I don't want anything you do now to impede your progress. You can't just duck under the ropes and evade responsibility because you don't want to do what you're told. Do you understand?"

"Who would've thought this was one of those great things?" Excelsior asked Acerus, bringing the telling of his story to a close. "Inheriting the lifeforce of the god who created an entire star system."

"Your father was a wise man," Acerus answered. He looked like he was about to say something else, but suddenly, the light from the iridinsect changed from a warm and content yellow to gray.

"What is it, Merlin?" Acerus asked the large insect, his voice dropping to a whisper.

Excelsior walked up to the windows and looked outside. The houses all around the immediate area went just as dark. Zorribis, still standing by near Acerus' home, was looking around as well.

"There's a Krunation here," he whispered.

The next moment felt like everything moved in slow motion. Excelsior's focus drifted from his friend to a clear patch of land between two small houses facing Acerus's. He saw a shade of dark green among the darkness, then a burst of bright light heading right for him.

No, not him. To the right of him.

"Acerus!" Excelsior yelled, while stepping to the right and allowing his uniform to absorb a powerful laser bolt, which nearly knocked him off his feet. He could hear a gasp from the High Elder behind him.

"Excelsior! Are you all right?"

"Y… yeah, I'm fine," he answered while rubbing his chest and grazing his fingertips against a hot area right in the middle.

The silence outside now gave way to a loud group of chattering, and Excelsior could see Zorribis running toward the clearing. Two older Denarian males exited their homes on either side of the clearing and joined him.

"What is happening?" Acerus asked.

"Stay here," Excelsior said, drawing his sword and leaving through the front door. "I'll take care of this."

CHAPTER FOUR

"**E**xcelsior! We have him!"

Zorribis yelled out while the two Denarian men stood on either side of the attempted assassin. The one on the left, with cropped short blonde hair and striking sky blue eyes, was showing off a broad chest through his tight silver shirt and looked almost as tall and foreboding as Nocterar. The one on the right had a slick bald head and was shorter and less well-defined physically. Each was holding and squeezing an arm, while the larger one on the left held a blaster rifle.

Excelsior ran up to them, his sword gleaming in his hands, and stopped when he noticed the size difference between the Denarians and this... this very small Krunation. His loose gray uniform looked brand-new as it draped over his wiry build. The blaster rifle kept away from him looked almost the same size as his entire body.

"He's just a kid," Excelsior said.

"Who is still an excellent marksman," Zorribis added, pointing to the mark on Excelsior's armor.

"Who are you?" Excelsior asked.

No answer came, so the two Denarians holding the young Krunation's arms pulled harder on them, causing him to wince.

"Answer him!" yelled the one on the left.

"Wait! Stop," Excelsior commanded. "Keep hold of him, but don't hurt him."

"This weapon was aimed at the High Elder's home," the Denarian on the right said, pointing toward the rifle in his neighbor's hand. "He wanted to do much more than this."

"But he didn't," Excelsior answered. "Acerus is fine now and he'll continue to be fine." He turned his attention back to the small Krunation. "I'm gonna ask you again. Who are you? What's your name?"

The Krunation spit out his response. "Sivtra."

"And who sent you here?" Excelsior asked. "Hodera? Connoram?"

Sivtra let out a laugh, prompting the two Denarians to pull tighter on his arms. "Ha! Connoram? Never."

"Connoram would never send someone to assassinate an Elder," Zorribis said.

"You got a point," Excelsior replied. He turned his attention back to Sivtra. "So Hodera sent you, huh? Guess she didn't want to waste any soldiers so she gets someone who's expendable?"

"No!" Sivtra declared. "General Hodera knows I am not expendable!"

"Then it would upset her if something terrible would happen to you," the Denarian to Sivtra's left growled.

For a moment, a vision flashed before Excelsior's eyes. A memory. Not one belonging to Semminex or even

Valertus, but of his current host Matthew Peters. He saw this situation before: two larger and more intimidating young men looking down on someone weaker and scrawnier than them. And he saw it many times in many different ways. Some involved beatings. Others only wedgies.

Excelsior held in a gasp. He saw Matthew's high school friend Thomas in Sivtra's position, and the ones threatening him were playing the roles of the popular jocks Nick and Kelly "The Kraken."

"Hey..." Excelsior started, then turned to Zorribis. "What are their names?"

"The one on the left is Malitus, and the other one is Branerik."

"Malitus!" Excelsior yelled, getting his attention. "Don't threaten him like that!"

Malitus shot Excelsior a glare. "He is just another Krunation, no matter his age. He does not deserve any sympathy from me."

"He does from me," Excelsior answered. "I don't care what species he is, I'm not gonna let you kill a child."

"You care about killing Krunation children?" Malitus' voice raised and he let go of Sivtra's arm while squeezing the confiscated blaster rifle. The two stood a distance apart, but Excelsior could see the color in Malitus' eyes was changing, darkening.

The quiet Branerik's arm slackened and Malitus pointed accusingly at Excelsior. "And yet our savior was not there for us while our fathers and children were taken as high as Klierra Peak to build Nocterar's castle! Where were you when the altitude crushed them? When their screams were heard through all of Edenaria?"

Excelsior had no answer. But he could suddenly hear those very screams in his head, the same ones loud enough to make him lose his balance on Klierra Peak.

"Stand down, Malitus!" Zorribis ordered. "You know there was nothing that could have been done. Semminex was still in his cell, and it would be hundreds of Earth years..."

"Thousands," Excelsior corrected him.

"Yes, thousands of Earth years before this young man became Excelsior's new host. Valertus may have failed us, but Excelsior did not."

"Failed?" Excelsior whispered. He never heard it like that before. He knew Valertus was overrun by Krunations, but was there a way he could have succeeded and maybe ended Nocterar's reign before it started?

"Malitus!" Branerik interrupted. Excelsior looked past Malitus and back to Sivtra, who was pulling himself away from Branerik and stepping backward into the shadows. "Grab his arm before he escapes!"

Both Malitus and Branerik lunged toward the darkness, but both came up empty-handed. "Where did he go?" Malitus yelled. "He cannot have gotten away!"

"Quite the gift he has," Zorribis observed, his voice as calm as Malitus's was heightened. "Excellent aim and the ability to blend into his surroundings? Hodera has quite the assassin under her tutelage."

Malitus aimed the blaster rifle toward the shadows. He turned around and walked out from in between the two houses, into the open.

Zorribis called out, "Malitus! No! You do not know where he is!"

"I think I see something," Malitus said, holding up the blaster rifle and aiming it in the direction of another home. Excelsior ran up to him, held up his sword, and brought it down on the rifle, cutting it into two pieces and rendering it completely useless.

"What are *you* doing?" Malitus yelled.

"What are you doing?" Excelsior yelled back. "We don't need you shooting all over the place and putting a hole in someone's home. For all you know, he's on his way back to Nocteris."

"Because you allowed him to escape." Malitus threw down the rest of the rifle and moved so close to Excelsior, they were practically nose-to-nose. Excelsior noticed the color in Malitus' eyes still shifting, turning a deep red. And the more Malitus' eyes changed, the louder in volume his voice grew. "Is this how you honor those who died before us? Who suffered under their rule?"

Excelsior kept his lips tight, hiding his clenched teeth. The desire to lash out at this man who has been nothing but antagonistic rose in his chest, but a voice from within – a motherly voice – interrupted his thoughts.

"He is in pain, Excelsior," said Elder Klierra. "He has seen so much you have not. Now is not the time to engage him in anger."

Excelsior took a deep breath and sheathed his sword. "You know how you honor the ones who died before you?" he asked. "You go back to your home, you get some sleep, and tomorrow, you help us prepare for the Bonding Ceremony." He motioned to Zorribis. "Very soon, we'll be celebrating the biggest day in this man's life, and it wouldn't have happened if the ones who died didn't light the path for us to follow. We made sure they didn't die in vain, and Denarians everywhere can breathe in the open air, thanks to them." His voice softened even more. "So please, you and Branerik, go home. I'll alert our security team to keep an eye out for Sivtra. He doesn't have a weapon anymore. If they find him, I'll make sure he's imprisoned. Okay?"

The proposition hung in the air. Keeping his lips shut tight, Malitus nodded his head, and Excelsior saw the color in his eyes fade from red to its normal blue. He turned away and walked toward his home. Branerik did the same while nodding to Denab IV's savior and the Bonded-to-be Zorribis, leaving them alone in the middle of the now-quiet village.

"So who was he?" Excelsior whispered. "And why'd he keep going after me?"

"Just like he said," Zorribis whispered back. "He was in the division of prisoners assigned to the top of Nocterar's castle. Everyone sent to the higher levels were at risk of not coming back. None who worked at the top ever did."

"When I first saw him, I thought he'd be ideal to be trained by Nosgood for the security team you mentioned. But then I saw how his eyes changed. He must have been turned down."

Zorribis nodded. "Shame. He would have been a fine soldier."

Excelsior watched Malitus walk into his home and shut the door without turning back to face them. For a moment, silence hung in the air and he and Zorribis stood together, looking around the village. Excelsior took the time to ponder everything he experienced for the short time he was on this small planet. Defeating Nocterar. Freeing the Denarians. Regaining the connection with all of the continents. Restoring life to a destroyed Sancterrum tree. But there was also the screaming from the top of Klierra Peak. The woman on Nelleram crying. The Krunation child who wanted to be an assassin. Malitus accusing him of letting Denarians die in vain.

"Is everything alright, my friend?" the telepathic voice of Acerus filled his mind. "I heard yelling."

"Yes, everything's fine," Excelsior responded. "I'm sorry we bothered you."

"No bother at all," Acerus said. "Considering this sudden turn of events, I feel it is necessary for you to wear your armor at all times. Including your helmet. We have seen complacency work against us in the past."

"I understand," Excelsior said, grateful the uniform designed for him was as comfortable for him as a T-shirt and sweat pants on Earth.

"And as we discussed earlier, I feel the need to ask. How would you like to be remembered? As an inspiration? Or a cautionary tale?"

Excelsior smiled. Acerus knew him too well. "I look forward to finding out."

"Yes?"

Sivtra sat in the seat of his one-man transport floating along the surface of Denab IV's waters, looking down at a small gray screen attached to his left wrist. He was fighting to catch his breath ever since he pulled himself from the clutches of Malitus and Branerik, and used his ability to blend into his surroundings to escape capture.

It took several hours for Sivtra to hide his transport from Krephthera near a rocky terrain close to the ocean and walk to the main village of Edenaria, the same amount of time for him to get back to his transport, climb inside, and initiate contact with General Hodera.

"General, I bring some very useful news that could bring the end of Excelsior and the Denarian Elders."

From the small image on the communicator, Sivtra could see a hopeful smile on Hodera's face. "Would this be news of a successful Elder assassination?"

Sivtra winced. "No, General. I tried, but Excelsior took the blast meant for Acerus. And my blaster rifle was destroyed."

"What?" There was no longer a smile on Hodera's face.

"But I have learned of something better. Preparations are being made for a Bonding Ceremony between two Denarians. It will take place within the main village of Edenaria, and all of the Elders, as well as the top representatives from the neighboring lands, are expected to attend."

"A joyful occasion," Hodera mused. "Reveling in their own success, congratulating themselves for driving us out of power. A much greater opportunity to eradicate the entire Denarian virus from this planet. Sivtra, you have done well. Now join us at Nocteris. Your new home is waiting for you here."

"As you wish." Sivtra remained calm on the outside. Inside, he was leaping up and down with his fists raised in the air.

"If only all Krunations from Krephthera could be like you, Sivtra," Hodera stated. "Tornatrax himself would approve of your actions."

The communication cut off, and Sivtra sucked in a deep breath at the mention of their master's name.

CHAPTER FIVE

Lokris ascended the steps to the chamber holding the tall rectangular inter-planetary doorway known as The Leap of Faith, her right hand rubbing across the pristine white fabric of her new Elder's robe. Her left hand clutched her walking stick and she raised it in acknowledgement to the two Denarians standing guard on each side of the chamber's entrance.

The guard on the right nodded and pressed the button behind him, opening the chamber. Lokris smiled, nodded, and walked inside, her old joints popping with each step.

The cold and metallic structure of the chamber was a complete contrast to the more wooden and marble motif of the Edenarian village, and it always fascinated Lokris to see it in action. The doorway itself was a large rectangular shape that went from the floor to the 9-foot-high ceiling, and since it was currently not in use, a silver-gray blast door was tightly shut. Attached to the wall on her left was a large flat-screen monitor with a golden orb attached to a console used to operate the actual doorway. She could never understand the inner workings of it, but considering how this was Excelsior's vision he made a reality while in Valertus's body, she took it for what it was: a gift from their god.

But being in the chamber also brought Lokris some unexpected baggage. She remembered standing behind the chair facing the directional orb and the monitor, her hands on either side of the late Krunation Emperor Nocterar's head. She remembered the threats from General Hodera to locate Danaak and Excelsior, and she remembered the process being so taxing on her body and mind, it killed her. She would have stayed dead if Excelsior – now in the body of Matthew Peters – didn't bring her back to life.

The sudden opening of the Leap of Faith shook Lokris from her painful memories. She smiled as a burst of light appeared and began to enlarge and transform itself into a humanoid shape. When the light faded, a beautiful young Denarian woman with short black hair stood in its place. She wore a long overcoat shimmering with various shades of orange, yellow, and blue. Underneath was a tight gray shirt showing off a very athletic figure, matching pants, and red shoes.

She yelled out with her arms wide open. "Lokris!"

"Arinna!" The two women embraced for a long moment. "Your timing is impeccable as always. So much has happened since you left Denab IV. So much happening, but first I must ask. Where did you get this coat?" She ran her fingers along the material on Arinna's coat. The fabric continued to change colors at her touch.

"Do you like it? The Emperor on Darenga VI gave it to me."

"But I thought you were going to the Knutrat system."

"I did, and I was going to come back, but it was advised I try another planet after Semminex left. Did he ever return? I cannot wait to see him."

"Well..."Lokris hesitated to find the right answer. "Well, the spirit of Semminex has returned."

"What is that supposed to mean?"

"I mean what I say. Excelsior has returned to us with a new host, but the memories of Semminex are with him."

Arinna's excitement dipped. "Hmmm. Such a shame. I was looking forward to seeing the Denarian who saved my life."

"He is still there. And even better than what he was before since he was not always a Denarian."

"Oh?" She cocked one eyebrow. "And where is the foreign land he's from?"

"I am sure you know of Earth?"

Arinna wiped away her skepticism in an instant, replacing it with wide-eyed wonder. "Earth! The new Excelsior is from Earth? I have always wanted to go there!"

"Well, you will have a lot to talk about when you see him. He is currently off to regain his connection with the rest of the planet. But you must tell me about your travels in the meantime."

"Absolutely," Arinna said. She wrapped her arm around Lokris's shoulders as the Elder led her out of the Leap of Faith. But as she looked to the sky, she suddenly stopped.

"What is it, child?" Lokris asked.

"The stars," Arinna said, her head still pointed up. "Where did they go?"

Lokris patted Arinna on her back and said, "Do not worry. This pale blue is how the sky looks on Earth."

"But not here," Arinna countered. "It never looked like this here."

"It was, once before," Lokris corrected her. "You were too young to see it. Come, you said there were stories for me. The stars will be waiting for you tonight."

Arinna nodded and Lokris could see the young traveler force a smile through her worry.

"Coffee's ready!"

If the smell of fresh coffee wouldn't bring a smile to Jason Peters' face, Becky's voice would. He looked at himself in the bathroom mirror and ran his hands through his hair, making sure not a single one was out of place, then switched off the light and walked into the small kitchen in their Manhattan apartment. His eyes roved over the gorgeous woman with the short blonde hair and slim frame standing by the kitchen counter, pouring two cups of coffee. She glanced over her shoulder at Jason, and he asked, "Miss, you wouldn't by chance have been jogging past the Metropolitan Museum of Art earlier today, were you?"

She let out a laugh. "Quite possibly the best pick-up line I could have ever imagined."

"I should hope so," Jason said. "It's been what, three years, and you're still here? Who would have thought I'd see you again? It must've been fate, right?"

"Either that or just plain luck you weren't killed by whatever was at Tollund Laboratories. How many people did it get?"

"I don't know how many scientists, but it killed four really good people. I still think about them."

"I'm sure, considering how much you write about them."

"I promised I would," Jason said. "Keep the memories of them alive."

Becky kissed Jason lightly on the lips. "You're doing a great job of it, sir. Three years of writing and it keeps getting better. And..." She reached for a letter sitting on top of a pile of mail. "I think you're about to find out how good your writing is."

"Hmmmm," Jason said as he reached for the envelope and saw the very familiar multi-colored logo on the upper left corner.

"What's 'Hmmmm?'" Becky asked.

"No phone call, no e-mail. And there's probably only one piece of paper in here. You think it's a form rejection or something?"

"Just read it."

With a curious glance, Jason reached for the envelope, opened it, and pulled out the letter inside. His eyes moved from left to right as he studied the paper, and after sucking in a large gulp air, he suddenly shot Becky a suspicious glance.

"What?" Becky asked, looking like she was trying to stifle a laugh.

"He called you, didn't he? Your dad called you and told you?"

Becky nodded and giggled. "I told him not to e-mail you. I wanted to see your face when you found out the news!"

Jason laughed along with Becky and threw his arms up in victory. "A green light. NBC is green-lighting the series!" He tightened his grip on the letter as though it were going to float away and prove itself a figment of his imagination.

Becky leapt into Jason's arms. "I'm so proud of you!"

"Can you believe this? It's like a big relay race. Matthew had the webcomic, then I get to put Excelsior on television. Maybe in two or three years, I hand him off to someone else and he goes to the big screen."

"We have to go out and celebrate," Becky offered. "Maybe apartment hunting? Something a little bigger than a one-bedroom on York Avenue? Does it say anything about how much you're getting up front?"

Jason glanced through the rest of the letter. "It doesn't say, but they still have to give me the contract, and I still have to get a lawyer to look at it."

Becky wrapped her arms around his neck and gave him a kiss on the nose. "Can you believe how quickly everything came together? It's almost like our lives shifted into another gear as soon as I met you."

"Well, it took a long time to be an overnight success. Besides, I got Matthew to thank for everything. I wish I could tell him all about it. He got it all started. I just did what I was told."

"Not quite. You told me back then, all he said was to keep the stories going. You're the one who thought of taking them to television."

"Only because your father is a development exec."

"Yes, and he knows a good story when he hears one. Stop selling yourself short and start enjoying the success. Did they say what happens next in the letter? I know Dad likes to rush news like this out so someone online won't spoil the surprise."

"Yeah, I have an interview in two days on The Today Show. And then in the evening, there's a special event at the observation deck at Rockefeller Center. You remember that place, right?"

"Oh, right," Becky said with a wide smile. "Top of the Heap or something."

"Rock. Top of the Rock," Jason corrected her. "You know, ROCK-efeller Center?"

"Whatever. I just remember it was really nice."

"Yeah, they're gonna have a fun reception there, and they want me to go over there today so I can pick out some illustrations they'll blow up as decorations."

"Ooooh!" Becky exclaimed and held up her hands. "The stuff upstairs in the closet? You can bring it, show it off."

"You're right. It'll look great, along with the illustrations and stuff."

"Awesome." Becky gave him another kiss on the lips. "So can I go apartment hunting today on my own while you're getting everything ready?"

"Sure," Jason said, then closed his eyes and kissed her back. He felt Becky pull away and slip a small box into his right hand. He opened his eyes and looked down at the box. "What's this?"

"We're not only celebrating the green light. It's two years of complete sobriety. No compromises. No bargaining."

Jason choked back a sudden wave of emotion. "You remembered. Although it should've been longer."

"Stop beating yourself up," Becky said. "Now, open your present."

Jason opened the box and held up a small, silver oval-shaped medallion attached to a thin cable chain. He looked closer at the medallion and saw the face of a short-haired man with glasses. "Ummm..."

"His name is Maximilian Kolbe. He's the patron saint of addicts. And journalists."

Jason let out a burst of laughter. "Ha! Best combination I've ever heard."

Becky took the chain from Jason's hands and wrapped it around his neck, clasping the two ends together. "Why do you think I got it? Now, you keep doing what you're doing, and Max will watch over you. And so will I."

Jason gave Becky another deep kiss, holding her close and as he held her tightly, his gaze suddenly locked on to the folded newspaper behind her. He looked over her shoulder.

She turned her head to try to follow his gaze. "Something wrong?"

"I don't know. Something familiar about this." Jason reached behind Becky and grabbed the paper. His eyes widened as he saw the complete picture of a lifeless reptilian/humanoid hybrid creature, its body lying on a steel table surrounded by a trio of scientists. The headline read: "'Ritgen-Man' Lifeform Returned to Tollund Laboratories by Homeland Security."

"Oh, my God," Jason gasped. "It's Danaak." He felt his stomach growing queasy.

"The thing from the lab?"

Jason nodded. "It says Tollund Laboratories actually petitioned to get a grant from the Department of Defense so they could further study the remains."

"Are you all right?" Becky asked.

Jason nodded. "I hope they don't make another mistake." His hand gravitated to the medal now around his neck. Thinking of Danaak's face staring him down, he could really use some support from Max.

CHAPTER SIX

The building excitement for the Bonding Ceremony in Edenaria's main village gave Excelsior a rush equaling his reconnection with the planet. Everyone worked together to create a truly remarkable event right in the middle of the village, and as Acerus suggested, Excelsior kept his uniform on for the duration of the setup, including his helmet. It helped endear him to the rest of the village, since they didn't have to ask if he was who others claimed he was.

Several assembled a collection of small lights bright enough to illuminate the entire area during the night. Others assembled a stone platform for the Elders to stand and look over all those in attendance. And two days before the ceremony began, the men and women who trained under Nosgood in the continent of Axsella to be Edenaria's security force returned and reunited with their families.

Excelsior participated in all areas, and he was relieved to see everyone he worked with smiled at him. During the preparations, no one saw much of Acerus. The High

Elder stayed confined to his home to rest, and the other Elders made a point to work with their fellow Denarians wherever they could.

On the day before the Bonding Ceremony, they were joined by a collection of ambassadors from the neighboring continents of Axsella, Rellata, and Collagra. The one from Nelleram – an older man with long silver hair tied back into a tight ponytail – introduced himself to Excelsior as Tecino. They only shared a brief moment together amidst all the activity around them, but Tecino made sure to say, "I believe Zorribis will be quite taken with the gift we have for him and Niterra." The glint in his eye stirred Excelsior's curiosity.

The Denarians working tirelessly in the village seemed to be the most anxious to experience what Collagra was going to bring to the ceremony. Excelsior could sense their mouths watering as much as his when they were told of what they could expect. He was feeling especially hungry when he heard the words "fire-roasted throngar."

The arrival of the ambassadors seemed to accelerate everyone's enthusiasm. And when Nosgood and Tecino from Nelleram worked together to perfect the apparatus at the bottom of the stone platform allowing it to float above the ground, the resulting victorious cry echoed through the village. Excelsior cheered along until he saw Niterra dressed in a flowing white robe walking with a stern purpose and calling out, "Elder Tricerus!"

With a sturdy and thick muscular build echoing the late Grannik, Tricerus looked like he was of an age similar to his assistants, but the graying hair revealed he was as old as the other Elders. Still, he stood tall and looked down his nose at the Denarian sharpshooter. "Yes, my dear?" he asked with a mixture of warmth and wariness. "Should you not be preparing for your ceremony?"

"This will not take long. You told me you would have your finest Farratulik greens as part of the main course. Where are they?"

Excelsior's heart sank as he saw Tricerus turn toward him for a moment, then look back down at Niterra. "My dear, I must apologize and assume full responsibility for the omission of the Farratulik greens. We timed their planting to coincide with the Bonding Ceremony, but unfortunately, we did not account for the recent..." He glanced at Excelsior again. "Noticeable changes in our atmosphere."

Niterra's shoulders slumped and she nodded. "I understand," she said and returned to her home. Tricerus and Excelsior locked eyes and the Elder of Collagra slightly shook his head before joining another Elder, the squat and scowling Quinterus. As Excelsior walked past them, he overheard Tricerus say to his colleague, "We expected them to ripen at their normal schedule, but they already started deteriorating. Their lifespan was only half as long as normal."

Quinterus shook his head. "A true Denarian would not allow this to happen."

Excelsior approached the two, recalling the Sancterrum tree he restored only a couple days before. "Excuse me, Elders. I overheard there are some problems with the crops? Maybe there's something I can do to give you the extra time..."

"Oh, I believe you have already done enough, Excelsior," Quinterus responded with some unexpected bite in his words.

Before Excelsior could ask what he meant, a very familiar voice from behind him spoke. "Elder Quinterus, may I speak with you?"

Excelsior turned around and was suddenly face-to-face once again with the blue-eyed Malitus. The tall Denarian's lips pursed shut as though he were holding back a barrage of inappropriate words aimed at Denab IV's savior. After a moment of uncomfortable silence, he finally said to Excelsior, "Pardon me, sir. So sorry to interrupt."

"Not at all, Malitus," Quinterus said. He and Tricerus started walking around the active village square. "We were leaving. Come join us."

Malitus shot one last glare at Excelsior as he passed him and walked with the two Elders. Excelsior could hear Quinterus saying to him, "I understand you and Branerik accosted a would-be assassin recently?"

"Yes," Malitus said. "And I would have ensured his demise if I was not interrupted."

None of the three looked back at Excelsior, who was now trying to channel a fragment of the happiness and excitement he felt just a few moments ago.

"Ready?"

The night before the Bonding Ceremony was not a good one for Excelsior. He was grateful to Zorribis and Niterra for allowing him to be a guest in their home, and he was especially taken by the care Zorribis took to create furniture so similar to what was on Earth. The couch was especially comfortable and long enough to provide plenty of room for him. And when the back folded out to create a bed the size of an Earth queen-size mattress, he was asleep very quickly. But the scowling faces and accusations of Malitus and Elders Tricerus and Quinterus were waiting for him when he closed his eyes.

"I believe you have already done enough."

"A true Denarian would not allow this to happen."

"I would have ensured his demise if I was not interrupted."

When he woke up the next morning, despite the comfort of the couch, Excelsior struggled to get out of bed. If two Elders and an Edenarian citizen had no problem confronting him like this, what would stop others from looking at him in this way?

Excelsior stayed on guard throughout the day of the ceremony, putting the final pieces together of his Bonding Gift for Zorribis and Niterra. But he kept looking over his shoulder to see if someone was giving him another snide comment or look of contempt. Thankfully, there was nothing. None of the Elders mingled with the Denarians, and Malitus was trying to talk to Nosgood from Axsella. In a way, he was looking forward to seeing them again so he could ask how he could have brought a Sancterrum

Tree back to life if he wasn't a real Denarian? If he wasn't fit to be Excelsior?

When the time came to prepare for the ceremony, Excelsior closed the box holding his Bonding Gift and walked back to Zorribis and Niterra's home. When he walked inside, he saw his friend dressed in a white silk long-sleeved shirt and pants with matching white boots, and Zorribis's smile grew wider with each step Excelsior took toward him. But when Excelsior looked down at his friend's hands, he saw they were trembling.

"Ready, Matty," he answered, his voice quivering.

"You all right?" Excelsior asked. "You're not getting cold feet, are you?"

"Cold feet?" Zorribis cocked his head. "My—"

"You're not considering not going through with this, are you?" Excelsior said, quickly cutting off his friend's inevitable question about American vernacular.

"Oh. No. Not at all. Just anxious to begin everything. Do you have the blinders?"

Excelsior grinned, holding up a simple white cloth which matched Zorribis's outfit. "Now remember, as soon as I put this on, you have to stay still. And you can't look outside either."

"I know, I know," Zorribis said with a hint of impatience. "Put it on."

Excelsior stood behind his friend and wrapped the cloth over Zorribis's face, covering his eyes. He pressed the two ends of the cloth together, and the ends attached as though they were stitched as such.

"I'll be outside waiting for you," Excelsior said. "Just wait until the gong is sounded before coming out."

"Matty, I think I know how these work better than you do."

"Right, right," Excelsior said. "I keep forgetting." He wanted to say, "That's what happens when you're not a real Denarian," but he held back. This wasn't the time for a pity party when there was a real party waiting to begin.

"I understand," Zorribis said, missing the worry on Excelsior's face. "Have you been experiencing any other memories lately?"

He nodded. "Kind of. Only the memory wasn't mine."

"Oh? What do you mean?"

"Well, after I was reconnected with the planet, I came across this tree. It was burned almost beyond recognition. I reached out to touch it, and I could see what happened to it play in front of my eyes. It... I couldn't believe it."

Zorribis's mouth dropped. "So you saw its memories? You connected with its core?"

"If that's what you call it, then yes."

"So in case there was any doubt about who you are and how important you are to the planet, you must know this is one of the rarest of gifts."

Did Zorribis know about the growing doubts in Excelsior's mind? Whatever the case, the groom-to-be looked less occupied with thoughts of the upcoming Bonding Ceremony and more with putting his friend's mind at ease. "It is said, those who can access the memories and thoughts of nature have been selected by nature to be their representative. It means you have earned their trust and therefore they have opened themselves up to you. Remember this when there are issues plaguing you."

"I will. Real quick, I got a question for you."

"What is it?" Zorribis asked.

"The Krunation kid who got away from us. Malitus told the Elders he would've taken care of him if I didn't get in the way."

"Malitus says a lot of things," Zorribis said dismissively.

"Yeah, but do you think they'd consider it an act of mercy by letting him go?"

Zorribis shook his head. "If Connoram sent him, yes. Hodera would see it as an act of weakness."

"Yeah, I thought so," Excelsior said. "But they're both on Nocteris, right? So word should travel quickly."

"Possibly. Why do you ask?"

"Well, if word gets around, then maybe it can be a first step to peace between the Denarians and Krunations."

"Are you sure they want peace? I doubt Hodera would want to sit across from you without trying to kill you."

"Then we should reach out to Connoram. Maybe he can see us letting him go in the same way as when he let you go when you were a kid."

Zorribis looked up for a moment, then responded. "If there is any chance for peace, it must be through Connoram." He smiled at Excelsior and added, "Now can you help me with putting these blinders back on?"

"In one second. I almost forgot. I have something for you. A gift."

"Gifts are given after the ceremony."

"I know, but this is for the actual ceremony." He held up the small box and handed it to Zorribis.

"What is it?"

"You're supposed to open it and find out."

The Denarian betrothed-to-be opened up the box and held up a small tool resembling a wristwatch from Earth. Zorribis examined it and asked, "Is this... is this a Krephth?"

"Kind of," Excelsior answered. Looking at the object brought up memories of the seventeen-year-old Matthew Peters taking a piece of Denarian technology and rewiring it to be safe for use on someone from Earth. "Keep this on your wrist, and when the ceremony begins, press the blue button."

CHAPTER SEVEN

"**W**ow, I can't wait for you to see this," Excelsior whispered to Zorribis as the sound of the ceremonial gong echoed through the clearing in the middle of the village. Small blue lights positioned around the village square illuminated the crowd of more than a thousand Denarians. Acerus, Tricerus, and Quinterus stood together on the floating stone platform, and Excelsior kept his focus on Acerus, quietly hoping he would stay upright.

"Send them out," Acerus announced.

The Denarians cleared a path as Lokris ambled into view. She was holding the hand of Niterra, who was dressed in white garb identical to the one Zorribis wore, complete with white blindfold.

Excelsior gasped when he saw this young and beautiful woman, whose hands were visibly trembling as much as Zorribis's were.

"What is it?" Zorribis whispered.

"Uh uh," Excelsior whispered back with a smile. "I'm not spoiling anything. You ready?"

Zorribis nodded and took Excelsior's arm. "I am ready."

Excelsior strode out into the crowd with Zorribis gripping his right arm. After taking several steps, he pulled his arm away, allowing the blindfolded Denarian to walk by himself through the crowd, which started to move as one to block both Zorribis and Niterra's paths, walking around to fill in any empty space in the area.

For a moment, Zorribis stood still in the middle of the fracas. From what Excelsior could see, it looked like he was trying to concentrate on Niterra's location. On the other side of the crowd, Niterra's arms were outstretched, and anyone she grazed her fingertips against, she shook her head and walked in a different direction.

Suddenly, as though nothing impeded their vision any longer, Zorribis and Niterra met in the center of the crowd and reached out toward each other. Excelsior approached them while the crowd fell silent, and a single tear rolled down Zorribis's cheek.

"I found you," Zorribis said.

"You never lost me," Niterra said.

Acerus beckoned for Excelsior and Lokris to lead Zorribis and Niterra to the Elders. As they did so, Acerus, Tricerus, and Quinterus surrounded the couple, and Lokris faced them.

"You may remove your blinders," Lokris said.

Zorribis and Niterra reached behind their heads and detached the blinders, then turned to face each other.

Excelsior gave Zorribis a nudge and whispered. "It's time. Turn on the gift."

"The what?" Zorribis whispered back.

"The Krephth. Press the blue button."

"Ahhh, yes," Zorribis held up his wrist and Niterra gave Excelsior an annoyed glance.

"Trust me," Excelsior whispered to her.

Zorribis pressed the blue button as instructed, and when the holographic image of a very young Denarian with shaggy blonde hair materialized, both Zorribis and Niterra gasped and their eyes welled up with tears.

Karini. Niterra's brother. Zorribis's friend. Excelsior watched their reaction with delight and gave the slightest of fist pumps.

Lokris addressed the crowd. "On this day, we enrich the life and history of Denab IV with the joining of this couple. Zorribis, from Ducera's clan of creators, the ones responsible for the architecture which gave us our homes, the machines which gave us our way of life. Niterra, from the late Klierra's clan of protectors, the ones responsible for our defense in the face of adversity from the Krunation Empire. A creator and a protector shall bond together before the eyes of our savior..." Excelsior blushed when Lokris mentioned him. "...And from this day forward, we open our hearts, our minds, and our arms to Zorribis and Niterra. Let this be the first step for a brand new clan." She then raised her right hand to the sky. "Ever Upward!"

The crowd lifted their hands and yelled back, "Ever Upward!"

"Look unto each other as eternally bonded."

They both gave one last glance at the hologram of Karini, then embraced once again.

"And now," Acerus declared before the enthusiastic crowd of Denarians. "Now... we invite everyone to share their gifts with Zorribis and Niterra. Fill their new home with love as they have filled Denab IV with their love." Acerus faltered and leaned on Excelsior's shoulder for support.

"Are you sure you're all right?" Excelsior whispered.

"As I said before, my friend. The days are simply growing shorter for me."

"My loyal Krunation soldiers. At long last, the time for us to strike has come!"

General Hodera stood proudly in front of a group of forty Krunations, all with their shoulders thrust back and heads held high. Some were baring their sharp teeth with anticipation of the upcoming slaughter. Standing in the front were Hodera's two escorts who traveled with her to speak with the Matera. Standing away from the group was the young spy Sivtra.

It took some time for Hodera to regain the swagger she was known to display in her demeanor, and her escorts ensured nobody could see her try to collect herself after the taunting by the Matera. Her time on Krephthera now seemed like a distant memory to her. All that mattered was this moment, and the mission she laid before all of the loyal soldiers she could gather.

"You have been cast aside for long enough. You, who once held this planet in your grasp, have been reduced to struggling to find your own food! Well, those days have passed, and now is the moment when you will take back

what was so wrongfully taken from you. Thanks to Sivtra."
Hodera motioned to the young soldier who smiled her.
"We will serve our Master Tornatrax with pride. And we
will avenge our fallen Emperor Nocterar!"

The soldiers cheered in response to Hodera's words.

"And now is the time when we end the life of the great
Excelsior!"

The cheering grew louder, and Hodera held her fists
high in the air. She turned to Sivtra and called to him
over the noise. "Well done, Sivtra. What do you wish for
your reward?"

"I wish to be your personal security."

Hodera cocked her head, motioning to her two
Krunation escorts. "I already have two soldiers as my
personal security, taller soldiers. You may be a better fit to
lead your own team of espionage agents."

One of her escorts walked up to stand beside Hodera.
"She is well accommodated regarding security, little one."

"Why do you call me 'little one?'" Sivtra asked him
as he stood up, proving he was, indeed, much shorter
than Hodera's escorts. He was even shorter than Hodera
herself.

"Is it not obvious?" the escort said, his laughter
mocking.

Before the escort could react, Sivtra quickly grabbed
a small blaster from a holster on his belt and fired two
shots, hitting the larger Krunation in each knee. With a
cry, the escort dropped to the ground, clutching his legs.

Hodera nodded and glanced at the wounded soldier.
"You have been demoted," she said.

"In more ways than one," Sivtra added as he walked up to the General and stood beside her with pride.

The cheering died down, and Hodera turned back to the crowd of Krunations awaiting their instructions. "It is up to all of you to ensure our Lord and Master's destiny is realized. Now, board the transports."

Every time the Krunation General saw the monstrous-looking barges floating above the land, she felt both impressed and proud of this achievement in her people's technology. Of course, it was technology obtained by imprisoning Denarians and forcing them to use their skills to bring the barges to life. These transporters were long and wide enough to comfortably fit up to two hundred soldiers. Even with only two hundred Krunations at the ready to fight and die for her and for their Lord and Master Tornatrax, she knew with her leadership, these Krunations were a greater threat than their Denarian oppressors.

The barges landed on the ground in a single-file formation. Hodera could hear the enthusiasm from her loyal troops as they entered and sat down, their weapons already set to fire. She licked her black lips in anticipation of seeing all those corpses at her metal-tipped boots and approached the entrance door of the barge in the front of the line, with Sivtra now at her side. Her hand brushed against the shiny surface of the barge, nodding in wordless admiration of the transporter's beauty. Despite the barges being locked away for so long, they stayed so clean she could see her own reflection on the metal. In fact the reflection was so clear, she could see the early stages of her skin molting.

Wait. Hodera stepped closer to the metal, and her eyes widened as she brushed her fingers against the patch of skin below her forehead. The crackling rang in her ears, and she turned away from the barge lest any of her soldiers see the horror in her eyes. On her fingertips were flecks of dead skin.

"No," Hodera whispered. She looked closer at her reflection and could taste the bile in her mouth when she saw the tan-colored skin underneath the scales. How could this be happening so soon, when she was in the prime of her life?

She looked up to the sky for an answer, and suddenly, there it was. Her eyes narrowed with rage, her hands balling into fists.

Him.

Of course.

That was what he was doing in the sky for so long. He couldn't defeat her in person, and so he had to alter the planet somehow to age her, expose her.

There could be no other explanation. And it gave Hodera another reason to hate him.

"General?" Sivtra asked. "Are you all right?"

"Excelsior," she hissed through her sharpened teeth, not acknowledging Sivtra's question. She looked up to the sky and whispered, "I swear to you, my Lord Tornatrax, Excelsior will pay for this."

CHAPTER EIGHT

The daylight draping over Edenaria gave way to night, and the celebration after the Bonding Ceremony continued on. Excelsior watched with delight as Zorribis and Niterra moved through the crowd at the village, hugging and clasping wrists with everyone around them. All the while, the bonded couple stayed close, a tight grip on each other's hand.

But as the celebration seemed to grow with the darkening sky, a hush fell over the previously raucous and jubilant crowd in the Edenarian village. Tecino slowly stepped up to Zorribis, Niterra, and Excelsior, who made sure not to miss the big surprise. A transparent box was in his hands, with a silver dagger floating inside.

"Tecino!" Zorribis exclaimed. "I am so glad you could be here."

"As am I, my friend," Tecino said. "And as I told Excelsior before the ceremony, I believe you will find this gift for you and your beloved quite special."

Zorribis and Excelsior looked closer at the pristine silver dagger with a golden handle, and Excelsior saw

Zorribis's eyes were welling up with tears. "Is this what I think it is?"

Tecino nodded. "Several of us were taken by Hodera, who forced us to create a sword made of the same metal used for the blade which pierced Excelsior's armor. To honor those who fell, and ensure this material could not be used a second time, we forged all of the remaining material into this." Along the blade were Denarian hieroglyphics spelling out the words, "Never again!"

The rest of the party continued with friendly conversation. Excelsior noticed Acerus standing by himself and was about to check in with him, when he felt a tap on his shoulder.

"Excuse me, Excelsior." Excelsior turned to face Tecino of Nelleram. He was smiling, his hand outstretched in friendship.

"Tecino," Excelsior responded while clasping the older Denarian's wrist. "A pleasure to finally meet you."

"The pleasure is all mine, sir," Tecino said. "And I am not sure you are aware of this, but I felt your presence when you came to Nelleram."

"When I came to Nelleram?" And suddenly, images from his reconnection with Denab IV flashed before his eyes. "Ahhh, yes, I remember now. Sorry, seeing as much as I did at once was a bit overwhelming."

"Understandable. I hope you liked what you saw."

"Very much. I'll have to make a proper trip there sometime. But since you mentioned it, I have a question for you. You said you felt my presence when I was passing through Nelleram, right?"

"Yes," Tecino said.

"Okay. Well, I noticed there was a woman on her knees in the middle of this clearing. And she was crying."

Tecino nodded. "There were many tears shed there."

"Why?"

"Because our village the Krunations invaded so long ago was originally there. Their homes were gutted from the inside, and by the time the Krunations took them away to build Nocterar's castle, they were reduced to charred shells of what they built."

"And so you tore them down?"

Tecino shook his head, looking at Excelsior with an almost accusatory glare. "We did not. Those were not just destroyed domiciles allowing us to build on top of them. They represented the remains of our fallen Denarians. But on the same day Nocterar was defeated and his castle came crashing down, a powerful wave of energy swept over all of Denab IV. It replenished the ground, but also wiped away all debris left behind."

Excelsior's face reddened underneath his helmet. He opened his mouth to speak, but nothing escaped his lips. The wave of energy came from his own sword, the blast wave doing as he commanded, and this man knew it. And everyone back on Nelleram knew it.

Tecino's face softened and the smile returned. "I see the innovation within you. In your eyes. Looking for the correct means to enhance the beauty of our village."

"That's how it is on Earth. Take what was destroyed, clear the rubble, build something brand-new on top of it," Excelsior said.

Tecino nodded. "So those who see what is, as you say, brand-new forget what preceded it?"

Excelsior pondered the question. "I... I can't say. If I knew, I wouldn't have—"

"My friend, you may be the creator of Denab IV, but you have much to learn about it," Tecino said. "We are aware of how young a planet we are, how small of a planet we are, and we consistently aim to improve ourselves in all areas but not at the expense of what came before us. Why do you believe the Elders occupy Edenaria? They could have been stationed anywhere." When Excelsior failed to provide an answer, Tecino spoke again. "Acerus is from the clan of educators, and it is because of their teachings, we have the ability to communicate telepathically with each other. Knowledge is the very center of our way of life, and so it is here where we have ambassadors from the rest of our world. Knowledge of our past will lead us into our future, and those who forget the past--"

"Are doomed to repeat it," Excelsior finished.

Tecino smiled again and patted Excelsior on the shoulder. "Maybe our worlds are not as different as I suspected. Enjoy yourself."

Excelsior watched the Denarian wander off into the celebrating crowd, and was about to rejoin Zorribis when something else stopped him in his tracks.

Someone else. A Denarian woman with short black hair, a thin athletic figure, and a long overcoat shimmering with various shades of orange, yellow, and blue.

"Wow," Excelsior whispered. She was beautiful, and somehow familiar.

But how? Who is she? he kept asking himself. Why do I know her face? His eyes widened as a long-lost memory awakened.

"Arinna."

Excelsior was no longer within the body of the gawking Matthew Peters but in his previous host, Semminex. He spoke the name of the woman Matthew was looking at, only Semminex was looking at a much younger version. Her hair was longer, hanging in front of her face, and she was sitting in a large chair with her wrists tied to its arms. Her legs hung close to the floor, her body not grown enough for her feet to reach.

"Arinna, wake up."

The young girl looked up at Excelsior, revealing tear stains down her cheeks. "Please help me," she forced out.

"What happened to you?" Excelsior asked.

"They... she... she killed my family. They want me for... for what I can do. Please help me before they come back."

Excelsior used his sword to cut her binds. "You will not have to worry about them. Nocterar has been defeated. The Krunation threat will soon be gone completely."

Arinna smiled. "Really?"

Excelsior nodded. "They will not be back here anymore."

"They..." The tears came back and rolled down her face. "Can I go home please?"

"Absolutely," he said, and he picked her up and held her tight as she wept on his shoulder.

"Arinna?"

She turned toward him and gave a warm smile.

Excelsior took a deep breath, rubbed his fingers against his already sweaty palms, moved his right hand up to his mouth and breathed into it, and took three steps toward this beautiful woman... and then turned around and took thirty steps away from her.

"Matty," Zorribis called out. Excelsior looked up at his friend and forced a smile. "What is wrong?"

"Nothing. Nothing's wrong. I'm fine. It's just..."

"Just what? Did you have another flashback? Something upsetting?"

"No. Well, yes. I mean... where's Niterra?"

"Enjoying the festivities with her friends," Zorribis answered. "So this flashback..."

"Well, yeah, I had a flashback, but it was nothing upsetting. Nothing at all," Excelsior waved his arm, dismissing Zorribis's concern. "Something, well someone... I..."

"Matty, I am your friend. You can tell me."

Excelsior pulled his helmet off and ran his fingers through his hair as though he were once again in high school. "Someone's here. I recognized her in a flashback. And it..." He searched for the right words, but somehow the ones he knew on Earth seemed to fit the closest. "Well, it freaked me out a bit."

"Who? Do I know them?"

"You probably do. She's over there." He cocked his head in the direction of the beautiful woman.

Zorribis glanced long enough to see her and then looked back at Excelsior. "Arinna," he said.

"I know who she is. That's not the point."

"Well, what is the point?"

"The point is, I looked at her and she, well, she smiled at me."

Zorribis placed a helpful hand on Excelsior's shoulder. "Matty, I know you spent a lot of time on Earth, but on Denab IV, smiling is a good thing."

"I understand, and smiling's as good on Earth as it is on Denab IV. But nobody ever, well, I don't remember a girl ever smiling at me like this before. I mean, look at me. I'm all nervous and sweaty."

"So let me try to understand this." Zorribis ran his hand over his chin and began to ponder Excelsior's predicament. "You are the current host of one of the most powerful lifeforces in the known universe. You have inherited the abilities and memories of your predecessors. You inspired this entire race to stand up and fight against their oppressors. You struck down the Emperor of the Krunation Empire, as well as his second-in-command. You are responsible for all of the peace and harmony we are experiencing on Denab IV. And the thought of talking to a woman scares you. Am I correct?"

"Yes."

Zorribis shook his head. "Do you remember what you told me about the day you touched the sword? When you were a child? How the sword called to your blood, and you couldn't resist reaching out to it? Even if it meant there was security all around, and you would get in trouble with the museum and with your parents if you disobeyed their instructions?"

"What about it?"

"The woman over there. There is no security around her, and you will not get into trouble if you said hello."

Excelsior nodded. "Good point. Where has she been all this time? Why am I only seeing her now?"

"She is an ambassador of Denab IV. Arinna can remotely control the Leap of Faith and use it to send her from planet to planet."

Excelsior nodded. "Makes sense why the Krunations would want her, then. I'm sure they wanted to recruit more species to their cause."

"They were not the only ones," Zorribis said.

"Elders!" A wheezing voice cut through the various conversations at the party and attracted both Excelsior's and Zorribis' attention. "Must... speak... Elders."

They turned to see a balding man similar in age to the Elders. He was dressed in rags, a stringy beard covering most of his face. His arms and legs trembled as he walked closer to the Elders, who stood together and looked at this old man with caution.

"I have travelled," he spit out his words. "He... He is coming. Please. I can... I can help..."His words stuck in his throat as he looked around the party with confused eyes. "Where... where am..." Tears began rolling down his cheeks and stained his already dirty beard. Several Denarians came to his aid and eased him away from the Elders.

"Who's he?" Excelsior asked.

"A drifter," Zorribis answered. "He has been seen outside the village from time to time. This is the first time he was this close."

"I wonder what he was talking about. 'He is coming?'"

"Not the first time we have heard him say it."

"So we shouldn't be alarmed?"

"Our guards know to respond to legitimate threats. We will be safe."

Excelsior nodded. "Then I guess there's nothing left but for me to... speak to Arinna." He began to put his helmet back on his head, but Zorribis stopped him.

"No helmet. This is not a war."

"You're right, you're right," Excelsior said, trying to calm his anxious nerves. "Acerus said... never mind, you're right. Okay, here I go."

Zorribis gave him an encouraging pat on the back and Excelsior could have sworn his friend was stifling a laugh. He took another deep breath and his knees trembled.

Arinna greeted Excelsior with an enthusiasm normally reserved for lifelong friends reuniting. "You are finally here!" she exclaimed, wrapping her arms around Excelsior and giving him a tight hug

"This is... wow," he managed to say. It seemed all of his nervousness was for naught.

"Yes, wow indeed," she said as she let go of him. "So I understand you are the same Excelsior I knew a long time ago. But not quite. Correct?"

"Uhh, yes. Yes, you're right," he said, trying to keep his smile from looking too goofy. The more he spoke, the less his knees shook, and so he took it as a sign to keep talking. Maybe it might even make him more confident. "It's more than just Excelsior in here," he said with a tap to his forehead. "Semminex, Valertus, and Matthew Peters are here too, and we're all happy to meet you."

Arinna gave him another small hug with a laugh. "Well, all of you. The feeling is definitely mutual."

"I understand one of Semminex's memories was of you? Back when you were a child?"

Arinna nodded. "You were my hero. If not for you, I might still be there, wondering when someone else would rise up in Nocterar's place and finish the job started on me."

"I wish I would have been there earlier," Excelsior said, thinking back to the other children left to burn in the Sancterrum tree.

Arinna opened her mouth, but nothing came out.

"Are you okay?" Excelsior asked, his fear of making a fool of himself replaced by concern.

She nodded, her expression lost. "Yes, sorry. I... I wish you were there earlier as well. But nothing can be done about it." Arinna looked up and cleared her throat. "Can we maybe talk about something else? I do have a question for you."

"Oh?" Matthew said, his mind suddenly relieved.

"Yes," she said, pointing at the sky. "Why do the stars look like this?"

"The stars?"

"Yes. Do you see how dull they look? This is how they used to look in the daylight. Now we cannot even see the stars during the day, and when night comes, this is how bright they get."

Matthew looked up, and his mouth went dry. He had to admit, the stars never crossed his mind. He started off on his quest across the world so soon after he arrived on Denab IV, and he was so used to only seeing stars at night on Earth, he never thought he could change the planet in any way. He thought back to the blast wave wiping away the sacred village in Nelleram. Was it possible Arinna wasn't the only one feeling this way?

Before he could dwell on this any longer, a low booming siren cut through the conversations in the crowd and the iridinsects overlooking the festivities changed their various colors to black.

"Oh, no," Excelsior said, placing his helmet back on his head. He turned to give Arinna instructions, but she was already heading to a group of worried children.

"Everything is all right," he heard her tell them as the mood of the attending Denarians went from celebratory to panicked. "We need to go to the Development Center for now. You will all be unharmed."

"There are some others over there." Excelsior pointed toward another group of children.

"I see them," Arinna assured him.

"I will help her." Lokris walked toward the remaining children with an intensity defying her age.

"Are you sure?" Excelsior asked.

Lokris waved him off. "Do not worry about us."

Excelsior nodded and unsheathed his sword, squeezing the handle in anticipation. "Elder Acerus," he called out. "You should get indoors."

"No, Excelsior," Acerus declared with a detectable wheeze in his voice.

"Elder, please!" Excelsior said. "We need to make sure you are kept safe." He glanced at Tricerus and Quinterus who were standing behind the High Elder. "All of you."

"Our fate will be the same as our Denarian brothers and sisters," Acerus insisted.

Excelsior wanted to plead with him again, but before he could say another word, Nosgood ran up to him, a blaster rifle in his hand.

"Krunation transports approaching, Excelsior."

"Your security team is ready?" Excelsior asked.

Nosgood smiled. "Armed and ready. It will be an honor for all of us to fight alongside you."

"The honor will be all mine, Nosgood," Excelsior said, and the two clasped wrists.

"And your security team will not be alone!"

Excelsior turned toward the source of the female voice, and saw Zorribis and Niterra holding hands while running toward the center of the village. They were still wearing the outfits they wore during the Bonding Ceremony with their blaster rifles hung over their shoulders.

The bonded couple gave each other a kiss on the lips, and Niterra broke away and started climbing up the side of a house.

Excelsior opened his mouth to say something to stop her, but what came out was, "Make sure you're high enough so they won't easily get you. Target anyone who gets close to the Elders. Where's Zorribis?"

Niterra stepped on to the roof and waved her left hand, then crouched down and ducked out of sight.

"What do you need me to do?" Zorribis asked.

"Stay by the Elders," Excelsior answered. "I have a feeling the Krunations are coming because they're all together. Hodera wouldn't want to pass this up."

Zorribis nodded and ran toward the Elders. Excelsior turned toward the Denarians surrounding him, and almost instantly, the boy who was scared to talk to a woman turned into a grown man, a leader. "Krunation soldiers are approaching. Your children are safe in the Development Center. Anyone else who can fight is welcome to join us."

Malitus raised his hand, his eyes colored blood red. "I will fight alongside Nosgood and my fellow Denarians."

Nosgood must have heard the same contempt in his voice Excelsior heard, because he replied with, "If you fight with me, Malitus, then you fight with Excelsior."

Excelsior turned away from the other Denarians, looked Nosgood in the eye, and whispered, "Thank you."

Nosgood nodded in return. "I will stay close to him."

As he finished his sentence, Nosgood and Excelsior turned toward the sound of the Krunation transports landing outside the village. They could also hear the chattering and hissing of soldiers exiting the transports, ready to attack.

"If you have weapons, now is the time to get them," Excelsior said to the Denarians stepping forward. "If you don't want to fight or if you can't, please stay in your homes." The men and women scattered to retrieve whatever blasters they had, while the rest obeyed Excelsior and ran to safety.

"I can fight!" Excelsior saw the old bearded man running toward him. "Please. Please let me! He is coming. He..."

With the old man's arms flailing about and his eyes still glassy, Excelsior noticed Branerik walking up, his rifle in hand. "Get him to safety," he commanded. Without saying a word, Branerik took the old man by his arm and led him out of harm's way.

It only took a few minutes for the Denarian men and women willing to fight to grab their weapons and return to the center of the village. The hissing of the approaching Krunations grew louder.

Excelsior faced the other armed Denarians standing alongside him. "This is our home, and this is a very important event for our friends. We will not sully it with a pile of dead bodies. Take aim at their weapons! We will protect ourselves, but we will not fire—"

"Death to all Denarians!" Hodera shouted as the Krunation soldiers emerged from outside the village.

Excelsior rolled his eyes and finished his thought. "—unless we are fired upon!" He held his sword in the air and yelled, "Ever Upward!" The Denarians repeated his call, drowning out the approaching Krunation soldiers.

CHAPTER NINE

The piercing sound of laser fire from the Krunations' weapons was music to Hodera's ears. She kept her distance from the fracas, standing behind her loyal cannon fodder like a queen on a chessboard, and casually stepped from one side to another when a soldier acting as her shield was struck down by a Denarian blast.

Hodera was overflowing with confidence as the transports landed close to the Edenarian village. If only she had a weapon large enough and powerful enough to destroy all of Edenaria in one blast, she thought. However, even without one, she was sure her soldiers could recapture the momentum the empire lost with Nocterar's fall.

But as soon as she heard the Denarians crying out, "Ever Upward!" Hodera's enthusiasm began to wane. They weren't taking anyone by surprise. They weren't interrupting a party. They were walking into a trap. The Elders were well-protected and Excelsior stood in front of his army, his sword deflecting her soldiers' laser blasts.

"Advance!" Hodera yelled to her soldiers, and they ran as one toward the Denarians, firing their blaster rifles along the way. But this seemed to only galvanize their enemies, especially Excelsior, who was no longer using his sword in defense from the lasers. He swung at any Krunation unfortunate enough to get close to him, and whether he sliced through blaster rifles or the hands holding them, the Krunations attached to both could live another day.

What went wrong? Her Krunations continued to be cut down while the Denarians were suffering minimal casualties. Was the shift in the air she felt affecting her soldiers' ability to fight? She wanted to use this opportunity to make a statement, to create chaos by robbing their enemies of their guidance, but instead she invited them to sharpen their skills and make sure they didn't get too soft now once they regained control over all of Denab IV.

And right in the middle of this chaos was Excelsior. Curse him, she thought. He was the living embodiment of everything she hated about this planet. Hodera craved order, discipline, and loyalty to a higher power. No matter what the Matera may think of her, she was the ultimate example of what Tornatrax yearned for in a Krunation.

And Excelsior? He was the opposite, allowing people to find their own destiny, to contribute to Denab IV in their own way, and most importantly, he encouraged his Denarians to stand beside him rather than have them looking up at him and swear their allegiance. To Hodera, this went against everything she was brought up to believe.

Suddenly, a laser blast grazed her ear. She looked up and saw someone positioned on the roof of the new home. Another blast would have struck her in the head, but Hodera ducked and almost fell as a result. She hissed in anger as she focused on who was firing on her.

"Niterra," she whispered. "And where is your beloved?" she yelled.

"Right here," Zorribis called out while firing several shots toward Hodera.

She ducked out of the way and dropped to one knee, staying behind three of her soldiers and allowing them to die for a worthy cause: keeping her alive.

"Zorribis!" Excelsior called out while standing and deflecting laser blasts from the front line. "Get back!"

"I will after she dies!" Zorribis shouted. He fired three more times, striking the rifles from the Krunations covering Hodera. Without their weapons, they scattered, leaving Hodera without any protection.

"I said, get back. Protect the Elders!"

Ahhh, Hodera thought. Opportunity. She pushed herself back to her feet, watching Zorribis the whole time. Once he turned his head back toward the Elders, and with a voice as calm as one could be under these circumstances, she looked to her right and said to no one in particular, "Now."

"Who are you talking to?" Zorribis snapped his head back in Hodera's direction.

Hodera remained still and gave a slight smile. "Just wait," she taunted.

"I said, get back," Excelsior yelled while tightening his grip on his sword. "Protect the Elders!"

The battle in the Edenarian village seemed to be a mismatch from the start. As much as Hodera must have thought her army was ready for an assault such as this, she was mistaken. The Denarian security force-combined with the volunteers who knew how to handle a blaster rifle-was too much for the Krunations who must have thought they would swoop in, strike as one, and leave his people for dead without knowing they were under attack.

But at this moment, in the middle of driving the Krunations back, Excelsior noticed something odd around the empty space to the direct right of Hodera.

Was the light... bending?

Before he could ask, a single laser blast appeared out of nowhere. Excelsior noticed its direction and gasped as he saw it heading toward an open space near the Elders.

A space Zorribis was supposed to fill.

Tricerus's deep voice crying out in pain cut through the sounds of the battle.

Zorribis and Excelsior both turned toward the Elder, who dropped to one knee while clutching his broad left shoulder. "No!" Zorribis said, lowering his blaster and returning to his post.

"Yes!" Hodera yelled back. Excelsior followed Zorribis toward the Elders, and he felt like an idiot for thinking this all-out attack was the only method she would use to get to them.

Another laser blast materialized, this one originating closer and to the left of the first, and it was heading straight toward Quinterus. Excelsior swung his sword and the destructive energy struck the tip, stopping the intended target from almost certain death.

"Thank you," Excelsior whispered.

"You could have done that earlier!" Quinterus called out while tending to Tricerus's shoulder. Excelsior squeezed his jaw shut and did his best to push past the Elder taking the opportunity to berate him. Again.

"Where is it coming from?" Zorribis called out to Excelsior while looking back and forth with his rifle at the ready.

Excelsior deflected another Krunation's laser blast with his sword, and Zorribis turned toward its source and fired. As instructed, the weapon was struck, and the Krunation holding it ran off to safety.

"Where is he?" Excelsior whispered over the constant sounds of laser fire and cries from both sides. He focused on any open space in the village, knowing it was only a matter of time before another blast would appear from nowhere. He looked to his left, then his right, then straight ahead past the tall Denarian with the blaster rifle standing in front of him.

There! It was only for a brief moment, but Excelsior could see it. Light was bending, something was moving, and it was only ten feet away from him.

He lunged forward, grabbed the Denarian by his shoulder before he could fire, and directed the weapon toward the ground next to the open space.

"There! Fire!" Excelsior commanded.

The laser fire looked like it harmlessly singed a patch of unoccupied ground, but Excelsior knew he was right the second he heard the man in front of him yell, "Where did he come from?"

The smoke cleared, and Excelsior could now see a Krunation down on one knee holding a blaster rifle.

A pretty short Krunation.

"You," Excelsior whispered.

But Sivtra couldn't hear him. He was too busy aiming and preparing to fire one last blast. And this one was aimed directly at Acerus.

"No!" Excelsior pushed himself in the line of fire and swung his sword as the third laser blast headed straight for him. He must have swung it right because the laser sped back to its source. Sivtra dropped his rifle and ducked out of the way. The laser struck a stone wall, leaving a black ashy mark.

Sivtra slowly got to his feet, leaving the blaster rifle on the ground. Excelsior looked directly into his eyes and shook his head in disappointment. But before he could make any additional motion toward him, he heard the angry voice of Malitus.

"You again!"

With eyes so red Excelsior could see them across the battlefield, the blonde-haired Denarian heading toward Sivtra must have been so filled with rage, he didn't see what was immediately ahead of him. Otherwise he would have avoided the writhing body of a wounded member of Nosgood's security team. He tumbled over and landed hard on his face.

Excelsior turned back toward Sivtra, but he was gone. Malitus provided enough of a distraction for the cunning Krunation to get out of harm's way. Excelsior cursed under his breath. The other Krunation soldiers weren't worth taking prisoner, but someone like Sivtra–who was obviously close enough to Hodera to be sent on missions by himself–would have been ideal.

"My apologies, Excelsior!" Nosgood yelled out while running up to Malitus. "He has been by my side the entire time before this."

Excelsior waved him off and re-focused his attention on the firefight going on around them. The final wave of Krunation soldiers was being pushed back. Nosgood's security team had done their job and done it well. Casualties were light, thankfully, and the Elders were safe.

He breathed a sigh of relief, then looked to his right and saw Zorribis standing there. His weapon was still pointed at the ground. The Denarian opened his mouth to say something, but the words must have caught in his throat because nothing came out.

The remorseful look in his eyes told Excelsior all he needed to know. He nodded and said, "Make sure they're okay," he said.

Hodera stood up straight and surveyed the situation. Her poor Krunation soldiers were either running away or wounded, and the Denarians showed no signs of letting the rest leave alive. She gnashed her teeth and clenched her jaw in rage.

"Sivtra!" she shouted while looking around. "Where are you?"

Sivtra materialized beside her. He was breathing heavily, and his face tensed at the look of anger on her face.

"Did you do as you were told?" she asked.

"I tried, General," Sivtra said, his voice cracking. "I did injure one of them."

Hodera nodded and her face softened. "Much better than anyone else here." She then called out "Retreat!" As one, the wounded soldiers began crawling toward the transports. Those still able to move began retreating as well, turning their backs to the Denarians who were too happy to shoot them down before they escaped.

The call to retreat echoed through the Edenarian village, and the Krunations still lying on the ground picked themselves up and ran to safety. Excelsior saw several Denarians aiming their rifles at the Krunations and ran in front of them with his arms spread. "No!"

"But they're getting away. They may come back again," Branerik yelled to him.

"And if they will, we'll be ready for them like we were today. But we're not going to shoot them in the back. We will defend ourselves!"

"They would have done the same to us," another unfamiliar Denarian called out from among the crowd.

"That's no excuse," Excelsior responded. "I'm not gonna let this world tear itself apart! You've all been here a lot longer than me and you shouldn't want that either."

Excelsior scanned the faces of everyone in the crowd. Some nodded in agreement and delight in winning the battle, while others showed skepticism, even anger. But all lowered their weapons.

"Good," he said with a sigh of relief. "Now, let's get back to the festivities! We're still celebrating Zorribis and Niterra!"

A half-hearted cheer rose from everyone, and it grew louder when Niterra walked up, her blaster rifle resting on her shoulder, and held up her fist in victory. She wrapped her arms around Zorribis and wiped his tears away.

"Are you okay?" she asked.

Zorribis shook his head. "I was so close to ending her. And yet I put my own Elder in danger by..."

Excelsior walked up to him and placed a reassuring hand on Zorribis's shoulder. "I know." He glanced at the Elders and smiled when he saw Tricerus back on her feet, still holding his shoulder. "How is everyone here? Nobody's injured?"

Acerus approached Excelsior. "Once again, we have you to thank for our safety and our protection. And hopefully those who escaped with their lives remember the lesson you taught our fellow Denarians. They just might...." The next words caught in Acerus's throat. He took a deep breath, pushing his words out. "... They just might... wish to make peace with..."

Acerus's eyes glazed over, and he collapsed to the ground. The festivities instantly came to a halt, and the smiles and laughter were replaced by shock and concern. Excelsior dropped to one knee to attend to the High Elder.

"What happened?" he asked Tricerus and Quinterus, who also crouched down to assist Acerus. "He wasn't shot, was he?"

"This has nothing to do with a laser blast," Quinterus declared, his tone bitter. "Acerus's body is deteriorating. We must take him to the Regeneration Chambers."

"No," Excelsior responded. He took the old man's withering body in his arms and stood up, looking around at all of the concerned men and women. Malitus was the closest to him, and he looked at Acerus, then back up at Excelsior. "What did you do?" he whispered.

Excelsior didn't answer. He turned toward his closest friend while cradling the High Elder in his arms. "Zorribis, do me a favor and get to the development center. Help Lokris and Arinna with getting the children back to their families. Then bring them back here."

Zorribis nodded, and he and Niterra ran off together, while Excelsior walked toward Acerus's home. With the villagers no longer in a celebratory mood, Excelsior could hear Tricerus and Quinterus's voices cutting through the silence.

"Deteriorating," Tricerus said. "Like our crops on Collagra."

"Yes," Quinterus replied. "And the rest of us."

CHAPTER TEN

"**W**hat do you want?"

Hodera looked at the Krunation soldier who dared to speak to her with utter contempt. He was taller than Hodera, but younger and definitely of a lower rank, and he was standing to the right of a large gray chamber door. Another Krunation not quite as tall stood on the left of the door. Neither showed any effort to move from their post.

"I wish to speak with Connoram," she spit out.

"He is not speaking to anyone right now," the soldier said. "Especially someone who refused his advice to not strike against the Denarians."

"Why am I even speaking to you?" she growled, her anger rising with each passing second.

"You are speaking to me because Connoram does not wish to see you," the soldier growled back.

"Let her in, Charak," a stern but fatherly voice commanded from the other side of the chamber door.

"Yes, my Lord," Charak motioned to the door. "He will see you now," he said with a smirk.

Hodera stormed past the two guards and threw open the door. No matter how much time Hodera spent in Connoram's quarters, she always felt as impressed as she did the first time she saw them. While the other Krunations were given a room consisting of one small bed, their daily food rations, a waste disposal center, and their spare uniforms, Connoram's space included enough room to house a small Sancterrum tree, similar to the kind Hodera burned so long ago. Above the tree was an opening in the ceiling, allowing for fresh air to enter and sunlight to shine down on it. She walked past it and rolled her eyes, wondering why Connoram would waste his time caring for something like this.

"Connoram," she said to the older Krunation looking through his wall-sized window.

Standing tall and proud, with not a wrinkle on his black uniform to be found, Connoram slowly turned his head in Hodera's direction and narrowed his eyes. "You went to the Denarian village, yes?"

Hodera nodded, trying to stand as straight as the old man.

"Despite my warnings not to do so," he continued. "When I told you how proud of a race the Denarians are, and how they do not appreciate sacred ceremonies being interrupted."

"The Bonding Ceremony was long-since completed," Hodera said. "We attacked during the celebration afterward."

"Still, you did this because?"

"Because we knew with a ceremony of this importance, everyone would be there. It was a perfect opportunity."

"An opportunity to do what?" Connoram's voice rose with impatience.

"To crush the Denarian people at the source," Hodera shouted. "If the Elders and Excelsior were eliminated—"

"This may be how Nocterar conducted business," Connoram said, walking toward her. He looked her in the eye. "It is not how I will, especially since the Empire is gone. Besides, the Bonding Ceremony is a sacred ritual, and there is no honor in taking anyone by surprise like that."

"This is not about honor. It is about re-establishing our place on this planet. The Empire is rebuilding itself, Connoram. Our forces are still strong in numbers—"

"Not anymore, according to what I have been told," Connoram shot back. "You have to think beyond what you have been taught all your life, Hodera. You have potential to be a great leader in this new age on Denab IV, but you cannot squander your potential on petty wars."

Hodera was tempted to punch Connoram right in his smug face, but a very familiar soft roar from outside caught her attention.

"Is that what I think it is?" she asked. She moved to the window and took a startled step back when a slow-moving, mammoth-like creature peered at her. Its blue eyes were the size of Hodera's head, and its black fur covered its entire head and body.

"Why do you have a throngar here?"

"Why not?" Connoram said, opening the window so he could reach out and caress its large head. The throngar closed its eyes in response.

"It would make a great dinner for all of your soldiers," she said, scoffing at this act of kindness.

"You go before she does," he told her, keeping his eyes on the unexpectedly gentle creature.

"How do you do this?" Hodera asked. "You have a Sancterrum tree in your quarters; you have a throngar outside. You go against everything you, as a Krunation, were meant to do."

Connoram let out a sigh of exasperation, then asked, "Do you ever stop and wonder why we were given such rigid commandments? Why our minds are conditioned to accept the orders of our god and nothing more? While the species we share Denab IV with are given the ability to find their own destiny and work alongside the god who created them?"

Hodera cocked her head, confused. "This is how you spend your time? Why would you choose to fill your mind with such waste? Unless you wish to think like that inferior race!" She turned on her heels and headed toward the door to exit the chambers, stopping before she reached them and facing Connoram. "Those who follow Excelsior choose to live in a straight line with no room for advancement. They choose to follow a god who enjoys being less than a god. Tornatrax gives us the chance to live beyond this planet. I follow what gives me the chance to be a part of greatness, not live among the squalor. And if you feel the need to live in the squalor with them, you have my permission and my blessings. But you will not bring your fellow Krunations with you."

Hodera turned her back on Connoram and left the room.

Charak walked inside the chambers as Connoram reached out and caressed the large throngar's head. "Everything all right, sir?"

Connoram kept his eyes on the throngar. "She will never understand, Charak. She is a powerful warrior, one of the best this planet will ever see. But she is not the leader our race needs at this time. She is as outdated as her beloved Nocterar."

Charak glanced at the Sancterrum tree. "I believe it has reached its full maturity."

Connoram glanced over his shoulder at the tree. "Well done, young one. You are correct. Where is Tarrax?"

Charak nodded toward the door. "Staying at his post. As always."

Connoram nodded, then gave the throngar one last pat. "Rest, my friend. Everything will be all right."

"I have never seen such a gentle creature," Charak observed.

Connoram turned away from the throngar and walked to the Sancterrum tree. He pressed his palm against the trunk and shut his eyes as he spoke. "Do not be afraid. I know the skin you feel is familiar, but I promise I mean no harm. All I ask is for you to reveal the truth to me. We have been told one truth by one god and a second by another. There must be a connection hidden from us. Only you and the consciousness you share can tell us. Only your secret can help this planet come together. Only your answers can heal this rift." Connoram held his hand on the trunk for several seconds before he finally let go.

"Do you feel any different?" Charak asked. "Have you heard anything yet?"

Connoram shook his head. "I can hear something, but I cannot decipher it," he said, his voice shaken. "Time is growing short. The planet is trying to send us a message."

"I have never known of our kind communicating with the planet," Charak said.

"Tornatrax was never concerned with this."

"Then it is good I am not seeking to learn from Tornatrax." Charak looked over his shoulder and felt a dreadful chill.

"Does this frighten you, child?" Connoram asked.

"I only fear for your safety," Charak answered. "If Hodera were to hear you say this..."

"Hodera knows where I stand," Connoram said as he grabbed his black overcoat and slipped it on, draping the attached hood over his head. "Whatever I do or say, it should be of no surprise to her."

"Are you going somewhere?" Charak asked, motioning to his commander's coat.

Connoram nodded. "There is only one lifeform on this planet who can help me find the answers I need."

"You know where he is?"

Connoram froze for a moment, and then his shoulders sagged. "The attack Hodera led was on Edenaria. I can begin there."

"Before you go," Charak began, his voice thoughtful. "Try touching the tree one more time. Ask it for Excelsior's location."

"There is no reason to," Connoram replied, impatient. "I cannot understand it."

"Yes, but maybe it can understand you," Charak said.

Connoram's lips curved and he hurried back to the Sancterrum tree. He pressed his palm against the trunk, took a deep breath, and spoke. "If you can hear me, please show me a sign. Any sign. Please."

An audible rumble emitted from the trunk of the tree. Both Charak and Connoram took a step back and looked at each other in shock.

"It worked," Charak whispered. "That could not have been a coincidence."

Tarrax peeked inside the room while still standing at his post. "Everything okay in here?"

Connoram waved him off. "We are fine, Tarrax. Thank you." He pressed his hand against the trunk once again. "I may not understand you. I may not yet know what you intend for me to do. But I know you can lead me to the one who can understand you. I ask you to please join with me and lead me to the one known as Excelsior. Please."

Another rumble came from the tree, and Charak and Connoram once again took a step back. But this time, a piece of a branch grazed against Connoram's head and dropped to the floor.

"It is not dying, is it?" Charak asked with concern as Connoram bent down to pick up the branch. It was no larger than the palm of the Krunation's hand.

"No," Connoram said, gazing down at the branch. It was vibrating as much as the tree. "I can still feel it." He pressed it up against his chest and winced as the branch seemed to attach itself to his flesh. He pulled his hand away and looked up at his soldier with a renewed vigor.

"I can feel it pulling me," Connoram said. "It can take me to Excelsior."

"You will need protection," Charak said. "I can go with you. Tarrax can stay here."

"No," Connoram said. "I can make this journey alone. I will need you to stay here and watch over the rest of our soldiers." He faced the younger Krunation, who kept his head high and his chest out, the model soldier. "You are a fine leader, Charak. If there was anything left of your father before I lost him, he would have been very proud."

"I must trust your opinion," Charak said. "There was nothing from him I would emulate."

Hodera stormed into her own quarters, which was twice the size of Connoram's, and stood in the middle of the room. The decoration was minimal, with a large black orb in the center of the table behind her. Nothing hung on the walls, and the only piece of furniture other than the table was a single-size bed without any kind of blanket. She looked around the bare suite and shuddered as she felt the presence of the quarters' former owner, Emperor Nocterar.

"How dare he," she whispered through her clenched teeth as the chill was replaced by the wave of anger toward her fellow Krunation. "The gall of him to suggest he knows what is best for our race, that he knows better than our god."

Hodera sucked in a calming breath and turned to face the orb on the table. She knelt down and placed her hands over it, and suddenly the room was fully illuminated by its otherworldly glow. She shut her eyes and spoke out, "I call out to thee, O mighty Tornatrax, ruler over the rightful dominant species of Denab IV. We have done as you commanded."

A gust of wind blasted from the orb, threatening to knock Hodera on her back, and a deep, sinister voice echoed within her head. "I am here, my dear Hodera, and I have sensed your wishes to continue my message. You have made me very proud."

Hodera smiled with satisfaction. "It will not be long, my Lord. In time, the wrong incurred upon you so long ago will be righted. You will be freed from your prison in deep space and able to strike the final blow against your captor."

"Your success relies on your ability to obtain what belongs to me, child. Your attack on the Denarians existed for one single purpose, to capture the sword of Excelsior." Hodera felt herself growing tense as Tornatrax's voice grew in anger. "And what did you do? You prepared an attack at a time when Excelsior was surrounded by his pathetic fellow Denarians. You acquiesced to defeat with this terrible strategy!"

"I only wanted to please you, my Lord. Only by attacking at full force would we—"

"There is no use being the dominant force if you do not have soldiers to dominate."

"I understand, Lord Tornatrax."

"Yes, but now is not the time to attempt another attack on Excelsior. Now, you must be mindful of the one called Connoram."

Hodera clenched her teeth and hissed. "Yes. He is not to be trusted."

"He has been corrupted, my dear. He believes only what has been told to him by the same race eager to send the Krunations into total annihilation. He has become a disciple of the enemy, and by commanding other Krunations, he is guilty of treason against his own race."

"He will be punished, my Lord. I will end this danger to the Krunations myself. Him and those lackeys of his, Charak and Tarrax."

"No, Hodera. Patience." Tornatrax's voice calmed, became more soothing. "I admire your will to do as I command. You will do well by my side in the new age of Krunation dominance."

Hope blossomed within her. She would stand by his side?

"But you must not attempt a civil war to reduce his power, my child. Do not engage Connoram and Charak when their soldiers are most loyal to them. You must test their loyalty. You must show them Connoram's way is a lie."

"It is not just his way," Hodera said through gritted teeth.

"Ah, yes. The Matera. I can feel your hatred, child. I know you believe they are obsolete."

Hodera dropped her chin to her chest in shame. Who was she to dictate her preferences to a god, especially one as mighty as Tornatrax? Who was she to declare what should no longer be utilized?

"And you are correct."

Hodera's head shot back up.

"Yes, you are correct. The Matera have been in their position of power for too long. A new era for Denab IV is ready to begin, Hodera. And with your help, that era can begin. When the time is right, you will know what to do."

Hodera smiled, more than a little intrigued at the possibilities. "And what of Excelsior, my Lord? With his sword in our possession, we can free you from your prison."

"Do not concern yourself with Excelsior anymore, Hodera. I will handle him myself."

"But... but my Lord, how can you do this from your prison?"

"Not all of me is here, child. The sword you possess has an element of myself attached to it, and so does something else. I can feel its connection. In time, it will grow stronger. And when my power is fully manifested, I promise you the moment of victory will be upon us very soon."

The cold, dark refrigeration facility remained silent; its capacity filled with artifacts from Earth's various continents, spanning centuries of history. Among them was a clear case with a thin layer of dust across it. Inside were the remnants of a vicious-looking reptilian humanoid with its head leaning back and its arms covering a large wound in its chest. However, its face—one expected to be frozen in pain considering the shape of its body—was a picture of peace. Its eyes were gently closed as though the creature was taking a restful nap.

Between its fingers, a clear residue could be seen around the wound its hands covered, and the residue began to emit a soft glow, the only light in the room. It grew brighter for a moment, then dimmed.

"Soon, my servant," a voice called out to the being within the case. "When the time is right, you shall rise once more. I have great plans for a warrior such as you."

CHAPTER ELEVEN

"What could have done this to you?" Excelsior asked as he laid Acerus down on his bed and gently held his hand. The door was left open, with Nosgood standing by the door and many Edenarian villagers looking inside.

Excelsior remembered the days before he began his reconnection with the planet, when he saw an aging, but still sturdy man, ready for the tasks ahead of bringing the Denarian race to full fruition. But after he returned, whatever light was in Acerus's eyes was fading fast, and he seemed content to allow it.

Excelsior was so preoccupied with his thoughts, he didn't hear Quinterus and Tricerus bursting in.

"Why are you here wasting time?" Tricerus asked. "He must be taken to the regeneration chambers immediately!"

"I said, 'no,'" Excelsior answered. "Acerus doesn't want to go there. He told me."

"Of course he did," Quinterus said, his voice dripping with anger and sarcasm. Excelsior was tempted to engage in an argument with Quinterus, but not now.

Fortunately for him, Acerus's eyes fluttered open. "No," he said, confirming Excelsior's earlier response. "My time... is short. If we are... to leave this planet... to others... then we... will not take it from them... in the future. Leave me here." He drifted back to sleep.

"What's wrong with him?" Excelsior asked. "How could someone deteriorate like this so quickly? This has never happened before."

"Are you sure you have never seen it?" Quinterus asked. "Not even on your precious Earth?"

"My precious Earth?" Excelsior repeated. "Quinterus, you may not believe this, but there is Denarian blood in my veins. I was born on Earth, yes, but Denab IV is my home."

"And your presence here may very well have doomed everyone on your home," Tricerus spoke up, the volume in his voice attracting the attention of everyone listening outside.

"Nosgood, please shut the door," Excelsior said.

"No, leave it open!" Quinterus countered. "The people deserve to know what their 'savior' has done to them!"

"Our crops are dying almost as quickly as they are harvested," Tricerus continued. "Acerus is in his final ten-day cycles, and it may be only one more cycle before he leaves us. Surely you must have seen this happen to Elder Klierra on Earth."

Excelsior shook his head. "No. No, she showed no sign of aging like this. She was... Danaak killed her before something like this could happen."

"Regardless of whether you saw it before," Quinterus said, anger rising in his voice. "You must know how fragile Denarians are when they are outside of their own atmosphere. Was it not you who created this planet? Was it not you who gave us life? Are you not 'Excelsior?' The father and savior of Denab IV!" When Excelsior failed to give an answer, Quinterus stepped up to him. "Are you not the one who came to us and invited us to share in your infinite wisdom? To thrive on a planet free from the oppression of the Krunations? To keep your legacy alive? And for what? So my son can give his life to send you here? So your presence will ensure nobody will survive to enjoy the peace of this planet? What kind of a god are you?"

Excelsior stepped back from the Elders and turned toward the crowd looking at him from outside the door. He could feel their accusatory stares, and he felt his whole body trembling with guilt. Was he really to blame for Acerus's condition? And was there a way he could fix it?

"You all believe I had something to do with this?" he asked the villagers. They, like Quinterus and Tricerus, remained silent.

He turned back toward the Elders and pointed at Tricerus. "Acerus began to feel this way after my arrival, right?" The large Elder nodded. "Then I think I know how to fix this," he said. He ran to the doorway and the crowd of villagers split apart, allowing Excelsior plenty of room to run out into the village and launch himself into the sky.

There it is, Excelsior thought to himself as he approached Klierra Peak. He felt his body trembling as he approached the top of the mountain. "Please," he whispered. "Please let this work."

Excelsior pulled his sword from his sheath and closed his eyes, holding the sword to the sky, and braced himself for what would follow. The screams of a distant past from so many Denarian men and women filled his head, and once again, his knees buckled. But he squeezed his eyes shut and kept the sword straight up. Even with the screams crippling his concentration, he expected the clouds to gather like a magnet over the sword. A bolt of lightning was supposed to come down and touch the blade, creating a wave of energy cascading over the sky.

But now... nothing.

Excelsior opened his eyes and glared at the sky. "Come on!" he yelled over the piercing voices, begging the clouds to come together as they should. Panic set in "Please!"

The clouds refused to answer, but the screaming intensified. Excelsior continued to hold his sword high and he yelled out to them, "I'm sorry! I'm sorry I wasn't here! I'm sorry I was gone for so long!"

"Matthew!"

Excelsior looked up at the sky, confused. In the midst of the cacophony of tormented cries, one singular, very familiar voice cut through.

"Matthew, please come down."

"Lokris?" he said out loud. Then he reached out with his mind. "Elder Lokris?"

"Come to the development center, Matthew. We are waiting for you there."

We. Lokris and Arinna were both there. And so were the parents visiting their children in the development center. He felt the dryness in the back of his throat that Matthew Peters always felt whenever his parents were about to scold him.

Just get it over with, he said to himself. You still don't know for sure if you were the one who's making crops deteriorate. Or caused Acerus's age to increase. Or... did he take the stars away from the daylight as well? But if he's not the cause of all this, then what is?

"Come to us, Matthew," Lokris said. "We have a problem in front of us. We must know how to solve it."

She did have a point. Whatever happened to Denab IV, Excelsior was the only one who could possibly fix it. He took a step off Klierra Peak and glided through the sky, heading back toward the Edenarian village.

Excelsior stayed as high as fifty feet in the air as he looked down on his beloved Denarians in the village. He could see some still keeping vigil outside Acerus's home, while others seemed to be either walking around with their families or chatting amongst themselves.

But one Denarian in particular caught Excelsior's attention. He recognized the bald head and sturdy build of Branerik, and he was standing apart from everyone, in the direct center of the village square. He was looking down at the large seal that matched what was on Excelsior's uniform, the one added to the village with the words "He Has Returned" carved into it.

And Branerik was... what was he doing? Was he praying to it? Was he trying to use it as some form of guidance?

No, he was using a small blaster rifle to shoot into it.

How dare he, Excelsior thought to himself. He looked closer to the symbol as Branerik walked away, apparently done with his handiwork.

The Denarian used his blaster to cross out the word "Returned" on the symbol, and added two more words underneath, so it now presented a different message.

"He Has Destroyed Us."

Excelsior started to fall, his concentration momentarily shattered. He shut his eyes and cleared his mind as quickly as when he fell from the top of Klierra Peak, and swooped back into the sky before any Denarian could look up and see him. Lokris was right. He needed answers now. And the development center couldn't get close enough for him.

Or far enough.

CHAPTER TWELVE

"**W**ow!"

Excelsior's jaw dropped when he stood outside a large white building with the words "Development Center" above the doorway. The same symbol on his uniform, the same one vandalized in the village square, was on both sides of the door, and Excelsior could see the roof was translucent, with bright yellow lights attached inside.

He shook all nervousness from his hands and entered the building. Inside were rows of clear orbs as far as his eyes could see. There were dozens of them, maybe a few hundred, and they looked large enough to contain a five-year-old Earth child. Three thick green vines were protruding from the ground underneath each orb, providing a cradle to keep them off the ground.

Excelsior stepped closer and his eyes widened when he saw what was inside one of the orbs. Something was moving.

No. Someone.

A child. A Denarian child. And from the looks of it, it was about three years old, maybe four. The three vines holding up the orb were connected to the child inside, and the vines looked like they were pulsating, transferring energy in and out.

"Ahh, good. You are here."

Excelsior was so fascinated by the Denarian children that Lokris's voice startled him. He looked up and his palms began to sweat as the Elder approached him with such speed, Arinna looked like she had to jog to keep up with her.

"Yes," he said, his eyes going back and forth between the two Denarians and the orbs attached to the ground. "So this is the development center Zorribis mentioned."

Lokris nodded. "Yes. Our next generation are cultivated here. When a mother is with child, the initial elements are deposited here and the child is born within the orb. The planet provides nutrients, water, even education for the first several years of its life. Then, when the child is ready, the parents bring them home, leaving a space in the center available for another parent-to-be to begin the process all over again."

"But we have noticed something while we have been here," Arinna added. "Do you see the vines? The energy cycling in and out of each orb?"

Excelsior crouched down in front of the one closest to him and saw three different streams of light in each vine. Two of them were traveling from the ground through the vine and into the orb, and the third was going in the opposite direction. "Yes, I see it."

"The light should be much brighter than it is now," Arinna said. "Like the stars above."

"So the kids in these orbs," Excelsior said while standing back up. "They're not getting as much of what they need?"

"It appears so," Lokris said. "And because of what is happening to the planet, it is likely more than us and these children being affected. The wildlife. The plant life. Even the Regeneration Chambers."

"I still don't know what it is," Excelsior said. "But whatever it is, I have to fix it. I went to Klierra Peak and held up my sword like I did before, but nothing happened."

"Of course," Lokris said, not showing any surprise by this news. "Such a change in our atmosphere cannot be solved so easily."

"So what do we do?" Excelsior asked, crossing his arms over his chest.

Lokris's eyes studied Excelsior, and she held up her right hand. "First, I need you to calm yourself. Take a deep breath."

He shook his hands and inhaled as instructed.

"Good. Now remove your helmet," she said.

He placed his still sweaty palms on his helmet and pulled it off, revealing the worried eyes of Matthew Peters.

"Drop the helmet."

"I can hold it," Arinna said. Excelsior gave the younger Denarian a nervous smile as he passed the helmet to her. She grabbed the helmet and took a step away.

Lokris gently pressed the palms of her hands against the young man's temples. "Now, I want you to answer a question for me. When you re-established connection with the planet, when did you feel closest to it? When you could picture every speck of land in your mind? Every single drop of water?"

"When I flew," Excelsior answered. "A bunch of different images went through my head when I went to Klierra Peak. Next thing I knew, I was staying in the air. That was when I felt the most connected. It felt like a large hand was cushioning me underneath and gliding me along the planet like I was a toy."

"Okay," Lokris said. "Now, close your eyes and allow every one of those images to fill your mind. Make sure you hold on to me."

His eyes darted over to Arinna again, but Lokris gave him a small slap on his right temple and said sternly, "Focus."

"Right. Sorry." Matthew wrapped his arms around Lokris, taking another deep breath and closing his eyes. "Okay. Here we go." He tightened his grip on Lokris and opened his mind to Denab IV once again. But this time, he felt a separate presence watching over him, and he briefly tensed up as though he were protecting his homework from a cheating classmate in the desk behind him. This must be what it felt like to be on the receiving end of the Enterrand Process, when a Denarian who had this special gift entered someone else's mind to unlock hidden information.

As Excelsior made his peace with what Lokris was doing, he allowed the familiar images to flood his mind. The mountains. The valleys. The caverns. The bodies of water. The Leap of Faith. The various Denarian clans. The

Elders watching over them. The people of Nelleram, both still living and long gone. The warriors of Axsella.

And then, for a flash, an image of somewhere else. A completely foreign location, with the sounds of cars driving by, buses stopping and opening their doors, people of all ages, colors, and creeds chattering among themselves. Someone walking on the concrete sidewalks of New York City, then looking down and glancing at their wristwatch to see the time.

As the final image flashed before Excelsior's mind, he felt his feet leaving the ground and his body floating in the air. He felt content, at peace with himself, as if no problems could ever exist as long as he stayed in the—

"Excelsior!"

Lokris's panicked cry snapped his eyes open. He looked at her face, which was stricken in fear, and was so startled by her expression, he almost dropped her. He drifted back to the floor, and she stepped away from him.

"The last image in your mind before you flew. That was from Earth, yes?"

Excelsior nodded. "Yes."

"Why?" Arinna asked. "Is there still a connection you have to Earth?" Arinna's soft, calming voice was suddenly replaced by concern. And something else. Was it jealousy?

"A connection? Well... maybe."

"Maybe? What do you mean?"

"I mean I... uh..." Excelsior stumbled through the rest of his answer, trying to find the right words. "I, well, told my uncle to continue the comic strips I made, to keep the name alive. And when he thought he couldn't do it, I... well, I gave him a little something."

Lokris placed her hands on Excelsior's shoulders and gazed deep into his eyes. "I want you to really think about this. Did you pass on any of your new powers, any trace of them at all, before you left Earth?"

Excelsior tried to gather up the right words to answer, but Lokris immediately placed her hands over his temples one more time and shut her eyes. In the young man's mind, he suddenly heard a voice from his recent past speaking to him. The voice of Jason Peters.

"So what happens to you now?" Jason asked.

Excelsior heard himself answer, "Zorribis and I have to go back to Denab IV. Acerus has sent our people to the Leap of Faith to bring us back, and there is no telling who is leading the Krunation Empire." He smiled at Jason. "Thank you. For everything."

Excelsior looked around and saw he was no longer standing in the development center, but in Tollund Laboratories in New York City. He was standing in front of Jason Peters, who had fresh wounds due to the battle with Danaak. Beside him stood Zorribis, ready to return to Denab IV to avenge the loss of his fellow Denarians, including Elder Klierra.

Excelsior held out his hand, and Jason shook it. Suddenly, the room was lit up by a bright light from Excelsior's hand. The light found its way into Jason's. Matthew's uncle looked down at their still clasped hands, and both could see goose bumps going up Jason's arm.

"I want you to continue the comic strip," Excelsior told Jason.

"What? No, the comics are yours."

Excelsior shook his head. "They need to keep going here. I'll do my part to generate the stories. You just keep your mind open, so you'll be able to get them. It'll be just like at the beginning when you helped me develop the comic."

"But how can we do this? You'll be on another planet."

"Like I said," Excelsior said as he looked down at their hands still clasped together. "I'll do my part. You just keep your mind open."

"Oh, no." Her voice dropped to a whisper, and she pulled her hands away. She took a step back and almost tripped over her own feet, but Arinna reached out and caught Lokris before she could fall.

"What is it?" Arinna asked.

"What? What did I do?" Excelsior's voice rose, and the sweat returned to his palms.

Lokris pointed at him. "You left some of your energy behind. You created a tether between the two planets, between Denab IV and Earth."

"And this is bad?"

"Very bad, bad for all of us." Lokris pointed to the transparent ceiling. "We can no longer see the stars during the day because Denab IV's atmosphere is shifting to accommodate you, because there is still a connection to Earth."

Arinna gasped. "This is why we cannot see them?" She grew angrier. "Why we are doomed to grow old and die at an accelerated rate? Because of your actions?"

Lokris turned toward Arinna. "Calm yourself, my dear. How could he have known this would happen? What we need to focus on now is how to repair the planet and guarantee its future. Excelsior, believe me when I say I understand why you did what you did. But this is your home now. These people need you, and they need you to sever this connection you have made with Earth."

"And this is the only option I have?" Excelsior asked.

"This is the only option we all have," Lokris answered.

Excelsior felt his guts tighten into knots. How could he have done this to all of these people? They spent one generation after another underground, struggling against the might of the Krunation Empire, keeping themselves motivated by the promise of Excelsior returning and leading them to ultimate victory. And after fulfilling the promise and returning to the people who loved him, he repaid their loyalty by speeding up their mortality and dooming every life on Denab IV to an early death. He couldn't even bear to look at Lokris and Arinna. He turned his head away from them, but the rows and rows of children in the development process pained him even more.

Meanwhile, Matthew Peters was contemplating the task ahead of him, and it made him feel nauseous. He had to go back to Earth, track down his uncle, take back the gift he gave him in order to maintain a connection with family, and then go back to Denab IV for good. By doing so, he would save everyone on this planet, but when the time came, would he have what it took to permanently close the door Matthew Peters's life?

Lokris interrupted his torturous train of thought. "It may not be a good idea for you to return to the village. We do not know if any other Denarians wish to confront you."

"Aren't we going to the Leap of Faith?" Excelsior asked, confused. "So I can fix everything?"

"No," Lokris answered. "How long have you been awake? I know this was your home planet, but we need a well-rested Excelsior for this mission."

"But Acerus—"

"Will last longer than you think. He has yearned this long for a peaceful Denab IV. I can promise you he will wait as long as it takes for you to do what must be done on Earth."

"He will not be alone," Arinna spoke up.

"What?" Excelsior asked.

"I will go with him," she confirmed. Her voice was steady, as if she was indifferent about what was happening and what was ahead of them. "He will need someone to get him back here. After he accomplishes his mission, of course."

"Of course," Lokris said. "Now make sure you both are well rested. There are beds available here, in the back room. I will inform the other Elders of what is happening, and neither of you should be disturbed. You will leave for Earth at dawn."

Excelsior didn't know how to take all of this. Earlier in the evening, he would have been delighted that Arinna was tagging along, but now? Now, she wasn't even looking at him, and he could only imagine the vitriol she was saving up once they were behind closed doors.

Lokris must have noticed how uneasy Excelsior was because she took his hand and whispered to him, "I understand why you did this. And I am proud of you for wishing to make things right." Excelsior could only nod in response. She turned to Arinna. "Take care of him."

"Oh, I will take care of him," Arinna said, shooting Excelsior a look strong enough to strike down a lesser man.

"Not like that," Lokris said. "If you spend a moment inside his head, you will see his intentions."

"If you declare it," Arinna said.

"Rest well," Lokris said, then turned and left.

Silence hung in the air for over a minute. Excelsior's legs felt like cement as he struggled to come up with something to say. "Thank you," he finally said. "For coming with me tomorrow."

"You gave me no choice," Arinna said in a cold tone of voice. "Who is to say you would not want to return home?"

"You're saying I was planning to abandon everyone to die?" Excelsior asked, the feeling in his legs coming back, but not for the reason he preferred.

"I am simply reminding you of what Lokris said. Denab IV is your home, whether you like it or not." She tossed his helmet back to him as an exclamation point.

Excelsior dug his fingers into his helmet and said, "Please, with everything going on, you don't have to remind me where my home is!"

"Nobody on this planet needs a reminder of where your home is," Arinna snapped back. "They can look to the sky and ask where the stars have gone!"

Excelsior dropped his helmet at his feet. "You want to do this instead of me? Valertus and Semminex are both gone. It's not my fault the sword called to me! I didn't petition for this job. And I sure wasn't looking forward to leaving everything I was back on Earth so I could come here and play the hero. I'm still trying to figure all this out. So if you want to give it a shot, if you think it's so easy, be my guest. At least you won't have Elders looking at you like you have no business wearing this uniform!"

Tears formed in Excelsior's eyes and he squeezed his eyes shut in response to the sudden sting. Arinna looked like she was about to say something snippy as a response, but kept it in.

After a moment, her voice softened. "I apologize."

"You what?" Excelsior expected the argument to continue.

"I apologize," Arinna repeated. "I understand you were not given adequate time to prepare for this monumental task."

"So you're not gonna kill me for taking the stars away?" he asked.

The color in Arinna's eyes gave a slight shift to red, then back to blue. "It would not be productive to kill you if I could. Your lifeforce would return to your sword, and we would need to wait until the next worthy person, Denarian or otherwise, was found. Who knows if we would survive with our planet's sudden... changes?"

"Good point. And speaking of the changes," Excelsior said while turning toward the rows of orbs. "What will happen to them? If the planet isn't giving off the same energy as before, how will they be nourished?"

"Lokris said the orbs holding the children inside can sustain them for a period of time, but it is finite," Arinna answered. "A matter of days. Maybe more for some, and maybe less for others."

"You don't have to worry about me not coming back," Excelsior said, more to himself than anyone else. "I won't abandon them. These kids will get the same opportunities as everyone else here. More, even. I don't see why we can't be gone long enough for the Krunations to take notice."

"I hope you are right," Arinna said, her voice not carrying as much confidence as Excelsior would have liked. "Your enemies will seek out any possible trace of you in hopes of destroying it."

His eyes rounded. "You don't think the Krunations will try to get to Jason before we can, do you?"

Arinna shook her head. "I cannot say. Hodera is leading the Empire right now, and she has become very unpredictable and frantic."

"I need to know if Jason is okay. Maybe we should just go to the Leap of Faith right now."

"No," Arinna ordered, pointing at him. "Lokris said you need your rest. You may be a god, but you are still flesh and blood. And you get tired just like the rest of us. We will rest now and locate him at sunrise."

She walked away, but Excelsior called out, "Wait!" Arinna stopped and turned around. "You studied under Lokris, right?" At her nod, he continued, "Well, is it possible for you to do what she did earlier?"

"The Enterrand Process," Arinna said. "She told me about it as well, how you brought her back to life after she was forced to do that. But you saw your uncle a short while ago. Do you think he is in danger already?"

"I don't know. But like you said about Hodera, she's unpredictable. And I need to make sure he's okay. Please?"

She contemplated him for a moment, then motioned him toward an overturned chair. "Sit down."

He sat, leaning his head back. She placed her hands over his head, her fingertips lightly pressed against his temples, and shut her eyes. He shut his eyes and waited.

And waited.

And waited.

"Open your eyes," she said. "And look into mine."

Excelsior obeyed. He didn't have to be told twice to look into Arinna's eyes, even if he didn't know the reason.

"Shouldn't my eyes be shut to make this work?"

"Not yet. Your mind is too erratic right now," she answered. "It needs to be relaxed. Now keep looking into my eyes."

After a long moment of silence, his shoulders, his neck, his head, and his mind began to relax. Everything moving at a rapid pace—the worry over Acerus, the accusations from the Elders, the atmospheric shift, the threat of the Krunations, the mission ahead—began to slow, no longer attacking him.

"Better?" she asked.

Excelsior took a deep, cleansing breath. "Better."

"Good," she said, grinning. "Now I can try again. Close your eyes."

He closed his eyes and waited again.

And waited.

"Do you see anything?" she asked.

"Not yet," he answered.

"Hmmmm," she said, and Excelsior felt her fingers pushing harder on his head. "How about now?"

"If you press any harder, I might see my skull crack," he said, wincing.

She pulled her hands away. "Sorry. It must not come as easily to me as it does to Lokris."

"It's okay," he replied. "I'm sure he's fine. So we'll go there, find him, get the energy back from him, and head home, right?"

"You may have the power of a god inside you, but you do not know the future," Arinna countered. "We should sleep."

"You're right," Excelsior said, giving the rows of orbs another look of concern. "Maybe I'll grab my bed and sleep out here with them."

"As you wish," Arinna said, walking to the back room.

CHAPTER THIRTEEN

Excelsior didn't realize until after he laid flat on the twin-size bed, the energy feeding into the orbs was emitting a soft hum echoing through the large development center. The sound was so hypnotizing, he felt his eyelids getting heavy and all stress leaving his body. He looked up through the translucent roof and gave a silent promise to the stars above: when he returned from Earth, they would shine brighter than ever.

The last thought running through his head before he faded off into sleep was, And they will be seen during the day again.

Suddenly, after what seemed like only a few seconds, Excelsior's eyes snapped open again. Something was wrong. The humming of energy feeding into the orbs was gone. The smell of thick ash filled his lungs. He let out a harsh cough, then leapt to his feet.

"Oh no," he choked out, and he spit more ash from his mouth as he saw its source. Where the orbs were once intact and pulsing with life-sustaining energy, every one of them was now shattered and laying in pieces on the ground, and there was no sign of the children inside. Where could they be? And where were all those ashes coming from?

Excelsior took another deep breath in shock.

"Arinna?" he asked, while running to the back room. It was a basic and sterile room with five flat monitors set up on the wall, displaying the rows of orbs from various angles. And Arinna's bed was placed right in the center.

He placed his hand on the blanket covering her shoulder, but instead of her smooth skin underneath the cloth, he felt his hand wrapping around a ball of... What was this? Excelsior pulled back the blanket and unleashed a cloud of more thick gray ash. He stepped back, startled. His hands grabbed the top of his head, and he cried out in panic. "Arinna!"

But there was no answer. All that was left of the woman floated in the air around him. He stumbled back and almost fell through the room's doorway.

A strong gust of wind blew in from the main room, and Excelsior could see a burst of white light accompanying it. He got back to his feet and walked toward the light coming from outside. He expected to see the village housing their Denarian neighbors, but instead saw a desolate wasteland. The houses were destroyed and pieces of them were strewn about on the ground, floating ash and dirt providing the only movement. The black night sky was gone, replaced by an oppressive orange with an unending series of pulsating, humming shockwaves emanating from the top of Klierra Peak in the distance.

Excelsior stood in front of the door, his feet frozen to the floor, and watched a cloaked figure in the distance walking through the storm of ash, getting closer and closer to the development center. Its head was covered by a hood; its face hidden in darkness. Whatever this being was, it pointed to Excelsior with a smooth Denarian-like hand.

"So this is what you have become, what our planet has become." The figure standing a short distance away from Excelsior spoke to him in a deep and raspy male voice that rang so clearly in his ears, he could have sworn this person was standing right beside him. Or from behind him. The voice was suddenly everywhere.

"And it could have been avoided, all of it, if you only listened to me," the voice continued. "If you indulged my wish to be proud of the greater glory we have attained. But you chose to reject it, to reject your very name. You allowed yourself to be a god of mediocrity. And then, when I could not feel sorrier for you, you chose to live among your own slaves."

Excelsior shouted, "The Denarians are not my slaves."

"Not anymore. You have lowered yourself to their level. And through your recent actions, you have condemned those very people to a quick and painful death."

Excelsior felt the verbal dagger stay embedded within him. "Who are you?"

The figure approached Excelsior, its face still covered but its voice as clear as ever. "You do not recognize me, do you? The voice within applauding you for creating a planet of perfection. The feeling of pride swelling within you. The same feeling you suppressed and expunged from yourself."

Excelsior approached the hooded figure, his fists clenched with anticipation. "I don't know what you're talking about."

The figure pointed its right index finger in Excelsior's direction. Its hand morphed from a human appearance to one green and scaly, its fingers long and thin. "You will know soon enough, my friend. And you will learn we belong together."

Suddenly, the figure's hand grabbed the hood and pulled it back, revealing a face that forced Excelsior to take a startled step back. The head was as green, scaly, and decrepit as the hand, but behind the scales was a very familiar face. He recognized the brown eyes even though he couldn't see any life within them. He recognized the mouth curved up into a smile, despite the sharp teeth. He'd looked in the mirror and saw a similar face staring back at him on Earth for almost eighteen years.

It was him. Matthew Peters.

The voice sounded nothing like his own. "We have always belonged together."

"No. Never!"

"Yesssss. And nothing you do will ever change this!"

Excelsior bolted awake, sucking in a deep breath of air and trying not to cry out and awaken Arinna. He sat up in the bed and looked around. Nothing seemed out of place. The smell of ash no longer hung in the air. The soft hum of the energy feeding into the completely intact orbs was echoing through the quiet room. He stood up and crept around the development center, doing his best to shake the image of Arinna disintegrating from his mind.

He peeked into the back room and let out a sigh of relief. There she was, asleep but very much alive, and Excelsior wanted to tap her on the shoulder and bring her out of her slumber so he could talk about what he dreamt. But then he remembered the journey ahead of them both, and he stepped away.

Excelsior wanted to sleep as well, but he couldn't be still enough long enough to relax. He needed to speak to someone, someone who wouldn't hate him for his actions, someone he could trust. Someone like....

The name came to him in a flash. Excelsior grabbed his helmet, exited the development center, and ran away from the Denarian village. A small light on a flat hill in the distance attracted him like a moth to a flame, and he knew who owned the light.

"How did you know I was here?" Zorribis looked up and smiled when Excelsior rounded the hill. The newly-married Denarian sat on the ground with pieces of parchment around him filled with various drawings Excelsior couldn't recognize.

"You told me about it yourself, how coming here helps you think."

Zorribis shook his head. "Matty, there has been so much in my head as of late, I do not think I remember anything from this past day."

"Well, you and Niterra were bonded today," Excelsior reminded him. "So shouldn't you be... I don't know, honeymooning?"

"Excuse me?" Zorribis asked, his expression bewildered.

"Sorry. I'm trying to come up with the right phrase. I guess, uh, consummating the bonding?"

"That is between myself and Niterra, Matty," Zorribis answered sharply.

"You're right. Sorry," Excelsior said, his face reddening under his helmet.

"But to answer your question," Zorribis added with a wicked grin. "Niterra is resting. I wanted to dedicate more time to my project."

"Your project?"

Zorribis held up a piece of parchment. "Are you sure you would like to see it?"

Excelsior nodded, then took the parchment from his friend's hands and studied it. His eyes narrowed as he stared at the design. "I don't know what this is," he said and handed it back.

"You do not remember the Libeli?" Zorribis asked. "The only flying creatures on Denab IV with the ability to reach the highest mountain?" Excelsior shook his. "They have been extinct for quite some time now."

Extinct. Even though he knew of millions of species that came and went on Earth, it was more difficult than he thought to wrap his head around the word. How could a species here be extinct? And what, or who, brought about its extinction?

"I am trying to alter the aircraft Niterra took from Axsella into something modeled after the Libeli. If it works, Denarians will have the ability to watch over Hodera and any other Krunation wanting to surprise us like they did earlier today. I also added some boosters to its speed capabilities. When it reaches a certain speed, a protective shield covers the seats so the passengers can fly as fast as they like without any issues."

"Very cool. But judging by what I saw tonight, it won't be long before we're all joining the Libeli in extinction," Excelsior replied, his shoulders drooping as he felt the weight of the world he called home coming down on him.

"What do you mean?" Zorribis asked, his eyes narrowing. "Is Acerus worsening?"

"Not yet. There's still a chance for him to survive, but I got..." His words got caught in his throat. "Oh, man, I got a big mess to clean up."

Excelsior sat on the ground beside his friend and let it all out. Acerus' rapid aging. The Elders lashing out at him. Lokris determining the cause of the atmospheric shift. The task ahead of him. And worse than anything else, the look of disdain Arinna gave when the truth came out.

Zorribis listened as each problem spilled from Excelsior's mouth, and the silence after Denab IV's savior finished hung in the air for almost a full minute. Zorribis shut his eyes for a moment, then looked at his friend and said, "I do not blame you."

"What?"

"You heard me," Zorribis said. "I do not blame you at all for this. You wanted to keep some form of communication with your family. If I had the option, if Hodera had not taken it from me, I would have done the same thing."

For only a moment, Excelsior could hear the same bitterness in Zorribis's voice during Hodera's earlier attack. Excelsior smiled and sighed in relief. He'd literally felt the weight of the world on his shoulders all night, and it seemed someone was finally on his side. But he still needed to ask. "Would you have done it even if you knew you'd be condemning everyone on your new home planet?"

Zorribis held up his hand. "Wait! You did not know this would happen. Whatever the Elders said, whatever Arinna said, does not matter. You were in a situation where you had to react, and consider the man who took care of you after your parents died. It does not mean you would have acted the same way if you were aware of the circumstances."

Excelsior gritted his teeth with anxiety without giving any kind of response.

"Matty?" Zorribis asked, his voice now carrying a trace of worry. "Am I correct in assuming you would not have acted the same way if you were aware of the circumstances?"

"You're basically asking me, a Denarian in a human's body, to choose between Earth and Denab IV. Let everyone here die or never see my family again."

"Matty, forgive me for saying this, but your hesitation disappoints me."

"Wait a minute," Excelsior said. "You said you didn't blame me for wanting to maintain a connection with my uncle. And now, because I'm taking my time considering a hypothetical question, I'm suddenly not worthy to be Excelsior?"

"Did I say you were not worthy?" Zorribis demanded, his voice rising. "Quite the contrary. I know you were occupied when Hodera's soldiers attacked, but Denarians from across the planet witnessed you showing mercy to Krunations. They have never seen that before, and they were impressed with your actions. Whether you like it or not, you are worthy of being Excelsior, of leading Denab IV to a greater age. We expect you to do what is necessary to solve this problem, because many of us look forward to a time when Denarians and Krunations can live together in peace."

"I am. Believe me, I am. I already know what needs to be done, and I swear it's going to happen. But answer this for me."

"Yes?"

"Say I pull it off. Say Jason gives back the power I gave him, I return here, and everything is okay again. What happens next? You say I'm supposed to lead Denab IV into a new age. How can I when I don't even know the basic do's and don'ts of this job?"

Zorribis shook his head. "Matthew, stop. The more you think this way, the more you will convince yourself the sword made a mistake by selecting you. You must put an end to that right now. The sword. Does. Not. Make. Mistakes. You have already done what your predecessors could not, and you have the trust of your people."

"I had their trust," Excelsior countered. "From what I saw earlier tonight, the Elders have no problem letting them know what I did—"

"What do I have to do to make you see things as they are, instead of how your fear tells you they will be? What do you wish me to say? You are a failure as Excelsior? You have doomed us all to an early death and should be cast out? I will not do that! It accomplishes nothing, and neither does this conversation. No matter what you may think, you are the savior of Denab IV. Act like it!" The last few words hung in the air for a long moment. Then Zorribis said in a much calmer tone, "Matthew, you had what it took to hold that sword. You need to convince yourself you have what it takes to keep it."

Deep down, Excelsior knew his friend was right. He was feeling sorry for himself, and he was not giving himself any credit for wanting to fix the problem he'd created. He nodded to Zorribis, his mouth pulled down in deep thought. Suddenly, his eyes lit up and he grinned.

"What is that look?" Zorribis asked, confused.

"You're right," Excelsior said. "About everything. You say I'm supposed to be a leader. Well, I have an order."

"An order for me? Yes, sir. What would you like?"

"First off, don't call me sir."

Zorribis laughed. "Yes, Excelsior."

"Second of all, I want you to get this machine, this Libeli impersonator, as functional as possible."

"It is nearly there," Zorribis said. "It cannot reach the heights of Klierra Peak, but it will suffice. Where do you need it to go?"

"You will fly it to Nocteris."

"To the Krunations." Zorribis balled his hands into fists. "To Hodera?"

Excelsior shook his head. "No. In fact, I want you to avoid her at all costs. If you see her walking toward you, you walk away from her. Hide if you must."

"Hide from Hodera?" Zorribis's enthusiastic tone dropped, and a hint of anger heated his voice. "Matty, I was a child. I never intend to hide from that beast again."

"You have your order, Zorribis." Excelsior said, and he felt his spine straightening. "This mission is not about Hodera. I want you to find Connoram."

"And when I find him?"

"If he is anything like you said he was, then he wants to meet you. The last time I left this planet, one race almost wiped out another. I don't want that to happen again."

"I understand," Zorribis said. "Niterra and I will meet you at the Leap of Faith to say our goodbyes, and I will watch over Denab IV while you are gone. Just make sure you do not stay on Earth for thousands of years again."

"You got a deal," Excelsior said, smiling at his friend. The two shook hands and Excelsior pushed himself off the ground and into the air, leaving Zorribis alone to accomplish his second task. He looked down at the ground below and allowed the paralyzing stress to slowly dissipate from his body. But when he turned to his right and saw a figure on a one-person glider, he momentarily lost his concentration and began to fall from the sky.

With the ground speeding toward him, Excelsior shut his eyes, did his best to relax, and let the images of both Denab IV and Jason flood his mind. He felt his power of flight getting stronger, and he swung his legs toward the ground, touching down safely in the path of the approaching glider.

Excelsior felt a rush of panic when he saw whoever was approaching him was wearing the same black coat and hood the Krunation doppelganger wore in his dream. He wasn't dreaming this, was he?

The question was answered when the figure pulled back his hood and revealed the face of an older Krunation, one with molting reptilian skin and wrinkles around his eyes. And even though Excelsior never saw this man before, he had a hunch who he was.

"Connoram?"

Denab IV's savior saw the Krunation step off the glider and hold up his hands, his face displaying a warm smile no Denarian was used to seeing. "I mean you no harm, Excelsior."

Excelsior held his hands up in return. "Neither do I. Especially not to you."

Connoram approached Excelsior and lowered his hands, placing one hand on the humming and vibrating object attached to his chest. "Thank you," he whispered.

Excelsior noticed the humming faded away, and whatever was attached to Connoram's chest detached and dropped to the ground.

"How did you find me?" Excelsior asked.

"With that," Connoram answered. "I owe you a great deal of thanks, as do many Krunation soldiers. Despite their actions earlier today, they are still alive because you showed mercy. May I ask why you let them live?"

Excelsior stared at the twig on the ground for a moment, then his eyes met Connoram's again. "It's my responsibility to lead this planet into a new age. And even if it may be short-lived, it can only be a new age—"

"If we meet that age together."

"Yes! Can you imagine Denab IV without this conflict between our two races? Without one completely exterminating the other?"

"That is why I am here, Excelsior," Connoram said.

"You have no idea how happy I am to hear this," Excelsior said with a smile on his face. "And you also have no idea how perfect your timing is. I just instructed one of my fellow Denarians to find you and bring you to the Elders. Someone you already know."

"I do?"

"Yes. Zorribis."

Connoram shook his head.

"He was running away from Krunation soldiers when he was a child. You pointed the soldiers in a different direction so he could get away."

"Ahhh, yes," Connoram said. "Yes, now I remember. But would you not be the ideal one to bring me to your Elders?"

"Normally, yes. But in the morning, I'm using the Leap of Faith to go to Earth. If this mission succeeds, our final days won't come for a very long time, and we can actually enjoy this potential harmony between our races. And since you're here, I can bring you to Zorribis tonight. He's just outside the village."

"No. You said he has been instructed to come to me, so let him come to me. I can assure you no harm will come to him."

"Okay," Excelsior nodded. He regarding the Krunation with suspicion. "So then why are you here, after nightfall, when everyone is asleep?"

Connoram took a step toward Excelsior, who flinched. He exhaled in frustration. This man let Zorribis go when he was a child, he told himself. He's not gonna ambush you. He wants peace as must as you do.

As far as he knew.

Excelsior's hand slowly moved to his sword, and he looked around as Connoram took another step closer to him. The Krunation noticed Excelsior's motion because he held up his hands one more time. "Please trust me," Connoram said. "I am unarmed, and no one has accompanied me here."

Excelsior relaxed his hand and stopped looking for any other Krunations. "I'm sorry," he said. "I don't mean to offend you. It's... I've never met a Krunation like you. One so eager to..."

"To evolve, yes," Connoram said. "To move beyond what our God originally planned for us. To communicate with the planet as you do. As the Elders do."

"Your God?"

Connoram nodded. "Yes. Our God. Tornatrax. The one responsible for our evolution, for our ability to climb from the oceans."

The name hissed inside his head. "Toooooornatraxxxxx."

"I know that name. It's what Candassus is reaching for, for the power of Tornatrax."

Connoram hesitated for a moment, then nodded. "As your story says, yes."

"Is that why you're here tonight?" Excelsior asked, stepping toward Connoram. "As you said, to communicate with the planet?"

"Denab IV is trying to tell us something. I can feel it screaming out to all of us. And I know it can understand my questions, but I cannot understand its answers."

"Do you think you know what it is?"

"Yes. I began hearing a strange humming coming from the Sancterrum Tree in my quarters."

"Wait!" Excelsior said. "You have a Sancterrum Tree?" It was one thing to know Connoram had a part of Denab IV's plant life in his care, but it was something else to hear this Krunation actually knew the name of the tree.

Connoram nodded. "And a throngar," he answered. "Were it not for them, it is likely our stronghold on Nocteris would have been wiped away along with the structure built on Krephthera."

"You sure you didn't keep a throngar just to keep your fortress safe?"

"Of course not!" Connoram said, sounding more than a little offended. "As I was saying, I first heard the humming after I researched the history of Denab IV, specifically the time when the swords of you and your enemy surfaced."

Excelsior nodded. He didn't want anyone to know he only recalled the time when he was Semminex, and even that era was spotty at best in his mind.

"The humming reminded me of something I was told by the Denarian Elder who watched over me when I was younger, when I was abandoned by my fellow Krunations to die. She said anyone could communicate with the animal life and plant life of Denab IV with enough discipline. Even a Krunation."

As Connoram spoke, Excelsior began to hear a humming in his head. It was quiet at first, but the more the Krunation talked, the louder the humming grew. Where was it coming from? He bent his knees and squatted lower to the ground. As he did, the humming became clearer, sounding like a voice, a very familiar female voice.

Excelsior pressed his hand to the ground, and suddenly he heard the unmistakable voice of Elder Klierra whispering in his ear. "Trust him, Matthew," she said. "He speaks the truth. Show him the way."

A wave of emotion washed over Excelsior. He looked up at Connoram with fresh eyes, the sudden waves of skepticism toward this Krunation gone forever.

"Yes," Excelsior said, the word almost catching in his throat as he choked up. He composed himself and stood, reaching for his sword and offering it to Connoram.

"Take it," Excelsior said.

"What?"

"I said, take it,'" Excelsior repeated. "Take the handle, close your eyes, and clear your mind."

Connoram wrapped his hand around the handle and squeezed it, reverence written on his face. Excelsior let go and the Krunation held the sword up to his face, examining it.

"It is beautiful," he whispered. "You realize I could penetrate your armor with this sword and ensure victory for the Krunation Empire, yes?"

"Yes."

"And you still approve of me holding this?"

"Yes."

"Why?"

"Because I know you won't," Excelsior said.

Now it was Connoram's turn to be skeptical. "How do you know?"

"If you would, you wouldn't be here." Excelsior heard another humming from within his head, most likely a voice of approval from the planet. "Just hold up the sword, close your eyes, and relax. Clear your mind."

Connoram did as he was told, and Excelsior stepped up to him and placed his hand around Connoram's hand on the sword handle. He shut his eyes and felt a warming glow flowing from the sword, enveloping both men.

"Stay still," Excelsior whispered when he felt Connoram flinch. The glow lasted for another several seconds, then faded.

The two men opened their eyes, and Excelsior took the sword from Connoram's hand and sheathed it. "Do you hear the humming again?" he asked. Connoram nodded. "Good," Excelsior said. "Now bend down and place your hand on the ground."

The Krunation dropped down to one knee and pressed the palm of his right hand against the earth. His eyes widened, and he sucked in a deep breath of air. "Oh my..." Tears flooded his eyes, and he started at Excelsior in shock. "I hear it. I hear a voice."

"And what is it telling you?" Excelsior asked.

"It is telling me..." Connoram paused to listen. "It is telling me... there is... much work to do. And little time to do it."

"There definitely is," Excelsior confirmed. "With your guidance, this work can be done. The planet can give you the answers you seek. And when Zorribis comes to you, the first steps to peace can be taken."

Connoram nodded and smiled at Excelsior. "You have given me a truly special gift," he said. "It will be my honor to bring the Krunations to you." And in an unexpected gesture, Connoram gave Excelsior a slight bow.

"It will be my honor," Excelsior countered, beckoning the Krunation to stand up straight, "to see our races come together."

Excelsior extended his hand in friendship, and Connoram eagerly took it.

"I must return to rest myself," Connoram said. "You should rest as well. You have quite a journey ahead of you, a monumental task."

"We both do," Excelsior said, and he took to the sky, waving goodbye to Connoram as he flew. His heart felt like it was soaring even higher than his body, feeling more than ever like the god he was always supposed to be.

Connoram hurried to his glider and headed back in the direction toward Nocteris. Once he was out of sight, a small pile of rocks a short distance away began to distort and a short, scrawny form stepped from them. The Krunation soldier pressed a button on his left wrist and spoke. "I found him, General Hodera."

"And where was he, Sivtra?" Hodera asked through his communicator.

"With him," Sivtra said with contempt. "With Excelsior. He even held his sword for a moment but gave it back. He even..." Rage built within Sivtra's young voice. "He even bowed before him."

"Traitor," Hodera hissed. "Then the time to act is now. Return at once, Sivtra. You have done well."

CHAPTER FOURTEEN

"You seem happier this morning," Arinna said as she and Excelsior walked toward the Leap of Faith. "Did you sleep well?"

Excelsior considered telling her about his dream, the conversation with Zorribis, and the meeting afterward with Connoram. But instead he nodded his head, biting the tip of his tongue to keep from smiling. He wanted to wait to tell Arinna everything until they got to the Leap of Faith, so he could tell her in front of Lokris, Zorribis, and Niterra. Excelsior remembered the look she'd given him. The look that wondered why someone would jeopardize the lives of everyone on a planet to maintain contact with one man from Earth.

The two approached the Leap of Faith and saw Lokris standing by the doorway to the building. Alongside her were Zorribis and Niterra.

Lokris smiled when she saw them. "Are you both ready?"

Excelsior nodded. "I still feel the connection with Jason. It won't be difficult to find him." His gaze shifted to Zorribis and he asked, "Are you ready?"

Zorribis and his wife nodded.

"Ready for what?" Arinna asked.

"They have a mission, as we do," Excelsior answered. "He and Niterra will go to Nocteris to speak with Connoram."

"Connoram?" Arinna asked with wide eyes. "You know of Connoram?"

"He saved my life," Zorribis said. "I can finally thank him."

"We should all thank him," Arinna answered. "He saved more lives than you know."

Excelsior could see the gears in her head turning as she faced him.

"When did you... how did you...?"

"While you slept," Excelsior said. "I paid Zorribis a visit and gave him some instructions." He looked at the other man. "Oh, and Zorribis, he will be waiting for you."

"How do you know?" Zorribis asked.

"He paid me a visit last night as well." Excelsior gaze flicked to Arinna. "Also while you slept."

"He was in my home? And I was not awoken?"

Excelsior shook his head. "We met outside the village. He was looking for me, saying he was researching the history of our planet, and he needed me to help him."

"Shame," Arinna said. "It would have been an honor to meet him. Zorribis, this should help you."

She reached behind her neck and unhooked a thin chain hidden by the shirt she wore. In the middle of it was a golden hexagonal pendant. She handed it to Zorribis. "Give this to him. He will know what it means."

Zorribis glanced down at the pendant and squeezed it in the palm of his hand. "I will," he said. "You both be safe." He smiled at Arinna as he said, "You will love Earth."

"I look forward to seeing it," Arinna replied.

Zorribis turned to Excelsior. "Your home will be waiting for you."

Excelsior nodded, understanding what Zorribis meant. The two couples embraced each other, and Lokris led Excelsior and Arinna inside the Leap of Faith chamber. The door slowly shut behind them.

Lokris walked to the back of the chamber and pressed her hand on the glowing control orb in the middle of the console. She beckoned Excelsior over to her and pointed to the orb. "Just press your hand there and concentrate. Once your destination is set, the doorway will open."

Excelsior did as he was instructed, and the monitor above him immediately began its connection. He shut his eyes and concentrated, and he felt his mind leaving his body, an all-too familiar feeling, one he experienced when he left Earth and traveled to Denab IV through the Leap of Faith. This time he felt himself traveling from the Denab star system all the way to Earth to North America to New York City to...

"Midtown. 5th Avenue and 50th Street," Excelsior said out loud. "Why is he there?" Was Jason taking the day off from work to do some sight-seeing? He remembered his uncle always complaining about tourists clogging up the streets of Manhattan day after day, so why was he at Rockefeller Center? At Tourist Central?

"Do you have a lock on him?" Lokris asked.

"Yes," Excelsior answered.

"Now, is there a place you know where you can materialize without many natives seeing you?"

"I think I know one," Excelsior said. The image on the monitor moved below Rockefeller Center to the area known as the Concourse shopping level. It locked on to an empty broom closet. "It'll be a tight fit, but it should work."

The Leap of Faith doorway began to open and Lokris beckoned Excelsior to step away from the console and move to the center of the room. "I will make sure your travel goes safely," she said.

"You should stay close to me," Excelsior told Arinna. "There won't be much room."

Arinna asked, "And how is it you know about this?"

"I hid from my parents when we went shopping there."

Arinna wrapped her arms around Excelsior's waist, and he blushed as he felt her grip tighten. The two took three large steps and leapt into the doorway together, immediately transforming into beams of energy speeding through the cosmos.

CHAPTER FIFTEEN

"Connoram is not seeing anyone right now!" Charak's order rang uselessly in Hodera's ears, and she pushed past him and the quiet Tarrax as she entered Connoram's chamber.

"I want to give you one more chance," Hodera said as she quickly walked over to Connoram's desk, where he stared at the blank wall in front of him. "My spy has told me the Elders are beginning to weaken, especially Acerus, their High Elder. They have even begun turning against Excelsior, thinking Acerus's age is accelerating because of him. Their minds are preoccupied; we can attack them now and be done with the Denarians once and for..." She stopped when she saw that Connoram failed to notice her entrance or address her pleas. He hadn't even bothered to turn his head in her direction. How rude was this creature?

Hodera waved her scaly hand in front of Connoram's face. Nothing. The only movement came from his arms. His right hand was moving across a page of parchment, and when it was filled, his left hand would swipe the parchment off the desk. He would then grab another sheet with his right hand and begin filling the empty space on that page.

"What are you doing?" Hodera yelled at him. "You are not even listening to me, Connoram. You are missing our moment of victory, which is almost before us. Instead, you are... what is this?"

As Connoram pushed the completed page away from him, Hodera walked around him and grabbed it before it hit the ground. Her eyes scanned the sheet and then narrowed with anger.

"What do you think this is?" she hissed at him. "What do you intend to do with this? Use it as a means to beg the Denarians for mercy? To undo everything we have done? Everything we have learned? Everything that is the Krunation way of life?" Her hands began to squeeze at the parchment. "You cannot do this. You must be stopped!"

Before she could tear at the parchment, Connoram sprang from his seat and – without even looking in her direction – struck her across the face with his fist. Hodera stumbled back and fell to the floor, using her tongue to wipe away the green blood leaking from her mouth. "If I knew you could hit like that," she said, grinning. "I would not have spent so much time hating you."

"Leave me alone," Connoram said, then went back to his writing.

"So you can do what? Continue writing your intent to surrender to the Denarians? So you can send your Krunation soldiers to their death while you stand safely at Excelsior's side?"

Connoram gazed into her eyes.

She spat, "Oh yes, Connoram. My spy is very informative. He even alerted me of how you have been conspiring with the enemy. Suddenly your intentions seem so clear, do they not?"

"You may believe whatever your heart tells you," Connoram said. "But you will never be correct if it is with Tornatrax. Now I say again, leave me alone." His eyes fell back to the parchment in front of him, and she noticed his concentration was so intense, she might as well be invisible.

Hodera reached toward the sheath on her belt and revealed the sword she cradled when Nocterar's castle fell; the same sword Nocterar himself held during his final battle with Excelsior. She cleaned the blade every night, ensuring there wasn't a bit of dust or discoloration on any part. It gleamed as it reflected off the sunlight pouring into the chamber from the open window.

"You are so occupied with your treason, you will not even feel my blade penetrate your back," she warned as she held the sword up above her head.

The bellowing from the throngar outside startled her. She turned and pointed at the window with her sword. "And you will be next," she threatened.

"Step away from the general," Charak ordered. She turned to see him aiming his blaster rifle at her. "I told you, he does not wish to be disturbed."

"How dare you point your weapon at me. I am the last great hope for this entire empire!"

"You are the obstruction to the last great hope for this planet," Charak answered. "If you raise your sword, I will fire." He aimed right at her head to show he wasn't joking.

"Such a fool," she said and walked past him. "A waste you will never be like your father."

"My father was a power-crazed psychotic," Charak spit back at her.

"As are the greatest of us," she said. She began to walk away, but turned back toward Tarrax, who remained silent as always. "And you, Tarrax. I assume you agree with your partner here? Defending your precious commander?"

Tarrax didn't say a word. With a swift movement, he reached into the holster attached to his belt, pulled out a blaster pistol, and aimed it at the general's head.

Hodera smiled. "Such spirit. Shame to waste it on guard duty." She took a step backward, turned around, and walked down the hallway.

CHAPTER SIXTEEN

Excelsior opened his eyes and was greeted by total darkness. He could feel Arinna's body tight against his, but he couldn't see his surroundings.

"Are you okay?" he whispered.

"Yes," Arinna whispered back. He felt Arinna's head leaning on his shoulder, and he began to tremble as they both tightened their hold on each other.

Matthew's hand dropped to her waist and he felt something small and metallic attached to it. "What's that?" he whispered.

"My micro blaster. I never go to a different planet unarmed."

"What are you two doing in here?"

The light from the Rockefeller Center concourse shopping area immediately poured into the broom close, and the two Denarians faced an older, tall male security guard with glasses.

"This is a custodian's closet, not a place for a make-out session," the security guard warned.

"Yes, sorry," Excelsior said as he looked at the man's name badge. "So sorry, Mr., uh, Burris. I wanted to show... show my... my girlfriend around for a little bit. We're leaving now."

"Don't let me catch you getting into trouble again, okay?" the guard said before studying both of their outfits. "Aren't you trying out your Halloween costumes a bit early?"

"Yes!" Excelsior said. "That's what we're doing. We always like to plan ahead of time."

The guard shook his head and walked away. Arinna stepped out of the closet and asked, "Halloween?"

"An excuse for people to dress like us," Excelsior said. "I can sense Jason around here somewhere in this building. We should start looking for him."

Excelsior took Arinna's hand and led her through the labyrinthine concourse level of Rockefeller Center. They lost count of the amount of left and right turns before finally reaching a staircase to the outside level.

Arinna gasped as she stepped into the open area of Rockefeller Plaza. It was still very early in the morning—Excelsior noticed the clocks all read 7:15am—but the plaza was still littered with people of all races and colors. There were men, women, boys, and girls covering every inch of the famous area, and Arinna held on to Excelsior. "I've never seen so many people before. Where are we?"

"New York City," Excelsior said with more than a touch of pride. "Matthew Peters grew..." He cleared his throat, and even though he still wore the uniform of Excelsior, he felt his host's inner self emerge, making him feel completely like Matthew Peters for the first time since the fateful night at Tolland Laboratories.

"I grew up here."

"Incredible," she said with wide-eyed wonder. "Almost like an echo of the species I encountered on all of the different planets since my travels began."

"Well, it is called the 'melting pot.'"

"Mom! Look. Excelsior!"

The voice behind Matthew and Arinna sounded no more than ten years old, and when Matthew looked over his shoulder, he saw the face of a young boy who saw his hero come to life. The boy had thick, dirty blonde hair and gold-frame glasses, and he was wearing a long-sleeved tee-shirt that was an obvious parody of the I-Heart-NY shirt Matthew saw on tourists everywhere all his life. This tee-shirt read I-Heart-D4.

"Now, now, Jonathan," they heard the kid's mother say. "You know he's not really Excelsior. He's only in those webcomics you read." The mother looked up at Matthew and Arinna and said, "I'm sorry if he's bothering you. He's a really big fan."

Matthew couldn't suppress his wide smile. "I understand. I'm glad he enjoys them."

"Do you mind if he gets a picture with you two? Like I said, he's a really big fan."

"Not at all," Matthew said. "We'd be happy to." He reached out to the kid and put his arm around him, then pulled Arinna close so the three were in a tight frame. The mother reached into her purse, took out her smart phone, and aimed it at the three of them.

"What are we doing?" Arinna asked.

"You're holding still and smiling," Matthew answered.

Arinna placed her hand on the boy's shoulder and the three of them flashed toothy grins. The mother snapped her picture, and the kid immediately turned around and wrapped his little arms around Matthew's neck.

"Thank you!" he yelled into his ear.

Matthew laughed as he hugged the child back, then let him return to his mother.

"I told you he was a fan," the mother said with an amused smile.

The kid began speaking fast. "I love the story when you and Nocterar had the big battle in his castle and then he was all like..." He held out his hand like a claw and pushed it out as though he were firing a blast from Nocterar's crystal, yelling "Naaaaaahhhhhhhhhhhh" all the while to provide the necessary sound effects. "And you had to keep jumping out of the way," the kid continued, jumping back and forth. Matthew folded his arms and grinned as he watched the show. "And then you went up to him and started," He threw his fists to the left and right, beating up an imaginary Nocterar. "Boom! Boom! Boom!"

The mother shrugged her shoulders. "It's okay. You can nod and smile. I do."

"No, it's okay," Matthew said to her. "I know what he's talking about." He crouched down to look the kid in the eye, removed his helmet, and said, "That was a really tough battle. Nocterar was one of the biggest enemies I've ever faced, if not the biggest. But when you face your tough battles, you can't give up. You have to keep fighting. Especially when you're fighting for the future of everyone on your planet."

The kid nodded, his eyes round. His reaction told Matthew nobody talks about these stories with him. "I'm sure you're gonna be as good of a fighter as I was back then. If anyone like Nocterar comes at you, you gotta protect your family."

"Even my big brother?" the kid asked.

Matthew laughed. "Yes, even your big brother. I wish you were on Denab IV fighting with me, but I'll have to settle for you working with me down here. Sound okay?" He held out his hand for a high-five, and the kid gave him the biggest high-five he could. Running a hand through his hair, Matthew watched as the kid ran back to his mother even more excited than when he first saw them.

"So are you here for the big announcement about the TV show?" the mother asked.

"TV show?" Arinna asked. Matthew was thankful for Arinna's question, so he wouldn't have to explain why he was in Rockefeller Plaza dressed the way he was and not know about a television show.

"You know, the new TV show they're doing on you. The guy who writes it is on the Today Show."

"Ahhh, yes!" Matthew said, trying to cover up his ignorance and realizing why he was pulled to this area in the first place. "Yes, yes that's why we're here. To meet Jason Peters and thank him for everything."

"Well, have fun," the mother said, then told her son, "Wave goodbye to the nice man."

"Goodbye Excelsior!" the kid shouted as they passed Matthew and Arinna and continued walking through the plaza.

Matthew placed the helmet back on his head, looked around the plaza, and pointed toward a large group of people on the Forty-Ninth Street side of the building. "We should go over there, where The Today Show broadcasts, and Jason's gonna come from the entrance on that side once the interview's over."

The two began walking, and at the halfway point, Arinna pointed toward the Fiftieth Street walkway where they'd encountered the mother and son. "What was that all about? How did he know about you and Nocterar?"

"I spent over five years writing and drawing my own stories about Excelsior. I thought he was just a character I created. Didn't know they were really his memories."

"Love the costume!" a fan yelled out, interrupting his train of thought.

Matthew waved in their direction. "Thank you!"

"Where'd you get it?" another fan asked.

"My friends made it for me," he answered.

"Can they make one for me?"

Matthew and Arinna gazed at the large monitors overlooking the Forty-Ninth Street side of Rockefeller Plaza and saw a long, blonde-haired head filling the screen with a white, toothy grin. "And welcome back to 'The Today Show.' It's 7:20am on Wednesday, May 14, 2014. I'm Kathryn West, and we have a special treat for you."

"Oh my God," Matthew whispered.

"What is it?" Arinna asked.

There it was. The ultimate reminder of the mistake he made, and it was on the television screen for all to see. "The date. It's only 2014. I've been gone for six months, so

five years should have passed, but it's been only three..."
Once again, he felt the weight of two worlds on his
shoulders.

Kathryn West continued with her introduction. "If
you or your kid is into comics, then you've probably heard
of our next guest. He is the writer and artist behind the
webcomic sensation 'Excelsior,' and he's also the creator
of the upcoming science-fiction / fantasy series coming
to NBC based on the same webcomic. Please welcome
Jason Peters. Jason, it's great to have you here."

The camera pulled back to reveal Jason sitting beside
Kathryn, wearing a navy-blue sweater vest over a button-
down shirt and slacks. His smile almost matched Kathryn
in its intensity. "Great to be here. Thank you very much
for having me."

Matthew smiled when he saw the former chairman
of the "What Not to Wear Society" learned how to
color coordinate and found the right kind of diet. Of
course, Jason's slimmer and more athletic figure may have
been attributed to what was gifted to him at Tollund
Laboratories, but whatever the case, it was working.

Kathryn opened up the interview. "You've really come
out of nowhere with this 'Excelsior' comic. Tell us a bit
about it."

Jason stuttered through his breakdown of the comic,
and Matthew kept his eyes on the screen, silently willing
him to explain it the right way. "Well, it really started
with my nephew, Matthew. He spent seven years working
on this, uh... sprawling epic tale about this warrior from a
faraway planet called Denab IV, struggling to, uh, keep his
people alive against a constant threat. I can't tell you how

many nights he and I kept picking away at this storyline and building up all these characters, and after all those years, he finally got an audience. But it was bad timing because he had to leave with other family members when his momentum started to build."

"And now here you are, making a television show," Kathryn countered. "It sounds like a relay race in the family, how one member starts the characters, then gets the webcomic going, and then it gets passed off to another family member who gets it on the screen."

"Kind of, yeah," Jason agreed.

"Would something like this cause some friction in the family? Maybe some egos getting in the way?"

"Oh, no," Jason said, shaking his head. "We're all in this together. We're all in the proper mindset. And he, uh, would be here instead of me if he wanted to handle this. But he put so much into this character and so much into this world, so by the time it started picking up, he said he was burned out, and, uh, gave me his blessing to take it from there and keep it alive."

"Well, wherever he is, I'm sure he's very proud of how far 'Excelsior' has gone," Kathryn said with an even bigger smile.

"I agree," Matthew whispered.

"So when does 'Excelsior' premiere?" Kathryn asked.

"Well, the latest I've heard is, uh, it's getting a Friday night slot, but I'm still optimistic about our chances. We should be going into production in the next couple of months, so the pilot episode can be ready for airing by this January. I hope everyone out there's excited as I am. I can't wait to see how this character evolves in this medium, and I'm, uh, looking forward to seeing everyone's reaction."

"Well, we definitely wish you all the best," Kathryn said and shook his hand, then looked into the camera and continued the pitch. "We've been chatting with Jason Peters. The series is called 'Excelsior,' and while you wait for its January premiere, get yourself acquainted with the webcomic at TheExcelsiorJourney.com. And we'll be right back after these words. You're watching 'The Today Show.'"

"So what happens now?" Arinna asked when the monitors cut to black.

"He finished his interview, so he'll come out over there," Matthew answered, leading the two of them toward the Forty-Ninth Street side entrance.

"Awesome costume, man. Excelsior's dope!" one fan yelled.

"Thank you," Matthew said with a smile and a wave.

"You are what?" Arinna whispered.

"He thinks I'm dope," Matthew answered. "Don't worry. It's a good thing."

Arinna shrugged as the two stopped outside the NBC Studios door. Matthew smiled when he saw Jason emerge from the doorway while signing autographs from fans.

"Is that him?" Arinna asked, stepping forward.

Matthew grabbed her by the arm and eased her back. "Give him some time. Let him enjoy himself." The Excelsior within him wanted badly to step through the small crowd, grab Jason by the arm, and convince him to give back the gift he gave him, but Matthew Peters felt only one sentiment.

"Are you okay?" Arinna asked when she saw the faraway gaze on Matthew's face. He was looking past Jason, past the fans, and suddenly he saw himself dressed similarly to his uncle, standing outside NBC Studios and signing autographs for his adoring fans.

"That should be me," Matthew whispered to himself. He kept the smile on his face, but inside, he felt a burning desire to pull his helmet off and yell, "I am the creator of Excelsior! I am Matthew Peters. If you want an autograph, you want it from me."

But he did what he felt was right for everyone. He held back and gave Jason the time to bask in the glow of Matthew's hard work.

Arinna whispered into his ear, "Come back to us, Excelsior."

Matthew blinked and looked at her. "What was that?"

"Wherever you were, we need you here."

He nodded, eyes darting back to Jason finishing up his latest round of autograph signing. "Hey, great costume!" he shouted in Matthew's direction.

Matthew hesitated to speak, wondering why Jason wasn't recognizing his nephew, but then remembered the helmet covered his eyes. He smiled back. "I thought you'd like it."

Jason's eyes widened and he walked toward Matthew. "Wait... are you...?"

Matthew pulled off his helmet, revealing the rest of his very familiar face and greeting his uncle with a child-like smile. "Matthew?"

The young man nodded.

"Matty!" Jason yelled and wrapped his arms around his nephew, embracing Matthew for a long moment.

Turning his head, Matthew could feel tear stains forming on his shoulder. "Are you all right?" he asked.

"I'm sorry," Jason said as he wiped his eyes. "I just... What are you doing here, man? You look terrific."

"So do you," Matthew replied, putting his hand on his uncle's chiseled shoulder. "And it looks like you finally got some taste in clothes."

"Oh, you can thank my girlfriend for that."

"Girlfriend?"

"Oh, yeah. You were already gone by the time we met. She was one of the cops who came in the lab after you left. No idea what was going to happen, and boom! There she was."

"Guess the universe is doing a good job of keeping you out of trouble."

"And I'm sure you had something to do with that, my omnipotent nephew," Jason said with a laugh and a slight punch to his shoulder. "Is it weird I still remember you as this scrawny little kid?"

"Believe me, sometimes I wish I was still a scrawny little kid," Matthew answered, which provoked an annoyed glance from Arinna.

"If you were, the world you spent so much time writing about would not exist anymore."

"Whoever she is, she's got a point," Jason said while holding out his hand. "Hi, I'm Jason Peters, the brother of Matthew's father."

"I'm sorry," Matthew said to both of them. "This is Arinna. She's my chaperone on a mission I'm on."

"Chaperone?" Jason asked, then asked Arinna, "You don't think he went through everything he did just to stay here, do you?"

"One can never be too sure," was all Arinna said as an answer, prompting a look of slight annoyance from Matthew. She shook Jason's hand. "It is an honor to meet you. I have heard much about you."

"All true, I hope," Jason said. "Don't make this question think I'm not happy to see you both, but what's this mission you mentioned?"

Matthew looked over Jason's shoulder and saw a few fans still hanging around, waiting for Jason to redirect his attention back to them. "Can we go somewhere a little more private?"

"Absolutely," Jason answered, then waved to the long white limousine waiting for them several feet away on the curb. The driver inside waved back and drove up to meet them.

"You really have upgraded," Matthew said. "Too good for the subways now?"

"It's the network's car. Get in. I got some news. Not sure if you're gonna like it."

CHAPTER
SEVENTEEN

Arinna stared out the window of the pearl-colored stretch limousine as it drove on to the Queensboro Bridge. Matthew noticed her eyes were wide as the two of them soaked up the surroundings: the different cars, the various types of people crossing the streets and making their way up and down the sidewalks, the buildings needed to sustain housing for more than eight million residents of this small island and its neighboring four boroughs.

"This is amazing," she said. "All the planets I have been to, there is such a limited number of cultures and types of people. Some only have two or three families occupying their land. Seeing all of these people, with their various accommodations, I can understand how someone can so easily lose themselves in a place like this."

Matthew agreed. He was back on Earth for less than an hour, and at this moment, it seemed like he never left.

"You should see the Village," Jason replied. "At least in this part of Manhattan, there's a grid so you don't get lost as much."

Matthew added, "We used to joke about how the Village's streets were set up to scare away tourists so the locals would have an area of Manhattan all to themselves." He turned back to Jason. "So what did you have to tell me?"

"I saw a story in the newspaper recently. One mentioning the 'Ritgen-Man.'"

"Danaak?" Matthew said.

The name prompted Arinna to turn away from the window and stare at Jason in shock. "What about him?"

"You know about Danaak too?" Jason asked her.

Her hands clenched into fists. "I know what he was capable of doing."

"So you know how Danaak was taken by Homeland Security after he was killed, right?" Jason asked.

"No," Matthew answered. "I wasn't here, remember?"

"You're right, you're right," Jason said. "I keep forgetting you were gone by then. Anyway, the cops came in around the time when Katherine's body turned into ash, just like Karini, Grannik, and Radifen did, and not long after, some government agents came in. They took Danaak's body, and the last thing I heard, it was gonna be examined by Homeland Security. But according to the article, Tollund Laboratories lobbied for 'Ritgen-Man' to be released back to them after all their examinations. They still wanted to be the ones to study an actual alien lifeform and use it as their own personal fundraiser by letting the public see him."

"You would think they'd learn from their past mistake," Matthew said with contempt in his voice. "So Homeland Security just gave it back to them?"

"Not at first. The article said they did a bunch of tests, scans, everything possible to make sure it wasn't gonna be a threat. And then they gave it back to them."

"So where is he now?" Arinna asked.

"Back at the lab. The article was meant to be a pitch for tourists and families to come out and 'see the proof we're not alone in the universe.'"

"Your people still think you are alone in the universe?" Arinna asked

"Some of them do," Matthew answered. "We have to see for ourselves if Danaak is dead. Take us over to the lab."

"Well, hold on, Matty," Jason said, holding up his hands. "First of all, you're not going anywhere dressed like Excelsior. You're gonna cause a scene, no matter what you're there to do. We're gonna get you in some regular clothes. Your old stuff may be a little too small for you now, but I got some stuff at the old place." He glanced at Arinna. "I don't think we have anything that can fit you, but you should be fine. You can make your look work."

"Thank you, I think?" Arinna said.

"You're welcome, and second, you still haven't told me why you came back to Earth in the first place. You couldn't have heard about the party going on tonight for the show."

"Well, yeah, we didn't hear... party? There's a party for the 'Excelsior' series?"

Arinna rolled her eyes.

"Oh, yeah. NBC set up a private party at Top of the Rock."

Arinna tapped Matthew on the shoulder. "Matthew? Matthew, you have to tell him."

"Tell me what? What's wrong?" Jason sat back in his seat, moving away from Matthew and Arinna.

"You're right," Matthew said to Arinna, snapping out of his gaze once again. "Jason, ummm... you remember the 'gift' I gave you before I left?"

"How could I forget? If you didn't give that to me, I wouldn't have turned my life around. I got a second chance, and I owe it to you, man. I owe it all to you."

Matthew started to speak, but he stopped, the words stuck in his throat. He turned to Arinna, who motioned for him to continue speaking. "I.... I need it back."

"Whoa. What?" Jason pressed his back against the seat as Matthew held his hand out to him. "What do you mean, you need it back? Why do you need it back?"

"Because I didn't know what it would mean to Denab IV if I gave it to you. By giving you a piece of me, it created a tether between the two planets. And since I'm originally from here, the atmosphere of Denab IV started to shift to match the atmosphere of Earth. You remember how worn out Katherine was feeling?"

"Yeah, she told me about the different atmosphere."

"Right. Now picture that on a global scale. Everyone is getting older quicker, and if I don't break this tether, everyone on Denab IV is gonna die around me." Jason's eyes widened, and Matthew lowered his gaze to his uncle's right hand. "Look at your hand," he said.

Jason glanced down, his mouth dropping open in shock. "What... what's going on?" A faint outline of a star was now on the palm of his hand.

"You see?" Matthew asked. "There's a little bit of Excelsior in you, just like there was in me after touching the sword. See? Look at this." He held up his own right hand and showed the same star outline he had on his palm for years. It was slightly thicker than Jason's, and there was a diagonal line running through it, the scar left by Danaak during the battle at Tollund Laboratories. The closer Matthew moved his hand to Jason, the brighter both outlines grew.

"So now what?" Jason asked. "Am I just gonna walk around with a glowing hand?"

"Of course not," Matthew replied, holding out his hand to him. "Shake my hand and everything's fixed."

Jason held out his hand but then pulled back, and the glowing of the two hands reduced. He looked at his nephew with glazed eyes similar to Matthew's expression from earlier. "How do you know this?" he asked. "Maybe by you being Excelsior, you've been the tether. Did you ever think about that?"

"Of course, I have," Matthew answered. "But if I wasn't supposed to be Excelsior, I wouldn't have felt the sword calling to me in the first place."

"But you were still born here, on Earth. No matter who else is in there with you right now, Earth is always gonna be your home planet." Jason could see Arinna was annoyed by that statement, and so he added, "No offense."

"None taken," she said in a flat tone of voice, then turned her head back toward the scenery outside the car.

"Doesn't matter now," Matthew said. "I have a responsibility to Denab IV and its people."

"Now, say I do this," Jason mused. "We shake hands, you get your gift back, you go to your new home, and the atmosphere still hasn't changed. What are you going to do then? Drop in and give it back or something? Say, 'No harm, no foul?'"

"What is your problem, Jason?" Matthew asked, his voice rising. "You have the opportunity to save an entire planet, and you don't have to do anything close to what I did. I had to kill two of the biggest Krunation enemies in existence, and now I have Elders considering turning against me. I can't have that. Excelsior can't have that. And the rest of the Denarians can't possibly have that. I can't let them down, and I need your help to make this happen."

Jason hesitated. "Well... can you blame me? After so much happening here? What if giving this back to you screws up my head in some way? What if it's so wrapped up in me, it creates some weird lasting effect? This isn't like anything we've dealt with on Earth. This is an otherworldly type of power. This ever cross your mind?"

Matthew took a deep breath and admitted, "No. No, I didn't think about anything else when I did what I did. All I wanted was the best for you, the same way you wanted the best for me. It was an impulsive idea, yes. But it was done with nothing but the best intentions for you. Now I'm asking you to do the same."

"And if I do this, then I'm never going to see you again. Grandma's never going to see you again, and she's been waiting to see you."

"What do you mean, Grandma's been waiting to see me?"

"I mean, where do you think we've been going this whole time? You're not just going to the apartment to get a change of clothes. You're gonna see Grandma too. She actually called me and asked about you this morning before my interview."

Matthew's eyes suddenly lit up. "Grandma's here?"

"Sure. After Grandpa died—"

"Grandpa died?" Matthew exclaimed.

Jason nodded. "Maybe three months after you left. It was only a matter of time with his condition. You know how it is. I brought her back from the West Coast so she could have her old place back. I was moving in with my girlfriend, and I didn't want to put the place up for rent, so it worked out great since it keeps family members close." Jason smiled. "These days, you gotta keep family close, you know?"

Matthew took a deep breath, then held out his right hand one more time. The glow returned to both his hand and Jason's. "Look, I didn't want to leave, but I had to. There's too much on my shoulders, and I can't walk away from that. If I did, I wouldn't be able to live with myself. I'm asking you to help me out one more time, and I'm asking you to see this through my eyes. The gift I gave you ensured the Excelsior comic would continue. Well, now it has. You got a TV series from it."

"You don't think I know what I have from this?" Jason's climbed again. "And you think I don't want to give it back to you because of it?" He then pointed to Arinna and asked in the same agitated voice, "Something funny?"

Matthew turned to look at Arinna and saw she was trying to stifle a laugh. "Apologies," she said. "This reminds me of a species I recently visited on Elres III. They were so transfixed on their sides of their conflicts, they never saw the answers were right in front of them the whole time. They needed an outside source to identify them."

"And I take it you're the outside source here?" Jason asked.

Arinna nodded. "No matter the format in which you choose to tell the stories of Excelsior, their quality can only improve if you have assistance from someone who has actually been on Denab IV."

"True," Jason said suspiciously. "But Matthew's not gonna be here."

"Correct," Arinna said. "But he can use his artistic skills to create a map of the entire planet."

Matthew's eyes lit up. "Genius! Okay, I got a proposition for you, Jason. You shake my hand and give back what I gave you, and in return, I'll put a map together and prepare a bunch of stories to keep you going for at least two seasons, maybe even three if you use some stories as two-parters. Your writing staff can take them in whatever direction you want."

Jason looked at Matthew's hand, his expression thoughtful. "Hmmmm."

"Think about it," Matthew said. "You get to keep your show going, I get to keep my people from dying so quickly, and everyone's happy."

Jason pointed at Matthew. "Tell you what. I got a counter-offer for you. We're coming up to Grandma's house now, so you take some time with her, change into something less Excelsior-like, put together some ideas, check out Danaak's remains and make sure he won't be an issue, and then come to the party tonight at Top of the Rock. I'll make sure you're both on the guest list." He turned to Arinna and added, "You'll like it. Lot of people having a good time, and you'll get to see some of the stuff from Katherine's place."

"The stuff from Katherine's?" Matthew asked. "The stuff she brought over from her apartment?"

"Yeah, it's at my place," Jason said. "There's some kind of device; she never got to tell me about it. We can set it out as a prototype prop for the show. And maybe she..." He nodded toward Arinna while keeping his eyes on Matthew. "...will be able to let me know what it is. Then, after the party's done, I'll shake your hand and give you what you want. In case something goes wrong, it won't be in front of the big network guys. Sound like a deal?"

Matthew exchanged glances with Arinna, who nodded and asked, "Does this mean we can see more of the area?"

"I think we can set up some time for sight-seeing. Okay, Jason, you got a deal." He held out his hand one more time, but Jason balled his hand up into a fist, then held it up to Matthew.

"Sorry," Matthew said, grinning. He balled his hand up into a fist, and they gave each other a light fist-bump.

The car slowed and stopped on near Northern Boulevard in Woodside, Queens. Jason opened up the door. "Perfect. I feel much better about this now. So why don't you guys give Grandma a big hug for me and let her know I'll call her before the party starts?"

"You're not coming in?" Matthew asked.

"I can't. I gotta meet with the executives and make sure everything's ready for tonight. You know how it goes."

"Oh yeah," Matthew said. "As soon as you turn your back, something goes wrong. So hopefully this deal won't do the same to me."

"Will you stop worrying and go see Grandma? She can't wait to say hi." Jason gave Matthew one last embrace, then turned to shake Arinna's hand. "And it was lovely meeting you too."

Arinna smiled at him and the two stepped out of the limousine. Before Jason could shut the door, Matthew asked, "So what time are we meeting you?"

"The party starts at six. Make sure you have your uniform and the sword with you. The execs will love seeing those."

Matthew nodded and shut the limo's door, and he and Arinna watched it drive away.

"That was an excellent job," Arinna said. "The way you coerced him into agreeing to give back the gift."

Matthew shrugged. "I couldn't force him. There had to be a compromise."

"None of your predecessors could have done that," she said. "Although it does worry me that the potential genocide across Denab IV was being used as a bargaining tool for Earth's entertainment."

"It's not just that," Matthew said. He wanted to go into more detail, but instead, he said, "Come on. Grandma will be thrilled to meet you."

CHAPTER EIGHTEEN

The start of the journey from the Denarian village of Edenaria to Nocteris was quiet for Zorribis and Niterra. As soon as the two said goodbye to Matthew and Arinna and watched them go through the Leap of Faith, Zorribis led his beloved to the hill where he and Excelsior spoke the night before, and they climbed into the aircraft he was trying to enhance. Niterra sat in the pilot's seat with Zorribis directly behind her.

What the aircraft lacked for altitude, it more than made up in speed. Within one Earth hour, which was becoming dangerously close to matching one Denarian hour, the two were close to the halfway point of their journey when Zorribis let out a gasp and yelled, "Look! Over there!"

"What is it?" Niterra asked.

"We have to land at the Caverns of Yelsew. The humming from the crystals powering the regeneration chambers, I do not hear them!"

Niterra immediately set down the aircraft. It landed with a thud strong enough to throw the two Denarians off if it weren't for the clear protective shield they bounced against.

"I think the landing cycle needs some extra adjusting," Niterra said.

"May be the least of our worries," Zorribis said. "Listen. The crystals are silent."

The two stepped out of the vehicle and ran inside the caverns, slowing down when they saw the inside of the cave was pitch black. Zorribis reached for his belt and pulled out a handheld spotlight. It activated, illuminating their path.

"So many memories here," Niterra said while walking behind Zorribis.

"Some I would prefer to forget," Zorribis said, bringing his light up and down on the walls. The light grazed over the damp dust and rock, and occasionally the large crystals that once illuminated the caverns. "A little farther now."

Zorribis brought his light down to their feet, and after a minute of fast-paced walking on the dirt-covered ground, they came to a stop right in front of a deep pit with one long steel rod reaching down to a platform positioned five tronks below the surface.

"The mechanism has to be somewhere," Zorribis said as he moved his hand along the wall closest to him. When he found a metallic panel embedded in the rock, he pressed his hand against it and the platform started to rise.

"What if the crystals are not working anymore?" Niterra asked. "What if all the work we did to restore the broken chambers was in vain? What will we do?"

"I just want Elder Ducera to be okay," Zorribis said, the only answer he could conjure.

The platform holding two regeneration chambers finally arrived. Zorribis handed his light to Niterra, stepped on to the platform, and opened the white diamond-layered chamber closest to him. He dropped to one knee and reached inside, expecting to feel the Elder's sleeping body. Instead, his hand went past the ceremonial wrappings to the bottom of the chamber.

"Gone," Niterra whispered.

"No," Zorribis countered as tears streamed down his face. "She is still here." He held up his closed hand as proof, and dark ash seeped through his fingers.

Niterra ran to Zorribis and wrapped her arms around him, the two of them openly weeping the loss of an Elder, one who watched over Zorribis when he was a scared orphaned child, and helped make him the man he was today.

"What do we do?" Niterra asked.

Zorribis looked up at his spouse, his eyes as red as hers. "We do what Excelsior said. We speak with Connoram."

CHAPTER NINETEEN

"Matty?"

Grandma's hair looked grayer than Matthew remembered, and he could have sworn she was half a foot taller than what she was now, but her eyes were still full of life and her smile could change the mood of any crying infant. She reached out and embraced her grandson with a tight hug.

"I'm so happy to see you," she said, loosening her grip and gazing up at Matthew. "You look terrific. You look so tall! But we need to get you inside or else the neighbors will worry about why you're dressed like Excelsior."

"Jason told you about Excelsior?"

"He didn't have to, hon," Grandma answered. "I've known about him for years. Oh, and who's this?"

Arinna smiled and reached out her hand. "My name is Arinna. I am... a friend of Matthew's from..."

She looked to Matthew and nudged him to think of a proper location, but Grandma answered, "Denab IV?"

Arinna looked at her in shock. "How did you—"

"I saw it in your eyes. Now please come in, both of you. I have so much to show you."

The two walked inside, and Matthew smiled with nostalgia as he looked around the living room. Everything looked as it did when he was there only a few Earth years ago. All the protective plastic on the furniture remained intact; the tea cups and saucers on the end tables had the same blue patterns. He even recognized the slight layer of dust on the windowsills. The only new items were the various-sized picture frames displayed on a long table in front of the window.

"I never thought I'd be so thrilled to be here," he said to Arinna. "So many years, I'd be upstairs, writing and drawing in my own little world."

"But it wasn't just your world," Grandma said. "Was it, Matthew?"

"It sounds like you have known of Denab IV and Excelsior for a long time," Arinna noted. "Even longer than Matthew."

"Maybe you should sit down for this," Grandma said. "I thought you'd be here, so I made you some tea."

"With milk?" Matthew turned to Arinna. "She made it for me when I was a kid."

Grandma retreated to the kitchen and stayed there for a moment as Arinna curiously looked at the pictures. "What is her name? Grandma?"

"Margaret," Matthew answered. "Or Peg, for short."

"How do you get Peg from Margaret?"

"Yeah, how does that happen? I don't know."

"So here we are," Grandma announced as she emerged from the kitchen, holding a tray with three white teacups and saucers on it. "Now, Arinna, I'm not sure what Denarians drink these days, but I think you'll enjoy it. My grandmother made it for me like this."

As Arinna took the teacup from the saucer, she pointed toward one of the pictures on the table. "Thank you, Margaret. I have a question—"

"Peg, sweetheart. Call me Peg," Grandma interrupted. "Oh, Matty, I almost forgot. I'm a little rusty on my Denarian and my microwave keeps flashing some weird Denarian symbols. Can you take a look at it?"

"Sure, let me see." Matthew walked into the kitchen and called out. "It keeps flashing twelve. But I think I can fix that."

"Oh, good. It's been flashing it the whole time I've been back. I'm sorry, sweetie. What were you going to say?"

Matthew looked at the keypad on the microwave, and his fingers glided along the keypad, punching in a long and complex code. At the same time, he listened to the conversation in the other room.

"Oh, yes. Ummm, Peg. This older woman. How do you know her?"

"Oh, yes. She's my grandmother."

"You do know she was an Elder, yes?"

"She's what?" Matthew stopped entering the code on the microwave and ran into the living room. "Grandma, your grandmother was an Elder?"

"Of course, dear. How do you think you were able to hear the sword in the museum when nobody else could? Did you think this whole time it was just a coincidence? Did you think you could eat all that fast-food junk and not gain any weight because you had good genes? Well, maybe you did."

"Fast food?" Arinna asked.

"Don't get me started on their eating habits," Grandma told Arinna. "It's a good thing both of you have good women to help you with food not in a foil wrapper or a thin pizza box."

"Arinna and I are just friends, Grandma," Matthew interjected. "But wait, don't change the subject. You knew about Denab IV all this time and you never told me?"

"I couldn't, dear. I wanted to tell you when you were old enough, but your mother and father wouldn't let me. Your father was always very practical, his feet on the ground. Your uncle, well, he was always a dreamer. I was tempted to tell him all about it, but he never seemed like he could handle the responsibilities." She pointed to the sword that was safe in its sheath attached to Matthew's belt. "And speaking of that, you might be interested in this."

"What do you mean?" Matthew asked suspiciously.

Grandma beckoned Matthew and Arinna to the wall next to the kitchen. For all the years Matthew spent in this home, this particular wall was blank, but now it had a large painting hung on it, a pristine framed 1900s N.C. Wyeth painting. "Recognize it?" the older woman asked the two Denarians.

"I do," Matthew said, looking closer. "I read about it in class. 'Sword Excalibur Rising from the Lake,' right?"

"Right. This was in Dr. Sierra's apartment. It was delivered to Jason after her apartment was cleaned out."

"Why this?" Arinna asked.

"Its connection with Denab IV," Grandma answered. "Take a closer look at the sword in the Lady of the Lake's hand. Look familiar?"

Matthew stepped closer and his mouth dropped as he noticed the intricate details of the cross guard. But it had to be a coincidence.

"Huh," he said. "Funny, it looks like—"

"It is," Grandma said, her gaze moving from the painting to the sword embedded in the sheath attached to Matthew's belt.

"It can't be," Matthew said, shaking his head. "The sword was a legend, a myth."

"Every myth has to start somewhere, Matty," Grandma said with a smile. "This one started on Denab IV and found its way into the hand of a king before disappearing, never to be found, until a team of excavators led by Dr. Sierra uncovered it."

"And you never mentioned this to anyone at the museum?"

"Of course not," Grandma said sharply. "I was sitting on the volunteer board. If I mentioned to them that the sword was Excalibur, or it was really an alien sword, or the Lady of the Lake was a Krunation—"

Matthew waved his hands. "Whoa! What are you talking about? The Lady of the Lake?"

Grandma laughed. "What other race could stay underwater for so long?"

Matthew looked up at the ceiling, then back at the painting, and laughed along with Grandma. How could he have not seen this, after all this time?

"I had to keep my mouth shut," Grandma continued. "They said the sword was of 'an unknown origin,' and it was the smartest people in the room who said it, so I nodded and smiled like everyone else."

"If she is a Krunation," Arinna began, pointing to the hand of the Lady of the Lake. "Then where are her scales?"

"It's a painting, sweetheart," Grandma answered. "If it were a photo, you would've known it was a Krunation. Just like how you can tell who's a Denarian."

"How so?" Arinna asked.

"Come here," Grandma directed Arinna back to the table of photographs. "Look closer at the picture of my grandmother."

"So you knew Sestera," Arinna said as she picked up the picture and held it up to her face. "This image is monochromatic, but her eyes look light blue."

"You Denarians should get your pictures taken more," Grandma said. "Can you imagine what people would think when they saw what was really in that painting? Scales on the hand holding the sword? Merlin's eyes light blue?" She then reached out to Matthew and gave him another strong hug. "Oh, I'm so happy to see you, Matty. I thought I'd never see you again."

Matthew returned the hug. "I thought the same thing. About all of you. Is it okay if I show Arinna around? I need to make a quick phone call and change into something. Jason said he had some clothes here."

"Of course, sweetie," Grandma said. "I do have to make a run around the corner. Would you like something to eat? I'm sure you're hungry."

Matthew smiled at Arinna. "We are, but we'll wait for Palermo's to open. They don't have pizza on Denab IV."

"Peet-za?" Arinna asked.

"Trust me," Matthew said. "Zorribis and the rest who came here before couldn't get enough of it. You'd think it was made on Collagra."

CHAPTER TWENTY

"Armfather, you have two guests."

Charak led Zorribis and Niterra into Connoram's quarters, and judging by the look on the old Krunation's face, their arrival took him by surprise. He looked the two Denarians up and down.

"Thank you, Charak," Connoram said, then rose from his desk. "Do I have a reason to draw my weapon?"

"I hope not," Zorribis answered. "We brought no weapons with us."

Connoram's smile was warm. "Your leader told me about you. Zorribis, yes?"

Zorribis nodded and stepped forward. "Yes. You saved my life when I was a half-size, and I never said 'Thank you'. If it were not for you directing the Krunation guards away from my trail, I would have been dead."

"Those were Hodera's men following you; the same who took your family's lives. You always had my sympathy. No child should have to be subjected to that, no matter if they are Denarian, Krunation, or any other race."

"Is that why you let me live?" Zorribis asked. "Because of what Hodera did to me?"

"Not quite," Connoram answered. "I made a vow to someone, someone very special, and thanks to Excelsior, I now have what I require to fulfill the vow." He turned away from the two Denarians and gathered a small pile of loose parchment pages strewn across his desk.

"Are you all right, Armfather?" Charak asked from the doorway.

Connoram waved him off without turning around. "We are fine, Charak. The time has come for our journey."

"Yes, sir," Charak said, leaving.

"What did he call you?" Niterra asked. "Armfather?"

"Yes. Now, I assume you wonder why you are here."

"Because Excelsior sent us here," Zorribis answered. "To bring you to the Elders. He said you were researching the history of Denab IV?"

"Yes," Connoram confirmed. "So much discovered, thanks to him. Do you see these pages?" He held up all of the parchment in his hands, each piece filled with the old Krunation's writing. "Until now, Excelsior was the only lifeform on this planet with the capability of receiving this information. If all of this is true, then there are elements of our planet's history hidden from us, and it might be what is needed for both the Denarian and Krunation races to come together and face this planet's future in peace."

"You understand Excelsior has left the planet, yes?" Niterra asked.

"Yes," Connoram answered. "To find the solution to the atmospheric shift. If both he and I are successful, then he will return to a changed world; one changed for the better."

"We are already too late for at least one Elder," Zorribis said, tears forming in his eyes once again. This time he forced them back. "Elder Ducera died already."

"You have my sympathies," Connoram said while bowing before Zorribis and Niterra.

Niterra reached into the front of her shirt and pulled out the six-sided pendant Arinna gave her. "A fellow Denarian wanted us to give this to you."

She detached the chain, pulled it off her neck, and handed it to Connoram, whose eyes widened as he held it in the palm of his right hand. "Sestera," he whispered. "Yes, my vow to you will be fulfilled."

"Elder Sestera?" Zorribis asked. "You knew her?"

"As I saved your life, my friend, she saved mine."

The door to Connoram's quarters opened, and Charak leaned in. "Tarrax and I are ready, Armfather."

"Thank you, Charak."

Zorribis shot Connoram a suspicious glance. "Ready for what?"

"We must go to the Elders at once," Connoram answered. "There is very little time."

"The Elders are in a very fragile state, especially Acerus," Zorribis said, taking a step away from Connoram. "We can take you there without your soldiers."

"My friend, you know I mean your people no harm. But I cannot say with the utmost confidence that your fellow Denarians do not intend to harm me. My soldiers are coming with me as protection, not for warfare. If you can trust me with this luxury, I can repay you in kind."

"I grow impatient, my child." Hodera sat quietly in the middle of her chambers, her nerves quaking as the voice of Tornatrax filled the room. "I sense more dissension within the Krunation Empire. The Denarians are at their most vulnerable, their savior has fled them once again, and nothing is being done."

"My Lord," Hodera pleaded. "I will not fail you! I have promised you I would retrieve what Excelsior took from you. It is only a matter of time."

"Time is a luxury you do not have, Hodera. I can sense the damage done to the planet's atmosphere, how it is shifting to match another, far inferior planet."

"You can feel it happening?"

"Denab IV is my planet as much as it is Excelsior's, child, if not more so. My influence lies deep in the water, and those resources are waiting for you to take them. As your soldiers betray you, you must take advantage of the shifting atmosphere and greet your new children who are evolving as I speak."

"Yes," Hodera said. "Yes, as everyone ages faster, we will gain more followers ready to do your bidding."

"And you must be there for them, as I was for your dear Emperor Nocterar. And you must ensure they are kept as pure of mind as you were, away from the corrupt teachings of Connoram."

"It shall be done, my Lord Tornatrax. The mission has already begun, and Connoram will never be able to spread his written lies."

"I am pleased to hear this. And if your mission is successful, you shall be granted the ability you so crave. The power to override the influence of the Matera. And an army of your own waiting for you to lead them."

Hodera gasped. "An army of my own, my Lord?"

"Oh, yes. They are already on the planet, waiting for you beneath the surface of Denab IV's waters."

Hodera bit down on her lower lip. Everything she ever wanted was so close for the taking, if only this one mission succeeds. So close.

Her eyes snapped open when she felt a sudden itch on her arms. She looked down at them and recoiled at the sight of her typically shiny scaly skin beginning to dull and flake off of her body. She quickly stood up and ran her hands across her face, feeling pieces of her skin flaking off, revealing a flesh-colored layer underneath.

Hodera balled her hands into fists and silently cursed Excelsior for doing this to her, for taking away her beauty as he took away her ability to hold on to her loyal soldiers, who abandoned her for the traitorous Connoram.

"You will pay for this," Hodera hissed. "You will both pay for this."

CHAPTER
TWENTY-ONE

"Tollund Laboratories, how may I help you?"

Matthew paced around his bedroom, running his fingertips along his bed and the walls of his old bedroom. He held the home phone in his other hand to his ear. Jason's black T-shirt stretched out against his muscular frame, and the jeans were a surprisingly comfortable fit. Arinna watched him pace while sitting at his computer desk, still wearing the same outfit she wore on Denab IV.

"Yes, I read Tollund Laboratories now has the remains of the 'Ritgen-Man' discovery. Is this true?"

"Yes it is," the female operator said in a matter-of-fact tone. "We have opened the exhibit to the public, and it is encased in glass. There is no life at all in the body, and no harm will come to anyone. We only ask for a suggested donation at the door to assist the families of those lost in the infamous attack."

"Of course," Matthew said as memories of Elder Klierra, Karini, Grannik, and Radifen flashed before his eyes. None of them deserved their fates. "Thank you very much. And what time does the exhibit open today?"

"Three to six pm," the operator answered. "We believe it was the estimated time when 'Ritgen-Man' first awoke in our laboratory."

"How fitting. Thank you again."

"You're welcome," the operator said. "Have a good day."

"You too." Matthew hung up the phone and checked the clock in his room. "We have a lot of time, and Grandma should be back with food soon. I can work on the map if you want to lie down. Grandma won't mind if you used her bed, so you can stretch out a bit."

Arinna shook her head. "If it's all right with you, I'd like to lie here." She motioned to his bed, and Matthew felt heat flush his face when he realized this was the first time a woman asked to lie down in his room.

"Ummm... sure." He motioned to the bed, and Arinna sat on it, pulled her shoes off, and then stretched out as much as possible on the twin-sized bed. "It's comfortable?" he asked.

"It feels wonderful," Arinna said. "Much softer than the beds on Denab IV. It reminds me of the sleeping quarters I used on Golgonoth VII. Considering how cold they were, I was surprised how soft their beds were. Felt like I was sleeping on a cloud."

"Well, I never thought it was quite cloud-level, but I hope it works for you. If you need anything, I'll be here working on Jason's map."

"How are you 'working on it?'"

"Back when all of this was just a webcomic, I downloaded this really cool map-building software. I could keep track of where everything takes place, but I only knew so much of the planet since I kept all the action limited to only a few areas. I've reconnected with it, so I can give Jason a lot more detail than before."

"I understand," she said, then leaned her head back on the pillow and shut her eyes.

The computer on his desk started and, not surprisingly, took several minutes to boot up. Once the desktop wallpaper appeared, which was a crude rendering of the symbol on Excelsior's uniform, Matthew clicked on the cartographer software. A new document opened, and he narrowed his eyes while focusing on the screen. All he needed to get the map going was to draw the first line.

But that didn't happen.

For fifteen minutes, his mind drifted back and forth between the task in front of him and the question nagging at the insecure side of him, the Matthew Peters side.

Why me?

Why were all the pieces put into place for him?

Tension tightened his neck, and as he massaged the back of it with both of his hands, he turned to his left and saw it for the first time since he was last in his room.

It was a sketch of Excelsior—the simple design which flashed in his mind the night after he touched the sword at the Metropolitan Museum of Art. Matthew felt those triangular eyes on him, and he knew what it was thinking.

That's not Matthew Peters. That's Semminex. Semminex was the big hero of the webcomics. Semminex ensured Denab IV would live on by putting Nocterar and Danaak out of commission.

Semminex rescued the young girl who grew up to be the woman lying on Matthew Peters's bed.

Clenching his teeth, Matthew snatched the sketch off the wall and tore it into pieces.

Arinna sat up in bed. "Are you okay?" she asked.

Matthew tossed the pieces of the sketch to the desk and put his hands on the back of his neck again. "Yeah. Sorry."

She walked over to Matthew and stood over him. She pointed to the torn up picture. "What is that?"

"Just a sketch I drew. About ten years ago, right after I was at the museum when I touched the sword."

Arinna looked closer. "This is you, yes? Excelsior?"

Matthew nodded. "It's Excelsior, yeah."

"Why did you tear it up?"

"He was staring at me."

"The drawing?"

He started rubbing his neck harder. "I know, I know. Sorry, I didn't mean to wake you."

"Maybe you should go downstairs," Arinna suggested. "Take some time away from the monitor." She gave a slight smile. "And I will have more time to sleep before we visit the laboratory."

Matthew smiled back. "Maybe you're right." He left his bedroom and walked downstairs. He was relieved to see Grandma wasn't back from grocery shopping yet, so he could sit down on the couch and be alone with his thoughts.

Even if the thoughts weren't very calming.

Matthew studied every inch of the Wyeth painting. He could see the hand of the Lady of the Lake holding Excalibur from the water, and he could picture the hand with scales and sharp fingernails. He wondered what Merlin and Arthur must have imagined when they saw it in real life. And he wondered why Arthur–one of the true legends in Earth's history–was allowed to wield the sword without having access to what lay dormant inside, while a 10-year-old boy who grew up in Queens was chosen to become a god in human form.

What would his life be like if Arthur was chosen instead? Or, at least, what would it be like if he hadn't gone to the museum that day?

"Matty?"

Matthew leapt to his feet, startled by the voice of Grandma, who was standing behind him holding two plastic bags filled with groceries.

"Oh, hi, Grandma," he said.

"Where's your friend? Arinna?"

"She's upstairs, taking a nap. We're gonna head over to Tollund Laboratories for a little while when she wakes up."

Grandma nodded and walked past Matthew, placing the grocery bags on the table in the kitchen. "Are you okay?" she asked from the other room. "It looked like you were off in your own world or something."

"My own world," Matthew said. "Funny. My own world isn't doing so well."

Grandma walked back into the living room. "Okay. Tell me, what's wrong?"

He stood up and pointed at the sword in the painting. "That. That's what's wrong."

"What about it? It's a beautiful painting."

"No, not the painting," Matthew corrected her. "The sword. The being inside. The whole Excelsior package. He's doing all the work; I'm just along for the ride. And whenever I chime in, I screw something up. Because of me, I might have ruined the whole planet. Who else gets to claim something like that?"

"You're not screwing anything up. If you were a screw-up, you wouldn't have this power in the first place. You've used it. You know how it works. And you already know what you have to do to fix your problem. So why are you still worrying about it?"

"It's... well..." He looked upstairs, then back down to Grandma.

"It's about who's actually using this power, right?" Grandma asked. "Who gets the credit for it, right? You or Excelsior?"

"Kinda. Well, yeah. I seem to keep getting in the way. I didn't have to give Jason some of my creativity."

"You didn't do that," Grandma interrupted.

"What are you talking about?"

"You can't give someone your creativity. Muses don't even do that. They inspire creativity in others."

Matthew let that soak in for a moment. "Well, then what did I do when I shook his hand? What did I give him?"

"You didn't give him anything," Grandma answered. "He may have thought you gave him something, and maybe it gave him the confidence to get the TV series going, but he was going to continue the comic no matter what."

Matthew's knees felt weak and he ran both hands through his hair. "So, what you're saying is, I set up a tether between these planets and endangered the lives of everyone on Denab IV, and there was no need for me to do it?"

"You didn't know that, Matty," Grandma insisted.

"I know. Everyone keeps telling me! But look at this mess! Was I at the right place at the right time? Or..." His eyes narrowed as he turned back toward the painting.

"Matthew, if you spend all your time trying to justify your position, you're going to make yourself crazy. The bottom line is this: yes, you were born with Denarian DNA. And yes, you were on a field trip to the Metropolitan Museum of Art where the sword was waiting for you. But here's the thing you don't get."

"What don't I get?"

Grandma pointed toward the plastic-covered sofa. "Matthew, sit down."

"Why?"

"Sit down," she repeated. Matthew could tell her patience was wearing thin, so he walked over to the couch and sat down. The sound of the creaking plastic echoed through the quiet apartment.

Grandma sat in the club chair opposite her grandson. "Remember when I said I was on the board at the museum? How I had to keep my mouth shut about the sword when I saw it? I got to see you grow into a gentle, caring young boy with big ideas. You read a lot, you watched movies a lot, you were really into science fiction, and you kept telling me about how much you wanted to make the world a better place." She pointed to the sword. "If the sword only responded to someone with Denarian DNA, I would have sent Jason to the museum in a second. In a second."

"Then why didn't you?"

Grandma shook her head and shut her eyes. "Because he wasn't the one. It responded to someone it deemed worthy to become Excelsior. You. It may mean a whole lot of new responsibilities, but if it didn't think you were up to the challenge, it wouldn't have called to you. So relax. You didn't have everything handed to you. You were the right man to hold the sword." She used her finger to poke him in the middle of his chest. "You are the right man to be Excelsior. So stop beating yourself up. There's nothing you can do, except take back whatever you gave Jason. Focus on that, and everything on Denab IV will be fine."

Grandma stood up and kissed Matthew's forehead. "I'm gonna put the groceries away. You do whatever else you need to do, but make sure you say goodbye before you go." She walked back into the kitchen and started unpacking the bags.

The creaking of the middle stair prompted Matthew to turn around, and he saw Arinna standing there, looking down at him. "Sorry. Did we wake you up?"

Arinna shook her head.

"You heard all that, didn't you?" Matthew asked.

Arinna nodded, and Matthew never felt less like Excelsior.

"So, yeah. I'm sorry I brought you here and everything. Turns out I didn't even have to create this tether in the first place. If I left him alone, nothing around here would change. Heck, if I never went to the museum and touched the sword in the first place, two planets would have been better off."

"Do not apologize. Jason is family," Arinna said while walking down the rest of the stairs. "We do things for family we would not normally do for anyone else."

"Like give yourself up to General Hodera so your siblings can be safe?" Arinna nodded without giving a verbal answer. Matthew felt he may have crossed a line, so he quickly added, "Again, I'm sorry."

"I said, do not apologize," Arinna said. "I cannot speak for Earth, but I know Denab IV is better because you are there."

Matthew's mouth hung open as he tried to process what she told him. Was this the same person who condemned him for taking the stars away? Now, all of a sudden, Denab IV is better off with him? What did she mean?

"What do you mean?"

"I will always love my Denarian brothers and sisters," Arinna began. "But visiting other planets and other species on a regular basis allows for a broader perspective. And we need a broader perspective in our leaders, especially in Excelsior. You do not see all of the Krunation race as something to be extinguished, you show mercy on them. And you consider the well-being of your loved one here. You do not force him to relinquish what you gave him."

These were encouraging words, but they didn't seem to penetrate the wall of woe Matthew built for himself. He walked toward the stairs. "We might as well go back upstairs. I still have to figure out how to get this map made for Jason, so I can cut the tether and be done with all this."

"Wait," Arinna said, holding out her hands and blocking Matthew from walking upstairs. She placed her hands on his shoulders. "Take a deep breath."

"Why?"

"Because your mind needs to be cleared."

"Good point," he murmured, then took a deep breath as instructed. He had to admit it helped. He didn't feel as tight in his shoulders as before.

"Good. Now, do you remember what to do?" she asked.

"Look into your eyes," Matthew confirmed, giving a little smile. "This part's pretty easy."

"Now hold still."

Matthew concentrated on Arinna's eyes as she applied a little bit of pressure on each side of his head. After several moments, the doubts, the fears, the thoughts racing through his mind, all slowed down to a crawl.

"Better?" she asked.

"Much," he responded in a much sturdier tone of voice.

She pulled her hands away. "Do you believe you can create his map now?"

"Sure."

Arinna turned around and walked upstairs ahead of Matthew. The two re-entered Matthew's room, and Arinna stretched out on the bed again and closed her eyes.

Matthew sat back down in his chair and turned his attention toward the monitor. The empty blue background called to Excelsior's energy, and he felt his eyes glaze over as he rested his right hand on the computer's wireless mouse. His fingers clicked the left and right buttons at all of the right moments, and the map burst to life on the screen.

"Wow," Matthew whispered. He sat up straight and pushed his shoulders back, an unfamiliar feeling of confidence washing over him.

Knowing Arinna believes her home planet benefits from his presence didn't hurt either.

CHAPTER
TWENTY-TWO

"**E**lders, you may want to see this."

Tricerus glanced up when he heard Nosgood's warning, and his sudden movement broke Lokris's concentration as she sat beside Acerus, holding his hand and feeling his grip constantly strengthen and weaken. The other Elders sat near the High Elder's bed, occasionally taking time to step away and ease the pain in their aching joints.

It was quiet in the Edenarian village ever since Acerus's collapse. The ambassadors from the neighboring continents returned to their homes to share the news, but Nosgood chose to stay behind, sending some of his soldiers back to give the message for him. He took his position outside Acerus's home, standing at the ready.

The popping in Lokris's knees echoed in the room when she stood and turned her head toward the source of the noise. She cautiously stepped outside and turned to Nosgood. "Something is coming," she said, stepping out from Acerus's home.

"Krunations!" Lokris heard the exclamation from Malitus, who was running from his home with his blaster rifle in hand. He dropped to one knee, aiming his weapon at the low-flying, wide aircraft holding an older Krunation and two younger ones on either side of him.

Before Malitus could fire, Nosgood ran up to him and quickly knocked the weapon out of his hands. "Do you see any aiming at us?" Nosgood asked while pointing at the approaching aircraft.

"No, Nosgood," the emotional Denarian said. "Not yet."

"Then we will hold our fire until they do otherwise," Lokris instructed while walking past the two, standing directly in front of them. "And if they wish to engage, the first one they will strike will be me."

"Not quite, Elder," Nosgood said as he walked away from Malitus and stood alongside Lokris. "They will have a choice over which one to shoot."

Lokris gave Nosgood a faint smile, then pointed toward the smaller flyer leading the Krunations. "Looks like one of your aircrafts," she said.

"It is. Niterra borrowed it." From a distance, both could see Zorribis waving one of his arms. "I see her. And Zorribis."

"Why are they with the Krunations?" Branerik asked while walking from his home, his blaster rifle in his hands. "Have they been taken prisoner?"

"They would not have been given their own aircraft to fly if they were hostages," Nosgood answered. "Besides, Hodera is not the type to take prisoners. She would prefer to kill us on sight."

"Hold your fire!" Zorribis yelled to the Denarians. "They mean no harm!" Niterra landed her aircraft while the Krunation transport came to a rest beside them.

"How do we know?" Branerik asked, his rifle aimed at Tarrax, who stood to Connoram's left.

"Because these soldiers have sworn to abide by my commands," Connoram answered. "And they have been ordered not to fire on any Denarians, except as self-defense. So if you wish for them to fire on you, you are more than welcome. All you need to do is strike me down."

"I recommend you refuse his offer," Zorribis said, motioning for the Denarians to lower their weapons.

"Why are you here?" Malitus asked.

"Zorribis has granted me an audience with Acerus," Connoram said. "It is very important I speak with him as soon as possible before it is too late."

"Too late for what?" Nosgood asked.

"We understand the High Elder is dying from the sudden atmospheric shifts. Another Elder, Ducera, has died already." A shocked murmur went through the crowd of onlookers. "In time," Connoram continued, "the rest of the Elders will join him in death, as will every other lifeform on this planet, Denarian and Krunation alike. You must have felt the effects of the shifts by now."

The younger Denarians turned to each other and nodded, several of them pointing to their joints.

Lokris stepped forward and looked into Connoram's eyes. "I can see the shifting has not been kind to you, Connoram." She gave him a warm smile. "But I have seen that light in your eyes before, and I am happy to see your time with Hodera has not extinguished it."

"Quite the contrary," Connoram answered. "Working alongside her has done nothing but increase the hunger to bring Denarians and Krunations together."

"Everyone please step back," Lokris ordered her fellow Denarians. They obeyed and cleared a path so the three Krunations, followed by Zorribis and Niterra, could enter Acerus' home.

"Did you ever think this was possible?" Lokris asked Nosgood as they walked in behind Zorribis and Niterra. Nosgood shook his head no.

"Lokris, has your logic betrayed you?" Quinterus asked, pointing to the Krunation leader approaching him. "How could you possibly bring Krunations to the home of the High Elder?"

"Because Connoram is not like any other Krunation," Lokris answered.

"Connoram?" Acerus's eyes slowly opened. "Help... help me to... my feet." He extended his arms, motioning for someone to assist him.

Zorribis and Niterra walked to opposite sides of the bed, and each took one of Acerus's arms. They gently pulled him up and helped him stand.

"We have you, High Elder," Niterra whispered.

"Thank you, my child," Acerus spoke, his voice wheezing. He lifted his head up and stared at Connoram. "Come closer."

Connoram stepped forward and looked into Acerus's ancient-looking face, which grew older with each passing minute. "I know you," Acerus said. "You... you saved us."

"He what?" Tricerus asked. "What does he mean?"

"The caverns," Acerus forced out, then sank back on his bed.

Connoram held up a six-sided pendant around his neck; a pendant identical to the one owned by Arinna.

"Sestera," Lokris whispered, covering her mouth in shock.

Connoram lowered his arm. "A long time ago, as the war escalated between our races, I was abandoned to die by my fellow Krunations. The only one to take pity on me and nurse me back to health was a Denarian Elder, Sestera. She opened my mind to the possibilities of our two races living in peace on the same planet. She was a brilliant woman, capable of changing even the most hardened minds, and she challenged me to look beyond everything we were taught about your god Excelsior and our god Tornatrax. I felt my mind expand beyond anything I once thought capable while spending time with her."

Connoram held up the pendant one more time. "Before we parted ways, she gave me this pendant as a symbol of trust. She believed I was beyond the ambitious, yet petty ways of Nocterar, Danaak, and Hodera. And when I knew of Nocterar's intentions to eradicate the entire Denarian species, I recruited several of my soldiers to assist Sestera with relocating a group of Denarians, including all of you, into the same caverns used to house your regeneration chambers."

A hush fell over the room, and Acerus forced himself back to his feet. "Yes," he whispered. "Sestera... had the idea... but you turned the idea... into reality."

"It was necessary," Connoram said. "I told Nocterar no one would build his city of Nocteris or that monstrosity of a castle he wanted if the Denarians were exterminated."

"We owe you our lives, Connoram," Lokris said. "You are an ideal ambassador to your race, and an example of what can be found within. How can we possibly repay you?"

Connoram glanced over his shoulder and called out, "Charak! Please bring me the parchment."

Charak stepped forward with a stack of the parchment papers tied together. "Yes, Armfather."

"Thank you," Connoram said as he took the stack from the younger Krunation's hands.

"Armfather," Acerus said.

"Yes," Connoram said. "When he appeared before us, Tornatrax declared we are an extension of the power coursing through him, and he displayed that power with his right hand glowing with immense energy. The arm directs the hand, and the shoulder directs the arm."

"So you are the shoulder... and Charak is the hand..." Acerus took a deep breath, then continued. "Who is the arm?"

"The arm is no more," Charak said. "He was a maniacal force of nature, seeking to eclipse the legend of Emperor Nocterar."

"Danaak?" Niterra asked Charak. "Danaak was your father?"

Charak stood stone-faced. "He chose not to think of me when he was on Denab IV. Therefore, I choose not to think of him. We only look to the future for this planet."

"And to realize that future, we must look to the distant past," Connoram said as he held up the parchment. "For as long as we have been alive, we have known of two gods overseeing Denab IV: Excelsior, who watched over the Denarians on the land, and Tornatrax, who brought about our evolution from the water. We have known our two races were fated to spend their time on this planet at odds with each other. While Excelsior trained the Denarians to cultivate the land, Tornatrax encouraged the Krunations to conquer, to spread his influence throughout this planet. Denarians were born to serve Denab IV, but we were born to rule it."

"We know all of this," Tricerus said. "And yet you claim to have a new revelation about our past. You may not have noticed, but our High Elder is dying."

Connoram's attention immediately turned toward the painting on the wall of Candassus and Abrattus. "You are familiar with that story, yes?" he asked Tricerus through gritted teeth. "According to your interpretation, from what I see in this piece of art, the Krunation Candassus was tempted by the power emitting from the sword and became the vessel of Tornatrax's lifeforce on the planet. He then killed Abrattus and took the first steps toward finding and destroying Excelsior."

"It was a cautionary tale," Quinterus interjected. "The tale of Candassus and Abrattus was meant to show these two races were fated to always fight, with little to no chance for peace."

"Our version was quite different," said Connoram. "According to the story we have been told, both men raced to reach the sword, and it was the Krunation-already gifted with greater strength and speed than the Denarian—who reached the sword first. And the lifeforce of Tornatrax was his reward."

Acerus shook his head. "No. No, these two men... they were friends. Tornatrax forced Candassus to destroy Abrattus."

"They were more than friends, High Elder," Connoram said as he held up the parchment. "They were brothers."

CHAPTER
TWENTY-THREE

Zorribis's eyes darted back and forth between the Elders standing dumbstruck around the weakening Acerus, Connoram, and the parchment manuscript held out in the Krunation's outstretched hand. He studied their looks of anger and denial by this sudden revelation, expecting them to immediately accuse the older Krunation of trying to lead the Denarians astray, but surprisingly, they didn't.

Acerus leaned forward and squinted as he read what was written, this supposed new interpretation of everything they were taught. He took one small, labored step forward to read the text better, and his eyes widened in surprise. "Where did you... get this?" he whispered.

"You lie," Tricerus pointed his finger at Connoram. "You are here only to disrupt what we know. You are here to divide us!"

"What you know at this time is the same as what we know!" Connoram shot back. "And what we know is whatever finite time we have on this planet has lessened and continues to lessen. Our fates are intertwined, and so we must meet our end with peace rather than a continuing war we can no longer afford."

"And this is how you intend to make peace?" Quinterus asked.

"Let him talk, Quinterus," Ducera interjected.

"No," the Elder snapped. "He claims he wants to make peace and brings soldiers with him."

"I come in peace but not in stupidity," Connoram said. "I trust my guards to do what they must, but they will not engage you in battle until noted. Besides, what would stop you from striking me down if I came unarmed and without any soldiers?"

"Enough!"

Everyone stopped when Acerus barked out his order. He took a moment to catch his breath, then spoke again, "I have seen this writing before... I have written this... a long time ago."

"You?" Tricerus's voice dropped in confusion and disbelief. "What do you mean?"

"You have... a different handwriting, yes?" Acerus asked Connoram, who nodded. "Before Excelsior came to us... He gave me the gift to let the planet speak through me... and I wrote something like this."

The High Elder's gaze drifted as he spoke. "You have the same ability?"

"For a long time, I could hear rumblings, gibberish," Connoram said. "But I could not interpret what was said without Excelsior providing the gift; the same he bestowed upon you. I finally established a connection with the Sancterrum Tree I have in my possession."

Acerus's mouth curled into a smile. "Amazing."

"We are more alike than you think, High Elder," Connoram said. "After Tornatrax took Candassus's body for his own and destroyed his brother Abrattus, he returned to their home and murdered his entire family, completely eradicating the existence of a male Denarian and a female Krunation who found each other and wanted to spend the rest of their lives together. By the time Tornatrax found them, neither had the skin tones differentiating the two races." He looked past Acerus and asked, "Zorribis, will you hold this, please?"

Zorribis stepped forward and took the manuscript out of Connoram's hands, freeing the Krunation to roll up the sleeve on his shirt. His soldiers gasped as they saw his normally green and scaly skin was flaking away, giving way to a smooth, pale blue skin. He looked down at the arm, then into Acerus's eyes. "May I see your arm, High Elder?"

Acerus nodded, and despite his weakened state, managed to roll back the sleeve on his left arm, revealing skin with the same color and texture as Connoram.

"How is this possible?" Quinterus asked, then turned his attention to Acerus. "And how could you not tell us? We lead by following your example, your teachings." He pointed to the painting on the wall. "And yet you continue to give credence to an altered legend instead of fact! To keep this from us—"

"For your own safety," Acerus said, which silenced the room once again. "I wanted to, please believe me. But when I saw..." His ancient eyes welled up with tears as he pressed on. "When I saw what the Krunations did...

to Valertus... to our fellow Denarians... I could not. If I encouraged peace with a race wanting us annihilated, the Denarian race would have welcomed its own extinction." He took a deep breath and spoke directly to Connoram. "This reconciliation could have occurred much earlier... and I regret not being in your position." His voice dropped to a whisper as he added, "You are as brave a soul as your mother."

The revelation forced Connoram to stumble back. His eyes widened, and he whispered back, "You knew my mother?"

"Knew her," Acerus said. "And loved her."

"Liar!"

Everyone turned to look and saw the Krunation soldier to Connoram's left was pointing at Acerus. He had such a deep, authoritative voice, Connoram and Charak looked at him in shock at his sudden exclamation.

"Tarrax!" Connoram said in a chiding tone of voice.

But Tarrax was still staring straight ahead at Acerus, and with his gaze not leaving the High Elder, he reached for the holster on his belt and pulled out his blaster pistol. Before anyone could react, a shot rang out from Tarrax, burning a hole in Acerus's stomach.

Acerus looked down in shock, and his hands trembled as they covered the gaping wound.

"Acerus!" Lokris exclaimed, running up to the High Elder and assisting him into his bed.

"No!" Connoram screamed at Tarrax. "What have you done?"

"We are victorious, Connoram!" Tarrax declared while turning the pistol toward his chest. "Our mission is complete! Hail Tornatrax!" he yelled before pulling the trigger. His death was instantaneous, as was the dissolving of his body. The black cloud of ash remaining was the only proof someone else was standing next to Connoram at all. The blaster pistol dropped to the ground and broke into two pieces, emitting a couple of sparks before going silent.

"An ambush!" Tricerus turned toward Zorribis, eyes filled with contempt. "You allowed this to happen by trusting this untrustworthy race!"

"No, Elder!" Connoram cried while holding up his arms in surrender. "You know I had nothing to do with this terrible attack."

"These are your trusted servants," Tricerus replied. "Just as you said!"

"Get them out of here," Quinterus commanded the villagers. "Nosgood, summon your guards. Take these two prisoner."

"No," Zorribis said to the Elders while pointing to Nosgood. "Nosgood, let them pass."

Nosgood looked back and forth between Zorribis and the Elders. "You know me, Nosgood," Zorribis pleaded. "And you know Excelsior would ask this from you as well."

"Nosgood!" Quinterus interrupted. "I am an Elder. You listen to me. We command you to take these Krunations prisoner!"

"Not all of us, Quinterus!" Lokris yelled from Acerus's bedside. "Nosgood, do as Zorribis asked. Let them pass."

"Yes, Elder Lokris," Nosgood replied. He stepped aside at the doorway and called outside, "Stand down!"

Zorribis nodded to Nosgood and said, "Thank you," then turned to Connoram and Charak and whispered, "Get out of here."

"Nosgood, what are you waiting for?" Quinterus called out. "Seize them!"

But Nosgood didn't leap at the Elder's command. He stood still as Zorribis and Niterra led Connoram and Charak to the door.

"Now it is my turn to be in your debt," Connoram said to Zorribis while lowering his arms

"That has nothing to do with it," Zorribis answered. "You showed your trust in us by being here. We will trust in you. Whatever will happen in the immediate future between our races will not happen here and now."

Connoram nodded. "I see my decision to let you live has not been in vain," he said as the two Denarians quickly escorted the Krunations to their transport and watched them head back toward Nocteris.

CHAPTER
TWENTY-FOUR

"**E**veryone is here to see him?" Arinna and Matthew stood near the front of the long line outside Tollund Laboratories. She held a cardboard take-out box in her hands with a slice of pizza inside. Matthew wore a backpack stuffed with his Excelsior uniform and helmet, the handle of his sword slightly protruding from the opening. He looked back and forth between the large crowd of people in front of them, and the line already around the corner behind them.

"They're not quite here to see Danaak. It's a chance to see an alien for the first time in their lives, if not the only time in their lives," Matthew answered. He looked to his left and saw a group of students from nearby Columbia University walking to the back of the line. Matthew pointed to the large group of people and the various tents, sleeping bags, blankets, and pillows along with them. "Everyone in front of us slept overnight for this. Reminds me of college students sleeping outside Rockefeller Center for Saturday Night Live tickets."

"I still do not understand how your people can believe they are the only forms of life in the universe," Arinna said. "Do they not know how vast it is?"

Matthew shrugged. "It's a good thing you didn't watch any of the twenty-four-hour news channels here. You'll get debates about climate change, the age of the planet, how big space is. People arguing for the sake of arguing."

"Reminds me of my short time on the planet Dribkcom," she remembered. "There was only one humanoid species there, but nobody could agree on anything. Everyone was too preoccupied with themselves, there was no room for a race like the Denarians, who only thrived when everyone worked together. Out of all the planets I visited to establish a harmonious relationship, I spent the least amount of time there."

"I don't blame you," Matthew said. "I'm surprised you wanted to come here. Hell, I'm surprised I was looking forward to being back here."

"Of course I wanted to come here," Arinna said. "We needed to ensure your return to Denab IV. And knowing the kind of man you are, I thought it would behoove me to see the planet responsible for making you this way."

"Really?" Matthew asked. "You sure you don't mean the kind of man Excelsior would make of me?"

"Did you hear me mention Excelsior?"

"Well, no, but..."

"Then you should not mention him either."

"Good afternoon, everyone," the tour guide announced to the growing crowd. She was a tall, blonde-haired woman who attracted the attention of several males on the line. She held a gray clipboard in one hand and a silver clicker in the other. "My name is Kristin, and I'd like to welcome you to Tollund Laboratories for our Ritgen-Man exhibit. Now, unfortunately, due to the high level of demand to see the exhibit, and due to the limited amount of space open to the public, we can only accommodate the first fifty people in this line. So I must ask for those past the first fifty people to try again tomorrow or later this week. We will do our best to accommodate you, and on behalf of everyone at Tollund Laboratories, we apologize for this inconvenience."

No, Matthew thought as sweat began to collect in his palms. He never got top grades in math, but even he knew he and Arinna were well beyond the fifty-person cut-off point, and he wouldn't accept this. He couldn't. He needed to figure out a way inside.

"Did anyone ever tell you how fascinatingly beautiful you are?"

Matthew's accelerated state of panic was stopped when he heard the man with the glasses and graying hair leaning over Arinna's right shoulder and trying to keep his tongue in his mouth. His eyes looked glazed over, a drunken smile across his face.

Arinna looked behind her and smiled a forced smile. "Thank you," was all she said, but judging by the man's goofy grin, she might as well have told him she loved him. She turned back to Matthew and rolled her eyes. "Just like the race on Dranadon."

"Dranadon?" Matthew asked.

"Primitive culture. They based all of their decisions on their basest instincts. When I was there, anytime I came close to them, they would stop what they were doing and pursue me. Apparently, Denarian DNA causes a pheromone-like reaction."

"Can you tell me your name?" the old man drooled.

"As I was saying." Arinna cocked in the man's direction.

Matthew looked past Arinna, "Ummm, sir, the tour guide said none of us will be able to get inside to see the exhibit. Maybe it's time for you to go home?"

The man cocked his head back and forth as though he were a confused dog, then frowned at Matthew. "Don't tell me what to do, you little punk!" The man reached out over Arinna's shoulder, and gave Matthew an off-balanced shove. Matthew took a step back and bumped into a mother of two toddlers, but the man stumbled and, as Arinna moved out of the way, dropped to one knee.

"Sorry," Matthew said to the mother, who turned around after he bumped into her. She looked like she was about to yell at him, but stopped and sniffed the air. Her face went from angry to pleasantly intoxicated.

"Oh, that's all right, handsome," the mother said. She ran her left hand up Matthew's arm and gave his bicep a light squeeze. "Oh wow, very nice," she added. "Where do you work out? Maybe we go to the same gym."

He glanced at her left hand. "Oh no, I'm from out of town. And besides, I don't think your husband would like it if he saw this."

The mother waved her right hand dismissively while squeezing his arm with her left hand. "Oh, don't worry about him. I never do. So where are you from?"

Matthew turned back to Arinna and said, "Safe to say I'm definitely Denarian now. I never got this kind of reaction when I was in school."

The mother shot Arinna a look of jealousy. "Who's she?" she asked.

A sudden thought came to Matthew, and he pulled the woman's hand away from his arm. "I'm sorry, could you excuse me for a moment?" He jogged up to the front of the line where Kristin stood with her clipboard tucked under her arm and the silver clicker at work, monitoring everyone passing her.

"Excuse me, Kristin, right?" Matthew said.

"I'll be with you in one moment, sir," Kristin said, her head facing the clicker as one guest after another walked past her in a single file. "Forty-eight, Forty-nine, Fifty," she counted, then held up her arm to block the next person from entering. "I'm sorry, Ma'am," she said to a redheaded woman who was the unfortunate number fifty-one. "We have to ask you to come back tomorrow."

As Matthew watched Kristin break the woman's heart, a sudden flash of recognition came to mind.

"But I'm leaving to go back to Richmond tomorrow," she said. "And my flight leaves in the morning. This is the only time I can go!"

"I'm so sorry, Ma'am," Kristin replied. "This is the policy. There's nothing I can do."

"Wait, weren't you in my homeroom class?" Matthew blurted, pointing to Kristin. "You used to sit with Lisa and Jen and—"

"Sir, I'm sorry," Kristin interrupted, keeping her focus on the redheaded woman. "I'm going to need you both to..." She suddenly inhaled Matthew's scent, and she turned her attention to him. "I'm sorry, can I help you?" Her frustrated tone drifted away, and she grinned.

"Uh, yeah," Matthew started, still trying to get used to women paying attention to him. "I was saying we were in the same homeroom class. You may not remember me. Matthew Peters?"

There was a drunken lilt in Kristin's voice. "Oh, yes, I definitely remember you, Matthew. Who could forget you?"

Until now, Matthew knew the perfect answer. He felt his temperature rising a few degrees, and he adjusted the collar on his shirt. "Thank you. Yeah, I remember you too. Anyway, I was wondering if you could do me a favor."

"Anything," Kristin said.

"Well, see, my... associate and I, we have a very small window of time to complete an important project, and a major part of it is getting into Tollund Laboratories to see the Ritgen-Man. If there is any possible way we can come in, you'd guarantee our project's success." Matthew took a step toward Kristin. "Something I will never... ever... forget."

The redheaded woman's mouth dropped open in disdain. "Oh no!" she yelled. "If anyone is getting in, it's going to be me and my family. I have a flight scheduled for tomorrow morning to go back to Richmond, and I'm not leaving without seeing this exhibit."

"Ma'am, I'm sorry, but there's nothing I can do for you," Kristin said. She turned to Matthew and her voice softened. "Matthew, like I told this woman a moment ago, we can only allow fifty people to enter at once. However, if you contacted the facility ahead of time, I can check our VIP list to see if you are on it." She turned away from the redheaded woman and gave Matthew a quick wink and a smile.

His eyebrows raised. "Oh, yes. The VIP list. Thank you very much for reminding me."

"Okay, then," Kristin said as she pulled the clipboard from under her arm and flipped up the top page. "And your last name is..."

"Peters," Matthew answered. "Matthew Peters."

"Ahhh, yes," Kristin said. "Peters, Matthew, plus one. Yup, it's right here." She reached for a walkie-talkie attached to her belt and spoke into it. "M.O.D., please advise I'm letting two more individuals in the exhibit. They're on the VIP list."

"The what?" the voice on the other end asked.

"Ten-four," Kristin said, turning down the volume on her walkie-talkie. "Okay, you're all set to go in, and I hope you have a great time," she said with a smile. "Maybe I'll see you again when you're finished?" She gave Matthew another wink.

"Maybe," Matthew said, returning the smile, then making his way back through the line to retrieve Arinna.

When he made it back to his original place in line, he stifled a laugh when he saw three different men surrounding Arinna. One was even wearing a three-piece suit and carrying a briefcase, and he must have walked by when he picked up the Denarian's scent because he was holding out his business card to her when Matthew arrived.

"Sorry, guys," Matthew said as he held out a hand to Arinna.

"Oh good, you're back," the mother said with a smile.

"Sorry, I'm spoken for," Matthew said to her, trying to let her down as softly as possible. The look in her eyes showed it still stung, but there were more pressing matters ahead of him.

Arinna smiled and extended her hand, and the two walked down the line toward the entrance. Matthew felt her grip on his hand tighten as they made their way to the door, and he shot her a grin.

"Right this way, Matthew," Kristin said with a renewed excitement in her voice. She stood in front of the door, holding it open for him and Arinna to walk inside. "And this is your colleague?" she asked.

"Yes," Matthew replied. "Yes, my colleague."

Kristin nodded in return. He didn't have much experience when it came to women, but even he could tell jealousy was suddenly in the air. He looked down, realized he was still holding Arinna's hand, and gently pulled it away. Arinna looked down, then back at Matthew with a confused glance.

Eager to break the sudden tension, Matthew asked, "So, the VIP access? What is it?"

"You have me as a tour guide," Kristin answered brightly. "And since I'm here, there is no need to go through security. Now, if you'll follow me, please." She walked in front of the two, and Arinna leaned toward Matthew.

"Are you okay?" she whispered.

"Yes," Matthew whispered back. "I can get us closer to Danaak. Just trust me."

As the three of them made their way up the stairs and into the main hallway, Matthew saw the fifty men, women, and children in a single-file line, waiting to see the proof mankind was not alone in the universe, no one knowing a Denarian and a human with Denarian blood walked among them. And at the end of the long line, waiting for them all, was him.

"This is the main lobby of Tollund Laboratories," Kristin said in a well-rehearsed tone. "This is where Ritgen-Man unleashed a terrible wave of carnage, killing several of our employees, including Dr. Franklin Ritgen himself. It is unclear how many more people he killed in addition to them, since the weapon he unleashed resulted in a total annihilation of his victims."

"I know," Matthew murmured. With each passing step, the memories flashed before his eyes. Karini, Grannik, and Radifen being blasted into oblivion. The glowing red hand of Danaak and his delight in executing his friends. His uncle Jason being knocked to the floor. Elder Klierra trying to kill Danaak and sacrificing herself to save Matthew.

"Such a monster," Arinna said, shaking her head.

"Very much so," Kristin replied, as though she were still reading off of her script, but regretting doing so. "Shame I never had the chance to meet Dr. Ritgen before... well, you know."

"I'm sure he was a great man," Matthew said as they continued to walk past the line of chattering people. Finally, as Matthew caught a glimpse of what awaited them at the end of the hall, he felt his breath being sucked out of him. His feet felt as heavy as anvils.

Three Earth years passed, and yet it felt like it all happened an hour ago. Matthew remembered facing

Danaak, declaring he wasn't afraid of him. He remembered his nerves then betraying him as the Krunation looked into his eyes, into his very soul, and saw the fear he tried to mask. He remembered how Radifen called out Danaak to fight him, and how Danaak destroyed him with a blast of power from his hand. How Matthew cried as Klierra bled to death in front of him as his uncle lay unconscious a distance away.

More than anything, he remembered the helplessness as he saw the wound caused by Klierra healing, knowing it wouldn't be long before Danaak rose again and obliterated Matthew. He wished his realization of what it took to awaken Excelsior's lifeforce within him came before it did, before it was too late to save his friends.

"And this," Kristin said with a mixture of bravado and disgust. "This is what is known as the Ritgen-Man. To this day, we know nothing of its origins or how it came to be on our planet, but we know it landed sometime between the fall of the dinosaurs and the rise of man. When it was discovered in its preserved state three years ago, the earliest reports say it was found with deep tears in its chest and abdomen, as though it made a fatal mistake of attempting to exert its power over an animal and paid the price for its hubris."

"Yes," Arinna said with a nod. "This sounds like Danaak."

"Who?" Kristin asked.

Arinna's words snapped Matthew into the present. "Reminds her of someone we know," he said.

"Someone we knew," Arinna added, correcting Matthew.

"Oh, okay," Kristin replied.

"Can we get a little closer?" he asked, pointing to the velvet rope positioned two feet away from the glass case holding Danaak's remains.

"Well, we really don't allow anyone to go past the rope," Kristin said. "We understand people would want to get as close as possible to an alien, but we have a digital insert of the alien we include in a special souvenir photograph." Matthew was sure she could see the look of disgust on his face, and she quickly added, "All proceeds go toward the families of the victims from the Ritgen-Man attack."

Knowing this calmed him down, but still, who thought this was a good idea? "We'll pass. I don't want to take a picture of him. There's something I need to see. I knew one of Dr. Ritgen's colleagues. She suspected something about Ritgen-Man, but she couldn't confirm it."

Kristin put her hand on Matthew's arm. "You knew someone who worked with Dr. Ritgen?"

He nodded. "Yes. Dr. Sierra. Katherine Sierra." It felt strange saying the name Elder Klierra adopted for herself, but Kristin gasped when he said it and moved closer to him.

"What was she like?" Kristin asked.

"She was..." Matthew struggled to find the right words. "... an inspiration."

"I feel the same way," Kristin said as her hand moved up and down his arm. "You're so lucky to have known her. The work she did with Dr. Ritgen was unprecedented. She was my idol."

"Mine as well," Matthew said. "Remember what I said outside about how we're working on something very important. Seeing the Ritgen-Man up close will give us the answer we needed." He stepped closer to her, making sure Kristin could smell him even more.

"And I won't be able to thank you enough for your help," he murmured, prompting another look of confusion from Arinna.

Kristin blushed. "Well, I don't see the harm in letting you under the rope since I'll be here. Considering you're a VIP guest and all."

Matthew turned to Arinna and mouthed the words, "Trust me," then turned back to Kristin and took her hand. "I really appreciate this."

He followed Kristin as she walked up to the velvet rope, unhooked it from its brass stanchion, and stepped aside for Matthew to walk past her. Matthew beckoned to Arinna to follow her.

"Hey, why do they get to go closer?" a middle-aged man at the front of the line yelled. "I paid my ticket too!"

"I'm sorry, sir," Kristin said with practiced ease. "They are liaisons of Tollund Laboratories, taking care of the latest safety precautions. We wouldn't want anything to happen to any of our guests."

Matthew walked up to the glass case holding the infamous Krunation and looked him up and down. There were enough scales on Danaak's face, chest, and uncovered arms to show his alien origin, and the rest of him was covered by a gray and black shirt, matching pants, and black boots.

He shook his head and said to Arinna, "They let him keep his Krunation uniform."

"Krunation?" Kristin asked from behind them.

"Never mind," he said, moving closer to the lifeless body. His focus was aimed at the wound in the Krunation's chest he caused, and he held back his urge to smash the glass, unsheathe his sword, and cut off the Krunation's head. Instead, he pressed his hands to the glass and whispered, "Sleep well, Danaak."

"Yessssss."

Matthew jerked his head around when he heard the soft hiss of a voice behind him. "What was that?" he whispered.

"What was what?" Arinna whispered back.

"You didn't hear that voice? That hiss?"

Arinna shook her head. Matthew turned back toward Danaak's body in time to see a slight glow emanating from the fatal wound in his chest. He shot Arinna a look and pointed toward the wound, whispering again. "Did you—"

Again, Arinna shook her head. "I saw nothing. Are you all right?"

"I think so," Matthew said, uneasy. When he turned back to the alien corpse, there was no sign of life from it at all. He cocked his head at Danaak in confusion.

"Don't worry," Kristin said as she approached the two. "If the Department of Defense saw any sign of a threat, they wouldn't have released the body back to us."

"Maybe you're right," Matthew replied. He shot Kristin another smile. "Thank you again, Kristin. I'll leave some very positive feedback with your manager."

"I hope that's not all you'll be leaving," Kristin said with another flirtatious smile. "Maybe a phone number?"

"Maybe," Matthew said as he and Arinna made their way back up the hall toward the exit doors. Kristin gave him one last wave goodbye.

CHAPTER
TWENTY-FIVE

"**H**ow is he?"

Zorribis walked into Acerus's living quarters with a cold gelatinous ball and handed it to Niterra, who knelt beside the High Elder's bed. Acerus was lying face-up, his eyes relaxed, his gaze focused on the ceiling. A brown blanket covered his wounded body. Niterra took the ball and pressed it on Acerus's forehead, where it spread out above the High Elder's eyes.

"The wound has been dressed," she answered. "His breathing is slowing down. It is not as erratic as it was before. But I have never seen a blast like that, and the wound seems to be growing."

"Growing?"

"Look for yourself." Niterra slowly moved the blanket aside to reveal a large, white wrapping around Acerus's midsection and pointed to a thin area of blackened skin above them. "The initial blast was small, but it has been spreading since I applied the bandages. It will not be long before it spreads farther through his body."

Zorribis gasped when he saw what could only be described as the infection eating away at the body of the High Elder. And his shock was only compounded when, despite such a terrible wound, Acerus began to stir.

"My.... love...."

"What was that?" Zorribis asked.

"He said, 'My love.' The only noise he has made since you escorted the other Elders out," Niterra answered. "He would cry out for someone, but when I tried to get him to speak, he would stay silent."

"'My love,'" Zorribis repeated. He contemplated those words for a moment. "His spouse, I would assume. He had one, right?"

Niterra shrugged her shoulders. "None anyone here knew of."

"Maybe you should try answering him."

"Me? As though I were his love?"

"Try it," Zorribis said. "You might prompt him to say something else."

Niterra hesitated, then moved herself closer to Acerus and whispered in his ear, "I am here."

Acerus sucked in a deep breath, and his eyes sparkled with a vigor no one saw from the High Elder in a very long time. "You... are here... with me," he said with a smile. "You are so... beautiful."

Niterra blushed. "You think I am beautiful?"

"Oh, yes," Acerus answered. "Always. And your time on this planet... in these... bodies of water... They are different from... Denab IV."

Niterra looked up at Zorribis, who asked, "Earth?"

Acerus held up his right hand and caressed Niterra's cheek. "Your skin... your scales... so much... softer."

"Scales?" Niterra repeated.

"It is her," Zorribis said. "Connoram's mother. A Krunation."

"What should I say?" Niterra asked, turning to face Zorribis.

"Tell him it is from the water."

Niterra nodded, then smiled at Acerus. "The water, my love. It has softened the scales and..." She struggled to find the right words. "It has rejuvenated me."

Acerus smiled again. "Yes... I wish... I wish I could stay with you. But my world, it needs me. I have done... my part... to watch over the boy. And in time... he will ensure the return... of Excelsior's sword... to you."

Niterra gave Acerus a confused look. "Boy?"

Acerus nodded. "Such a fine lad... that Arthur."

Zorribis repeated the name to himself. "Arthur. I must ask Matthew about him when he returns."

Suddenly, Acerus winced in pain and let out a slight moan. He squeezed his eyes shut for a moment, then opened them again. When he looked up at Niterra, he cocked his head slightly and asked, "Niterra?"

"Acerus? You can see me?"

Acerus nodded. "Yes. Was... Why are..."

"You have been injured, High Elder," Zorribis answered. "Lokris led the other Elders from your quarters so you could rest. We have been watching over you all this time."

"I fear I have been more than injured, my friend Zorribis," Acerus said as his face grew paler. "And I also fear... I fear..." He shut his eyes and let out a soft sigh.

"Acerus?" Niterra asked. "High Elder?"

Acerus's eyes flicked open again. "He is... coming." A single tear rolled down the old Denarian's cheek. "I am... so sorry. I was not worthy." His eyes shut again, and his body relaxed as Acerus drifted off to sleep.

"No," Zorribis said as Niterra reached for his shoulders. "Let him rest."

Niterra looked back at her spouse. "What do you think he meant? 'He is coming?'"

Zorribis shook his head. "I am not sure, but the Krunation who shot him yelled 'Hail Tornatrax' before he died. Could Tornatrax be the one coming?"

"It cannot be. He is destroyed. The legend claimed this."

"The legend claimed many things," Zorribis said. "Connoram must have more answers than we thought."

"Then the three of you will be in good company," came a voice from behind them. Zorribis and Niterra turned around and both held up their hands in a surrender position. Malitus was standing in front of them, his blaster rifle pointed right at Zorribis, and his eyes a fiery red. Branerik stood behind him, giving shallow breaths and trembling as he aimed at Niterra's head.

CHAPTER TWENTY-SIX

"**Y**es."

Hodera trembled as she heard the delighted voice of Tornatrax echoing through her quarters. The booming exclamation was so strong, it shook the Krunation's flaking skin, and she stood and looked into the orb.

"It is a success, my Lord! The High Elder is mortally wounded. He will live long enough to see you return to your rightful place, and then he will be cast into oblivion, but he will leave space for Excelsior when he joins him."

"I am proud of you, my child," Tornatrax said. "You have seen this mission through to its culmination, and now I can feel my powers growing in strength. I can feel the planet drawing me closer."

Hodera's eyes widened. "I can feel you getting closer, my Lord. My connection with you is growing stronger as well."

"Then it is time for your reward, as promised."

"A reward?"

"Yes, child. We have much to celebrate. Your mission was a success. The Denarians are in disarray. And my personal instrument of destruction has been found on the desolate planet Excelsior's current host called home."

"'Destruction,'" Hodera repeated. "Please tell me more, Lord Tornatrax."

"All in due time, child. All in due time. But I will say the current host of Excelsior's lifeforce continues the trend of his predecessors and even the pure form himself. Once again, he is the catalyst of his own demise."

Was what he said true? Between Acerus's incapacitation, Tornatrax getting closer to Denab IV, and now Tornatrax finding the means to defeating Excelsior on Earth, were the Krunations about to reach a total victory over the Denarians? Would Hodera's Lord finally be granted what was rightfully his, and would she be the reason all of this happened?

"But there is still more to do," Tornatrax added, bringing Hodera back down from her emotional high. "What must be accomplished on Earth cannot be done without assistance."

"The Leap of Faith," Hodera said. Was this the opportunity Tornatrax mentioned? Would she get to look Excelsior in the eye and watch his ultimate defeat? "It is currently under surveillance by the Denarians, but I know the chamber and the surrounding area very well. I can send myself to—"

"No, Hodera," Tornatrax said, voice hard. "You will send two of your finest warriors, but you will not send them to Earth. You will send them to me."

Now she couldn't hide the disappointment in her voice. "Why not me, my Lord? Whatever you would have our soldiers do, I can accomplish on my own."

"Because you are far too valuable, child. The task ahead is equally important. Your soldiers will be sent to join with me but only for a limited amount of time. At the proper moment, they will be sent to Earth to do what is meant for them."

"And what is meant for me?" Hodera asked.

"Place your hand on the orb."

Hodera hesitated for a moment, then stepped forward, dropped down to one knee, and placed her right hand on the top of the orb. Complete euphoria swept over her entire body as a jolt of electricity shot from the orb into her hand. She looked down and sucked in a deep breath, keeping her eyes on her flaking, scaly skin. To her great delight, the dead skin was replaced by the gorgeous scales of a newborn Krunation baby. She ran her hand through her hair. It was smooth and thick.

Master," she whispered. "Thank you."

She ogled her hands. Where they were once aging, they were now glowing with invigorated youth. And one hand in particular, her right hand, was actually glowing.

"You are more than just restored, child," Tornatrax assured her. "You have eclipsed the Krunation Empire. You stand on the dividing line between lifeform and god. The evolution of this species is now in your hand. And you know where it belongs."

Hodera's eyes glowed with anticipation. "Krephthera," she said.

"Your army is waiting for you there. My time is near, Hodera. But your time is now!"

The light filling the room faded, and once again, Hodera was alone in her quarters. But she never felt more joined with someone else. Not even when she served the Krunation Empire under Nocterar. "Sivtra!" she yelled.

The diminutive Krunation spy cracked open the door to Hodera's quarters and peeked in. "You summoned me, General?"

"We are going to Krephthera," she said with a slight smile. "You and me."

Sivtra nodded. "I will prepare my transport."

"No," she said. "Prepare one of the barges. We will need the extra space."

Sivtra nodded and turned to leave, but then stopped and cocked his head at Hodera.

"Something else?" the Krunation General asked.

"You," Sivtra responded with a lilt in his voice. "You are... beautiful."

Hodera smiled, walked over to Sivtra, and gently pressed her right hand against his cheek. "Yes, I know," she said softly. "Now prepare for launch."

CHAPTER
TWENTY-SEVEN

"**W**hat is this, Malitus?" Zorribis kept his hands raised, as did Niterra. He spoke in a flat tone of voice, trying his best to not sound too agitated and prompt a flinch from Malitus's trigger finger.

"This?" Malitus asked. "Our atmosphere is changing! Our age is accelerating! Our High Elder is dying! This is what happens when someone not from Denab IV is given the power of Excelsior! And he came here with you! You who brought Krunations to Acerus's home!"

"Connoram had nothing to do with this," Niterra said in the same calm tone as Zorribis, while using her head to motion to Acerus lying beside her.

"You believe him?" Malitus's voice grew louder. "You believe a Krunation over your own kind! You allowed an assassin near the Elders! We could have lost all of them at once!"

"Do you not see what happened?" Zorribis responded. "That was Hodera's soldier."

"An Elder, our High Elder, was attacked by a Krunation, and you still defend them. You have no place here anymore, Zorribis, and we are here to escort you from Edenaria."

Branerik kept his eyes and blaster rifle on Niterra as he reached behind him and opened the door to Acerus's home. Zorribis looked past the two Denarians and saw a small mob of villagers waiting.

"And you have convinced them of this as well?" Zorribis asked.

"There was little convincing needed," Malitus answered. "We were attacked. Our attackers escaped. You aided in their escape. If we were uncivilized, we would have condemned you to death already."

"Considering how armed you are, I find this hard to believe," Niterra said.

"Enough!" Malitus yelled. "Both of you will come with us now. Leave Acerus alone."

Zorribis and Niterra looked at each other. "If this is what they want," Niterra concluded.

"Then we should abide by their wishes," Zorribis agreed.

Malitus and Branerik stepped away from the doorway, leaving it open for Zorribis and Niterra to slowly step away from Acerus and exit his home. They kept their arms up as they made their way through the small grouping of Denarians ready to tear them apart.

And standing in the back of the group, stone-faced, were Quinterus and Tricerus.

"Is this what you did while we were caring for Acerus?" Zorribis asked them. "Spread lies about the two of us? About Connoram?"

"Do not speak to the other Elders," Malitus said while walking behind Zorribis and Niterra, still aiming his blaster rifle at them.

Tricerus held up his hand. "It is alright, Malitus," he said. "Zorribis is unsure where his loyalties lie."

"My loyalties lie with all of Denab IV, Elder!" Zorribis said. "And with anyone who wishes we live out the rest of our days in peace."

"And we believe Connoram is innocent in this attack," Niterra added. "Please let us prove this to you by bringing him back here."

"And why, may I ask?" Tricerus spoke, his voice dripping with sarcasm. "Do you believe he did not accomplish his task? Would you have preferred he destroy us all?"

"That was not his task and you know it," Niterra yelled at the Elder.

"Be mindful of how you speak, child!" Tricerus roared at the younger Denarian. "You may be of the same race as we, but you are not immune to our demands of respect."

"Your demands?" Zorribis asked. "Elder, please look around you! We are being banished from our village. Denarians are turning against one another. This is precisely what General Hodera would want. Connoram is seeking to unite us all in uncertain times."

"He is seeking to infiltrate and destroy our kind from the inside," Quinterus corrected the Denarian. "I would ask if you saw this yourself, but since I know you have, I must only assume you do not care what happens to us as long as your dear Krunation friend—"

"Quinterus! Tricerus! Stop all of this!"

Everyone turned to see Lokris and Nosgood pushing their way through the mob of Denarians. "What is going on here?"

"These two have revealed themselves to be traitors to the Denarian race!" Malitus yelled while poking the barrel of his blaster rifle into Zorribis's back.

"They are nothing of the kind," Lokris yelled back. "If they were, I would not have allowed them to care for Acerus by themselves." She turned to the crowd and yelled out, "Zorribis and Niterra are not your enemies! Neither is Excelsior! And neither is Connoram!"

"We can bring him back here," Zorribis said. "We know where he is. He and Charak returned to Nocteris."

Quinterus sneered as he said, "Then go to Nocteris and bring him here. And only him. If he is innocent as you say, he will behave as such. If not, he will not leave Edenaria alive."

"One condition," Niterra said, holding up one finger. She exchanged glances with Zorribis. "He must be able to bring Charak with him."

"No," Tricerus said. "No soldiers. No escorts. No one to do his bidding."

"Charak is Connoram's descendant," Zorribis said. "He will wish to keep him close. Bringing him will only increase our chances for peace."

Tricerus and Quinterus exchanged looks of disgust.

"Elders. Nosgood. Anyone who can hear me, please respond! This is Kaprus. We are under attack!"

The panicked cry of the Denarian soldier filled Zorribis's head, and he could see this distress signal was being sent to as many of them as possible.

Nosgood spoke aloud. "Kaprus is guarding the Leap of Faith." He then closed his eyes and reached out telepathically. "Kaprus, this is Nosgood. Can you hear me? Are you and your men all right?"

"Nosgood, there are only five of us on guard here. A squadron was led to the other side of the continent. Hodera is... By the blood of Valertus."

"Kaprus, what is it?" Lokris reached out as well. "What is Hodera doing?"

"Hodera is leading scores of a new breed of Krunation! I have never seen this many since—"

Everyone in the village covered their ears as they heard a cry of pain echo through their heads. Lokris dropped to one knee. "Kaprus! Kaprus, can you hear me? Please answer me!"

There was no response.

"Scores of Krunations?" Quinterus asked. "How? Their squadrons have been limited ever since Nocterar fell. And the ones left in the water to evolve were nowhere near maturity."

Lokris replied, "If our planet was as it should be, they would have remained un-evolved. Unfortunately, this is no longer the case." She shut her eyes again and pushed her mind's reach toward the Leap of Faith. After a long moment, she shook her head. "I cannot sense them."

"Hodera," Zorribis said. "She is the real enemy! We need Connoram on our side more than ever now."

"Then it shall be done," Lokris said. "Zorribis and Niterra, you will go to Nocteris and find both Connoram and Charak. If they can defend us against Hodera and her army, then so be it. We deserve to have peace in these ending days."

"Your will be done, Elder Lokris," Zorribis said before bowing to Lokris, then to the other Elders around them. He and Niterra ran to their aircraft, and Zorribis felt a combination of relief for escaping from Tricerus and Quinterus's angry mob and dread for what was happening at the Leap of Faith.

"If the Leap of Faith is in Krunation hands, how will Excelsior and Arinna get back?" Niterra asked.

Zorribis shook his head. It was his only answer.

CHAPTER TWENTY-EIGHT

The darkness. The calm. The quiet. For the dead, it is a relief. Internal and external struggles coming at every turn for living creatures everywhere are no more. Hopes, doubts, fears, pain, love, hate, all gone. Nothing matters anymore. And so the darkness is the cocoon in which the dead wrap themselves, and nothing but comfort awaits.

Throughout the universe, very few lifeforms found a way to conquer death itself and return to walk among their peers. On Earth, the first man who died and rose again became the central figure of a worldwide religion. The second also became famous, but more so because he was the first sign of intelligent life from another planet. To humans, he was known as Ritgen-Man, but to the planet Denab IV, he was Danaak.

For several thousand years, Danaak stayed in a fossilized slumber after chasing Excelsior from Denab IV to Earth and being confronted by a ravenous four-legged animal. The power in the jewel he stole from the incapacitated Emperor Nocterar, however, kept Danaak's lifeforce trapped within his body. Once he was freed three Earth years ago from an expedition led by Dr. Franklin Ritgen, the energy awakened the Krunation, and he was able to continue his personal mission to eradicate Denarians and their god Excelsior from the universe.

Unfortunately for Danaak, the mission was a failure. He may have taken four Denarians—including Elder Klierra—with him, but he couldn't stop Excelsior from awakening inside Matthew Peters and thrusting his sword into the Krunation's chest. The pain of the blade penetrating his scaly body was excruciating, but once Danaak felt the savior of Denab IV pull the weapon out of him, he felt something unexpected.

He felt peace. He felt calm. He felt all of his troubles drift away, and death greeted him like an open blanket on a winter's morning. Danaak never felt more content, and nothing made him happier than knowing this was where he would spend eternity.

"Danaak."

He knew that voice. He recognized the familiar hiss. But it couldn't be. Danaak was dead. Nothing from the land of the living could reach him. Not even Tornatrax.

"Danaak."

The voice was getting louder, and Danaak felt the blinding glare of life accompanying it.

Go away, he wanted to say. Leave me alone. But he felt the force pulling him from the tranquility of death, and he saw the hand of his god reaching out to him.

"Hello, my friend."

Danaak's eyes shot open, and for the first time in three Earth years, he looked around. He did not see the glass case to which he was confined all this time, but the pinpoints making up the unending number of stars and planets in the universe. He floated in the emptiness of space, recognizing where he was. His mind was connecting with another, as when Nocterar arose and sought the jewel Danaak stole from him. But while Danaak remembered the icy cold grip of Nocterar around his neck, the touch of Tornatrax was gentle yet firm, like a mother prompting their child to wake up for school.

Danaak felt his mouth open, and he wheezed out the first words his mind would generate. "Wh... Why?"

"Why have I awoken you?" the disembodied voice of Tornatrax asked. "My friend, we have much work to do, and I can think of no better lifeform in this universe to carry out the mission I have for you."

"N... No," Danaak struggled to say. "I... was... finished."

"Danaak, you can never be finished. Even in death, you remain the most intimidating and dominant force in all of the mighty Krunation Empire. You, who were not granted dominion over your race, sought that responsibility, and your actions created an impact which remains to this day. You have survived death once. Now you must do it again."

"Please," Danaak said. "Leave... Leave me alone..." He yearned to be released once again, to retreat back into the eternal blanket of darkness and peace, but he also remembered Tornatrax was not someone to disobey. If this absolute force of power could make a connection like this, then what else could he do?

"Wh... what do.... you want?" Danaak asked with resignation in his voice.

"There is something here on this planet," Tornatrax instructed. "Something indigenous to Denab IV but is here instead. A sword. I can feel its presence near the area where your body still lies, and I know it is still in the possession of Excelsior."

"Excelsior?" Danaak asked, and then his mind was flooded with memories. Of striking down the child Matthew Peters in Tollund Laboratories and mocking him for daring to stand up to him. Of watching with horror as Excelsior was reborn through Matthew. Of the desperation he felt as Excelsior walked closer and closer to him as Danaak fired one energy blast after another from his jewel. And finally, the sword being thrust into his chest, killing him once and for all.

Or so he thought.

"You remember what was done to you before, yes? You remember what was taken from you? Both here... and on Denab IV?"

Danaak squeezed his eyes shut for a moment. He yearned to scream, "I remember what was given to me by surrendering my life, and now you are asking me to give my peace of mind back and return. It cannot be done!"

"You believe it cannot be done. You doubt me."

For the first time since seeing Excelsior absorb the energy of the stolen jewel with his sword, Danaak felt a tingling of fear crawl up his spine. Did he hear my thoughts?

"You carry my mark on your body, my friend. All I needed was to get close enough to establish my connection with you."

Carry his mark? Danaak looked down and saw the deep gash in his chest left by Excelsior's sword, but he cocked his head in confusion when he saw a thin resin wrapped around the gash. It glowed yellow and felt warming to the Krunation, and his eyes glazed over in ecstasy as the resin leaked into the wound and began to fill the hole.

"Do you feel my touch, Danaak? Do you feel the sensation you have not felt since your defeat? And now, the time has come for you to rise once again."

The stars and planets surrounding Danaak slowly dissolved, and suddenly he was in the dark hallway of Tollund Laboratories. He smelled the ashy remains of Karini, Grannik, and Radifen. He heard the last breaths of Elder Klierra. He felt the warmth of the glow enveloping the young Earth boy, Excelsior reawakening within him.

From there, it was only fear and pain. Fear of Excelsior walking to him, his sword absorbing the energy Danaak fired. Pain from Excelsior plunging the glowing sword into his chest, then pulling it out.

Danaak dropped to the floor. His eyes closed.

And then his eyes snapped open again. He shifted his hands and pressed them against the thick and airtight Plexiglas case, arms pinned down by his waist. He looked around the dark hallway and saw the red carpet leading to him, the velvet ropes, the framed posters featuring him lying dead for all to see.

After everything, was this Danaak's ultimate legacy? To be known as... what was it, Ritgen-Man?

Oh, yes. It suddenly made sense to him. Another flash of an old memory appeared before his eyes, of the short, arrogant man who took credit for Danaak's reawakening on Earth. "I am not afraid of you. I uncovered you! You, you belong to me!"

Danaak felt a rush of adrenaline as he remembered silencing Dr. Franklin Ritgen forever.

"You remember that feeling, Danaak? Ultimate power, righteous domination over all lesser beings."

"I do remember," Danaak whispered, his vocal chords regenerated. If he concentrated hard enough, he could sense the jewel's power, and he wondered if he would ever feel it again.

"I can bring it back to you, my friend. You can feel my power coursing through every molecule of your body. With my assistance, you can fulfill your destiny of a Krunation reign throughout the universe."

The rush gave way to frustration as Danaak found himself once again in the thick Plexiglas cell, and he could suddenly no longer hear the tempting voice of Tornatrax within his head. It sounded more distant. Where could it be?

"Do what you were born to do, Danaak."

There it was. The voice. But now it was coming from outside the case, echoing through the hallways he stalked only three Earth years ago. The rush of reliving his conquests gave way to frustration, and Danaak could hear the cracking of his knees as he pressed them against the front of the case, pushing with his hands at the same time. If I am to be here, he said to himself, I will not be confined to this tomb.

"Yes, Danaak. Come back to me. Come back to the world that is ready for your rule."

The encouragement of his god's voice inspired the Krunation to push harder, and he gasped with delight when he felt the Plexiglas case begin to crack and give way. He gritted his teeth and pushed with all his might one more time, and the front of the case cracked open. Danaak fell from the case and crashed to the floor. As he laid on the cold tile, he took in a deep breath of fresh air and contemplated his situation.

He was dead. And now he was brought back to life. Again.

A mix of emotions ran through his head. But how? And why? And why was he so calm about this?

Like all Krunations before him, Danaak's birth and initial rebirth were accompanied by a violent lashing out at anything and anyone around him. He remembered how particularly ferocious he was to the young men and women working with his body in this facility. But now... there was no rage in his mind. There was only—

"Hello?"

An old male voice interrupted Danaak's pondering. He looked up and saw some kind of authority figure with a short-sleeved, dark blue button-down shirt, a gold badge on the left side of his chest, matching blue pants, and a flat cap on his head. Through the sunlight peeking through outside the building, Danaak could see the wrinkles on his face, reminding him of the Elders on

Denab IV. He expected to feel hostility as he did in the past, but now there was no animosity whatsoever.

The guard stopped and let out a gasp. "Whoa! Who broke into this?" He looked around in a panic, breathing heavily as he approached Danaak now lying still on the floor.

The room fell silent once again, the guard standing still to listen for the footsteps of the possible vandals. When no answer came, he said out loud, "Maybe I should put it back."

Danaak could hear the words of the security guard and, with a sudden burst of strength, he leapt to his feet, grabbed the guard by his shirt, and pushed him up against the wall.

The guard let out a scream of shock and fear, and Danaak could somehow hear the words of his god cutting through the noise.

"Silence him!"

With one hand still pinning him against the wall, Danaak used his other hand to cover the guard's mouth. The guard was still screaming, but now it was muffled.

"No! Silence him the way you know you can."

Danaak stared at the terrified old innocent man. That's what he wants, he thought. That's what I would have wanted. To kill him without a second thought. To send him to the peaceful darkness from which I was pulled only moments ago. Would he be doing him a favor by extinguishing his life?

The screaming from the guard stopped as Danaak pulled his hand away from his mouth and balled it into a fist. The guard's eyes grew wide, and the Krunation could see him moving his lips, but no words escaped.

"Do it. Now, Danaak!"

Danaak brought his fist forward, but instead of slamming into the guard's head, it made a hole in the cement wall to the left of him. The guard's mouth stopped moving, and his whole body trembled in terror.

"Go," Danaak commanded, and he let go of the guard, who slowly stepped away from the Krunation, then broke into a full sprint and disappeared down the hall.

"What are you doing?"

"He is an innocent lifeform," Danaak answered the voice inside his head. "He did not deserve to perish."

"I tell you who is deserving of death and who is not. You are here. You are alive once again because your god demands it."

"Then my god will tell me why you demand it," Danaak replied. "Whatever plans you have for me, whatever mission you have felt worthy of my awakening, tell me now."

"You are not the only one who has been awakened, Danaak. I have been slumbering in a prison fashioned by your sworn enemy for eons. I was dormant, helpless to inspire my beloved Krunations to victory over their oppressors. But because of Nocterar's defeat and Excelsior's way of casting out his enemies, I am no longer dormant. My lifeforce is approaching Denab IV with each passing moment, and my consciousness has found my most loyal subjects: you and the female Hodera."

"Hodera," Danaak whispered. "She is still alive?"

"Oh yes, and as you slept, she has continued the fight in my name. Because of her, the Krunation Empire is not yet extinct."

Danaak gritted his teeth in anger, not at anyone around him, but at the taunting voice within him. "I was put to rest because of Excelsior, as you were."

"Yes, Danaak. And now we are both awake. We have been denied what is rightfully ours for too long. With you, my instrument of destruction, we can accomplish what we set out to do."

Danaak relaxed his fists, allowing his hands to fall open. "No."

"No?"

"In another time, I would have yearned for this opportunity. But my time has passed, Tornatrax. I only wish for you to release me to my prize of death."

"You dare give me orders? You are nothing but an insect, Danaak."

"Then let this insect die as so many others have in this universe!" Danaak shouted, his voice echoing through the still halls. "I am of no use to you, so let me—"

The Krunation's demands were stifled by an excruciating sensation similar to two large hands slapped on Danaak's head and squeezing. He let out a cry of pain and dropped to one knee. "Yes," he whimpered. "Please kill me."

"No, Danaak."

The sensation lessened and then increased again.

"You will stay alive for as long as I wish it. Even if you are the only lifeform remaining on this primitive world. Death will be out of your grasp for all eternity. You will never feel the comfort of life's release again, unless you do my bidding."

The pain lessened once again and Danaak whispered, "The pain..."

"I can make it go away, Danaak. I can make it all go away. All I require is for you to follow my instructions."

With his jaw locked, he shook his head. All he craved in his mind was release. Release from it all. Release from Tornatrax's grip on his mind. Release from the pain. Release from this short new life.

"If you will not do it for yourself, do it for your son."

Those five words cut through the torment like a burst of ice water through a wildfire. "Do it for your son," he said. With those words came the baggage of images locked from his mind.

His son. Charak.

He had a son.

"Charak," Danaak said. "He is still alive?"

"He is, Danaak. I know your affection for him. I know it goes beyond the typical affection Krunations feel for their bloodline, and I know of the vow you made to him so long ago. The vow you would make Denab IV a better place for him. If you help me, you will accomplish the mission you left unfinished."

Danaak rose to his feet, a tear dripping down his scaly cheek. "All if I do your bidding," he confirmed.

"You have my word, my friend."

The Krunation took a deep breath to consider his god's offer. "If I do as you ask, there will be no taking of innocent life. They will meet their end in their own time, and I will meet mine once again."

A long pause, then Tornatrax spoke once again. "Very well. You will be under no obligation to take any lives."

"Then I accept. How do we start?"

"It has already begun. I can sense our ultimate prize a short distance from here. You must leave now if there is any hope of us reaching it in time."

"Then I will go underground. The humans were not welcoming when they last saw me. I must stay out of sight until the proper moment."

"Very well."

"But before I do..." Danaak examined the guard still lying unconscious on the floor. "Those should be a correct size." He reached down, grabbed the guard's pants and shoes, then put them on, leaving behind the shirt.

Suddenly, Danaak felt a sudden sensation in his right arm, as though he were a living puppet and Tornatrax was pulling his strings. His hand began to glow and point down at the floor beneath him. "What are you doing?" he asked.

"We are going underground. Just as you wish."

A blast of energy shot from Danaak's hand to the floor at his feet. He felt his body dropping as the energy continued on through each level of concrete, past the street level, past the basement, until finally he came to a stop in a large subway tunnel. His feet crashed into the collected rain water alongside the underground train tracks, and Danaak let out a sigh of satisfaction as the reptilian creature felt the coolness of the water.

"Where do we go?" Danaak asked.

"I will guide you."

CHAPTER TWENTY-NINE

"**W**e have arrived, General."

Hodera's eyes opened. Once the transport took off from Nocteris, the General moved to the back, sat down, and glided her hand back and forth in front of her eyes, and she bit her lower lip in anticipation of what was to come. Ever since she first heard the legend of Tornatrax, how the possessed Candassus grabbed Abrattus by the throat and obliterated the Denarian, she yearned to unleash destruction on the entire species. And now, finally, she could do it.

Only in a much different way than originally intended.

The transport scraped the ground of Krephthera, and Sivtra activated the landing gear, setting the controls to stop and opening the hatch. Hodera stood, smelling the contempt in the air, and walked from the back of the transport to the entrance ramp.

"To the Matera, Sivtra," Hodera said.

"It will be my pleasure to lead you, General," Sivtra said with a smile on his face and, seemingly, an extra spring in his step. He armed himself with a blaster rifle, and the two stepped into the muck, the squishing sounds echoing through the still air.

The farther they walked, the more she saw the prying eyes of the various custodians watching over the hatchlings. No matter how many times she'd visited there, she always felt the same questions hanging in the air. Why was she there? What could she want? Was she not supposed to be dead by now? Why was this abomination even allowed to live?

The patch of dry land in the center of the swamp came into view, as did the uneven beams holding up the orange window, which now had a layer of algae so thick it was blocking out almost all of the sunlight. Hodera turned toward the deep waters and the growling and hissing of the amphibious creatures making their way to the surface. The noises from the water were so loud the custodians watching over the hatchlings backed away. Hodera could see rows upon rows of teeth from hundreds of the predators gazing back at her, as though they were fully aware of the gift Tornatrax had bequeathed the Krunation General, and they were anxious to see what would happen with it.

The hissing attracted the attention of the oldest Kitera, who alternated between looking wide-eyed at the water and turning back toward the younger Mynera. Hodera turned her head toward the female students still training to be the next ladies-in-waiting, while the current Kitera prepared to eventually take the place of the Matera. When the time came, of course.

Hodera never thought this time would come anytime soon, considering how strong of a grip the Matera had on their position. But looking at the Kitera's face, which was shedding so much it seemed to be peeling off, Hodera could have sworn this one would die before she had the chance to take a Matera's position.

"And so you return," the Kitera called out to the Krunation general. "You have such contempt for us, and yet your visits are becoming more frequent."

"Trust me, Kitera," Hodera hissed at her. "This visit will not be very long. And if I were you, I would..." She shook her head, baring her teeth in a grin. "I would never be you, but I would suggest you stay out of our way."

"Our way?'" the Kitera yelled as Hodera and Sivtra walked past her. "Sivtra, we have given you so much responsibility, so much protection, so much favor from the Matera, and this is how you repay us? Why have you chosen to align yourself with such a beast?"

Sivtra glanced over his shoulder. "Because she has chosen to align herself with me."

Hodera gave a warm smile. There was no better way to her heart than unquestioning loyalty.

They continued on until they reached the very center of the land mass and the four-woman audience Hodera craved. She pushed her shoulders back, took a moment to bathe in the remnants of the faded orange light, and spoke. "General Hodera has news for the Matera."

"The Matera are not interested in what you have to tell us," the four Krunation females answered as one. From where Hodera was standing, their gold gowns looked more faded than before, and more of the dull scaly skin on their faces was flaking off. Their voices no longer had the dream-like enrapturing lilt. Instead, they sounded rough, almost hoarse. "We have said before, your requested army cannot be rushed, and you will be notified when they are ready for you. Not before. You have no reason to be here."

"On the contrary," Hodera answered. "I have a multitude of reasons to be here. And they are all here… at your feet." She outstretched her arms, but instead of aiming them at the hatchlings and slate-colored eggs, she pointed down toward the creatures floating along the surface of the water.

"You are aware our god made his selections for a reason," the Matera said. "We are the fittest. We are the ones chosen to carry on our beloved Tornatrax's legacy."

"So you believe," Hodera said as she stepped to the edge and placed one foot in the water. Her nerves tingled from the icy liquid.

"What are you doing?" the Matera asked.

Hodera stepped farther into the water, keeping her eyes on the four Krunation females standing still. The creatures surrounded her, but none made a move to attack. They floated, waiting, as though they already knew and respected Hodera's rank.

"You know little of our god," Hodera said. Her right hand emitted an ethereal yellow glow, and she held it up for the Matera to see. "He is demanding. He is impatient. And so am I." She slammed her hand into the water, and a wave of orange light burst from her palm in a circular shockwave similar to the blast she saw Excelsior unleash on Klierra Peak after Nocterar's defeat.

Hodera clenched her jaw, her eyes not leaving the four women. After a long moment, the temperature of the water began to rise until the lake bubbled, but Hodera felt no scalding. Her immediate surroundings were as cool and comfortable as ever.

"What are you doing?" the Matera asked, their voices shrill. The one in front even dared to lean forward toward the water.

"Fulfilling our god's true wishes."

The creatures writhed and hissed, and Hodera looked down, gasping with delight. Appendages quickly grew on their bodies, swallowing up their fins. Necks emerged from under their heads, and their bottom halves split and grew into legs.

"Rise, my friends!" Hodera called out to the creatures. Their newly grown arms began flapping around, their fingers flexing.

The Matera stood still, each with the same worried expression on their faces. Sivtra let out a chuckle as he yelled over the sounds from the water, "This must be what it looks like to know you are obsolete!"

A series of splashes was followed by the shrieking of the creatures no longer confined to the water. They bared teeth twice as large as Hodera's and Sivtra's, and they were so pointed, Hodera almost pitied the poor souls who would get their limbs too close to them.

Almost.

The creatures had broad, strong chests with arms bulging with equally impressive muscles, and with the exception of the varied scale patterns along their skins, they looked indistinguishable from each other. It didn't matter to Hodera if she couldn't tell each one apart. What mattered was how her forces compared to the typical Krunation warrior.

To Hodera, they were terrifying and perfect.

Cutting through the noises made by the creatures, the Matera shouted, "What have you done? You have defiled our god with your actions!"

Hodera pulled her hand from the water, which was still glowing with energy, and her face tightened with rage as she pointed to the empty spot in the Matera's pentagonal arrangement. "Is that what you told my mother?"

With her hand now glowing brighter, Hodera pointed her index finger toward the Matera in the front. All of the creatures stopped wading in the water and turned their attention to the platform of land in the center of the swamplands. They hissed in unison as ten of them approached the land mass. Then another ten followed and started to climb over the first ten. Then twenty more emerged, and they climbed on top of them and reached the ground where the Matera still stood.

Hodera folded her arms across her chest and watched with a satisfied grin as her new army continued climbing over each other to finally reach the Matera. "Tear them apart, my children. Their time has ended!"

Without warning, the gleeful voice of Tornatrax filled Hodera's ears. "Well done, my child. Because of you, Krunation evolution has reached a brand new stage."

"And what shall be next for us, my Lord?" she whispered.

"The Leap of Faith. Your next instructions will come in time. For now, you must ensure the doorway is in Krunation hands."

"Understood, my Lord." Hodera paused to soak in this very special moment. The Krunations who were earlier staring at her in contempt were now running for their lives from her new army. Oh, the plans she had for them.

"What shall we do now?" Sivtra asked.

"You said you have aligned yourself with me," Hodera said. "This has not changed?"

"Of course not."

"Good," Hodera said. She glanced at where the Matera were once standing and raised her voice to compensate for the screams. "Once they are finished with their meal, we have more business to attend to, and it starts at the Leap of Faith."

"I look forward to being a part of this glorious new era," Sivtra said.

Hodera gave him a sly smile. "Trust me, you will see the moment when it all begins."

The screams from the Matera faded away, and Hodera quickly climbed up the land mass which once commanded such reverence, shooing away her new soldiers. They stepped aside, some dropping back into the water, and Hodera reached down, snatched the golden crown she'd coveted so much from the now-motionless Matera, and plucked out the red jewel. With her fingers now stained with blood, she looked down at her diminutive servant and tossed what remained of the crown to him.

Hodera let out a shudder as she pressed the jewel against her chest, and it let out a soft sizzle in response.

After a moment, she pulled her hand away and the jewel fused into place in her flesh. "Ahhh, yes," she exhaled. With her outstretched hands stained in the Matera's blood, Hodera called out to Sivtra, "Yes, young one! And now, I have one more message to deliver, a special message for the Kitera and Mynera."

"The Mynera?" Sivtra asked as he almost dropped the crown, the shock in his voice betraying the bluster he showed a moment ago. "But they are just children."

"Children who will grow into Kitera," Hodera said. "They are no longer any concern of yours." She pointed toward the crown in his hand. "The Matera wore that, and now you will."

Sivtra held up the crown. Hodera nodded, and he placed what was left of this Krunation status symbol on his head. A trace of thick, cold blood dripped on his forehead.

One more order came from the Krunation standing atop the land mass. "Prepare us for launch. This will not take long."

And then, as Sivtra stood still and watched, Hodera pointed her right index finger in the appropriate direction.

CHAPTER THIRTY

"**Y**ou made it!"

Matthew saw Jason clap his hands while approaching him and Arinna in the lobby of Rockefeller Center. He embraced his uncle, and Matthew noticed Jason was keeping his right hand from getting anywhere near his.

"Did you see him?" Jason whispered.

Matthew nodded his head. "He's dead. Danaak's not a problem anymore."

Jason let out a sigh of relief. "Phew. That's the last thing I'd need."

"Last thing anyone needs, let alone us," Matthew replied. "So you know the deal we have, right?"

"Yes, yes, I know. And I'm not reneging on the deal, so don't worry."

"It's not about the deal. It's about the gift. It's not exactly what you thought it is."

Jason held up his hands and did his best to keep his voice down. "Matty, we have an agreement. We get through tonight, and I'll give it back to you, no questions asked. But I need to make sure everything goes smoothly."

"But—"

"Matthew!" The authority in his uncle's voice hadn't been heard since after his parents died. Matthew stopped talking and let Jason speak. "I'm sticking to the agreement we made before. You just stick to yours. Now, do you have the files you said you'd make?"

Matthew nodded without saying another word, reaching into his pocket and pulling out a small, black USB thumb drive. He held it up, then handed it to Jason.

"Awesome! And you have the uniform?"

Matthew nodded again. "The sword and the helmet are in my backpack. I have the uniform on under my clothes."

"Got a print-out of the map?"

"Sure," Matthew said. He reached into his pocket again and unfolded a piece of white paper. Jason let out a low whistle as he held it in his hands, his gaze going from one continent to another.

"You called these the Lost Islands?" Matthew's uncle asked, pointing to the small patches of land far apart from their neighboring lands.

"I didn't name them. My people did."

"Can I change the name? ABC's gonna be upset."

Matthew shrugged his shoulders. "Do what you want. It's your show."

Jason patted Matthew on the shoulder. "Thank you." He then put his arm around his nephew and said softly to him, "I know what you're thinking. You think I'm gonna let you down again like I did before. You think I don't care about you or your friend or Denab IV since you don't live here anymore."

"That's not true," Matthew said.

"You're right," Jason said. "It's not true. I care about all you guys very much. Especially you. But we're dealing with a power which never should have been here. And I don't want to risk anything happening to either of us right now. They're setting up the launch party upstairs, and the last thing anyone wants to see is me stumbling around with my brain fried because of something going wrong. You know what I mean?"

Matthew looked back at Arinna, then at Jason, and nodded again. "Okay, I trust you. I never questioned you. It's..." He thought for a moment. Was this a good time to tell Jason about the Denarian DNA inside him?

"What?"

Matthew shook his head. "It's nothing. I'm worried about my people back on Denab IV. And..." He gazed at Arinna who stood a few feet away. "I want to make sure Arinna sees the stars during the daylight again."

"Wish I could see them too," Jason said with a smile. "But while you're here, you might as well take her up to the 70th floor. Who knows? Maybe some sparks will fly."

Matthew looked back toward Jason and asked, "No, I don't think so. I mean, yeah I'll take her up there, but, uh, no sparks."

"How do you know?"

Matthew shrugged his shoulders. "Just a hunch."

"Same hunch you used as an excuse to not ask out any of your classmates? Who was the girl you told me about? Rachel?"

"What about her?"

"You never asked her out. For all you knew, she was waiting for you to make a move and you didn't--"

"I had to leave the planet," Matthew exclaimed. "Not the same thing. She came here to take me back with her once we finish everything here."

"Okay. So at least talk with her and see what happens. I know you know how to talk."

Matthew smiled. "Kinda."

"Okay. So here's what's gonna happen. You come upstairs for the party, meet my girlfriend Becky, make your appearance with the whole Excelsior uniform and helmet and sword, everything. You let me show you off for the executives and party guests, and then you put your clothes back on over your uniform and take her upstairs. You chat, you watch the sunset, you'll have a beautiful woman with you, and who knows what'll happen? No point in playing any stupid hard-to-get games, just talk to her. Understand?"

"And then afterward—"

"Yes, and then afterward, I'll give you back the gift and let you both go off on your merry way. Maybe when you go back, you'll have a clearer idea about everything."

Matthew had to admit Jason was right. And he felt a sudden peace of mind as well as a renewed enthusiasm for the festivities ahead. "Can you still believe all this is happening? Me where I am, you where you are?"

"I keep waking up in the morning thinking this is all a dream," Jason said with a touch of pain and longing in his voice. He reached toward the medallion around his neck and rubbed it between his thumb and index finger. "Like there's really a completely normal life going on. Like I sobered up before going to rehab, and your mom and dad are still alive."

Matthew nodded. He knew what Jason was talking about, and he remembered what he said to the High Elder Acerus about the moment he touched the sword as a child in the Metropolitan Museum of Art. "I've been thinking about the same thing recently. What if I stayed home instead of going to the museum? Or what if I listened to Mom and stopped drawing 'those stupid characters?' Did you know she wanted me to go to law school? Can you even picture me being a lawyer?" He shook his head and looked down at the floor.

"Matthew?"

Matthew turned back in her direction and was shocked to see her standing next to him.

"Are you okay?" she asked.

"Yeah. Yeah, I'm fine," Matthew answered, and he turned back to Jason. "Just thinking about..."

"We were talking about family," Jason said, stepping in. "His father always told him everyone lives their life as either an inspiration or a cautionary tale, and it's up to you to decide how you want to live."

Matthew shot Jason a confused look. How did he know what his father would say?

"And how his parents would be proud of everything he's done, and everything he's doing."

Arinna smiled at Matthew, and once she looked away, Matthew whispered to Jason, "How did you know Dad said that?"

Jason whispered back, "Our dad would say the same thing to us all the time."

CHAPTER
THIRTY-ONE

"Charak!"

The mix of pain and panic in Connoram's voice prompted Charak to rush into his armfather's quarters with his blaster at the ready. He was expecting to see someone—Denarian or Krunation—with a weapon drawn to use against the older commander and let out a slight sigh of relief when he saw Connoram sitting alone at his desk. But then he saw Connoram had both hands pressed against his own head and a look of intense agony on his face.

"Armfather!" Charak yelled. "What is wrong?"

"The... The planet..." Connoram forced out from his gritted teeth. "It is in pain..."

Charak watched Connoram push himself up and stumble to the Sancterrum tree. He ran up to him and heard him whisper, "Please tell me. Please tell me what is happening." After several seconds of silence, he sucked in a deep breath. "How is this possible?"

"What is it, Armfather?" Charak asked, concerned.

"Hodera. Somehow she has created—no, this cannot be right."

Charak squeezed the barrel of his blaster. "What did she do?" The young Krunation's face twisted into a furious sneer.

Connoram pressed his hand against the trunk of the Sancterrum tree. "She has created monsters from the creatures in the deep waters of Krephthera." His eyes closed, and he shook his head. Charak could tell he was forcing back tears. "The Matera. The Kitera." Tears leaked from his eyes and rolled down his cheeks as he choked out the next words. "The Mynera. All gone. They have already conquered the Leap of Faith."

Charak's eyes filled up with tears, and he wiped them on his sleeve. He shook his head in disbelief. "How could she have done this?"

"Tornatrax," Connoram replied. "It was a gift from Tornatrax. He is getting closer—"

He stopped, both he and Charak turning their heads toward Connoram's door. "Do you hear that?"

Charak nodded. "Whatever those creatures are, they are coming. We have to leave."

"You have to leave," Connoram ordered.

"What about you?"

"Our soldiers will be here to defend me, and I can take care of myself. But you must get back to Zorribis. I will send you in the right direction."

"How?"

Connoram pulled his hand away from the tree trunk. "You know how. But we must do it now. Time is running short."

CHAPTER
THIRTY-TWO

"**L**adies and gentlemen, my name is Amanda, and I would like to welcome you to Rockefeller Center here in New York City." The operations manager connected to the Top of the Rock Observation Deck spoke with Jason, Becky, Matthew, and Arinna on the mezzanine level of Rockefeller Center. If they were one of the thousands of regular guests going to the observation deck, they would be on the line to their right at the main elevator. Instead, as part of the gala upstairs, these five people stood in a separate area in front of an elevator labeled "A Bank."

Jason was dressed in a black tuxedo with a black bowtie, and on the lapel was a small round pin with the logo of Excelsior on it: the tip of the sword in front of a purple background with the three lines coming from the blade. Each line signified the three elements of Excelsior: strength, leadership, and innovation. Becky wore a silky purple blouse with black pants and black high heels. Matthew and Arinna wore the same clothes as before, but underneath Matthew's clothes was the uniform of Excelsior. The helmet and sword stayed in his bag out of Amanda's sight, and Matthew felt relieved he wouldn't have to go through the typical security protocols at Top of the Rock. He chuckled to himself while imagining his explanation to the security team why a grown man was walking around with a helmet and sword.

Amanda continued her address as they waited for the elevator. "Once this elevator arrives, it will take approximately forty-three seconds for you to reach the sixty-seventh floor. As a representative of Top of the Rock, we believe you'll find everything to your liking. The entire back area is closed to the general public, and we have tables, chairs, and the displays from NBC set up as they requested. During the gala, if you would like to visit the sixty-ninth and seventieth floors, you are more than welcome to do so. Please keep in mind, those floors are open to the general public as well. And since we expect to have a beautiful sunset tonight, I hope you won't mind it'll be more than a little crowded."

"Trust me. We can handle a big crowd," Jason said, smiling at Becky. She smiled back.

The A elevator arrived. The doors opened, Amanda stepped aside, and Matthew held out his arm to Arinna. She smiled and took it, and as they walked into the elevator, Matthew saw Jason give him a look he could only interpret as "Told ya so."

Amanda held the door open. "Okay, folks. We hope you have a wonderful time, and don't forget to look up."

"Why should we look up?" Arinna asked after the elevator door closed, and three seconds later, her question was answered when the four of them were greeted with a special forty-three-second-long video projected onto the elevator ceiling. Matthew smiled with pride at the video, recognizing all the various moments in history as televised on NBC from the 1950s to the present. He glanced over at Arinna, who was staring with wide-eyed wonder. The video came to an end just as the elevator decelerated, reaching its destination. Arinna turned to Matthew and said, "Your world may not be as advanced as others I have seen, but you are definitely not as primitive as you think."

"You might think differently once you see some of the shows we have on cable," Jason interjected. "We're not getting visits for a reason."

The elevator door slid open, and the four were greeted with a wide smile by another Top of the Rock representative. She wore a gray jacket with matching pants, and a gold name badge on her lapel with "Dana" engraved in it.

"Good evening, everyone. My name is Dana, and on behalf of Top of the Rock, we'd like to welcome you to the sixty-seventh floor. If you'll step this way, I believe your party is expecting you."

"Thank you," Jason said and they made their way toward the back of the room. Matthew's jaw dropped when he saw the setup in the center of a Swarovski crystal wall. The stage was two feet off the ground and completely silver, and along the wall were two long monitors, showcasing various pieces of artwork Matthew recognized—from his earliest drawings to the ones of the Elders completed the night before Elder Klierra came into his life.

"Amazing, isn't it?" Jason asked as he put his arm around his nephew. "I'm glad you're here to see all this, Matthew."

"Yeah, I am too," Matthew said, his eyes glued to the displays. He refused to say out loud what he was actually thinking, but all he wanted to do was get through this party so he could fix whatever was so messed up on Denab IV. Who knew how much worse things were getting there since he left?

"These drawings look like the ones in your home," Arinna said to Matthew. "Very impressive. May I have one?"

Matthew blushed. This was the first time any woman ever asked for a copy of his art. If only his mother could see him now. "Sure," he said, as he felt a nudge from Jason.

Matthew nodded to his uncle as Arinna asked, "So where is the device you mentioned?"

"Oh, it's over there," Jason said, pointing to a table to the left of the stage. On top was a small wooden case the size of a shoebox. On its center was the circular emblem of Excelsior surrounded by glimmering jewels.

Arinna glided her fingertips across the top of the box. "I have not seen one of these in a very long time."

"You know what it is?" Jason asked.

Arinna nodded. "A larger version of what our ambassadors used in times of emergency. It amplifies our telepathic ability so we can communicate to Denab IV from a different planet."

"Does it still work?" Matthew asked, walking over to the communicator.

"We shall see," Arinna answered. She opened the box, closing her eyes, and Matthew watched all tension leave her body. The orb in the middle of the box began to rise, then glow, and finally morph into the face of one of the Elders.

"Elder Lokris," Matthew looked up at Arinna when he heard her voice, but her lips hadn't moved.

"What was that?" Jason asked, looking around.

"What was what?" Becky asked Jason. "Are you okay?"

Jason nodded. "I'm fine. Thought I heard a voice in my head."

Matthew's eyes narrowed when he heard Jason.

Lokris looked up when the telepathic connection was made, then closed her eyes and responded to Arinna.

"Arinna! Are you with Excelsior?"

Matthew said, "I am here, Elder."

"Matthew, how are you doing this?" Jason asked, now turning around to see if his nephew was standing behind him.

"Okay, you're really starting to worry me," Becky said to him. "Why don't you lie down?"

"I'm fine, I'm fine," Jason said, waving her off.

Matthew looked back to the communicator and shut his eyes to reach out again. "Elder, how is Acerus?"

"He is… he is not well. Much has happened here."

"Is everyone else safe?" Arinna asked. "Has Zorribis reached Connoram?"

"I can answer both with a conditional 'Yes.' A Krunation soldier sabotaged the summit between the Elders and Connoram, and Acerus was badly injured as a result of it." Arinna and Matthew exchanged worried glances as Lokris continued. "The Elders chased Connoram away, but Zorribis and Niterra are convinced he was not responsible, so they are traveling to Nocteris to bring him back."

"We'll get back as quickly as possible," Matthew said. "I'll be able to retrieve the gift from my uncle very soon, and then--"

"Matthew, do not return until we allow it," Lokris instructed with an urgent tone, and suddenly the connection was broken. Arinna and Matthew's eyes both snapped open.

"What happened?" Matthew asked.

Arinna shut her eyes again. "Elder Lokris? Elder Lokris?" Opening her eyes, she shook her head. "No response."

"You can still take us back to Denab IV whenever you want, right?" Matthew asked. "Should we maybe see what's going on over there?"

Arinna shook her head. "It is possible the Leap of Faith has fallen to Krunation control. Whatever the case, we should remain here and stay alive. The Elders would not forcefully keep you on a different planet. Leave it to them." She then looked to Jason. "I can stand by the communicator during the celebration and keep it safe. My clothes reflect what Denarians wear in your interpretation."

"And you still have the micro blaster you mentioned before, right? You didn't take that off and leave it at my house?"

"Of course not," Arinna answered. "It never left my side."

"Good. If Krunations are plotting to take over the Leap of Faith—"

Arinna held up one hand. "I was thinking the same thing, but I will not use it unless it is necessary. Jason said there will be many innocent people here, and I do not want to do anything to jeopardize their safety."

Matthew nodded. "Fair enough." He faced Jason and Becky. "I'm going to change now." He walked to the elevator bank to deliver him two floors down to the restrooms. The uniform under his clothes may have been made from otherworldly lightweight materials, but it never felt heavier.

CHAPTER THIRTY-THREE

The sound of the heavy feet smashing into the puddles of green water echoed through the empty subway tunnels. Danaak strode through the underground maze with a tugging in his chest, as though he were at one end of a string, and the other end was yanking him from one area in Manhattan to another. He stayed quiet the entire time, content Tornatrax allowed him not to kill. He could tell the god would not be so flexible with any other demands, and he winced at the thought of the excruciating pain Tornatrax gave him.

Finish it, he told himself. Do what he wants you to do, and he will reciprocate with your freedom. You will be at peace, and no one—physical or ethereal—will ever disturb you again.

"Stop here."

Danaak stopped and waited as he heard his echoing footsteps fading in the distance, mixing with the chattering of unsuspecting humans going about their day.

"Why?" he whispered.

"You will have what you need to accomplish your mission very soon. Your partner on Denab IV will send it to you."

"What will I need?" Danaak asked.

"You will know when you see it."

Danaak could almost see a smile cross Tornatrax's invisible face, as though he were refusing to spoil the surprise. "Rest, my friend. Rest and wait."

"Well done, my children. This was almost too easy."

Hodera stood in the center of a pile of carnage made up of Denarian soldiers tasked with defending the Leap of Faith. She wiped her sword clean across her sleeve and gave the jewel fused to her chest a brief rub while watching the lifeless Denarians dissolving into ash.

She heard the hissing and growling of her hulking Krunation minions and delighted as they wiped Denarian blood from their chins and picked at their teeth. Once her sword was again in pristine condition, Hodera stepped up to the doorway to the chamber and examined the torn apart doors.

Sivtra, still wearing the crown taken from the Matera, walked up to Hodera and nodded at the Krunation minions standing by, waiting for their orders. "Definitely exceeding expectations," he said.

"They are, indeed. And more are coming. I can feel them evolving and rising up as we speak. It will not be long before the shockwaves felt at Krephthera will be felt throughout the entire planet."

She pointed to the squadron of Krunation soldiers on her right, and her hand began to emit a yellow glow. "Return to our home. You know what must be done." The eyes of the Krunations she addressed began to glow an equally bright yellow, and after a moment, they turned and strode away from the chamber as though they were guided by a remote control.

Sivtra nodded as Hodera's warriors drifted into the water and out of sight. "It will not be long before the Denarian military answer this attack," he warned.

"Then we must ensure this does not happen," she said.

"Yes, Gener—behind you!"

Hodera turned her head toward the Leap of Faith doorway in time to see the blast from Sivtra's weapon strike a Denarian soldier in the stomach. The poor fool doubled over and rolled down the stairs, landing hard on the ground.

"Must have been hiding inside the chamber," Sivtra said, the barrel from his rifle still smoking.

"Well done, Sivtra," Hodera said, placing her hand on the young Krunation's forehead. "These are your next instructions," she whispered into his ear. "You are to follow them without hesitation."

"Yes, General," Sivtra replied, his voice suddenly drifting as though he were talking in his sleep, his arms dropping to his side.

"Now, go to Axsella at once," she said, pointing at the transport. Sivtra turned, walked away from the Leap of

Faith with his rifle still in his hand, boarded the transport, and left.

"Your service to Tornatrax will always be remembered," Hodera said as she watched him leave. "As well as your service to me." After allowing a moment of silence, she turned toward the remaining soldiers, and with her hand still glowing, ordered, "The six of you in front, step inside the chamber." Their eyes glowed, and the six Krunation soldiers ascended the steps and stood at the doorway.

Before she could take her first step up the stairs, Hodera felt someone grasping her leg. She looked down and saw the wounded Denarian soldier struggling to hold on. The smoke from the wound in his stomach clouded the air as he said between short, sharp breaths, "You will not... succeed... Hodera."

The Krunation general sneered as she pulled the sword from the sheath attached to her belt. The Denarian's eyes widened and she hissed at him, "Such heroic nonsense." She casually lifted the sword above her head, swinging straight down. Hodera pulled the blade from the middle of a pile of ash which was once a Denarian, sheathed the sword, and turned to address the rest of her squadron.

"The rest of you will stay outside the chamber. Let no one pass!" Hodera climbed the stairs and walked through the doorway, her mindless soldiers striding behind her.

"So beautiful," she whispered as she approached the console operating the Leap of Faith. The silver walls, the luminescent orb in the center, the massive metallic cover over the inter-planetary doorway. Excelsior definitely knew what he was doing when he created this place.

Hodera placed her hand on the orb in the center of the console and closed her eyes. As she concentrated, the screen above the console flashed to life and zoomed past the Denab Star System toward the Milky Way Galaxy, then reached the third planet of an insignificant solar system, and finally came to rest on New York City.

"This will work, my Lord?" Hodera asked.

"Do not doubt me, child. My instrument of destruction is awaiting this as we speak. The Leap of Faith will deliver the sword to him."

Him. "Who is he?" she asked, the gears in her head turning. Did another Krunation go to Earth after Danaak? To succeed where he failed? Or was it Danaak himself?

"Another time, Hodera. Send the sword. Now!"

The cover slowly opened, revealing a force of pure energy with the blue and green planet Earth seen in the distance. Hodera unsheathed her sword once again and held it up to the Leap of Faith. She pulled her arm back, holding the sword like an athlete on Earth competing in the Olympics, and launched it through the doorway.

"Well done. And now you must wait. When the time is right, I will summon you once again to send your loyal soldiers to join with my servant on Earth."

"By your demand, it shall be done, my Lord," Hodera said, smiling. Her grin faded when she looked down at her hands and saw her skin was flaking off again. She gritted her teeth in anger. If only she could be there to witness Excelsior's final defeat. He owed her that much.

CHAPTER THIRTY-FOUR

"Ladies and gentlemen, if I can have your attention please?"

The voice of Becky's father speaking into the microphone silenced the chattering crowd, and they all turned to the stage in front of the crystal wall. Mathew—dressed in his full Excelsior uniform and wearing his helmet—could feel all their eyes gravitating toward him in particular. Even though he wore this his entire time on Denab IV, he still felt silly outside his normal surroundings. *Now I know how cosplayers feel when they're within the confines of Comic-Con and then go out into civilization in their outfits,* he thought.

Matthew glanced at Arinna, who was standing beside the communicator with a proud smile on her face, and gave a light wave. She waved back, and his stomach did another back flip. He turned toward his uncle, who was fidgeting behind Becky's father on the stage, and nodded his head. Jason sucked in a deep breath and nodded back.

"I want to say how happy I am to have you all here this evening," Becky's father said once the party attendants quieted down. "And I know you're as excited for this program as I am. But first, a quick note about what you're seeing here." He motioned his arm in Matthew's direction. "This is basically a prototype of what Excelsior will be wearing in the upcoming series. I'm sure it won't be the finished product. It'll remain true to the spirit of the character while being quite a bit thicker and sturdier, not as flimsy."

Matthew rolled his eyes. The Krunations' weapons on the series should be able to handle such "flimsy" armor. That's what Excelsior needed to handle himself better in battle. Bulk. Why didn't he think of it before?

"Now, please allow me to introduce to you the reason we're all here. He is the custodian of the popular webcomic and the creator of the upcoming television series, 'Excelsior.'" At the mentions of both the comic and the series, Matthew glanced back at Jason and shrugged his shoulders. Jason shrugged back.

"Please welcome Jason Peters!" Becky's father walked off the stage and, as the crowd applauded, let Jason step up to the front. He gave a broad wave to everyone there, and then gave one in particular to Becky.

"Thank you very much, sir," Jason said, shakiness evident in his voice. He cleared his throat, and when he spoke again, it was with a noticeable increase in clarity and confidence. "Thank you to everyone for being here. This is a very special evening, the culmination of over ten years of hard work. And while I couldn't be more excited to see where this character will go on the small screen, I also couldn't be prouder to see the work of someone very close to me see this kind of validation."

Matthew turned to Jason with a smile and listened as his uncle continued his speech. "I understand my position in the development of 'Excelsior.' I know I wasn't born with the same creativity of my nephew. I know I wasn't the one who put pen to paper and spent seven years getting this character and his world just right. But after my nephew decided to step away from being a writer and artist, he knew he had something with 'Excelsior,' and he not only wanted it to succeed, but he also wanted to keep it in the family. So I'd like you all to give a round of applause to the true creator of Excelsior: Matthew Peters."

Jason started clapping, and the rest of the party attendants applauded in kind. Matthew clapped along with everyone else, refraining from puffing out his broad chest, and glanced at Arinna, who was also clapping and smiling at him.

The next half-hour dragged on for Matthew. After Jason finished his thanks to everyone for attending, the partygoers started a line to take pictures with the "model" in the Excelsior costume. The first couple took Matthew by surprise when the husband reached into his inside jacket pocket and pulled out a telescopic stick attached his smartphone to the end, held it up so all three of them were in the picture, and pressed a button on the stick's handle. Looks like I missed the next step in state-of-the-art technology, he thought to himself.

"Matthew." The whisper from Jason snapped Matthew back to reality. He blinked and looked to his right and saw his uncle standing right beside him, giving him a gentle nudge. "You okay?"

"I'm fine," Matthew whispered back. He looked around the busy room. "Where's Arinna?"

Jason pointed to a mass of men gathered around the communicator's table. "I have a feeling she's over there. Denarian DNA, I tell you. Potent."

Matthew nodded. "Especially hers."

"You said it. Although from what I saw from some of those wives and girlfriends getting pictures with you, yours is kinda strong too. I thought one of them was gonna be a little extra frisky."

"Really?" Matthew blinked again. "I didn't even notice."

"Well, you looked preoccupied. They tried talking to you, but you never answered."

"Oh, sorry," Matthew said. "How many more couples need pictures?"

"They're done. They're all partying. Go ahead, get some quiet time with Arinna. Once the party's over... well, you know."

Matthew nodded. "Yeah, I know." He didn't want to push the topic again since both of them knew he was on the cusp of accomplishing his mission on Earth, but he was also about to cut the tether between Denab IV and Earth forever. "And the communicator will be okay?"

"It'll be fine," Jason said. "Anyone tries to walk off with it, security will stop them before they take another step. Now go, get your moment before the sun goes down."

Matthew took a step toward Arinna, then paused and looked back at Jason. "How did you—"

"Oh, please. Give me some credit. Now go."

CHAPTER THIRTY-FIVE

"**N**ow is the time, my friend!"

Danaak sat cross-legged in the dank waters underneath the Rockefeller Center subway station, his eyes shut as though he were back in the comforting arms of the afterlife. Just accomplish this mission, he told himself. You have been chosen to be an important element in your god's plans. Do what must be done, do not sway, and you can finally leave this universe once and for all to Tornatrax's influence.

The voice of the Krunation god filled Danaak's head and he awoke, glancing at the subway tunnel ceiling. His eyes widened as he saw a blue electrical charge appear, then grow brighter and larger, until a burst of light cascaded over the Krunation.

Danaak held up his right arm and felt the cold steel of a weapon falling into his hand. He clasped the handle and lowered his arm, examining the sword and paying particular attention to the jewel at the end of the handle.

"Ahhh, yes," he whispered to himself. "I remember this very well."

"As do I. I remember the carnage you unleashed. How glorious to grant you that power."

Danaak smiled and ran his finger along the blade. "This... feels... good..."

"It does, Danaak. And it can feel even better when this power is wielded up there. You are my personal instrument of destruction. You are the key to my victory."

"Instrument of destruction?" Danaak asked.

"Oh, yes, my friend," Tornatrax said. "All you require is the anger strong enough to succeed."

A wave of energy flowed from the sword and into Danaak's arm, and suddenly his mind was flooded with images of Excelsior advancing toward him and thrusting the blade of his sword into his chest. He felt the pain, nothing more.

"Let us explore a little further."

Danaak felt another burst of pain as more images flashed in front of him. "What... are... you doing?"

"What must be done."

Another burst of pain, this time from a creature of unknown origin on Earth tearing into his mid-section. Danaak placed his hand on his body and traced his fingertips along the scars. The pain subsided, as did the vision.

"Maybe further back, to a time when more... emotional pain was felt?"

"Please, do not do this," Danaak whispered. And then he felt the energy pulsating through his head, as though the simple act of asking for mercy disgusted Tornatrax.

"So you still remember."

A quick flash in front of Danaak's eyes was all he needed to conjure up the memories.

The pain.

The agony.

The sight of her lying on the floor.

Not moving.

Not breathing.

And the sound of the Krunation soldier assigned to protect her, yelling, "Excelsior! He did this!"

Danaak squeezed his eyes shut, trying to push the image from his mind, and as his fists clenched, something he hadn't felt since his life ended came rushing back to him.

Anger.

Pure anger.

And Tornatrax could feel it.

"Yes. And now rise, my friend! Your destiny is waiting for you. As is mine."

CHAPTER
THIRTY-SIX

"**N**iterra, look!"

Zorribis, sitting behind Niterra in their transport, pointed to their left. A squadron of Krunations were standing in a perimeter surrounding the Leap of Faith chamber. Three soldiers stood against each other in front of the broken entrance doors.

"It fell to their control so quickly," Niterra exclaimed. "Do you think the Elders are preparing a counter-attack?"

"We will know in a moment," Zorribis replied. He shut his eyes and he could hear his own voice filling his head. "Elders, is there anything we can do to prevent the Leap of Faith staying in Krunation control?"

"Negative, Zorribis," the voice of Tricerus said. "Nosgood has gathered a battalion of Edenarian soldiers, and they are about to engage. Worry about your precious Connoram instead."

"Have you been able to make this rise any higher?" Niterra asked.

"Not yet. But we can go faster. Press the button on top of the console."

Niterra pressed a small red button, and a clear field of energy surrounded the two Denarians, keeping them safe as the aircraft accelerated past the Leap of Faith. Niterra turned her head toward the chamber and smiled when she saw the first of the Denarian battalion arriving on the scene.

"I hope they will be okay," Niterra said, unable to hide the nervousness in her voice.

"Oh, no." Zorribis pointed toward the land in front of them and saw even more Krunations climbing out of a glowing body of water and running in the direction of the Leap of Faith. "Look at them!" he said with a mixture of disgust and fascination. "Those are not typical Krunation soldiers."

"They look..." She struggled to come up with an ideal word. "Inhuman. As if they have been rushed through evolution."

"Whatever they are, at the rate they are moving, they will arrive at the Leap of Faith while the Denarians are battling the ones already there." Zorribis squeezed his eyes shut and concentrated again. "Elder Tricerus, please order your soldiers to retreat. More Krunations are preparing to ambush them."

The silence hung in the air for what seemed like an eternity. Zorribis and Niterra looked at each other.

Finally, they heard the Elder's voice once again. "Fear not, Zorribis. We have alerted Nosgood, and he has adequate soldiers at his disposal."

"They will not have enough time, Elder," Zorribis answered. "The Krunations are already on their way."

Niterra shook her head. "This is what Hodera wants."

"Elder, we can see Hodera used the atmospheric change to her advantage," Zorribis added. "If you keep sending Denarians after her horde, she will grow more to overwhelm us. Please instruct them to retreat."

"Concentrate on your own mission, Zorribis," Tricerus's voice boomed. "Our soldiers have been more than capable of handling the Krunation threat. This will be no different."

"Relics," Niterra said through gritted teeth. She turned to Zorribis and smiled.

"You do not even have to read my thoughts," Zorribis said to her, smiling back and reaching to his left. He unlatched a blaster rifle from the vehicle.

"We are still concentrating on our mission," Niterra justified out loud. "We simply want to make sure our blasters are functioning properly."

"Correct," Zorribis said. He placed his hand on his beloved partner's shoulder and pointed forward. "Land there."

"My pleasure." She directed the aircraft to a smooth patch of land next to a large rocky area. She eased it to the ground and shut down the engines. The aircraft landed, and the two climbed out, Niterra grabbing her blaster rifle in one swift movement. They both looked over the rocks at the Krunations walking and growling, and Niterra placed the barrel of her rifle on the rock in front of them.

"Do you have your targets?" Zorribis asked.

She nodded. "All of them head shots. Do you think Excelsior will be angry with us?"

"If we do not do this, many more Denarians will be attacked."

"Understood." She squeezed the trigger several times. Zorribis kept his eyes on the large battalion of Krunation soldiers and saw five of them drop lifeless to the ground.

"Impressive," he said quietly.

"You sound so surprised," Niterra said, keeping her eye at the rifle's scope and continuing to fire.

Zorribis positioned his rifle and started firing as well. Another five Krunations fell, then ten. Then ten more. Zorribis and Niterra took a moment to glance at each other and smile. Oh yes, Zorribis thought to himself. This is definitely the one I want bonded to me for all time.

They turned their attention back to the Krunations and continued firing. As more fell, Zorribis noticed they made a decent dent in the armada's numbers, but more than half of the enemy made it past their gauntlet of blaster-fire unscathed, while continuing on to the Leap of Faith.

Niterra lowered her blaster rifle and peeked once again above the rocks. She whispered, "I hope Nosgood and his men will be able to—" She gasped when several Krunations turned in their direction, then looked down at their fallen comrades, and let out a screeching roar to each other. "I believe they see us," Niterra said.

Zorribis stood and fired three more shots. Three more Krunations fell.

"No reason to stay hidden now," Zorribis said over the blasts. Niterra stood up and joined her lifemate in firing on the Krunations, which were now running in their direction and scattering so it was more difficult for the two to strike them down. And to Zorribis's horror, some of them made a wide turn and were now behind the two Denarians.

But they didn't attack them from behind. Instead, the cluster of Krunations approached Zorribis's aircraft and brought their fists down on the control console.

"No!" Zorribis yelled as he opened fire.

The bonded Denarians positioned themselves so they were standing back-to-back and firing at the approaching warriors.

"I do not wish to regret this decision, my love," Niterra shouted out over her shoulder.

"Neither do I," Zorribis said.

CHAPTER
THIRTY-SEVEN

Matthew's timing to get Arinna up to the seventieth floor couldn't have been better. He scrambled to stuff both his sword and helmet back into his backpack and throw his button-down shirt over his Excelsior uniform, then took his friend's hand to pull her away from another batch of hopeful suitors. Once they were away from the party, Matthew told Arinna, "I hope you're ready for this."

They stepped inside the small elevator. After a moment, the door opened and the two were greeted by a beautiful glow shining over Matthew's hometown. His eyes filled with tears as he not only indulged in the sunset, but looked around and saw hundreds of different men, women, and children from all parts of the world enjoying the view along with them. He never allowed himself to forget–even when he was eager to lose himself in his webcomics—people were coming from everywhere to spend time where he lived.

"Beautiful!" Arinna exclaimed while inching closer to him among the crowd. "As an ambassador to Denab IV, I have seen views like this on so many planets, but they were always taken for granted by their inhabitants. I appreciate your people..." She stopped herself for a moment and then continued, "I appreciate the people of Earth take the time to recognize this gift of nature."

"They're still my people. I may have a new home, but they're still my people. I'm still of the same flesh and... well, they're still my people. And my family is still here."

"Of course," Arinna said with a nod. "There will always be something special about the first place you called home, like Denab IV will always be for me. I hope it can be the same for you."

"I know what you mean," Matthew responded. "Believe me, I'm very much aware of what needs to be fixed there. This place will always have a place in my heart, but Denab IV is my mess, and I will clean it up. I'm not Clark Kent or Peter Parker."

"Who?"

"Fictional characters," Matthew said. "They gave up their powers so they could live a normal life and everyone around them got hurt because of it."

"I see," Arinna said. "Is this a normal thing to do on Earth? To walk away from responsibility?"

"Well, not exactly," Matthew answered. "Politicians, maybe, but dropping everything in someone else's lap was never my style, especially after becoming Excelsior. Now, if I was never him in the first place–"

"You are still thinking this?" she asked. "Must I clear your head again to stop you from thinking such non-productive thoughts?"

"No, no. You're right. I'm not gonna dwell on it anymore. I promise, and I hope this plan works. We get the energy back, we go home, we get the planet back in working order. And maybe afterwards..." Matthew's voice trailed off.

"Afterwards?" Arinna asked.

"Well," Matthew stumbled with his words. This was the moment he waited for since his mind was cleared in his grandmother's home. He looked into Arinna's eyes and smiled. She smiled back. "Well, I was thinking, once we get back, and all this is behind us, maybe I can take you out somewhere on Denab IV. You and me, together." He froze when he realized he couldn't think of anything else to say at that moment. Silence hung in the air for what seemed like an hour while he waited for Arinna to say anything.

She smiled again. "Yes," she said. "I would like that very much."

"Really?" he blurted out. "Even after the whole stars thing?"

Arinna laughed. "After you bring them back, of course."

"Of course," Matthew said. "Now, look straight ahead. You don't want to miss this."

"Does it normally get this active?" Arinna asked as the sun continued to set over the New York City skyline. The tourists were now getting close enough to invade personal space, and Matthew pulled her closer to him so she was positioned in front of him. He looked down when he felt someone squeezing his right hand, and smiled when he saw her hand.

Maybe there was something other than the gift that Matthew needed from Jason. He made a mental note to ask Zorribis where he should take her on their date once everything was set right.

"What was that?"

The sudden sound of a woman's scream shattered Matthew's concentration, and when he looked around for the source, every noise came slamming back like a stereo being turned on after it was left at maximum volume.

"Something is wrong," Arinna said as the two looked around. They ran to the edge of the south side of the building and looked down on the 69th floor, which was packed with panicked tourists who could only point, scream, and snap pictures.

Matthew gasped when he saw cars and people scattering away from the plaza area below. One explosion followed another, knocking people off their feet, but when he looked around, he couldn't see anything firing down on the street. Whatever was causing this destruction, it was coming from underground. A burst of energy shot out from a crater-sized hole in the middle of Rockefeller Plaza, and came to rest above the seventieth floor. Everyone shrieked in a panic, and the noise was so overpowering, Matthew could barely hear a deep, booming voice from within the light.

"All who call Earth their home, leave this area at once!"

"They're here," Matthew said. "The Leap of Faith has fallen."

The entire floor erupted into bedlam, with people either shoving their way down the narrow stairwell leading to the sixty-ninth floor or cramming themselves into the elevator.

Matthew turned to Arinna, who was also looking up at the light in horror, and yelled, "Go downstairs. Find Jason and Becky!"

"What about you?"

"I'll join you in a little bit," Matthew replied, opening his backpack. "Make sure they're out of danger. And be careful when you go down there. People on Earth aren't used to these kinds of situations. You're gonna need your blaster."

"Not yet," Arinna assured him. "Too much panic. Trust me."

Matthew nodded. "You're right, but please be careful."

Arinna gave Matthew's hand one last squeeze and joined the mob trying to get downstairs. Once she was out of sight, Matthew pulled his shirt off and tossed it to the floor, then grabbed his helmet and sword. He slipped the helmet on his head with one hand.

"Whatever you are," Matthew said softly. "I will not let you hurt anyone. Not on Earth. Not on Denab IV. Never."

CHAPTER THIRTY-EIGHT

As the voices of fear and panic faded while the last of the people ran down the stairs, Matthew paused to soak in the stillness on the seventieth floor. He slowly backed away from the ball of energy hanging over the building and peeked over the top of the stairwell to make sure everyone was on their way to safety. The last thing he saw before walking back to the center of the platform was a tall, thin man wearing a gray suit placing two stanchions at the bottom of the stairwell, extending the retractable belt so the entrance to the top floor was blocked off, and calmly walking away.

"They're gone!" Matthew shouted at the energy, holding his sword in both hands and bending his knees, easing himself into a fighting stance and feeling the lifeforce of Excelsior return to the surface. Whatever this being was, he knew he needed to be at maximum capability.

The energy's response to Excelsior was a powerful blast knocking Denab IV's savior off his feet. He landed hard on his back and winced while still holding his sword.

"So you're one of Hodera's soldiers?" Excelsior said, pushing himself back up. "Sent through the Leap of Faith?"

"I am beholden to a master, Excelsior." The ball of energy descended, speaking with a mixture of voices. One was the same deep boom it emitted after its arrival, but the other was a higher, hissing voice that seemed to grow louder the closer it came.

"But it is not Hodera!"

Excelsior stood at the ready and the otherworldly energy faded away, revealing a humanoid figure holding a sword in its scaly-skinned hand.

A very familiar scaly-skinned hand.

Excelsior sucked in a deep breath and scrambled to his feet, his sword aimed at his adversary. He opened his mouth to say something, but his mind went blank.

The figure casually held his sword out, and the tips of the two swords touched, emitting a small spark. "You thought you were the only one whose lifeforce could be re-ignited?"

Finally, the word came from Excelsior's mouth.

"Danaak!"

Sivtra sat quietly in front of the transport's console, the Matera's blood-stained tiara still sitting on his head, and his hands wrapped tightly around the controls as he kept it steady. His eyes were glassy, and he didn't blink for the entire time he grew closer to his intended target.

This is for the greater good, he told himself. This will ensure Tornatrax's influence will be forever felt throughout all of Denab IV. Excelsior is no savior. He has doomed his own people to an early death by being here. He is not fit to lead. He is not fit to even follow. He is a danger to be eradicated. Tornatrax must do it, and we will be rewarded for our faithful service to him.

The same sentences ran like a loop over and over through his mind.

There it was; the large bunker of Axsella. Sivtra heard a voice in his head growing louder, a hissing voice. "Here it is, young one. Your destiny approaches. Hodera will be pleased with your ability to do what no other Krunation could do. Not Danaak, not Nocterar. Increase your speed, and complete your mission."

Sivtra pushed the throttle of the transport as far down as it could go, and the barge sped up, aiming right for the entrance to the bunker. The sunlight bounced off the metallic material of the stronghold, and it shone into Sivtra's eyes like a Kitera forcing the underlings to awaken every morning.

The sudden light caused the young Krunation to blink for the first time, and he looked around in his seat, confused. "When did I get here?" he asked himself. "How did I get here?"

Then he gazed ahead and saw the bunker getting closer as the transport was not slowing down. He cried out in terror. "What am I doing? Why am I doing this?"

Sivtra pushed himself out of his seat and immediately felt the g-forces pushing him down. He clenched his jaw and squeezed his eyes shut while trying to pry himself away from the front of the transport as it continued to speed forward, apparently on some form of auto-pilot.

Suddenly, an image flashed before his mind. One of Hodera pressing her hand against his forehead and whispering how much it would pleasure Tornatrax if he did as instructed.

Suicide.

After everything he did for General Hodera, after all of the information he provided, after pledging to her cause, Sivtra's mission was to die. He was as expendable to her as one of her new minions.

Sivtra slammed his hands on the control console, but nothing helped. The transport was speeding to the bunker. He pressed the buttons to disconnect the auto-pilot several more times, but to no avail, and before long he was close enough to see Denarian soldiers running out from the entrance. Some were even running back in and bringing out other soldiers.

This was not a familiar sight for Sivtra. He was so used to seeing Krunations concentrating on saving their own lives and disregarding anyone else, and yet these were supposed to be the enemy.

As though someone yanked a blindfold off his eyes, Sivtra blurted out loud, "Connoram was right!" And here he was, about to commit such a terrible atrocity in the name of someone who was only too happy to send him out to die.

No.

With a swipe of his hand, the tiara flew off his head, bouncing on the floor and coming to a rest underneath his boot. Sivtra brought his boot down as hard as possible, smashing it to pieces. Then, with all the might his diminutive frame would allow, he jerked the controls so hard, the transport suddenly swerved and careened against the corner of the bunker. Chunks of metal and concrete crashed down to the ground, but he couldn't tell if there were any casualties.

Sivtra tried pressing the button to lower the ramp while it was still in motion, but the controls wouldn't respond. He looked up in time to see the water ahead, and he shut his eyes in resignation. No, there was no escape, but at least Sivtra knew he didn't take any Denarians with him into oblivion.

The impact from striking the water jerked the small Krunation's body forward. Then all went black.

CHAPTER THIRTY-NINE

"Is it time, my Lord?"

Hodera looked up at the ceiling of the Leap of Faith Chamber with two loyal Krunation soldiers on either side. She stood in front of the inter-planetary doorway with eager anticipation, knowing the Krunations waiting for her outside could handle the approaching Denarians.

"Yes, child. Send your warriors through. My colleague has reached his destination."

With a triumphant smile, Hodera pressed her right hand to the forehead of one Krunation, then the other, and after a momentary pause, the eyes of both began to glow.

"You have your instructions?" she asked.

The Krunations nodded, and Hodera walked back to the console, pressed her hand to the main controller, and watched as the Leap of Faith activated once again. The two Krunations stepped up to the doorway, and Hodera called out to them one more time. "Remember. Seize and capture! As much as I would enjoy it, no exterminations."

Both Krunations nodded, stepped through the doorway, and vanished.

And as the Leap of Faith shut down, Hodera heard a distinctive, arrogant voice.

"Attack!"

"Ahhh, Nosgood," she said to herself in a playful tone. She turned and walked to the broken door leading outside.

Doing her best to stay out of sight, Hodera leaned against the door and peeked through one of the many cracks. Seeing her Krunation subjects engaging the Denarian soldiers brought a rush of pride, especially when she noticed how many wounded Denarians were on the ground, or how many dead ones dissolved into ash. Yes, there were Krunations as well, but she knew it was only a matter of time before the next wave would reach the Leap of Faith.

"Come out, Hodera!" The taunt from Nosgood singed her ears. "Come out here and face us like the leader you think you are."

She ached to step outside, to join the fracas, but resisted. The new order on Denab IV needed her guidance on the planet's surface, as well as Tornatrax's influence above it.

"In due time, Nosgood. At a time of my choosing, not yours!"

CHAPTER FORTY

"**H**ow is this possible?"

Excelsior gripped his sword with both hands and pointed it in Danaak's direction, doing his best to squelch the fear making him tremble.

"Your god gave you power, young man," Danaak spoke calmly. "My god pulled me from death, which I must say was quite a discomfort, and gave me life once again."

"Your god?"

Danaak nodded. "And now, as he bid it, I have a task to complete."

"To kill me, right?" Excelsior asked.

"You will meet your end in due time," Danaak answered. "But something else must be taken before your life." He tapped the tip of his blade against Excelsior's sword, then pulled his arm back, and swung his blade toward Denab IV's savior. Excelsior blocked the blow, and the two old adversaries engaged in battle on top of Rockefeller Center.

Arinna reached the sixty-seventh floor and saw Jason standing on top of the stage area, his hand rubbing a small medallion around his neck. Becky was working with the security officers and Top of the Rock staff ushering people into the elevators.

"Becky!" Arinna yelled.

Jason turned his head in Arinna's direction and waved to her. "We're okay!"

Arinna ran to them, and she could hear Becky speak in a very calm, yet authoritative, tone of voice to the Top of the Rock host standing by the elevator.

"How many people can these hold?" Becky asked.

"Sixteen," the host replied as people pushed and shoved their way inside.

"Make sure the priority is given to older and lesser-abled people," she instructed. "If people look like they can take the stairs, direct them to the stairs."

"Matthew is upstairs," Arinna said. "He will join us momentarily." Suddenly, a voice in her head made her stop in her tracks. She held out her hands to keep Becky and Jason from walking anywhere else.

"Oh, no," she whispered.

"What is it?" Becky asked. "Are you okay? You're not hurt, are you?"

"It cannot be," she said, looking back at Jason and Becky. "I am fine, but we must get you both to safety. I will watch over you—"

The sound of intense crackling electricity above cut off Arinna's instructions, and she looked up to see a very familiar pattern of light. "The Leap of Faith is open!"

She reached for Becky and Jason and ran away from the opening in the ceiling. "What are we doing?" Becky asked.

"We need to get upstairs," Arinna instructed. "We will be--"

A loud thud, followed by Becky's scream, interrupted Arinna's train of thought. "What are those things?" Becky yelled while pointing at the stage behind them.

Arinna looked over her shoulder and saw two massive Krunation soldiers standing there. Before she could answer, Jason yelled out, "Krunations!" He shuddered and followed it up with, "I think!"

"Upstairs!" Arinna called out to the two of them. "Now!"

She grabbed Jason and Becky by their wrists and led them back up the stairs. Behind them, Arinna could hear the raspy growl of the Krunations, followed by their footsteps cutting through the noise of the panicked crowd.

And those footsteps were getting louder.

CHAPTER FORTY-ONE

"**Y**our soldiers impress me, Hodera."

The Krunation general stepped away from the broken Leap of Faith doorway, satisfied with the carnage her freshly evolved warriors were creating. She nodded at Tornatrax's compliment. "They please me as well, my Lord. I trust the ones I sent to your associate are performing equally well?"

"Very well, indeed. And now, place your hand on the console. When the time is right, you will bring home your soldiers and my... associate."

"As you command, my Lord." Hodera swaggered toward the console, hips moving in a rhythm with the music of her Krunations' roaring. She placed her hand on the console and waited.

The hissing and roaring of the Krunation warriors grew louder in Zorribis's ears as he and Niterra pressed their backs harder against each other. He could also hear the crackling of the control console of the Libeli-inspired aircraft, which made him wince.

"They are getting closer!" Niterra shouted over her shoulder, and Zorribis gulped. These Krunations were playing with their food. They were low to the ground, their knees bent in a position allowing them to spring up and pounce at any moment. They showed off their sharp, pointy teeth, snapping their jaws shut over and over, while circling their prey.

"Beloved..." Zorribis began, still shooting in all directions.

"No!" Niterra said. "This is not our time! They will not be the last thing we hear!"

Suddenly, where there were fifteen Krunations in front of Zorribis, there were twelve, then ten. Their lifeless bodies dissolved into ash before they could hit the ground.

"I hear less growls over there," Niterra said without turning her head. "I know you have exceptional aim, but—"

"Not this good," Zorribis said. He continued firing at the Krunations approaching, looking around whenever possible to see what was thinning out their enemies.

A piercing screech prompted Zorribis to look up, and he squinted from the blinding sunlight. But what he saw after his eyes adjusted made his mouth drop open in shock. A majestic-looking creature soared through the air, huge wings spread out. It had a bulky triangle-shaped torso and a long, narrow head. It glided through the air without any effort, and there was only one creature on Denab IV with the capability of reaching such heights.

"A Libeli," Zorribis breathed.

As if it could hear him calling its name, the creature let out another screech, banking toward the two Denarians on the ground. As it approached them, Zorribis identified what looked like a man on its strong back, and the man was aiming some kind of weapon in their vicinity. Zorribis held up his blaster rifle but was too late to stop the man from spraying several blasts toward them. He shut his eyes and felt Niterra pushing her back against his, the two of them bracing themselves for the inevitable end.

The blasts ringing in his ears stopped. Zorribis opened his eyes and saw the remaining Krunation warriors littering the ground. They were motionless and disintegrating into ash. Zorribis rubbed his nose as he accidentally inhaled some of the smoke.

"What is happening?" Niterra asked.

"Who are you?" Zorribis cried to the figure on top of the Libeli.

The creature came to a stop on the ground, its four limbs bending at the knees. The figure climbed off without any difficulty, its silhouette in a perfect position to shield Zorribis from knowing the stranger's identity.

Then, from the mysterious figure, came a very familiar voice. "Someone my Armfather holds in high regard."

Zorribis blinked again. "Charak? What has happened?" He pointed to the large rifle in the Krunation's hand. "And what is that?"

Charak nodded to the rifle. "A larger version of what was used to wound your High Elder."

"And more powerful, I assume?" Niterra asked. "Acerus is still alive, and there is nothing but..." She and Zorribis both looked around and saw the Krunation corpses had already disintegrated.

"We can thank Hodera for this. The weapon used on Acerus was meant to prolong his suffering. This was meant for a quick and painless death."

"Showing mercy for your fellow Krunations?" Niterra asked, her temper suddenly rising. "While a Denarian is lying in pain?"

"Would you prefer they died a slow death while tearing you apart?" Charak said and Niterra flushed.

Zorribis walked toward the creature standing behind Charak and cautiously ran his hand along the side of its head. Its body gleamed white and was covered by soft, furry scales. Its four brown legs were long and muscular and the same color as its sharp beak. A large silver saddle with four seats was connected to its back and latched around its stomach.

"I thought the Libeli were extinct," Zorribis said as he looked into its soft blue eyes.

"Nearly," Charak corrected him. "My Armfather Connoram discovered one while in the forest. Somehow it survived Nocterar's wildlife purging when he rose to power. It was tired, scared, and alone, and so Connoram and some of his soldiers transported it to a safe haven within Nocteris. Since it was on his side of the stronghold, Hodera never found it. But when her soldiers attacked our army—"

"Wait," Zorribis said, holding his hands up. "Did you say Hodera attacked Connoram?"

"Yes," Charak said. "Before they could break into his quarters, he instructed the Libeli to take me to you. You showed mercy when the Elders could have ordered us killed."

"Is he still at Nocteris?" Zorribis asked.

"Yes," Charak said.

"We must go there immediately. Can you assist with the repairs of my aircraft?"

Charak shook his head. "No time. The Libeli can fit us all."

CHAPTER
FORTY-TWO

"Impressive, Excelsior."

The two swords clashed together, unleashing a sea of sparks, and Matthew felt his fear dissipate and his fighting skills take over. He successfully blocked each thrust from Danaak and stood his ground as the Krunation continued stepping forward.

"Glad you approve," Excelsior growled through gritted teeth, and he felt the overwhelming strength of Danaak pushing him back step by step. The concrete of the 70th floor barrier stuck into his back, and he was relieved it was there, keeping him from landing flat on his back on the 69th floor. Danaak moved closer, and Excelsior recalled a similar moment at Tollund Laboratories, when this same Krunation was so near his face.

Excelsior looked past him and saw the Empire State Building lighting up along with the rest of the city skyline. To his surprise, the antenna's chosen color for the evening was purple, the same purple as Denab IV's sky. It was as if the building was cheering him on as a representative of New York City.

Keep fighting, Excelsior told himself, and he turned his body ninety degrees and pushed back as Danaak swung his sword. The blade missed him, but struck the concrete barrier, leaving a gash in its wake. Excelsior brought his own sword up over his head and down hard, but Danaak recovered his balance and blocked the strike.

The duel continued back and forth, neither man yielding to the other, but questions filled Excelsior's mind. How was Danaak revived? What is this mission he mentioned? And most importantly, did Arinna get to Jason and Becky safely?

"Matthew!"

Excelsior looked past Danaak and saw Arinna, Jason, and Becky frantically running up the stairs.

Arinna shouted, "Krunations were sent through the Leap of Faith!"

"Get your blaster out," Excelsior called out. "Keep them safe."

Danaak held his sword with both hands and swung hard toward Excelsior, who once again blocked the blow, but not in time to avoid being struck on his left shoulder.

Excelsior winced and brought his right hand up to the wound, still using his left to squeeze the sword and continue blocking Danaak's persistent swings.

"So you no longer bleed the blood of this planet," Danaak said after another swing was deflected, lacking the glee Excelsior expected to hear.

"This is the last of my blood you'll see, Danaak," Excelsior said, stepping forward and forcing the Krunation back with one swing after another with his sword.

Suddenly, they both stopped as a hissing, demonic voice filled their heads, a voice familiar to both of them. "He killed her, Danaak. He spilled her blood."

"What was that?" Excelsior asked, blinking.

"A reminder," Danaak said, his mouth curling into an angry sneer. "You took her from me."

"What? What are you talking about?"

"Oh, you know," he said as he bared his teeth and held up his sword again.

"Yessss," the voice whispered. "Your son will be so proud."

"Matthew, get out of the way!"

Excelsior turned and saw Arinna holding her micro blaster, and she was aiming it at Danaak, waiting for the ideal shot. But when she called out her warning, one of the pursuing Krunations grabbed her arm and yanked the gun from her grasp. The Krunation looked down at the gun and aimed it at Arinna's head, and immediately roared in pain, dropped the gun, and clutched his skull.

"No exterminations!" boomed an angry voice filling Matthew's head, and apparently the heads of the invading Krunations.

Arinna reached once again for her weapon, but the Krunation still standing intercepted her. He grabbed her arm, swung her into the elevator door, then shoved her to the floor. Her head smacked the cement. The invader grabbing his head stood back up and shook his head.

"Arinna!"

Excelsior lunged in her direction, but Danaak kicked out, his foot slamming into his helmet. The force knocked Excelsior off-balance and he dropped down to one knee.

"Matthew, look out!" Jason called while running to his nephew, but he only got three steps before Hodera's Krunations seized him by both arms. Excelsior pushed himself to his feet, swinging his sword from left to right, but Danaak knocked it away and thrust his weaponed arm straight forward.

Excelsior's whole world stopped. His right arm stayed outstretched with his hand still clutching his sword. He turned his head and saw both Jason and Arinna. Both of their faces displayed sheer horror, and he heard Arinna let out a weak scream.

He glanced down, and his eyes widened. Danaak's sword penetrated his armor. He felt the tip of the blade pierce his flesh, and cried out in pain as his enemy pushed the blade another inch inside his stomach.

He could have killed me, Excelsior thought. Danaak could have skewered him, his lifeforce would return to his sword, and Matthew Peters would live no more. Why was Danaak not taking this ultimate opportunity? Was he toying with him?

Danaak's blade slid free, and Excelsior's knees buckled. Danaak watched him fall to the concrete floor. His emotionless voice boomed loud enough for everyone on the floor to hear. "Even in your frail mortal form, Excelsior, you will still live. My god does not desire me to send you to follow my beloved."

"I... I don't know... what you are... talking about," Excelsior wheezed, clutching the open wound in his stomach.

"What is done is done," Danaak said. "But there is more to do. My god wants you alive long enough to see me complete my tasks."

"To take... my sword?"

"Actions have consequences, young one," Danaak replied. "If you did not bequeath some of your power, I would have been given a different task."

"Don't give it to him, Matthew," Jason said. He squealed in pain as one of the Krunation soldiers holding him tightened his grip on his shoulder.

"Leave him alone!" Becky ran to one of the Krunations, throwing a punch across its jaw. But before she could pull Jason free, the other Krunation grabbed her by the shirt and shoved her to the ground. Becky's head collided with the barrier.

Danaak nodded at the Krunations. "To answer your question, I am here to take your sword." He then stood up and pointed past Excelsior. "And him."

He was pointing at Jason.

"Me?" Jason asked, his jaw slack.

"No," Excelsior protested with a strained voice. He squeezed his eyes shut. He couldn't fight back. He couldn't save his friends from the Krunations. And he couldn't stop Danaak from bending down and pulling his sword from his grip. The seventeenth floor was suddenly filled with an ethereal glow, and when it faded, the Krunation soldiers and Jason were gone.

Danaak whispered to Matthew as he crouched down in front of him, "Someone wishes to speak with you."

The Krunation's eyes began to glow, and Excelsior's mind was filled with a terrifying voice.

"So it is you."

"Who... who are you?"

"You know who I am, Excelsior. And because of your own actions, a terrible injustice will at last be corrected. Because of your own actions, you will look into the eyes of your loved one and see your enemy staring back at you."

"You... can't... do this."

"Yes, I can. You have denied us both of our battle's end for far too long, and now you must pay the price for your folly."

The glow in Danaak's eyes faded, and he stood up with a sword in each hand. "You will find your own way to Denab IV, Excelsior. When you do, prepare yourself. He will be waiting for you." Another burst of light appeared, and Danaak was gone. Matthew rested his head back on the floor. Blood slowly leaked from his wound, and his eyes glazed over.

"Jason?" he heard Becky call out. No answer. "Jason? Where are you?"

"What is... Matthew?" Arinna crawled to him and laid his head in her lap. "Matthew, speak to me."

"My fault," Excelsior whispered as his hands reached for his stomach. "I'm sorry... Jason."

Arinna pulled his hands away and tried to ease him to his feet. "Matthew, we have to get up. Becky, please help me. We have to get back to the communicator."

Becky pressed the down button on the elevator, then grabbed Excelsior's backpack and helmet. She stuffed the helmet in the pack, zipped it up, and strapped it to her back. Then, working together, Arinna and Becky eased Excelsior back to his feet and into the waiting elevator.

CHAPTER
FORTY-THREE

"Prepare yourself, Hodera. Victory is at hand for my vessel has arrived!"

A chill shot up Hodera's spine as she looked away from the console to see the Leap of Faith doorway activate once more.

She kept herself close to the console, despite the constant urge to walk up to the door of the chamber and watch her Krunation soldiers fighting off the two Denarian squadrons. The only two things keeping her there were her faith in Sivtra to cripple the Denarians' military, and Tornatrax rewarding her for her patience. So she took solace in listening to the carnage as the screams from the Denarians grew louder. Then, one by one, they fell silent.

Hodera reached the very limit of her patience when she heard a beautiful word from Nosgood. "Retreat!"

The timing of the Denarians' defeat was perfect since the light from the Leap of Faith burst from the doorway as the Krunations roared in victory outside. Hodera rubbed her hands together and watched her two Krunation soldiers walk through with Jason in their grasp.

"Where am I?" Jason asked.

Hodera approached Jason and grabbed him by his hair, inspecting his frail human form. "Much smaller than I expected."

Jason looked up and down at the Krunation general, and his mouth dropped open. "Hodera? You're General Hodera? And I'm on… Denab IV?"

"Ahhh, you know of us. Then you should be honored to know you are to be the recipient of the greatest force of power in the known universe."

"The what?" Jason's eyes bulged, and she could felt the fear rolling off him.

"Oh yes," she said, the volume in her voice raising with excitement. "Tornatrax is approaching our planet, and we will await his arrival together on the highest mountaintop." She took a step back from Jason, pointing her arms to the chamber's ceiling. "We will release his lifeforce from his prison, and through your sacrifice, he will be reborn to reclaim what has been so unjustly stolen from him!"

"No! Take your hands off of me."

Her eyes narrowed as she stepped forward again and backhanded Jason across the face. His head fell forward, and he lost consciousness.

"Fear not, my Lord. He is unharmed," Hodera said. "Now, where is your associate?"

"He is here, General."

Hodera's smile faded, and she folded her arms across her chest as the two Krunations stepped aside and Danaak walked through the doorway, still holding both swords. "Danaak. Alive, once again. This is, I believe, your third attempt to do something right?"

"Your kind words bring a smile to my face, Hodera," Danaak said, face grim. "Nocterar proved he had quite the sense of humor when he named you a high-ranking officer."

"Only because Nocterar knew I would do whatever it took to bring total victory to the Krunation Empire," she snapped. "I did not have to lurk about in the background and steal leadership when the opportunity presented itself."

Danaak shook his head. "Then you do not know what it means to be a Krunation."

"And you do?"

"I did," Danaak said. "Once. That Danaak is gone."

She cocked her head in confusion. "Then who is this being before me who wears the skin of the treacherous Danaak?"

"Someone who has grown tired of this constant conflict between Denarians and Krunations. Someone prepared to do one final bidding for his master before he can be reunited with the peace only death brings."

"Peace," Hodera said, shaking her head and sneering. "If you were not selected by Tornatrax to accomplish this mission, I would have cast you out as I did Connoram."

"Such contempt behind your eyes." Danaak stepped toward her. "Maybe now, after all this time, I can see why Nocterar took pleasure in watching you in battle."

"And now you see why we are victorious," Hodera replied. "You hear the cries of conquest outside, do you not? They are because of the warriors entrusted to me to pull from the waters of Denab IV. They have not only taken the Leap of Faith, but only a few moments ago, they successfully defended it from two Denarian squadrons, and they will continue to defend it against all intruders. They are aching for a final victory, and I am the one to give it to them."

"The final victory will only come when Tornatrax kills Excelsior," he corrected her. "And to make it a reality, he must return to Denab IV. Arinna is with him."

Hodera's eyes widened and she smiled. "Ahhh, the young ambassador saved by Semminex. I remember her well."

"Thanks to her gift, she will bring Excelsior back, but once they have returned, your underlings may do what they wish with her. And Excelsior has already been injured, so the battle should be a brief one."

"Injured?"

"He did not just hand me this," Danaak said, holding up Excelsior's sword.

Once again, Danaak held an advantage over her. Yes, she accomplished much, but he wounded Excelsior for a second time. She didn't do that. Nocterar didn't do that. Not even Tornatrax did that. An accomplishment like this could threaten her status.

Danaak must have seen the gears in her head turning because he added, "No one else needs to know of my achievement. I do not wish to wrest control over the Empire from you."

Reaching out, she wrapped her hand around the handle of Excelsior's sword. The two looked each other in the eye as neither one loosened their grip.

"You do not wish to wrest control? Then give me the sword," she whispered with pure contempt. She despised even having to stand so close to her rival. When he didn't answer, she yanked her arm back to try to pry it from his hand, and he released his grip. Hodera stumbled back and slammed the sword's blade into the floor to keep from falling down, then stood up straight and adjusted her uniform.

"You wanted to see me stumble?" she asked.

"I have a suspicion it will not be the last time I see that," Danaak answered.

Hodera snarled at Danaak one more time, then walked toward the broken doors. With one hand, she pried one of the doors open and exited the chamber. Pushing away her impatience with Danaak, she smiled at her beloved soldiers, all standing straight and ready for their next instructions. Their murmurs and grunts fell silent when she strode out to greet them, and even though these young lifeforms had never seen Excelsior's sword before, they must have known what it was. When she held it over her head in triumph, they let out a collective roar.

"We are victorious! As Tornatrax approaches Denab IV, we can feel his influence growing stronger within us all, and we now possess the means for our Lord's return. And now, we journey to the mountain they call…" She held back her disgust as she said, "Klierra Peak. And while you, my loyal subjects, keep any additional Denarians away, we will ascend to the very top and await Tornatrax's arrival.

And we will descend with our Lord ready to resume the battle Excelsior prematurely ended so long ago. At long last, we shall have victory!"

The Krunations raised their fists in the air and let out another roar as one. Hodera pointed to Klierra Peak and shouted, "Prepare yourselves, my friends! The Denarians' military resources have been compromised. Excelsior has been wounded. And it is only a matter of time before he returns to Denab IV. I depend upon all of you to guard this chamber, and when he dares to come through it, you may do whatever you please with anyone who accompanies him."

The Krunations murmured amongst themselves, an excited buzz flitting through the crowd.

"Excelsior must be brought to Klierra Peak, and when he arrives, Tornatrax will be waiting for him." She pointed the sword at the mountain and cried out, "To victory!"

Behind her stepped Danaak and the Krunations holding Jason, and the army of Hodera's minions cleared a path for all of them and Hodera to lead the march toward Klierra Peak.

"I can feel you approaching, my Lord," Hodera whispered. "And we are ready to greet you."

CHAPTER
FORTY-FOUR

As the Libeli carrying Charak, Zorribis, and Niterra descended from the air and landed safely on the ground outside the Nocteris stronghold, Niterra let out a loud gasp when she saw the ashy remains of Krunation soldiers.

"Oh, no," she said, grabbing her rifle. "Do you think he is still alive?"

"He has to be," Charak said, obvious worry in his voice.

Zorribis climbed off the Libeli and helped Niterra down as well. "We were instructed to bring him back," he told Charak. "Stay here with the Libeli."

The Krunation nodded. "Be safe."

Zorribis and Niterra ran through the broken doors, then down the empty halls of Nocteris, stepping over pieces of the Krunation stronghold's walls and ceilings.

"Connoram?" Zorribis called out, and almost tripped over a motionless Krunation body at his feet. Then he saw another several feet past him. And another. He bent down to examine them, since they weren't disintegrated like the ones outside. Their bodies were covered with deep slashes and their necks had holes in them Zorribis recognized as bite marks from Hodera's new army. The two Denarians exchanged worried glances and picked up speed.

"There seems to be more damage in this sector of the building," Niterra said. "I would assume Hodera arranged an ambush against him and his men."

"Connoram?" Zorribis called out again, trying to stifle the worry in his voice.

"Here!" An unfamiliar, raspy old voice called out.

"Who is that?" Niterra whispered. They followed the echoing voice, their blasters at the ready.

When they reached the end of one particularly winding hallway, they saw a rubble-ridden doorway with a low light coming from it. Zorribis whispered, "Connoram's quarters."

He began walking over the debris blocking their path, but Niterra grabbed him by his shoulder. "It could be a trap," she reminded him. "Keep your weapon drawn. I will stay out here."

Zorribis placed his hand over hers and gave it a squeeze, nodding. She pulled her hand away to let him step inside. He entered the large living quarters and gasped when he saw the level of destruction at the hands of Hodera's soldiers.

Tables were overturned, computer consoles were smashed into pieces, various pages of parchment were torn up and lying on the floor, and the large bed was titled on its side. There was even a huge hole in the floor past the fenced area leading to Connoram's pet throngar.

Zorribis followed the burning stench filling his nose, and his stomach dropped when he saw the charred remains of the large Sancterrum tree. He ran his fingers along the trunk, then sniffed them. His nose turned up at the chemical smell from the tree.

"The Krunation is here," the old voice said once again. Zorribis turned toward the source of the voice, both hands on his pistol, but when he saw who called out to him and Niterra, he slowly lowered his arms.

An old Denarian male sat on the floor. Connoram lay beside him, unconscious, and the man was using rags to bandage the Krunation's wounds. A small light was beside him, providing enough illumination for the old man to do his job effectively.

"How could they have burned this?" the old man asked, pointing at the destroyed Sancterrum tree. "I thought it was not possible for a Sancterrum tree to be harmed."

"If there is one thing at which Hodera excels, it is finding ways for indestructible things to be destroyed." Zorribis cocked his head left and right at the old man, as though his memory were a marble being led from one end of a three-dimensional puzzle to the other. "I have seen you somewhere," he said.

The man sitting on the floor had a long, gray, unkempt beard with stringy hair, and his torn and dirty robes suggested they were white and clean a long time ago.

"Yes, you have," the old man said, tying another bandage to Connoram's right arm. "I was one of the witnesses to your bonding ceremony."

"I remember now. You were trying to help when Hodera's soldiers attacked."

The man nodded and regarded Zorribis with sunken, tired eyes. "Please allow me to apologize for my behavior. I understand I was quite erratic. I had undergone a great deal of trauma because of the Krunations, and knowing they were near—"

"I understand," Zorribis said. "What is your name?"

The man opened his mouth to answer, but nothing came from his lips. The silence hung in the air for a long moment. "I... I do not know," he said. "Whatever identity I had... Whoever I was... it was taken from me."

"By the Krunations?" Zorribis asked. At the man's nod, he said, "And you know they were the ones responsible?"

"Yes," the man said. "The first sensation I remember is the tip of Danaak's blade in my midsection. The first memory I have is of Nocterar's voice, ordering my exile to the forest and assuring me Danaak would force his blade further if I should ever return."

"Nocterar let you live?"

"It was a surprise to me as well," the man answered. "Whatever state I was in, it must have been a fate worse than death."

Zorribis reined in his emotions. Hearing someone else's horror stories about Krunation tyranny brought up flashbacks of his own: his mother and father being exterminated by Hodera, Krunation soldiers chasing after him, and Connoram showing mercy by allowing him to seek shelter without pursuit.

"If this is what you know of the Krunations, then why are you here?" Zorribis asked.

"Because I know this one is different," the man replied. "During the time I spent in the forests, this particular

Krunation saw me several times, but he never ordered an attack. Any time one of his soldiers saw me, he ensured I was left alone. There were even several instances where food was left where he knew I would find it."

Zorribis nodded. "Sounds like Connoram."

"Because... it... is."

The old man and Zorribis turned toward Connoram, who started to stir. He slowly opened his eyes, rose, and surveyed the wreckage of his living quarters.

"Hodera did this," Connoram confirmed with tears in his eyes and a considerable limp in his stride. "She has been looking for any opportunity to destroy everything here. My work, the Sancterrum tree, the..." He walked toward the large hole in the floor. "The throngar."

"The hole was already there when I arrived," the old man said, getting to his feet. "There was no noise coming from below."

With a surprising nimbleness, Connoram scaled the fence blocking the Denarian wildlife from the rest of his quarters. He perched himself on top and pushed off, clearing the hole in the ground, and landing on his uninjured side with a hard thud.

"Are you all right?" Zorribis asked.

Connoram pushed himself to his feet and winced, holding his left shoulder and rotating his arm. "It has been a long time since I was this spry." He looked down the hole and dropped to his knees, slamming his fist on the floor.

"Is it...?" Zorribis asked, but the tears welling up in Connoram's eyes provided his answer.

"She was so peaceful," Connoram said, shaking his head.

"The Libeli is safe," Zorribis said. "Charak is outside with it."

Connoram turned to Zorribis. "Charak is safe?"

"He saved us. Likely from the same Krunations who attacked you. We have been asked to bring you back with us. Only you and Charak. The Elders believed us when we said you were not responsible for the attack on Acerus."

Connoram wiped his eyes. "We will go with you. But first, Hodera's army must be stopped. If we allow them, they will continue to unleash destruction on anyone standing against her, Denarian and Krunation alike."

"I know where they were going," the old man said. Zorribis and Connoram turned to stare at him. "The Leap of Faith."

"We disposed of several, with Charak's help."

Connoram nodded. "He has learned well. There is some of his father in him after all."

"Danaak?" Zorribis asked. "You say it like it is a good thing."

The side of Connoram's mouth quirked up. "You did not know him while Charak's mother was still alive." He turned back toward the Sancterrum tree and caressed its dead trunk. "I miss them both."

"We need to get to the Leap of Faith. Excelsior and Arinna are still on Earth. Once the chamber is freed from Hodera's grasp, we can contact him and maybe even retrieve him if he has accomplished his mission." Zorribis looked at the old man. "I would bring you back with us, but we barely have space for Connoram on the Libeli."

The old man held up a hand. "Connoram is alive. I have done what I needed to do."

Connoram pointed toward the overturned bed. "You may rest here if you like."

The old man shook his head and walked toward the exit. "Better to be on my own in the sanctuary of the forests than wait here for death at Hodera's hand." He bowed his head to Zorribis and Connoram. "I will pray to our god you are successful."

"I would pray the same," Connoram said. "But my god hopes we are not."

CHAPTER FORTY-FIVE

"**M**atthew."

The sound of Arinna's panicked voice, and her gentle slaps to his face, kept Excelsior from fading into unconsciousness. He felt two bodies hoisting him to his feet and leading him out of the elevator onto the 67th floor of Rockefeller Center. He looked to his left and saw Arinna trying to keep her composure, then looked to his right and saw Becky shaking with fear, tears streaming down her cheeks.

"I'm… I'm…" Excelsior sputtered to Becky.

Arinna squeezed his shoulder. "Matthew, please don't speak. We need to get back to Denab IV." She led the three of them to the crystal wall in the now-abandoned party room.

"Kru… nations."

Arinna nodded. "I know. We must get to the communicator first. It won't help us to return and suddenly face an armada of Krunation soldiers with their weapons aimed at our heads."

She gently pulled herself away from Excelsior, and Becky laid him down on the stage, cradling his head and using a nearby tablecloth to cover his wound.

Arinna placed her hand on the communicator, and Excelsior's mind was suddenly filled with her voice. "Elder Lokris, can you hear me?"

"No," he forced out, turning his head toward Arinna. "Zor... Zorribis."

She placed her hand back on the communicator and concentrated again. "Zorribis. Zorribis, can you hear me?"

"Anything?" Becky asked.

Arinna shook her head. "He is not an Elder. It is likely he will not hear me."

"Keep... trying," Excelsior wheezed.

"Matthew, please," Becky said, tending to his wound. "Shhh."

Arinna shot him another worried glance, then tried again. "Zorribis, this is Arinna. We are reaching out to you from Earth. We need your help. Please respond." Nothing. She pressed harder on the communicator and squeezed her eyes shut. "Please, Zorribis, my friend. Please respond. We need your help."

"Arinna?"

Excelsior could hear his friend's voice in his head. He exhaled softly and smiled.

"Yes, Zorribis. We can hear you."

"Are you both safe?"

"I am safe. Matthew is injured. We need to return to Denab IV right away."

"We are at the Leap of Faith, Arinna. The Elders warned us it has fallen to Krunation control. Allow us some time to deal with the soldiers surrounding the chamber."

The communicator went silent. Arinna pulled her hands away and walked to Matthew. She stroked his hair while Becky wrapped the cloth around his stomach.

"Did you reach them?" Becky asked.

Arinna nodded. "He is trying to free the Leap of Faith from the Krunations. Once he has, we can return home. But I can only know if I am in contact with the communicator, so we need to take Matthew to it right now."

Becky and Arinna got to their feet, easing Excelsior toward the communicator. They laid him down on the floor, and as Arinna pressed one hand on the sphere, she reached out and took Excelsior's outstretched hand.

"The chamber is secured," Zorribis said. "You are cleared to proceed."

Arinna looked to Becky. "They are ready for us now. We have to leave."

"Here," Becky said, pulling off her backpack and handing it to Arinna. "Please promise me you'll send Jason back," she said with fresh tears coming down her face. "Please."

"I promise you," Arinna said. She slung one backpack strap over her shoulder and squeezed Matthew's hand. "Time to go home, Matthew. Our home."

A bright light shone in Arinna's eyes, then cascaded throughout her entire body, wrapping itself around Matthew. The light grew brighter and more intense, and suddenly Becky was the only person in Rockefeller Center.

CHAPTER FORTY-SIX

"**L**ook!"

Keeping a firm grip on the Libeli, Zorribis motioned with his head beyond the Leap of Faith chamber. He sat between Charak–who was positioned on the back of the majestic creature with Hodera's prototype weapon on a strap slung over his shoulder–and Niterra, who was behind Connoram.

Niterra glanced over her shoulder.

"Do you see them?" Zorribis asked.

"Yes," Niterra answered. "Why are they walking away from the Leap of Faith?"

The Libeli softly dipped in altitude, and Zorribis could see Hodera flanked by several Krunation soldiers. Behind her, two soldiers were carrying an unrecognizable humanoid dressed in a black and white suit.

"They must have gotten what they wanted," Connoram said. "Or who they wanted. They have a prisoner with them."

"Someone from Earth," Zorribis confirmed. "The outfit is similar to what I have seen there."

Suddenly, both Connoram and Charak gasped. Niterra placed a hand on Connoram's shoulder. "Are you alright?" she asked.

"It cannot be," Connoram whispered while pointing to one specific Krunation staying several feet away from the marching army.

"Impossible!" Charak exclaimed, his voice suddenly in a panic. "He is alive!"

"Danaak," Connoram said. "My son."

"Danaak and Hodera are working together?" Niterra asked. "We need to stop them. Is there a way—"

"No more room on the Libeli," Zorribis said. "If we attempt a rescue, we could not guarantee safety for their captive."

"He is correct," Connoram said, his voice still shaken. "We are here to liberate the Leap of Faith from Krunation control. With Hodera and Danaak away from it, our chances of success have increased."

"Zorribis, this is Arinna. We are reaching out to you from Earth. We need your help. Please respond."

Zorribis nearly fell from the Libeli, and he grabbed the creature's furry scales to keep himself steady. He could hear it start to growl as he tightened his grip.

"He does not like that," Connoram said.

"I apologize," Zorribis said. "I think I heard Arinna's voice. Very faint, but I can hear her."

"She can communicate from Earth?" Niterra asked. "Are you sure it is not some kind of trap?"

"Only one way to find out," Zorribis answered.

"Please, Zorribis, my friend. Please respond. We need your help."

Zorribis squeezed his eyes shut and concentrated. "Arinna?"

"Yes, Zorribis. We can hear you."

"Are you both safe?"

"I am safe. Matthew is injured. We need to return to Denab IV right away."

"By the father of Valertus," Zorribis whispered to himself, then said loudly, "Excelsior is injured. We need to land now."

"Danaak," Niterra said. "He must have fought Danaak."

"Charak, is your weapon ready?" Zorribis asked.

"It is, yes," Charak responded. Zorribis could hear the Krunation shifting in his seat. He shut his eyes and concentrated again. "We are at the Leap of Faith, Arinna. The Elders warned us it has fallen to Krunation control. Allow us some time to deal with her soldiers surrounding the chamber."

"Forgive us, my friends," Charak said in a low whisper.

"Your friends? Those monsters?" Zorribis asked, shocked.

"They are still Krunations," Charak said, then opened fire. Hodera's soldiers dissolved into dust within seconds.

"Land over there," Zorribis instructed, pointing to the familiar-looking rocky terrain. "There are large rocks to shield the Libeli from impending harm."

Connoram obeyed, and the Libeli landed gracefully behind a barricade made of small boulders stacked against each other.

"It feels like I was just here," Zorribis said as he stepped off of the creature, the rest of the group following him. "Grannik, Radifen, Karini, and I used this to attack the Krunations and travel to Earth."

With all of their weapons drawn, they crept up to the entrance of the Leap of Faith doorway. Niterra slowly pushed the door open and peeked inside.

Empty.

"This is too easy," she said, walking around the chamber, looking for possible snipers.

Zorribis walked in behind his beloved and scanned the area, his pistol held out and ready. "I think we are alone," he said. "We should get them back now." He closed his eyes and concentrated again. "The chamber is secured. You are cleared to proceed."

"If Excelsior and your friend are in danger, they will need medical assistance," Connoram said. "Take him to your home on the Libeli."

"What about you and Charak?"

"Trust us." He motioned to Charak, and the two Krunations headed in the direction of Nocteris.

"What do you think they are planning?" Niterra asked.

Before Zorribis could answer, the Leap of Faith flashed to life and filled the chamber with its illuminating energy. The two Denarians turned around and watched as two beams of energy appeared and took humanoid form. When the light faded and the inter-planetary doorway closed, Arinna was kneeling on the floor with Excelsior lying beside her.

"We are here, Matthew," Arinna said, gazing down at the wounded young man clutching his stomach.

"Matty!" Zorribis cried. He sheathed his weapon and ran to his friend. Dropping to one knee, he gently pulled Excelsior's hand away from his stomach. "Oh no," he gasped. "What happened?"

"Danaak," Arinna answered. "We saw his corpse. He was dead. And now he is alive again."

"My... fault," Excelsior whispered as he faded in and out of consciousness.

"What is he saying?" Niterra asked as she knelt beside Zorribis. "His fault?"

"He keeps saying that. Blaming himself for his loved one being taken."

"Loved one?" The answer suddenly came to Zorribis. "Jason? They have Jason?"

"You know him?" Arinna asked.

"Yes. A good man. He helped us so much on Earth." He looked back down at the wound. "Matty, can you hear me?"

"I'm.... sorry. I'm sorry... Jason."

"Matty, listen to me. We will take care of you, and then we will all get Jason back." Zorribis took Excelsior's hand and squeezed it. "Do you understand me?"

"I..." Excelsior's eyes stared at Zorribis, but then he looked past his friend and his mouth curled into a smile. "I can?" he asked, nodding his head. "Okay." He let out a soft breath and closed his eyes.

Arinna looked up at Zorribis, stunned. "Is he...?"

Zorribis placed his hand on Excelsior's chest and felt it moving up and down. He let out a sigh of relief. "No," he said. "No, he is still with us. At least in body. We need to take care of him right away. Please help me with him."

"I know how to mend the wound. Where will we go?" Arinna asked, grabbing Excelsior's legs while Zorribis tucked his hands under his shoulders and lifted his friend.

"Back to our home in the Edenarian village," Zorribis answered as Niterra opened the door and walked out ahead of them, her weapon drawn in case of any sneak attacks.

"Are you sure?" Niterra asked. "Our neighbors will not be very pleased to see us."

"No time to worry," Zorribis answered. "He will get the rest he needs there."

"What do you mean, your neighbors will not be pleased?" Arinna asked.

"I can explain later," Zorribis said. "Come. We have transportation. And we need to contact Lokris immediately."

CHAPTER
FORTY-SEVEN

"There it is, Armfather."

Charak and Connoram managed to avoid any further confrontations with Krunations as they reached the area where the young soldier initially rescued Zorribis and Niterra. He pointed toward Zorribis and Niterra's immobilized aircraft.

Connoram ran past Charak and examined the console. "Not much damage, thankfully," he said. "A very basic setup. Zorribis said he made the alterations on his own as a personal project. Very impressive."

"Can you repair it?" Charak asked, circling the aircraft and keeping an eye out for any lingering Krunations.

"Not just repair it," Connoram said. "I can improve upon it, with your help."

"Behold, my friends. We have arrived."

Hodera outstretched her arms in delight as her crew of loyal soldiers, as well as the indifferent Danaak and abducted Jason, arrived at the mountain standing over all of Denab IV. This was the place. This was where it would all begin.

"You have made me very proud, Hodera," the voice of Tornatrax echoed in her head.

The female Krunation felt as though she could pick up this entire mountain by herself and hurl it in the direction of the Edenarian village. She gave a quiet chuckle as she imagined this coming to pass. But what was actually about to happen was even better than watching them be squashed in an instant.

Hodera held her head up and shouted, "I am ready for you, my Lord. We have the sword. We have your vessel."

Jason gulped loudly at the mention of "vessel."

"Yes, child. I am growing closer with each passing moment. And now the task before you is to hold the sword up high, higher than anything on this planet, and allow the energy stolen from me to activate. It will draw me to you."

"It shall be done, Lord. I allow you to lift me up so I may bring you to glory."

"No."

Her arms dropped to her side. "No?"

Hodera heard a stifled laugh behind her and darted around to see Jason gritting his teeth. Her hands clenched into fists. If this were any other person, she would have taken his head for daring to look at her differently. But her glare was enough to stop his laughing.

"My power in the sword will not activate until you reach the top of the mountain. You must climb, my dear."

The directive pierced Hodera's ego as she looked past Jason and saw Danaak approaching the captured human. "What about Danaak?"

"What about me?" Danaak asked. The energy surrounding his chest wound began to glow.

"The energy used to locate and revive Danaak flows within him. He will meet you at the top of the mountain," Tornatrax instructed.

Hodera unsheathed Excelsior's sword and held the blade up to Danaak. "What will stop me from cutting into you and taking the energy for myself?"

"Me," Danaak answered, unsheathing the sword he used to defeat Excelsior.

"Enough!"

The voice of Tornatrax boomed in both of their heads, and Hodera and Danaak took a step away from each other, lowering their swords and bowing their heads in pain.

Jason moved away from the two Krunations, but Danaak grabbed him by the back of his neck to keep him from escaping.

"Believe me when I say this," Danaak told Jason. "You will want to hold on to me. And you will not want to let go." He glanced at Hodera and said, "Make haste."

Danaak's feet left the ground, and he began to rise into the air. Jason wrapped his arms around Danaak's waist, and his eyes clenched shut.

"Don't look down," he whispered. "Don't look down."

Hodera choked back her disdain. She envisioned this moment ever since she first made contact with Tornatrax. Feeling his power flowing through her and lifting her off the ground, taking her all the way to the top of Klierra Peak, looking down at the puny lifeforms and basking in the power of Tornatrax as he made his glorious return.

She clenched her teeth and squeezed the handle of Excelsior's sword. "As you wish, my Lord," she said, continuing to trust what got her this far. She slid the sword into her sheath, then took a deep breath, dug her fingers into the rocky wall, and began to climb.

CHAPTER
FORTY-EIGHT

"I left as soon as I was contacted."

Lokris stood in the doorway of Zorribis and Niterra's home, and he stepped aside to allow her to enter. "Please come in," he said.

As she crossed the threshold into the small house, the large insect circling the ceiling and providing illumination changed color from a deep blue to a bright yellow. She looked up at the insect and smiled.

"It can sense a comforting presence," Zorribis said. "How is Acerus?"

"Fading too quickly," Lokris said. "The atmosphere has not been kind to him. Not to any of the Elders. In time, you will feel the same effects as we do. The aching. The fatigue."

"With your help, maybe these effects will not be felt by us for a long time."

"I hope you are correct. Where is Excelsior? And the others?"

"Excelsior and Arinna are in our sleeping quarters. Niterra is outside in the back. Would you like some water?"

"Yes, thank you," Lokris said as she walked into the room.

Excelsior lay still on the bed in the middle of the room, his eyes shut and his chest moving up and down in a steady rhythm. His shirt and the thin layer of armor underneath were off and lying on the ground, and a large cloth bandage wrapped around his mid-section. Arinna was sitting beside the bed in a chair, softly stroking his hair. She looked exhausted, and her hands were stained with Excelsior's thick Denarian blood.

"How is he, Arinna?" Lokris asked, placing a hand on the female Denarian's shoulder.

Arinna shook her head. "The wound is dressed and healing. He should have woken up by now, but there is no sign of it."

Lokris walked around the bed and bent down, placing here face mere inches away from Matthew's. She gently pulled up one of his eyelids, revealing Matthew's eyeball twitching back and forth.

"It looks like… It looks like he is reading."

"Reading?" Arinna asked.

"His body may be here with us, but his mind is… elsewhere," Lokris said. "But where?" She let go of Matthew's eyelid and stood up, pacing around the room.

"Elder?" Arinna asked.

Lokris waved her away and closed her eyes. "Where is he?" she whispered. The voice in her head brought tears to her eyes and a smile to her face.

"I am with him, dear sister. He is safe."

"What is it?" Arinna asked again.

Lokris nodded. "My sister," she said. "Klierra. He is with Klierra."

"With Klierra?" Arinna cocked her head. "But she is-_"

"No longer among the living, yes," Lokris answered. "But her blood awakened Excelsior within Matthew. Arinna, did he do or say something before losing consciousness?"

"He kept saying it was his fault. He kept apologizing."

"But then he stopped apologizing." Zorribis returned to the room with a glass of water in his hand. He handed it to Lokris, who drained it in one gulp.

"What do you mean?" Lokris asked.

"He looked past me and said, 'I can?' Then he said 'Okay' and smiled. That was all."

Lokris nodded and handed the empty glass back to Zorribis. "So something made him smile. Something to provide some kind of relief."

Arinna chimed in, "It might have to do with what he said to me." They both focused on her. "Matthew told me about how he sometimes wishes he never came in contact with the sword, since he would not have any responsibility to Denab IV."

Zorribis nodded. "He said something similar to me before you went to Earth."

"If he shared this information with you, he must trust you," Lokris said. "He may even be fond of you."

"I believe he is," Arinna said, and she reached out and ran her fingertips along the back of Matthew's hand.

"And I sense this is a mutual feeling," Lokris said as her gaze fell onto their hands.

Arinna paused for a moment, then smiled. "Well, there is potential."

"Then you must be the one to bring him back to us. Do you remember what I taught you?" Lokris asked. "The Enterrand Process?" When Arinna nodded, she said, "He has somehow retreated into himself. Use what you have learned to find him. You will likely have help."

"Help?"

"My sister is keeping him safe," Lokris said. "She would not hide him from us."

Arinna placed a chair right behind Matthew's head, sitting down with her knees pressed against the bed and her hands on his forehead.

"He may resist," Lokris explained. "But you must not allow him to stay where he is. We need him now more than ever before."

Arinna nodded, then took a deep breath and closed her eyes.

I hate them all, Hodera thought to herself as she continued her ascent up Klierra Peak. Excelsior. The Denarians. The Elders. The misguided Charak. His useless father Danaak. His treasonous Armfather Connoram. Even the soldiers she'd birthed with the assistance of Tornatrax weren't safe from her contempt because she knew they would outlive her on this planet.

Hodera looked down at her belt. A low humming noise came from the sheathed sword. Was what Tornatrax told her true? Could this ascent be awakening the power within?

The answer came to Hodera as she felt an invisible force pushing her farther up the mountain. She grinned as she thought of Danaak and the human expecting a shriveled up, out-of-breath Krunation greeting them at the top, and instead seeing a fully invigorated general ready to fulfill her destiny. Swinging up her hand, her palm came to rest on a horizontal flat surface. She did it. She reached the top.

Hodera savored the taste of victory as she saw Danaak standing at the top of the mountain beside her. Jason's wrists and ankles were now bound together and he was lying on the rocky surface. Danaak simply nodded to Hodera as she pulled herself up and stood tall on the top of Klierra Peak. She observed her surroundings. There was enough space to accommodate everything she needed at the top, no smaller than her living quarters in Nocteris. With a renewed strength in her arm, Hodera unsheathed the humming sword and held it to the sky.

A moment later, the jewel on the end of the handle flared to life and a beam of energy shot out from the tip of the sword. As the Krunation general held it high, she could hear a distant deep voice calling out to all on Denab IV.

"Yesssssss."

CHAPTER FORTY-NINE

"**W**here am I?"

Arinna opened her eyes and tried to survey her surroundings. Despite the darkness, she could tell she was no longer in Zorribis's and Niterra's sleeping quarters and she was alone. Spreading her arms out, she could feel walls against her fingertips. She groped around, hoping for some kind of light switch, and found one. As soon as the switch was flipped, a bright white light ignited. As her eyes adjusted to the sudden change, Arinna could see she was in the hallway of a house on Earth.

"Margaret?" Arinna called out.

No answer.

"Peg?" she tried again. Still no answer.

At the end of the hallway, the last door on the right slowly crept open. Arinna hurried toward it and pushed it open the rest of the way. She expected to walk into Matthew's bedroom as it was on Earth, and she wasn't disappointed. The bed, the dresser, the desk were all in the same place. But the walls were bare. The early pencil sketches of Excelsior. The various drafts of the Elders. The panels showing Semminex holding the sword and absorbing Excelsior's lifeforce.

All gone.

Arinna crept to the middle of the room and listened for any sign of life.

She let out a low whisper. "Matthew?"

Matthew's closet light switched on, and the door cracked open. Arinna walked to the closet, opened the door all the way, and looked inside.

"Matthew?" she asked again.

The clothes hanging on the closet rod were pushed to the left, and a young boy who looked no more than ten years old sat by himself in a chair with an open textbook in his hand.

"Matthew?"

The boy turned around and cocked his head. "Do I know you?"

Arinna crouched down and looked him in the eye. "You do know me, Matthew. Arinna. We were here earlier today. We were here together in this room. Your grandmother was here. She told you about your trip to the museum. You remember, yes?"

"Trip? To the museum?" he asked. Arinna nodded. "That happened earlier today, but Mom let me stay home."

"Stay home?" Arinna asked.

"Yeah," Matthew said in a nonchalant tone. "I had a bad dream and couldn't get back to sleep. I told Mom I wasn't feeling good, and she said I could stay home."

Arinna shook her head. "No. You did not stay home. You could not have stayed home."

"But I did."

An older male voice spoke behind her. She whirled around and saw someone who looked a lot like the Matthew she knew. He wasn't as tall, and he had a wiry build. She looked back toward the younger Matthew, but he was gone.

The older Matthew said, "I stayed home and went to school the next day. I didn't know what I was going to do with my life, but I knew I needed to buckle down, study hard, and get good grades to get somewhere in life. I got all As." He smiled to himself.

"I got a full scholarship to William & Mary," came an even deeper voice.

She turned back around and faced an older Matthew Peters, one in his early twenties. He wore a gray three-piece suit, and his short hair was slicked back. "And I pursued a law degree."

A silhouette of a thin, long-haired woman came into view beside him. Her back was turned so Arinna couldn't see her face.

"I even got engaged," he said, motioning to the woman.

The words stung Arinna, and her stomach sank. Was this really what he wanted? To give up everything he was and everything he would be to live a normal life and give his heart to this... this ordinary person? Was this his fantasy?

Arinna grabbed the shoulder of the woman standing beside Matthew and turned her around. There wasn't any face. It wasn't hidden in the shadows. There was only an empty void where eyes, nose, and a mouth should have been.

"Please listen to me," Arinna said as she refocused her attention on the now-adult Matthew. He looked at her, so she continued on. "None of this is you. None of this is real. You did not stay home when you were a child. You went to the museum. You heard the sword calling to you, and you answered its call, the first step toward fulfilling your true destiny. You inherited the lifeforce and power of a god! You saved our race from extinction. You ended the reign of Nocterar. You showed our leaders the potential for peace between the Denarians and the Krunations for the first time in their history. And..." She glanced back to the faceless woman, then to Matthew again. "And there may be no other way to remind you of this."

Before Matthew could protest, Arinna cupped the back of his head, drew him close to her, and kissed him. She kept her lips against Matthew's and wondered, if this didn't wake him up, what would? Would she have to hurt him? Scare him? Destroy the room around them?

Those questions were shoved aside when Arinna felt Matthew kiss her back. His arms wrapped around her, holding her tighter.

Ten seconds passed, and they both broke the kiss at the same time. Matthew opened his eyes and they now glistened with clarity and recognition.

"You..." Matthew struggled to say. "You...found me."

Arinna smiled in relief with a touch of euphoria. "Yes, yes I did. And your people need you now more than ever before."

Matthew looked down at the suit he was wearing. "Why am I wearing this?" He turned toward the faceless woman still standing beside him., "And who is this?"

Before anyone could answer, she vanished completely. Matthew added, "Or, should I ask, who was that?"

"I am sorry, Matthew," another voice from inside the closet said.

"Elder Klierra," Arinna exclaimed.

"You can hear her, too?" Matthew asked.

Arinna nodded, and she gasped when she saw the beautiful older woman with the short red hair stepping out of Matthew's closet. She hadn't seen Elder Klierra since she'd left Denab IV to begin the search for any sign of Excelsior on Earth, and she heard about her death at the hands of Danaak. And yet here she was, dressed in a flowing white gown and standing before both of them without as much as a blemish on her.

"It is good to see you again, Arinna," Klierra said. "And Matthew, I believe you remember seeing me while you were on the floor of the Leap of Faith chamber."

"Yes," Matthew said. "You told me I'd be relieved of any responsibility if I followed you. I could live my life without having ever touched the sword at all."

"Why did you tell him that?" Arinna asked with a frown.

"To keep his consciousness in a place where it could easily be found," Klierra answered, pointing toward Matthew. "His mind has been in chaos ever since Acerus collapsed, his confidence nearly shattered. I am sure you saw this. The constant doubting of himself and his abilities. The belief everything was handed to him and he was not good enough to carry on Excelsior's legacy."

"You helped me get past a lot of it," Matthew said to Arinna. "Doesn't mean they didn't go away completely, and I still want to have our date once we get everything squared away with Jason."

The words fell so easily from Matthew's mouth, as though he never had any problems with his confidence. Arinna smiled. Maybe the kiss shook something loose in him after all.

"Matthew, whatever you felt in the past is no longer relevant. You have returned to your people, and now you must take the necessary steps to save them, as well as your uncle."

"And one of those steps is to learn what's behind all this, right?" Matthew asked Klierra. "It's not just Hodera and Danaak. There's something else behind the scenes, something much bigger than them. Bigger than Nocterar."

"Oh yes," Klierra answered. "Tornatrax is much bigger than Nocterar."

"Yes, Tornatrax," Matthew said. "I know that name, but I don't remember ever writing it on Earth or drawing the character itself."

"And now it is my responsibility to inform you of everything you do not know, Matthew," Klierra replied. "When we are finished, you will be fully aware of what must be done to free this planet of Tornatrax once and for all."

"And you're giving me all this info now? Why?" Matthew asked, giving the late Elder a suspicious glare.

"Because your mind was so focused on repairing the damage to Denab IV, you could not fully process the kind of threat he is. Would it have been adequate to tell you this before you left the planet? Or while you were on Earth?"

"Good point," Matthew said.

The spirit of the deceased Elder pointed to Arinna and said, "You have done well, child. Now you must break this connection and return to those waiting for you. Tell them you have awakened Excelsior's spirit."

"We have very little time, Elder Klierra," Arinna said.

"And when I am finished showing him what he needs to know, he will be sent back to this very moment," Klierra said. "He will be safe, do not worry." She offered her hand to Matthew.

"It's okay," Matthew said to Arinna. "I'll be right there." He pulled his hand away and walked toward Klierra, who beckoned him to follow her inside the closet. As he entered, it slammed shut on its own, and Arinna was alone in the bedroom. She shut her eyes and felt the very familiar whoosh of her consciousness being sucked back into her own body.

The sound of the closet door slamming shut startled Matthew, and he looked over his shoulder in time to see it vanish into the darkness all around him. He stretched out his arms and expected to feel his clothes on hangers, but there was nothing.

"Hello?" he called out.

For a long moment, there was no response until he heard the reassuring voice of Elder Klierra. "I am here, Matthew," she said.

"Where are we?" he asked, eyes darting around and trying to find her in the blackness.

"Where it all began," she answered. "Life, the universe, everything."

"It's so dark," he said.

"In a moment, it will not be. You may want to shield your eyes."

"Why would I want to—"A blinding light cut across his vision. It was so bright, his eyes screamed in pain, and he quickly slapped his hands over them in a vain attempt to give them some sort of reprieve. His ears, however, were spared a similar punishment. "How long do I have to keep my eyes covered?" he asked.

"You may remove your hands now," Klierra answered. "We are not moving in real time."

Matthew lowered his hands, and with the universe now alive and illuminated, he could see Klierra standing beside him, wearing the same white gown as before. "If we aren't moving in real time, why didn't we start after the Big Bang?" he asked.

"Do you know of anyone who could claim they saw the birth of the universe for themselves?" Klierra said.

Matthew shrugged. Point taken.

"I also wanted you to see what happened immediately following the Big Bang." She pointed toward the sky where one silver shimmering orb hung. Beams of energy were pushed out from the orb, and those beams formed smaller spheres firing in all directions.

"What is all this?" he asked.

"The one in the middle is what the people of your planet call God," Klierra answered. "The ones firing outward are the Creators who are charged with developing various star systems. Each Creator was an extension of Himself, gifted with the ability to develop their own ideas and make them into reality."

He looked down at the surface they were standing on, then crouched and ran his hand along the cold dusty ground.

"Where are we now?" she asked.

"We are on a desolate, lifeless rock floating in space, becoming acquainted with its brand-new gravitational pull around a newborn sun." Matthew turned toward a yellow sun glowing brighter. "This rock we are on has settled into its place. There are three others closer."

"So we're on—"

Klierra held up a hand. "Not yet," she said. "This planet does not yet have a name, but it does have a purpose." One of the glowing spheres shot from the center of the universe came to a stop right above them. "And its purpose is about to be realized. Do you recognize it?"

"The sphere?" Matthew asked, confused. "Should I?"

"You should. It is you. That is Excelsior."

Matthew's eyes widened as he came face to face with the original Excelsior.

"Amazing, is it not?" Klierra asked.

Matthew could only nod. "You said this planet's purpose is about to be realized?"

"Oh, yes," Klierra said, alive with excitement. "Its purpose was to be a paradise, a jewel in the very heart of the universe. A living, breathing example of ultimate perfection. Its inhabitants would want for nothing. Its resources would never run dry."

As Klierra spoke, the sphere swept over the planet, leaving in its wake a translucent purple sky allowing the stars to be shown whether it was day or night. Mountains sprung from the ground and positioned themselves in their familiar formations, bodies of water formed, and the temperature rose.

Through it all, Matthew kept his eyes on the radiant sky. "So this is what the sky is supposed to look like," he said. "Before I came here."

Klierra placed a hand on his shoulder. "It will look like this again."

The development of the planet continued as though it were a recording played back on high speed, and Matthew watched with wonder as different forms of plant life sprouted from the ground. The forests gradually appeared in the distance, and blades of grass caressed his feet as they grew from underneath them.

"As the mountains were high enough and the oceans were deep enough, Excelsior felt the time was right to bring life to this planet," Klierra said, and the sound of chattering in the distance prompted both Klierra and Matthew to look over their shoulders and see different men, women, and children walking out of the forest and heading into the nearby waters to hunt for food.

"And they came from the ground as well, right?" Matthew asked.

Klierra nodded. "The first generation, yes. The rest were conceived by couples who found each other, and their children were developed as they are now. Outside of the body, but safe and thriving through the planet's means.

The vegetation. The wildlife. It was all for the people, and they were pleased and grateful for what they had."

"It looks like a worldwide Garden of Eden," Matthew said, impressed with how lush and beautiful everything was around them. "Only not one little garden and there's no forbidden apple on a tree."

"That is what Excelsior would call this planet," Klierra said. "Eden." Matthew shot her a confused look and Klierra nodded. "Yes, Eden. This name was given by God from the center of the universe. He saw the work Excelsior had done and was so impressed with it, He believed there was no better name for a place such as this. And Excelsior was so fond of the name he called the entire star system after it. This was Eden IV. This one giant land mass in the middle of the water was meant to keep the people in continuous contact with each other. The single continent became known among the people as Edenaria."

One group of people soon begat several groups, and then more, and as Matthew watched the planet continue to evolve around him, he smiled at how wonderful Eden and Edenaria were. This was what his home should have been all this time. Heck, this was what Earth should have been.

Klierra continued the story, her voice suddenly somber. "Generations passed with no conflict among the people. But with the planet as wonderful as it was, Excelsior was not aware the seeds of its eventual tragedies lay within himself."

Matthew turned to her. "What do you mean?"

"Look at the center again," she said.

He saw all of the spheres shot from the shimmering orb in the center were now going back into it. "What's happening?"

"Those extensions of God were only meant to be temporary, nothing more than to establish the universe. God Himself would oversee it as it matured."

Matthew nodded, starting to see where Klierra was going. "Excelsior was taking too long."

"Yes," she confirmed. "And by spending so much time overseeing his creation, and endowing so much knowledge to his people, Excelsior began to feel like one of them. He immersed himself in his work so much, he inevitably felt what people on Earth would refer to as one of the Seven Deadly Sins. Pride."

"What did he do?" The ethereal form of Excelsior hung in the air, burning with a glow as bright as the Eden Star System's sun. But once pride was mentioned by Klierra, the orb pulled back from the planet and condensed upon itself.

Klierra continued, "Excelsior tried so hard to suppress this feeling so he could continue his work without any distraction. All he wanted was to make the best possible planet for his people, but he suppressed the pride so deep within himself..."

Matthew gasped when he saw a segment of red and yellow energy within Excelsior separate itself from the source.

"It unexpectedly broke away from him and created its own entity; one filled with the emotions Excelsior sought to keep from his people."

"Tornatrax," Matthew whispered.

Both remained silent as the energy grew larger in size, but instead of taking the form of a sphere like Excelsior, the form of Tornatrax was of a long, twisted line resembling a combination of a serpent and a lightning bolt. It sped toward the planet and struck the very center of Edenaria. The ground rumbled and split into several smaller continents. They all drifted apart from each other, and three smaller islands broke apart from the larger Nelleram, positioning themselves far apart from all of the different continents.

"Tornatrax did not have the capability to create, as Excelsior did," Klierra said. "But what he could do was manipulate. He could pervert what Excelsior already granted life. And as Excelsior sought to create a world and be its guide, an example to follow, Tornatrax believed those on Eden should live as servants to him and should live only to do his bidding. He attempted to corrupt the minds of the men, women, and children, but he was unsuccessful when Excelsior assigned a group of men and women to be his teachers on the planet's surface."

"The Elders," Matthew said.

"Exactly," Klierra said. "Tornatrax could not turn Excelsior's people against him, so he sought to impede their communication with each other by separating the large continent into several smaller ones. And the servants he coveted were in the water surrounding the land."

As Matthew watched, the lesser lifeforms Excelsior created to inhabit the bodies of water on Eden took humanoid form and walked on to the shore of a land mass known as Nocteris. The sphere of Excelsior expanded once again over the planet.

When Matthew returned his attention back to the planet, his mouth fell open in shock. The serene beauty was replaced by burning forests and cries of terror in the distance.

"The first generation of these lifeforms knew only of subservience to their god and his wishes of destruction, and he led them around like the mindless beasts they were. They confined themselves to the most remote areas on the planet, and those who engaged them dubbed the area they called home 'The Cruel Nation.' Tornatrax took that name and declared his beings the Krunation race."

Matthew watched in horror as the battles between the Edenarians and Krunations raged on and took their toll on the planet's resources.

"Excelsior believed he failed his people by allowing this kind of danger to be wrought upon them. And so he considered this jewel to be a cursed planet. A baned planet."

"Baned?" Matthew repeated. "Denab."

"Yes," Klierra said with a nod. "He renamed the planet as a reminder to himself of how he failed in his mission." They both looked up at the sphere pursuing the energy bolt around the planet, causing chaos throughout Denab IV's atmosphere. "This was a time of chaos. Not only on the newly christened Denab IV but within the Kingdom of Heaven inside the orb at the center of the universe. God faced a betrayal by one of his greatest angels—"

"Lucifer," he chimed in. "He tried to de-throne God and was thrown out of Heaven."

Suddenly, the orb emitted a shockwave spreading throughout the universe. The sphere and energy bolt stopped in mid-motion. "What happened?" Matthew asked.

"God declared war would no longer be fought in His Kingdom," Klierra answered. "And so he issued a challenge to both Excelsior and Tornatrax. Both were sent down to the surface of the planet they both claimed for themselves, their lifeforces embedded in swords positioned at opposite poles. Whoever found those swords would be the hosts for these two gods, and they would engage in battle on the surface of the planet until one destroyed the other. The victor would rejoin the one God at the center of the universe knowing their influence would continue on Denab IV. The loser would be cast into oblivion."

Both ethereal forces folded into smaller beams of energy burying themselves into opposite poles on the planet, and suddenly Matthew and Klierra were swept off their feet. He saw the surface they stood on disappear in the distance. Within seconds, they were on the southern tip of Denab IV, and two young men were running to the spot where the energy of Tornatrax touched down. A beautiful jewel-encrusted sword rose from under the ground.

"Are they who I think they are?" Matthew asked, pointing to the two men admiring the sword.

"Candassus and Abrattus," Klierra said. "A rare breed of Denarian and Krunation sharing the same bloodline. Their immediate family lived among a small amount of the population staying away from the war."

"Brothers," Matthew said. "Connoram was right. Our races were closer than we thought."

"Yes, he was," Klierra said. "You were right to trust him."

He watched as the one with smoother skin, Abrattus, touched the sword and became instantly overwhelmed and transformed by its energy. The Denarian dropped to the ground, his body convulsing. The muscles in his arms and legs grew and his chest expanded.

A voice escaped from Abrattus's lips. A voice that was not his own.

A voice Matthew knew.

"Yesssssss."

Klierra continued. "Because Tornatrax's power was so overwhelming, any trace of Abrattus was completely destroyed, replaced by this dark god in human form."

Matthew turned toward Klierra, confused. "The legend said the Krunation touched the sword, not the Denarian."

"Unfortunately, Acerus altered the legend in an attempt to maintain solidarity among the Denarian people."

That revelation struck Matthew like a punch to the chest. "No! I can't believe he would do this. He could communicate with the planet, so he should have told the truth. Excelsior should have... I should have known he would do this before I made him an Elder, much less the High Elder. He was supposed to set an example for everyone."

Klierra saw the pained look on Matthew's face. "Please do not think any less of him. The High Elder fulfilled his obligations and ensured the Denarian people would stay safe during our darkest times."

"But if he didn't do this, there could have been peace between the two species before the rise of anyone like

Danaak or Hodera." He shook his head, wishing he could tell Acerus how disappointed he was. But at the same time, Acerus dedicated his life to keeping his fellow Denarians out of harm's way.

The two watched as the newly reborn Tornatrax grabbed Candassus by the throat, the destructive energy in his hand seeping into the young Krunation, completely vaporizing him. Tornatrax then pulled the sword from the ground and ran to seek his opponent. Matthew and Klierra followed him as he leapt into the air.

"While Tornatrax became familiar with his abilities on Denab IV, a young Denarian allowed the lifeforce of Excelsior to enter his body," Klierra said. Her eyes welled up with tears. "This young man was Valertus, my son. And instead of destroying any trace of him, Excelsior enhanced his virtues and gifted him with powers and abilities beyond any mortal."

Matthew and Klierra saw a young, strong Denarian male pull the sword from the ground and take flight. Klierra pointed toward a large, familiar-looking chamber being constructed not far from the tallest mountain on the planet. "Excelsior returned to his people and immediately set upon teaching his fellow Denarians to be better than what they were, to come together as one and never turn their backs to one another. He also believed the purity in the Denarians' hearts could benefit the rest of the universe, and he created an inter-planetary doorway for them. Acerus said it would require a leap of faith for other races to accept their way of life. Excelsior said this doorway is that leap of faith."

"Wow," Matthew whispered, then wondered. If he was the latest embodiment of Excelsior, then why wasn't he already familiar with everything Klierra told him? He put aside his concerns for the time being as he and Klierra were pushed ahead in time and location.

Klierra set the stage as Matthew watched the humanoid form of Tornatrax approach a Denarian standing tall and proud, holding a sword in his hand. "Finally, the moment came when Excelsior and Tornatrax met on Denab IV and engaged in battle."

The two came at each other with swords drawn, clashing. Matthew could feel Excelsior and Tornatrax attack each other with absolute hatred and contempt. Excelsior hated Tornatrax for smashing his beloved project into something he barely recognized anymore, and Tornatrax hated Excelsior for trying to suppress everything he was, ultimately casting him out and turning his back on the true purpose all gods should have. To be obeyed and worshipped.

"The battle raged on for many days," Klierra said, watching the two battle as day turned to night, then to day again. Giving into rage, Tornatrax lunged forward with his sword, but Excelsior spun around, knocked his adversary's weapon away, and followed through with a thrust of his own, his sword embedded into Tornatrax's stomach.

Matthew flinched while watching this very familiar maneuver. He looked down at his stomach, almost expecting to see Danaak's blade still cutting through his nearly impenetrable armor and resting inside his body.

He turned his attention back to the battle as it reached its sudden end. Excelsior was victorious. Tornatrax was defeated. Matthew watched the face of the fallen Krunation god, and he was amazed at how Tornatrax showed no fear but instead displayed a calm acceptance. A ghost of a smile flickered on his lips. Excelsior held his sword over his head, ready to deliver the killing blow and end Tornatrax's reign of tyranny over Denab IV forever. But to Matthew's surprise, the blow never came. Excelsior lowered his sword.

"What happened?" Matthew asked.

Before Klierra could answer, he saw Excelsior surveying the landscape, gazing up at the starry daylight sky, and then down again at his defeated opponent. A verse from one of Matthew's mother's many cast recording albums cut into his mind. "If you'd come today, you would have reached the whole nation. Israel 4 BC had no mass communication."

"He doesn't want to leave," Matthew deduced. "As soon as he kills Tornatrax, then he disappears and rejoins the collective of God. His influence will heal the planet, but—"

"But he would never be able to come back. He would never see his beloved Denarians again. He would never see the Leap of Faith reach its completion. And he would never see his planet once again reach the potential to be the paradise it was always supposed to be."

The image of Excelsior and Tornatrax faded away, and once again Matthew and Klierra stood together in total darkness. But this time, Matthew could see the deceased Elder looking back at him. The look felt almost accusatory, as he reflected on his thoughts and actions on Earth. How he tried to maintain a connection with his uncle. How he felt jealous of his uncle for taking his webcomic to television. How he wanted to throw away his responsibilities if it meant staying in New York. He didn't remember ever feeling that selfish before. Could this be an unexpected side effect of inheriting Excelsior's lifeforce?

"What did he do?" Matthew asked.

"Excelsior created quite the conundrum for himself," Klierra said. "He did not want to leave the planet he called his, but he also did not want the threat of Tornatrax to plague it anymore. So he fashioned an orb to serve as a prison for Tornatrax's lifeforce, one only Excelsior's sword could penetrate, and he used his sword to extract Tornatrax's lifeforce and inject it into the orb. Finally, he took the orb to the Leap of Faith and cast it into deep space."

"Unfortunately, by creating this loophole, Tornatrax's influence over the Krunations did not decrease. It grew. And because of Excelsior's newfound selfishness, the Krunations attacked and eventually overwhelmed the Denarians. They also took the life of Valertus, returning Excelsior's lifeforce to his sword. And there he remained captive, the two Gods of Denab IV trapped in their own prisons as the Krunations dominated the planet."

Matthew stayed silent as he digested the incredible amount of information given to him. The pieces of the puzzle in his mind clicked into place. He saw himself shaking his uncle's hand and unknowingly putting him in danger. He saw himself standing on the top of Klierra

Peak, and through no intention of his own, taking the stars away from the daylight. And then Matthew remembered lying on the floor, and Danaak telling him he was there for his sword. And Jason.

"This is what you meant, isn't it?" Matthew asked. "When you told me how my mission wasn't complete."

"Yes."

"Tornatrax wants a new body."

She nodded.

The next word felt like torture to say. "Jason."

"At their very core, Excelsior and Tornatrax are one and the same," Klierra said. "He has awakened, and he is approaching Denab IV as we speak. But while his lifeforce is trapped within the orb Excelsior created for him so long ago, his power is still within the sword they now possess."

"And he can sense the Denarian DNA I activated by creating the tether between our planet and his," Matthew added. Klierra's silence confirmed his suspicions. "So basically, all I have to do is free Jason and get the gift back I gave him, while Hodera and Danaak are holding my sword."

"And then you must complete the mission was left unfinished so long ago," Klierra said. "You must destroy Tornatrax, and it will take nothing less than the full power of Excelsior."

"The full power of Excelsior?" Matthew repeated. "But the only way his full power is released anywhere is when…" The next words caught in his throat, and he swallowed them, unwilling to say them out loud. He thought for a long moment, then asked, "What should I do, Mother Klierra? What can I do?"

Matthew yearned for Klierra to say something other than what he feared she would say.

But after a moment of silence, she shook her head." I am in no position to tell you what you have to do, Matthew. You are a leader of these people. You are the savior of Denab IV, and it is your responsibility to make the necessary decisions. That is all I can say."

Klierra held out her arms and beckoned Matthew to her, and the two came together in a tight embrace. Matthew shut his eyes and heard Klierra speak one more time. "I will always be beside you, no matter what you choose. I will remain beside you, and I will keep you safe. Your father and mother would be very proud of you. You are always an inspiration. Never think of yourself as a cautionary tale."

Before Matthew follow up on her statement, she was gone. The dim illumination was gone as well, and for one brief moment, Matthew never felt so alone.

But then he said out loud, "I'm ready to go home," and a blinding bright light enveloped him.

"He is awake."

It hurt for Excelsior to open his eyes, but once he finally did, his vision adjusted to focus on everyone in the sleeping quarters. He looked to his left and saw Lokris standing over him, a relieved smile on her face.

A glance to his right revealed Zorribis nodding his head, his arms crossed over his chest. "I knew you would come back to us, Matty," he said.

He looked up and saw the beautiful face of Arinna gazing down on him. She sat in the chair behind him and was caressing his head. Sweat poured down his face, and he reached for her hand and brought it to his lips.

"She told you what you needed to know?" Arinna asked.

"And more," was all he could say.

CHAPTER FIFTY

"I can feel him," Hodera whispered as she stood on the top of Klierra Peak. The sword of Excelsior was still held high over her head, and the beam of energy continued to pour from the sword into the sky. Danaak stood next to the still-bound Jason and watched the energy radiating from the sword begin to intensify. As Jason trembled in fear of what was to come, Danaak remained stone-faced.

A hot wind blew and black clouds filled the sky. All three looked up and a voice filled the air, one Hodera had heard in her own mind. Until now.

"Yessssssss."

"Armfather, that does not look promising."

Prompted by Charak's exclamation, Connoram looked up from tending to the small aircraft, his gaze shifting toward Klierra Peak where a burst of energy flowed from the very top. Gray and black clouds emitted from above the gargantuan mountain and spread throughout the dim sky. The wind intensified, giving Connoram a chill.

"We need to get back to the Denarians right away," the older Krunation said with a worry in his voice the younger one wasn't used to hearing.

"Is the aircraft operational?" Charak asked.

Connoram reached inside and pressed a button on the repaired console. He let out a sigh of relief the engines slowly began to hum.

"Get inside," Connoram said. Charak did as he was told, and the small aircraft rose from the ground. "I fear we may already be too late."

The shaken, weakened breathing of Acerus echoed through the High Elder's living quarters. Tricerus and Quinterus stood a distance away, both exchanging worried glances.

As the gray and black clouds choked the night sky and Tornatrax entered the atmosphere, Acerus's eyes snapped open, and his breathing became more violent. He opened his mouth and pushed out the words, "He... is... here."

His eyes rolled to the back of his head, and he let out one final breath. Acerus's body relaxed, then began to crumble and dissolve into ash.

After a long silence, the only sound filling the room was Tricerus's weeping.

CHAPTER FIFTY-ONE

"Elder Lokris!"

Zorribis and Arinna hurried to Lokris's side as she put her hand to her forehead and her knees buckled. They caught her before she fell and eased her over to the bed, where Excelsior was sitting up and putting his feet down on the cold floor.

"Are you all right?" Excelsior asked. He walked around the bed and knelt in front of the Elder.

Lokris shook her head. "He is gone," she said.

Silence hung in the room. Arinna choked back tears, and Zorribis bowed his head as he walked out of the room, hands on his hips. Excelsior took Lokris's hand and squeezed it. She squeezed his in return.

The Elder blinked back tears while looking into Excelsior's eyes. "And you? Are you all right?"

Excelsior nodded, and then he looked closer at the Elder's face. "Are those... Are those new wrinkles?"

"I am not worried about them," Lokris answered. "So you should not be. And speaking of eyes, I can see peace behind yours." Smiling, she added, "You saw my sister."

Excelsior smiled back, playing along with Lokris, even though the image of her face growing older and older with each passing minute was going to haunt him. "How do you know?"

"Klierra could always bring peace to the most chaotic of souls. And with the burden you are bearing, seeing you as calm as you are…"

"Tornatrax," Excelsior said. "I can sense him. He's back, and it won't be long before he'll be able to possess Jason. I have to get ready for him."

He grabbed his armor off the floor, stood up, and slipped it over his head. For a moment, Excelsior allowed himself to remember the first time Matthew Peters wore this armor, the moment when he felt both excited and somewhat embarrassed, as though he were one of the thousands of fans littering the halls of the San Diego Comic-Con. But now, with his objective laid before him, he knew he was the right man to save his uncle and stop the threat of Tornatrax. And maybe he could prove to the Elders what kind of a god he was.

"You will need a weapon," Lokris said. "And a simple blaster will not work for what you need to do."

The look they exchanged told Excelsior the Elder knew what was needed of him.

"What is she talking about?" Arinna asked with concern in her voice.

Lokris shook her head, and Excelsior smiled at Arinna. "I'll tell you in a bit. Can you check on Niterra and make sure the Libeli is ready? We'll need it for Jason's rescue." He turned to Lokris. "Hodera will likely summon her forces to Klierra Peak."

"And so shall we," Lokris replied.

Excelsior, wearing his helmet and armor, exited the front door to Zorribis and Niterra's home and saw Zorribis standing still, his head turned toward Klierra Peak. He gave the Denarian and tap on his shoulder, and Zorribis turned and smiled.

"Matty!" Zorribis exclaimed. "How do you feel?"

"Good enough," Excelsior answered. "And you?"

"I needed some air. Acerus..." His throat clogged, and he pushed the incoming tears down. "When I was growing up, he watched over me. He was the father figure I no longer had. Just as Ducera was like a..." The tears flowed down his cheeks.

"He was the father figure to all Denarians," Excelsior said with a nod, choosing not to say anything about what he learned about the late High Elder. "As was Ducera. And Klierra. And Sestera." He looked toward Klierra Peak and saw the clouds around the mountain thickening. "But if we do nothing, their deaths will be in vain."

"So what are we waiting for?" Zorribis asked.

"We're waiting for Tornatrax to get closer. The only way this ends is if he and I face each other, so I need something from you."

"From me?"

"A weapon. Not a blaster. It won't work against Tornatrax. It has to be from the same materials used for my sword."

"I may be excellent at what I do," Zorribis said. "But I cannot create a new sword for you in time to stop—" He looked up. "Wait, I think I may have something." He ran past Excelsior into his home.

Excelsior focused on Klierra Peak again, staring at the top of the mountain. His eyes narrowed as he saw the burst of energy coming from the sword and providing the only bright light in the area.

Suddenly, another object flying in the air grabbed Excelsior's attention. The small, familiar-looking aircraft was manned by two Krunations, and it landed right behind the house where Niterra was caring for the Libeli.

Excelsior walked around the house and saw Charak and Connoram climbing out of Zorribis's now repaired aircraft.

"You found us!" Niterra exclaimed.

"We assumed you lived at the home giving sanctuary to the Libeli," Connoram said.

"Excellent deduction," Niterra replied. "The aircraft is fully functional?"

"Functional enough," Charak said. "But with our help, it can reach its full potential."

Excelsior examined the repair job and grinned at Connoram.

"Welcome back," the older Krunation said. "We were waiting for you."

"You were right about so much," Excelsior said. He extended his hand once again in friendship, and Connoram reached out in return. The two clasped wrists.

"As were you," Connoram replied. He motioned to his younger counterpart. "Allow me to introduce you to my Arm-son, Charak."

"It is my honor, sir," Charak said, holding out his hand in friendship.

Excelsior took it. "The honor is mine. I knew Zorribis and Niterra would find you."

"They found us, yes," Connoram said. "And we went before your Elders, but one of Hodera's soldiers sabotaged the summit. Acerus was badly wounded, unfortunately."

"He died only a few moments ago," Excelsior said, his voice rough. "Another Elder is inside, reaching out to possible reinforcements."

"Then we have excellent timing," Connoram said. "I hold no allegiance to Hodera or the rest of the Krunation Empire under her leadership. Her soldiers are nothing more than mindless beasts. My soldiers were as strong in mind and spirit as they were in body. They took a great risk by aligning themselves with me, and I want their deaths to mean something."

Excelsior nodded. "I know what you mean. And I would like you, Charak, and Zorribis to join me on the Libeli at the top of Klierra Peak. Now, I understand the altitude is dangerous to Denarians, but it should be fine for Krunations, right?"

Connoram nodded. "Yes. And since there is this atmospheric shift taking place, I do not think they will be affected by such high altitudes."

"Good. I'll need your help to rescue my uncle. They're gonna use him as the new host for Tornatrax."

"We will be there for whatever you need," Connoram said, and he straightened himself up to stand as tall and proud as he could before the savior of Denab IV.

"As will I," said a voice behind Excelsior. He turned around and saw Zorribis holding a silver dagger in his hand. "Will this be an adequate weapon?"

Excelsior took it from Zorribis's hand and examined it. "This was your Bonding gift from your clan, wasn't it?" he asked. He looked closer at the sharp blade—the last remaining materials used to create Nocterar's sword—and saw the engraving of ancient Denarian hieroglyphics meaning "Never Again." When Zorribis nodded, Excelsior said, "This will be perfect."

"The Libeli is fed and ready," Arinna said, walking into view. She turned toward Excelsior. "May I speak with you for a moment?"

"Sure," he said. The two of them walked around to the front yard, and Arinna said, "Zorribis, Connoram, and Charak. Those are the three you want on the Libeli?"

"Yes."

"Why?"

"Connoram rescued the Libeli, so he would keep it steady while we're up there. Charak is an excellent shot with the weapon he took from Hodera. And Zorribis knows Jason and will be a familiar face to him after everything he's gone through."

"And I do not know Jason?" Arinna asked. "The Libeli can fit four people. I can help as well, and you can bring Jason down with you."

"No," Excelsior said in a stern tone of voice. "There needs to be room for Jason in case…"

The words hung in the air, daring one them to speak them. Finally, Arinna said, "In case you will not survive."

Excelsior nodded.

"So what would you like me to do while you are on Klierra Peak with the others?"

"Honestly? I'd like you to stay as safe as possible. I'm sure Hodera's going to send her army after everyone else on the ground."

"Do not worry about me," Arinna said. "I have been through enough. I will be fine."

"Right. You've been through enough. You survived being held captive by Danaak and Hodera; you went on to become a wonderful ambassador to our planet, and if we actually have our date, who knows what'll happen after that?"

Arinna stepped closer to Excelsior and said, "Promise me one thing."

"What?" he asked.

"Promise me you will do what you need to do with that," Arinna said, pointing to the blade in his hand. "And come back safely so we can have that date."

Excelsior hesitated. "I promise I'll do what I need to do."

"And come back safely," she repeated.

"Excelsior!" Zorribis yelled, pointing toward Klierra Peak. Excelsior and Arinna both turned and looked up at the sky. They were now in total darkness. The stars disappeared from sight, with the only real illumination coming from the energy in Excelsior's sword and the orb peeking out from behind the clouds. "Whatever you need to do, now is the time."

"The Libeli is ready for you," Excelsior said to Zorribis. "You, Connoram, and Charak will meet me at the top. The reinforcements should be at the bottom very soon." He turned back to Arinna and said, "I have to go."

Arinna gave him a tight hug and said, "Promise me you will be careful."

"I promise… I promise you will see the stars again." Arinna let out a slight laugh, and Excelsior smiled while taking a step back. He slid the blade into his belt and began walking toward Klierra Peak.

"Ever Upward!" Connoram shouted to him as he walked past.

"Ever Upward!" the rest of them chanted.

Excelsior turned back toward the Krunations and Denarians ready to fight for him and held up his fist. "Ever Upward!" Turning back toward the mountain in the distance, he broke into a run. As he ran, he allowed the familiar images to flood his mind.

The mountains.

The bodies of water.

The Leap of Faith.

The Denarian clans.

The Elders.

Jason.

Arinna.

He felt his feet leave the ground, and suddenly he was flying. He straightened his arms against his body as he accelerated, racing to Klierra Peak, and to the voices which almost crippled him the last time he stepped on the mountain's surface. The closer he got, the louder the screams of the Denarian ghosts became.

"Please," Excelsior said from within his mind. "I promise you will have your justice if you allow me the time I need."

For a moment, the screaming grew louder, but then—as suddenly as they started—they subsided. He breathed a sigh of relief as he continued his journey to Klierra Peak.

To Tornatrax.

"Excelsior is approaching," Danaak informed Hodera, who still held the sword high over her head, her gaze locked on the overcast sky above. "His Denarians will not be far behind."

"Then our soldiers will be waiting for them." Her eyes glowed and she whispered, "Come, my children. Denarians are coming to Klierra Peak. Ultimate victory is at hand."

CHAPTER FIFTY-TWO

"**N**osgood."

While soaring above the Leap of Faith, Zorribis spotted the defeated squadron of Denarian soldiers hiding inside the forest three tronks away. He directed Connoram to steer the Libeli down outside the forest. Arinna, Niterra, and Lokris were close behind on Zorribis's now-functioning aircraft.

Once they were all on the ground, Zorribis waved to the squadron and showed himself to them, shooing away Nosgood's drawn weapon aimed at Connoram and Charak. "Nosgood," he said. "Lower your weapon. They do not mean any harm." He kept himself on top of the Libeli—sandwiched between Connoram and Charak.

Nosgood's jaw dropped, and he lowered his weapon when he saw the creature they were riding. "I have never seen a creature like this! Where did it come from?"

"Another time," Zorribis answered. "For now, we should only be concentrating on Hodera. Look!"

Nosgood and his soldiers turned toward the Leap of Faith and saw the Krunations walking away from it.

"Whatever is left of her army is leaving to form a barricade between us and Hodera," Zorribis said. "I assume you received Lokris's latest communication to stay close, so we can all move on to Klierra Peak together."

"Correct," Nosgood confirmed. "We suffered too many casualties during the attack on the Leap of Faith. Hodera must have unlimited soldiers at her disposal. When one was struck down, three more were in its place. If there is a chance to avenge our fellow Denarians, we will be the ones to take it."

"Then you and Niterra can lead the attack on the ground."

Niterra smiled and leapt from the aircraft, her blaster at the ready. She exchanged a loving glance with Zorribis and mouthed, "Thank you."

Zorribis nodded and smiled before completing his instructions to Nosgood. "We will be flying above, assisting Excelsior at the top of Klierra Peak." He turned to Arinna, who was still in the aircraft alongside Lokris. "And we will ensure his safety."

CHAPTER
FIFTY-THREE

"**W**elcome! We have been waiting for you."

Excelsior gasped when he approached the top of Klierra Peak. There he saw his fears fully realized. Hodera standing tall, Excelsior's sword held over her head, and a bright energy shooting into the sky. The energy acted like a tractor beam for the orb holding the lifeforce of Tornatrax, and it penetrated the stratosphere of Denab IV. Beside Hodera was Jason, his arms and legs bound, his face pale with fear, and his eyes glistening. His mouth curled into a smile when he saw his nephew landing on the mountain. Standing next to Jason was Danaak, his arms folded across his chest, relaxed.

"You have come at such an opportune moment, Excelsior," Hodera said. She lowered the sword as the orb holding Tornatrax's lifeforce was now able to descend on its own. "You have arrived in time to see your future end. This atmosphere will continue to shift, just as you caused it. The Denarians you cared so much for will die quicker, and the God you thought could be contained will be free once again." She pointed toward the trembling Jason. "And the last thing you will see before you perish once and for all is the face of your loved one, smiling with satisfaction as he plunges your own sword into your chest."

A fierce wind blew as Tornatrax's imprisoned lifeforce continued its descent from space. The thick clouds announcing its arrival spread apart, creating a small, perfect hole in the sky. The orb was now fully visible for all to see.

"Excelsior!" boomed the disembodied voice from within the orb.

"Tornatrax!" Excelsior said.

Suddenly, a series of images flooded the mind of Denab IV's savior mind. He saw himself standing over the defeated Tornatrax in human form, his sword held high over his head, and finally lowering it. He saw various elements of Denab IV melding together and becoming the shape of a clear orb. He saw his sword embedded in Tornatrax's gut as the lifeforce of his enemy was sucked from his possessed body and into the sword, then thrust into the orb. He watched the orb fill with a dark mist pushing against its new prison. Excelsior pulled the sword out from the orb, and the hole immediately healed. Finally, Excelsior saw himself standing in front of the Leap of Faith, commanding four simple coordinates into the console: 0-0-0-0. Deep space. As the inter-planetary doorway opened, Excelsior threw the orb with the imprisoned lifeforce of Tornatrax through it.

"I see you now remember me," Tornatrax said. "The voice applauding you for creating a planet of perfection.

The feeling of pride within you. The same feeling you suppressed and expunged from yourself."

As Excelsior listened to Tornatrax, another memory flashed into his mind. A much more recent memory, one of Arinna's body floating away in ash, of Denab IV in ruins, of a dying Acerus pointing his finger at him and saying, "You did this." He shook the frozen images of his dreams away but couldn't lose the condemning voice of his other half.

"All you had to do was bring your sword down and end my life on this planet," he said. "You would have won, and your influence would have been felt by every living creature. You would have successfully avoided having to stand here, watching your loved one become my new avatar."

"I can't change the past, Tornatrax! And I can't wipe away the mistakes made by Valertus or myself. But I can stop you right now." He unsheathed the dagger Zorribis gave him.

"My Lord, this child bores me," Hodera said. "Are you sure you do not wish for me to kill him?"

"You may wound him," Tornatrax conceded. "I look forward to hearing his screams."

The orb now floated ten feet above Hodera's head. "I look forward to it as well," she added with a smile.

But as Excelsior crouched into a fighting position, Hodera remained still, as relaxed as Danaak. The wind died down, and Excelsior's ears were filled with the sound of chattering and hissing. He glanced over the edge of the mountain, and his eyes widened as he saw a swarm of Krunation soldiers scaling the rocks, stepping on top of each other, racing to reach the top. They looked up and let out a collective shriek of anger, then increased their speed up Klierra Peak.

Excelsior's eyes flicked back to Hodera, who wore an expression of smug contentment. "You should be pleased to meet my new army," Hodera said. "After all, with all you have done to this planet, you and I are both their parents."

"I thought you would have wanted to finish me yourself," Excelsior replied. "Or did you actually learn something from Nocterar?"

Hodera let out a laugh. "Nocterar? You believe your current situation compares to how you fared against Nocterar?"

"Well, he did have the guts to face me one-on-one, so I guess not."

"Trust me when I say, Excelsior, you do not need to concern yourself with me."

The hissing grew louder as the Krunations grew closer. Three of them reached the top and were pushing themselves over, baring their teeth, and roaring at Excelsior. He gulped when he saw the Krunations reaching for him. After Zorribis and Niterra's Bonding Ceremony, when they were attacked by Krunation soldiers which had a history of dealing with Denarians, Excelsior showed mercy. But these... these monsters, they knew nothing in their short lives except to do Hodera's bidding without question. Her bidding was the total extinction of the Denarian race, and he knew they wouldn't stop until she was satisfied.

Excelsior saw one of Hodera's minions reaching the very top, and so he kicked it in its teeth. It tumbled down the mountain, taking other Krunations with him.

The minions behind it climbed faster, and as they reached the top, Excelsior swung his dagger in all directions. He struck some and pushed them off the mountain, while others ducked out of range and connected with his body with their fists and claws.

"Get them, Excelsior!" Jason exclaimed.

Excelsior tried to will himself to flight to escape the brutal blows, but when the first image came to mind, he was punched from behind by one of Hodera's children. He dropped to one knee and another soldier pushed him down on his back, roaring with delight. Excelsior caught the attacking Krunation in the chest with his foot, then flipped him over his head. The soldier cried out as it fell all the way to the ground, but there was no time to celebrate the small victory as Excelsior pushed himself back to his feet. The hissing and high-pitched roaring seemed like it was coming from everywhere, as more of Hodera's inhuman army continued climbing to the top.

"You have our permission to wound him, children!" Hodera shouted over the melee.

Excelsior kept circling, continuing to swing his dagger at every Krunation in range. Finally, one of them struck him on his chin, knocking his head up, and pulled his helmet off. Excelsior turned as the Krunation threw the helmet over his shoulder. It dropped down the mountain and faded away from view. Another soldier struck his wrist, knocking the blade out of his hand. The Krunation picked the knife off the rocky floor and held the point up to Excelsior's neck.

"No," Hodera commanded. "I said, 'Wound him.' Do not kill him."

The Krunation looked at the blade in confusion, then at Excelsior—who was now imprisoned by two other soldiers, his arms clamped behind his back—and smiled as he slammed the blade into Excelsior's shoulder.

"No!" Jason cried out, squirming as much as possible, trying to pull himself free from the bonds. Danaak stayed still, his arms folded across his chest.

The chaos on top of the mountain died down, and the victorious Krunations turned their attention to the floating orb concluding its descent. "Do you see, my Lord?" Hodera asked Tornatrax. "Do you see your defeated opponent, waiting to be freed from this life?"

"I see him, my child," Tornatrax's voice boomed. "And the time has come for me to look on him with new eyes."

Hodera held up Excelsior's sword. "I could not agree more." She slammed the sword deep into the center of the orb. The energy within the transparent prison began to glow a deep red, and it swirled around the steel within.

"And now," Tornatrax commanded. "Our subject."

With a smirk aimed at Excelsior, Hodera turned to Danaak. "Place his wrists around the sword's cross guard."

For a long moment, Danaak didn't move.

"Did you not hear what I said?" Hodera asked. "Your god demands action from you!"

"You demand action from me," Danaak calmly replied. "You are not my god."

Suddenly, Danaak dropped to one knee and clutched his head. The voice of Tornatrax rang from the orb for all to hear. "You forget your place, Danaak! A lesson will have to be taught to you!" Danaak's screaming was almost loud enough to eclipse the roars from Hodera's minions, and it continued on for another fifteen seconds before he finally collapsed at Jason's feet.

"What a wonderful sight, my Lord!" Hodera exclaimed. She walked over to Jason, grabbed him by his wrist bonds, and led him to the sword protruding from the orb. She then hung Jason by his wrist bonds over the cross guard as ordered, and put an exclamation point on her actions by giving the unconscious Danaak a kick in his ribs.

"Matty!" Jason cried out. "Help me."

Excelsior struggled once again to break free, but the Krunations outnumbered him, and they used their advantage to keep him in place. "Get away from him!" he shouted.

Both Excelsior and Jason watched as the energy within the orb began to grow and envelop the sword's blade. The Krunations holding Excelsior reacted to the energy, crying out in triumph.

Hodera's voice rose above the screaming. "It will not be long now. Soon, the power of Tornatrax will be reunited with his lifeforce, and then nothing will stop him from being reborn through your loved one!" She pointed toward Excelsior like he was her own personal trophy, standing straight and tall like a dictator, her arms outstretched to bask in her glory.

Excelsior averted his eyes from Hodera's triumph, choosing instead to see Danaak still breathing while lying face down on the stone floor, but it was pointless. The moment was approaching. He could sense it, and he knew she could, too.

But over the shrieks and cries of the Krunations around him, Excelsior heard a much more human-sounding voice. He couldn't see where the voice was coming from, but he grinned when he heard Zorribis cry out, "I think not, Hodera!"

Hodera's smile faded, and she dodged as a blast of energy struck several Krunation soldiers at once. They cried out and quickly dissolved into ash, and Excelsior realized his right arm was now free. He reached for his left shoulder and yanked the blade from it, clenching his teeth in pain. While the other Krunations focused on this new enemy, he pulled himself away from their grasp. Staying down to ensure he wouldn't get hit by a stray blast, Excelsior looked past the Krunations, and what he saw truly lightened his heart.

Connoram was riding on top of a Libeli, with Zorribis sitting behind him and a younger Krunation—one who was definitely not one of Hodera's mindless minions—in the back. In the young Krunation's hands was a weapon the size of a small bazooka. Another blast of energy shot from the weapon, striking down more Krunation soldiers. Screams echoed through the night as they burned to ash.

"Matty!" Zorribis said.

Excelsior stood up and smiled. "And I thought I had a flair for the dramatics. Are you okay being up here?"

Zorribis nodded, his forehead wrinkled and his hands held tight to the Libeli. "As long as we do not stay up here long! Charak has something we believe is yours!"

The young Krunation held up Excelsior's helmet. "Did you drop this?"

"Thanks," Excelsior said.

Charak tossed the helmet to him, and once it was caught, he aimed his weapon toward the encroaching enemy soldiers. The blast disintegrated another batch of Hodera's monsters.

"No!" Hodera cried. "My children, surround the subject."

The surviving Krunation soldiers quickly positioned themselves around Jason, who was struggling to pull himself free from the sword and Tornatrax's orb. Hodera kept herself safely insulated within her squadron like the queen on a chessboard, and some of her soldiers added a couple additional inches to their height by stepping on the unconscious Danaak.

"Don't fire!" Excelsior ordered Charak. "You might hit Jason." He tightened his grip on his blood-stained dagger and charged the Krunations. "I'll deal with them!"

"We will assist with the rest," Connoram said, positioning the Libeli farther away from Klierra Peak.

Excelsior ran his blade through one Krunation after another, then stopped to look across the mountain. To his delight, he saw Charak firing his blaster at Krunations still attempting to scale the mountain. Connoram continued shifting the Libeli's position around the mountain so no direction was safe for them to ascend. After several of the deadly blasts, Excelsior noticed those enemies still on the mountain climbed down, and the ones on the ground dealt with the counterattack led by Nosgood.

"Go get 'em, guys," Excelsior said, turning his attention back to the Krunations guarding Jason. One after another, they fell to his blade, until he saw Hodera crouching down. She launched herself at him, knocking him down and pinning his arms to the rocky surface. "No!" she yelled with a renewed desperation. "It is my destiny to see this through. You cannot stop it. You will. Not. Stop. It."

She plunged her finger into the wound on Excelsior's shoulder, and he screamed in agony. He could hear both Connoram and Zorribis calling out to Charak to hold his fire.

"Yes," she said, grinning. "Your screams will be heard throughout this land very soon. It will be the last anyone on Denab IV, anyone in the universe, will hear of the great—" Her fiery gaze left his face, focusing on her left arm. Excelsior followed her eyes and saw the scaly skin on flaking away. She pushed her arm into Excelsior's face. "This is what you have done to all of us. And when you are expelled into oblivion, this shall be your legacy."

"I can feel it," called Tornatrax. Hodera and Excelsior glanced toward the orb and saw the energy within was growing, thanks to Excelsior's sword pumping its energy back into its rightful carrier. "I can feel myself growing stronger. It will not be long now before I am free. Before I am reborn."

Among the piles of ash scattered along the top of Klierra Peak, Danaak began to stir.

CHAPTER
FIFTY-FOUR

"**D**anaak!"

The older male voice caused Danaak to look up and push himself off the ground. He looked to his left and saw Hodera pinning Excelsior down on the stone surface. He looked to his right and saw three figures on the back of a winged creature powerful enough to reach all the way up.

Was that a Libeli? Aren't they extinct?

Danaak's eyes widened when the creature levitated closer to the mountain, and he saw two of the three riders had scales with faded horizontal black stripes.

"Father?" he asked out loud. "I was told you perished during an attack led by Nocterar."

Connoram shook his head. "A lie, my son! And not the last spread about me!"

"What do you mean?"

"Hodera destroyed the Matera while labeling me a traitor to our race! Our species has become endangered because of her. She wants us all as mindless beasts bowing to her command! And if Tornatrax is reborn through that innocent man, nothing can stop her from making this happen."

"He lies, Danaak!" Tornatrax snarled, and the sound of his voice pierced Danaak's skull once again. He placed his hands over his ears and squeezed his eyes shut. "You have secured your legacy as a true Krunation with your actions today. And when I am reborn, you will be the first to be released from this planet. You will no longer feel pain such as this. You remember what I promised you. What I promised your son."

"He is telling the truth, Father!"

Danaak forced his eyes open, and his mouth dropped open. He shook the pain from Tornatrax away. "Charak?"

Charak nodded and yelled out, "It has been too long, Father. Not since my mother was killed."

Danaak gritted his teeth and glanced at Denab IV's savior, lying on his back and struggling to catch his breath. "She was taken from me by Excelsior."

"No!" Charak said. "No, Excelsior was not there. I saw her die. It was by the hands of a Krunation soldier. Once blame was given to Excelsior, I could never give the blame to those deserving of it."

"What are you talking about?" Danaak asked.

Charak pointed past Danaak. "Hodera," he accused. "She gave the order!"

Hodera lifted her head and looked into Danaak's eyes with satisfaction while keeping Excelsior pinned down. "Now you know why your beloved left us."

Danaak's face twisted with rage. "You did it," he growled. "Why?"

"You should be thanking me, you ungrateful puppet," Hodera snapped, clenching her teeth. "Because of my interference, you became the greatest Krunation since Nocterar himself."

Connoram spoke again, his voice urgent. "Danaak, my son, I see you have left behind the tyrannical monster you once were. You can create a new legacy. Right now."

"No, Danaak," Tornatrax called out again, and Danaak's chest wound burned. His legs suddenly felt like they were fused to the mountain. "You will do nothing. You will wait."

"Do not wait, Danaak," Connoram demanded. "This planet depends on you!"

A bolt of powerful and destructive energy pulsed from the orb and flew straight toward the Libeli. Connoram grabbed the reigns of the creature and it lowered itself, barely dodging the blast. Charak gasped. A shard of energy had grazed his ear.

"Doing nothing is what must be done," Tornatrax declared.

Danaak turned toward his son caressing the wound Tornatrax delivered. "You said I would leave a perfect world for my son."

"I said this world would be as you envisioned it. Nothing more," Tornatrax corrected.

Danaak squeezed his eyes shut. After a moment, he felt the freedom in his limbs. "I will do what must be done, my Lord," he said with resignation in his voice.

"And you will be rewarded for doing so," Tornatrax answered.

Danaak nodded, looked into Charak's eyes and said, "Forgive me, my son." He turned his back on the Libeli, striding toward Hodera.

She glanced up and said with contempt in her voice, "I do not require help."

"I will not give it," he replied. And as he and Excelsior looked at each other, he added, "Not to the one who killed my beloved."

Danaak grabbed Hodera from behind, and with all his might, threw her into the barricade of Krunation soldiers. All of them fell as one, and Hodera's head smacked against the rocky surface.

Excelsior rolled to his feet, remaining in a defensive position, his hand still clutching the only weapon available.

Danaak ran to the orb soaking up the last of the power in Excelsior's sword, its energy within glowing brighter than ever.

"Danaak!" Tornatrax yelled with panic in his voice. "Stop!"

"Help me!" Jason yelled.

Before Danaak could take another step forward, his head was filled with more torturous pulses from Tornatrax. The pain was excruciating enough to make him drop to one knee, but this time, he continued to push forward.

"Hodera," Tornatrax commanded. "Hodera! Stop him! The transfer cannot be interrupted!"

Hodera's limbs trembled and thick blood oozed from her forehead. "What are you doing?" she asked Danaak while pushing herself to her feet.

"Hodera!" Tornatrax again commanded. "Destroy him!"

"With pleasure, my Lord." Hodera pushed herself to her feet and pointed at Danaak. "Soldiers! Destroy him for me!"

Suddenly, a series of blasts from the Libeli reduced the last group of soldiers on the top of Klierra Peak to nothing, followed by laughter from Charak and Zorribis.

Danaak unsheathed his sword, but Hodera grabbed his wrist and hissed, "Traitor!"

Excelsior pushed himself to his feet while favoring his injured left shoulder, and saw Hodera and Danaak were locked in a battle of their own. Hodera was prying Danaak's sword from his grasp, and the mental hold Tornatrax had on the revived Krunation was taking its toll.

Hodera pulled the sword away and held it up, prepared to give a killing strike. "I am only giving you what you wish, Danaak."

"Not like this," Danaak moaned through the pain. "I do not... wish to die... doing nothing."

"I hope you're ready," Excelsior said telepathically, and he could hear the ghosts of Klierra Peak stir and awaken. "You won't die doing nothing!" he yelled out loud.

Hodera turned around with the sword still held high. Excelsior's teeth were clenched and his left hand held his blade.

"And what do you intend to do?" Hodera asked, aiming the tip of her sword at the Denarian savior.

"This," Excelsior answered and slung his blade past Hodera. It landed at Danaak's feet, and he snatched it up.

Hodera looked over her shoulder at the Krunation now on his feet, holding the blade. "No!" she yelled. Danaak brought his arm up and swung down, smacking the tip of the small weapon against Jason's binds. They broke in two and Jason dropped to his knees.

"Traitor!" She held her sword high, about to cut Danaak in two, but Excelsior grasped her sword arm from behind, spun her around with his left hand, and pressed his right hand against Hodera's forehead.

"Now!" Excelsior reached out to the ghostly voices of Klierra Peak, and in an instant, they were directed from his head through his arm and hand, to Hodera's mind. She shrieked with pain as Excelsior yelled out over the weaponized voices, "Your children are waiting for you!"

With as much might as he could muster, Excelsior shifted his weight and pushed the Krunation general off Klierra Peak. She screamed as she fell, and Excelsior looked down to see her slamming her sword into the rock, stopping her fall halfway down the mountain. At least he'd bought himself, Danaak, and Jason enough time.

"Thank you," Excelsior said as a single tear rolled down his cheek and the screaming in his head finally ceased.

For a moment, all was quiet in Danaak's soul. He overcame the wiring of his god, withstood an attack by General Hodera, and freed Jason Peters from being possessed—and inevitably annihilated—by Tornatrax.

But this moment didn't last. All at once, the Krunation was wracked with the most excruciating pain imaginable as the voice of the Krunation god bellowed with rage.

"You traitorous piece of filth. You wish to be released from this life? You will never be released. You will remain here on this mountain for all eternity. The pain you feel now will be a happy memory compared to what you will feel until the end of time. And you will watch as the last of your family is exterminated."

Tears rolled down Danaak's scaly cheeks as he clutched his head and chest. His moaning fell to a whimper, and a scream was pulled from him. He looked up at Jason, who was standing still, watching everything unfold.

"Go!" he whispered, pointing toward the Libeli. He looked at Excelsior, tossed the dagger back to him, and cried out, "Get… him… off this mountain" as his body started shaking uncontrollably.

The Krunation looked up at the Libeli dodging pulses of energy coming from the orb, and saw Charak sitting in the back, his blaster rifle aimed right at him. Danaak straightened, his arms held at his sides, and pushed through the pain long enough to shout to his son, "Please!"

Charak nodded. "I forgive you, Father."

The blast from Charak's weapon struck Danaak directly in his gaping chest wound, and all the pain tearing through his body came to an end. His legs broke free from the rocky surface, and he looked to his son and whispered, "Thank you."

Danaak dropped off of the top of Klierra Peak and dissolved into ash before he could hit the ground.

CHAPTER FIFTY-FIVE

Excelsior trembled as he watched Danaak hold out his arms and beg his son Charak to end his suffering. The blast struck the Krunation in the chest, and as he fell off the top of Klierra Peak, his body was enveloped by the blast and turned into ash.

"Thank you!" Excelsior called out to Charak, sheathing the smaller blade into his belt.

Charak lowered his weapon. "We need to get you both off this mountain!"

"And hurry!" Zorribis said, doubling over with pain. "I can feel the altitude oppression."

"You just had to come, didn't you?" Excelsior yelled out with a smile.

"And miss your final victory over Tornatrax?" Zorribis yelled back, smiling while squeezing his mid-section.

A rumble emitted from the orb holding what was now a combination of Tornatrax's lifeforce and power. Excelsior ran up to the orb and clenched his teeth in pain from the shocks he received while grabbing the handle of his sword.

"Come on!" he yelled as the sword started to budge from its prison. A snakelike tentacle of energy shot out from the hole in the orb and nearly knocked Excelsior off-balance, but he held tight to the handle.

"Do you feel it within you both?" Tornatrax's voice said. But this time, the voice was softer, almost tempting. "Do you feel the lifeforce within you yearning for my touch? Yearning for the power only I can grant? Come to me, Jason Peters. Come to me, and you will have the greatness you always desired."

"Is that what you told Abrattus?" Excelsior yelled out, his hands on the handle of his sword. "Before you destroyed him?"

Another blast of electricity struck Excelsior in the chest, but he kept his hand on the sword and the momentum allowed him to pull it free.

"I got it!" he exclaimed, and his eyes went wide when he saw the orb had a hole in it, and the energy within caused Tornatrax's transparent prison to crack.

"Uh-oh," he said. "Jason, we gotta get you to the Libeli now!"

A burst of raw, concentrated electricity shot from the orb and Excelsior held out his sword to absorb the blast. Jason crouched behind his nephew, but the force began to push them back. Tornatrax's laugh boomed across the entire mountaintop.

"Jason!" Excelsior yelled over the continuous blast. "Touch the sword! You need to give me the gift back!"

"Are you sure I'm not gonna die if I do this?" Jason yelled back.

"No!" Excelsior answered. "No, I'm not sure! But it has to be done now!"

Jason placed his left hand on Excelsior's left shoulder, then reached out and squeezed the handle of the sword. A warm ethereal glow surrounded Jason's hand, traveled to the sword, and came to rest in Excelsior's hand.

"Whoa!" Excelsior exclaimed. A sudden shockwave burst from the sword, breaking the blast from Tornatrax.

For a moment, all was silent. The fiery red and yellow inside the orb faded to a dull gray. Excelsior looked over his shoulder and said, "It worked! How do you feel?"

Jason held his hands up to his face and smiled. "I feel... I feel fine. Did it work?"

"Oh, it worked!" Excelsior responded. "Do you feel any different?"

"No," Jason said. The cracked orb still hung in the air, but it looked like whatever life was inside it was extinguished. Both men breathed a sigh of relief.

"All that worrying," Jason observed. "Kinda anti-climactic, don't you think?"

Before Excelsior could answer, the dark gray force inside the orb erupted once again to a deeper red and brighter yellow, swelling and pushing against its confines.

"No!" Excelsior said. "No, it's not anti-climactic! Now, get on the Libeli! They need to get to the surface!"

"What about you?" Jason asked.

Another several cracks formed in the orb and another blast fired toward Excelsior. He held up his sword again to shield himself. "I'll be busy!"

"I'm not going without you!" Jason yelled out.

"There's no room for me! I'll meet you down there! Now, go! I'll cover you!"

Jason tapped Excelsior one more time on the shoulder and yelled out, "I'm very proud of you!" He ran to the Libeli and leapt on, landing in an open spot between Zorribis and Charak.

"Go!" Excelsior yelled, and he looked over his shoulder. The Libeli carrying two Krunations, one Denarian, and one human spread its wings and pushed away from Klierra Peak. The orb fired another quick burst of energy, which grazed the creature's wing. It let out a cry of pain.

"We must land now!" Connoram yelled out while trying to keep the Libeli stable despite its wound. Excelsior kept looking back and forth while holding out his sword to absorb as much of Tornatrax's destructive energy as possible.

"You can never get away, Excelsior," Tornatrax bellowed as the ball of energy continued to expand and the orb continued to crack. It would not be long before the full ferocity of Tornatrax was unleashed on Denab IV, unlimited by a host of flesh and blood. "This rock you call your home shall know nothing but darkness for the rest of eternity!"

"Never!" Excelsior yelled out and he swung his sword as hard as he could at the advancing energy.

"You cannot save your people," Tornatrax taunted. "No matter how hard you try, you can never reverse the damnation you have brought to this planet."

The energy from the orb ceased, and Excelsior looked over his shoulder to see the Libeli banking left and passing the mountain to begin its descent. "Good," he said as they flew out of sight. "Nobody can stop this."

Tornatrax's voice grew louder. "No, nobody can stop this! Once again, Excelsior, you could have finished me. Instead, you allowed my power to reunite with my lifeforce, and you have condemned your planet and all living on it to rot in darkness."

But then another voice filled his head, the calming voice of Elder Klierra as though she were whispering in his ear. "I am with you, Excelsior. I will always be with you."

Excelsior took a deep breath and tightened his grip on his sword. "I can do this," he said to himself.

"You can do nothing but watch as your failure is repeated," Tornatrax declared, and the mountain under his feet began to shake as the thunder above rolled.

"Repeated," Excelsior whispered.

He reached toward his belt and grabbed the dagger Zorribis gave him, then looked at the engraved hieroglyphics on the blade spelling out, "Never Again."

"Never again," Excelsior said, slamming the blade of his sword down into the mountain.

"Never again," he repeated, narrowing his eyes at the growing energy within the orb. He held up the blade.

"Never again."

He repositioned the blade, extending his arms out with both hands gripping the handle.

"Never again."

And plunged the blade into his own chest.

Pain lashed Excelsior, paralyzing him with the dagger sticking out of his chest, his hands trembling, and his legs locked in position. His mouth hung open, but not a single sound came from his lips. His eyes were wide, but he couldn't see a thing. For a long moment, Denab IV's savior heard none of the rumbling of thunder, the energy emitting from the orb, or the cry of the Libeli fading to a whisper in the distance.

Excelsior felt his extremities once more. His legs. His arms. His hands. His hands still holding the dagger. Glancing down, he squeezed the handle and pulled it from his chest. His hands felt so suddenly weak that the dagger fell and bounced off the surface of the mountaintop, falling down Klierra Peak. Excelsior grabbed the sword in front of him, screaming out in pain as he freed it from the mountain. He stumbled toward Tornatrax, the tip of the sword aimed right at his mortal enemy, and slammed the blade back into the hole in the orb.

"You think you can stop me by merely filling a hole?" Tornatrax bellowed.

"No…" Excelsior struggled to say, keeping the sword in place. But nothing happened. Did he make the wrong move? Did his actions once again condemn everyone on Denab IV to an early death?

Finally, Excelsior saw the blade start to glow, and with it, he felt a sensation very familiar to him, but new to Matthew Peters.

He felt his lifeforce leaving him.

Excelsior's legs buckled, his shoulders sagged, his head felt heavy on his neck, and his instinct was to let go of the sword. But he needed to hold on. With everything left in him, Excelsior tightened his grip on the handle and smiled when he saw the glowing white energy travel from the sword and into the orb itself. His mind also reached out to one specific Denarian waiting for him on the ground below. "I may have to postpone our date."

"What are you doing?" Tornatrax's voice lost its arrogance. Instead, there was concern. Excelsior even heard panic. And pain.

Excelsior was confident everyone else on Denab IV heard the cry of pain. And when he saw the deep red energy within the orb glow a warm yellow and white, he smiled.

From the cracks in the orb, white bolts of energy shot out. But instead of threatening to strike down anyone or anything in their path, they shot upward, ripping through the dark clouds hanging low in the sky.

"No!" Tornatrax screamed. "What are you doing?"

Excelsior clenched his teeth. Hold on, he told himself. Keep holding on. His weakening body trembled as he rasped to Tornatrax, "Let's.... find out.... together."

As the last bit of his lifeforce emptied from the body of Matthew Peters into the sword held by gods on Denab IV and kings on Earth, Excelsior looked to the sky and saw a bolt of pure white lightning slicing through the clouds and heading right toward them.

He shut his eyes.

He let go.

CHAPTER FIFTY-SIX

"**W**hat is happening?"

While the battle raged on top of Klierra Peak, Nosgood and his renewed Denarian forces led one on the ground. He and Elders Quinterus and Tricerus left Acerus's home not long after his death, and followed Lokris's instructions to come to Klierra Peak. They arrived in time to see Hodera's army either scaling the mountain or welcoming Denarians with another battle fierce enough to rival Excelsior vs. Nocterar.

But this time, Nosgood's forces were better prepared and fought her army to a stalemate with limited casualties. It stopped, however, when Arinna's panicked voice rang through the battlefield. She pointed up and the equally numbered Denarian and Krunation armies stopped fighting and turned their attention toward Klierra Peak.

For several minutes, they all stood still, their arms dropped at their sides, not a single word uttered. Not a cheer, not a gasp, just silence, except for the crackling heard at the very top of the mountain.

But then, as Lokris stood beside Arinna, she squeezed her eyes shut and whispered, "Never again. Never again." Her eyes snapped open. "We must get to safety, quickly."

"Why?" Arinna asked, fear rising in her voice.

"Please trust me," Lokris answered.

A buzz made its way through the crowd, which went from silence to concern to panic as two different energy sources above the mountaintop clashed, with one enveloping the other. They heard the cry of pain from Tornatrax. Then they saw the white and yellow bolts shooting into the sky. Finally, they saw the one white blast come back down from the clouds, striking the center of the orb containing the lifeforce and power of Tornatrax, causing it to detonate. The blast shook the ground beneath everyone's feet and decimated the top of Klierra Peak. Pieces of rock raining down on the Denarians and Krunations alike were no larger than stones that fit in the palm of someone's hand. Other larger pieces, thankfully, didn't injure anyone. Everyone fled from the debris, but Arinna kept her eyes on the sky, hoping to see Excelsior descending from the mountain. But there was nothing there, and no trace of any remains either. No uniform, no helmet, Valertus forbid a body part, nothing.

"What happened?!" Arinna asked.

Lokris looked at Arinna with tears in her eyes. "He sent a message for you," she said.

"Excelsior? Matthew?"

Lokris nodded. "He said, 'I may have to postpone our date.'"

Arinna's knees weakened as she looked back up at the sky. "No," she whispered while shaking her head. "No!"

Her anguish was interrupted by the cawing of the Libeli. Arinna wiped her eyes, looked up, and saw its wing was singed. It stumbled when it touched the ground, but it was alive, and so were Connoram, Zorribis, Charak, and Jason. Arinna and Lokris ran to them while the majestic creature crouched down and folded its legs inward, allowing its passengers to dismount.

Connoram pressed his hands, then his forehead, against the side of the Libeli's head. "Shhh," he whispered. "Rest, my friend. You have done well, and we will mend your wound." The Libeli rested its large head against Connoram's shoulder, and Connoram wrapped his arms around its neck.

Arinna approached Zorribis, who asked, "Where is Niterra?"

"Watching over Elders Quinterus and Tricerus," she answered.

"Help us with Jason, please," he instructed, and both Arinna and Lokris took the shoulders of the trembling and weeping Jason and set him down on the ground.

"Mmm....Mmmmatthew," was all Jason could say. Tears poured down his face, his mouth hung open, and his eyes were squeezed shut. He knelt on the ground, his hand pressed against his eyes.

Arinna looked back and forth between Jason and Zorribis. "What happened?" she asked. "Where is Matthew?"

"We do not know," Zorribis said. "The last we saw him, he was still on top of the mountain."

"You did not see him flying away?" Arinna grabbed Zorribis's shoulders.

"There was.... there was nothing left. No sign of him at all." Tears started swelling in Zorribis's eyes. He looked up at the mountain, now resembling a narrow volcano, and opened his mouth to speak again. Nothing came out.

Arinna turned to Lokris, who kept her eyes shut. "Please tell me you can find him."

Lokris opened her eyes, which were heavy with emotion, and shook her head. "Nothing. He is gone."

After a few moments of silence, tears slid down Arinna's face once again. She collapsed next to Jason, put her face in her hands, and began to weep.

"Zorribis!"

Niterra ran up to her lifemate, with Nosgood and Elders Tricerus and Quinterus behind her, and hugged him tight. She asked, "Where is Excelsior?" And Arinna could only continue weeping as an answer.

Lokris placed a nurturing hand on Arinna's shoulder and pointed to the sky that was getting brighter. "Look, Arinna!" she said. "The stars."

The three remaining Elders looked up as one, and Tricerus said, "He did it. The tether between the two worlds has been severed. Excelsior's actions have cured our world of the disease that sickened it. Denab IV will be restored as it should be."

Arinna gazed up and gasped. For the first time since she returned to Denab IV from her journeys as a planetary ambassador, she was finally seeing the stars the way she remembered them. And they were bright and beautiful, bringing a smile to the sea of sad faces standing at the bottom of the mountain.

"He promised me," Arinna said, the words getting caught in her throat as she spoke. "He promised... he would... bring the stars back." And then the tears stole her voice again. She wanted this to be a nightmare, but she knew in her heart everything around her was real, and there was nothing she could do about it.

Matthew–her friend, maybe even a lover if they had the time–was gone.

Quinterus placed a hand on Arinna's other shoulder and smiled at Lokris, nodding. "Truly this young man was worthy."

The Elder's calm tone was nauseating to Arinna. She remembered the aching Matthew felt as he tried to correct his mistake, to right Denab IV's atmosphere. He proved himself worthy time and time again in the couple of days she knew him, and yet here was this old man provoking the Edenarian villagers to blame Matthew for all of Denab IV's troubles, not even attempting to make his mission a little less torturous.

Quinterus and Tricerus. Both of them. She knew she would forgive them both in time, but at this moment, she wanted nothing to do with either of them.

"He always was," Zorribis said as he approached the Elders, Niterra walking beside him and holding his hand. "A shame it took you this long to see it for yourself."

Arinna nodded, letting him know she agreed with everything he said, even though she didn't have it in her to say it right now.

Lokris held up her hand. "Now is not the time, Zorribis."

"No," Tricerus interjected. "No, it is. It is the time to admit we were wrong about Matthew Peters and his intentions for Denab IV. Perhaps even our potential for peace."

"And it is up to all of us to ensure this potential is realized," Connoram said, stepping away from the Libeli.

Quinterus and Tricerus took one step back as Connoram approached them, Hodera's surviving soldiers behind him. Several of Nosgood's soldiers held up their weapons.

"Krunations!" Malitus yelled, his blaster rifle charged and pointed at Connoram's head, his eyes as red as ever. Branerik stood behind him, as always, but he kept his rifle up, not aiming at anyone.

"No, please," Connoram shouted, holding up his arms.

"Do not fire," Nosgood ordered his soldiers.

For a long moment, residual tension hung in the air between the two species, but one by one, the Denarians lowered their blasters.

"Do you see what happened?" Connoram asked the Elders. "Or shall I say, what did not happen?"

"No one fired," Tricerus confirmed.

Charak made his way to his Armfather. "No one fired because Hodera's soldiers never attacked. These Krunations are alive to do the bidding of Tornatrax, and Tornatrax is gone."

"Then what becomes of them now?" Tricerus asked.

"We teach them," Connoram replied. "We train them as Acerus would want them, to give them the ability to connect with this planet in a way no one in our species ever could."

"And you can do that?" Quinterus asked, as he joined the old Krunation.

"I can teach Charak," Connoram answered, motioning to Danaak's son beside him. "He can train them to defend themselves against any possible threat while I teach him what Sestera taught me. Once he establishes his connection with Denab IV, then he can work with them. The only way we can stop this from happening again and maintain Excelsior's influence is through education. Tornatrax sought to keep his subjects as nothing more than obedient. If it were not for the mercy that a Denarian Elder showed me, that objective would stay the same."

The remaining Elders all looked at each other and nodded in agreement.

"But what about Acerus?" Malitus interjected. "What about justice for his death? It was Connoram's soldier that--"

"Tarrax was not my soldier," Connoram said. "Hodera compromised him and won his obedience."

"Malitus, stand down!" Quinterus ordered. "I was wrong. We were all wrong. About Connoram. About Excelsior. About Zorribis." He looked up at the smoldering top of Klierra Peak. "About everything."

Malitus slowly lowered his rifle and the red in his eyes faded away.

"Admitting such is a crucial first step forward," Connoram said. "I see the potential for a bright future for Denab IV."

"Just as Matthew wanted," Arinna said. "He deserves to see this become a reality."

"It would be our honor to assist any way we can," Quinterus said, extending his hand in friendship.

"It would be my honor to accept that assistance," Connoram said as he clasped Quinterus's wrist, and the Elder responded in kind. Connoram glanced at Malitus and nodded his head. Malitus nodded back and walked away, and Branerik nodded and followed his neighbor.

"And while Charak teaches them…" Connoram began, when suddenly, he blinked several times and lost his balance. Charak caught him before he fell to the ground. "Thank you, Charak," he said. He continued, "And while you teach these Krunations, I will be resting. The atmospheric shift has ended and the planet will restore itself, but it has taken its toll on all of us."

"The regeneration chambers should be operating again," Zorribis said. "You can rest there."

Connoram nodded. "Thank you," he said, shaking the younger Denarian's hand.

"You will not have this kind of view of the stars since the chambers are underground, but—"

"I am aware of how the chambers work."

"Of course," Zorribis said, then motioned to the Krunations standing motionless next to the Denarians. "When do we start with them?"

"Immediately," Connoram said. "Time may have slowed down again, but we cannot."

Connoram and Charak both bowed in respect before the Elders, then walked to the Libeli. Zorribis took Niterra's hand, and they made their way to their repaired aircraft. As they mounted their respective means of transportation, Lokris announced to everyone still standing with a comforting hand on Arinna's shoulder. "Let this be the first step toward a new age. The sacrifice of Matthew Peters will not be in vain. The lifeforces of Excelsior and Tornatrax have joined once again, and the stars have shown us the true victor in their eternal conflict."

The Libeli squawked, and Charak took its reins. Connoram climbed aboard as well, and he said to Zorribis, "You should come with us. We need to track down Hodera."

"Can Niterra come as well?" Zorribis asked.

"Hodera will be brought to justice," Connoram said. "It will be difficult for that to happen if there is not a seat for her."

"Go get her," Niterra said, giving Zorribis an approving kiss on the cheek. He climbed aboard the Libeli, and with one more caw, the Denarian and two Krunations flew off toward the horizon, Hodera's soldiers turning and following them.

Arinna wiped her eyes, helped up a still grieving Jason, and stood next to Lokris with Matthew's uncle clutching on to her. Arinna's legs were still shaking as much as Jason's, and it was difficult to hold back her tears, but her vision was clear enough to see the thick, dark clouds above evaporating into the air.

CHAPTER FIFTY-SEVEN

"**A**rmfather." Charak pointed in the distance, keeping the Libeli close enough to the ground so it could use its talons to run instead of fly. The Krunations following were walking fast enough to keep up.

Zorribis followed Charak's finger, and his teeth clenched when he saw a very familiar female Krunation walking by herself, a sword in her hand. "She is still alive," he said with utter contempt, and he reached for his blaster pistol on his holster.

"No," Connoram told Zorribis. "Charak, stop here."

"Are you sure?" Charak asked as he cinched up on the Libeli to slow it down.

"Our new soldiers are not the only ones needing a lesson."

Charak nodded, and the Libeli came to a halt. Connoram stepped down and called out, "Hodera."

Slowly, the Krunation general turned around to face her rival. Hodera's outfit was torn, exposing one shoulder.

Blood dripped down her now deep red lips. She looked exhausted. She looked defeated. But when she saw Connoram was standing in front of what remained of her loyal and obedient army, she broke into hysterical laughter.

Connoram cocked his head. "May I ask what you find so amusing?" he asked.

She stopped laughing and wiped the blood off her lips. "You brought my minions to me. You may as well have handed me the weapon intended to end your life."

"Then command them to end my life," Connoram said, his arms outstretched. "I am unarmed. I will not stop you. And neither will Charak. And neither will the Denarians."

Hodera glanced at Charak, who nodded his head. She took a deep breath and pointed to Connoram. "You have been a worthy adversary." She then commanded to the soldiers standing by, "Destroy him, my children. Tear him apart."

The Krunations remained still. Hodera repeated, "Obey your master! Destroy Connoram this very moment."

Nothing.

"Why do you not obey me?" Hodera growled, her hands clenched into fists.

"The gift Tornatrax gave you is no more," Connoram answered for them. "They are no longer to be led around for your amusement. Their urge to kill has been removed, and in its place will be knowledge of their planet and the ability to choose their own destiny. I have chosen mine." He paused for a moment, narrowing his eyes. "You have chosen yours."

Hodera took a step back, holding out her arms. "So what do you intend to do now? Kill me?"

Connoram shook his head. "No. I cannot say the same for any other lifeform on this planet, nor any other planet in this known universe, but you can expect no retribution from me for your genocidal actions toward the Krunation race. However, you will not be welcomed in Nocteris because it is very likely our home is no more."

"What are you talking about?" Hodera asked.

"The Sancterrum tree and the throngar in my quarters were innocent lives. By caring for them as I did, I ensured our home would not be wiped clean by Excelsior's initial return. But you destroyed them both, leaving the Nocteris stronghold vulnerable to the blast which took Excelsior and Tornatrax. There is no place for you in this new era."

"This new era," Hodera said in a flippant tone of voice. She turned to walk away, but Connoram reached out and grabbed her wrist with his left hand, reached behind his back with his right hand, and pulled out a small handheld box with a button on top. He thrust it into Hodera's spine and pressed the button. She let out a whimpering cry and her body stiffened. Connoram pulled the box back and she dropped to the ground, limp but still living.

"Yes, this new era," Connoram continued, flipping Hodera on to her back. "This new era will include the Krunation species working with the Denarians to bring crimes against one or both species to justice. Your actions qualify for that."

Hatred filled Hodera's eyes. "You will remember this moment, Connoram. The moment when you had the opportunity to kill me, and you declined."

"Your time will come, Hodera," Connoram said.

"Oh, it will," Hodera said. "It will, indeed."

"But for now, Zorribis will take you into custody. We have room for you on the Libeli."

CHAPTER
FIFTY-EIGHT

"**H**e is awake."

At first, the feminine voice filling Sivtra's ears sounded like it came from several tronks away. But as he came back to his senses, the small Krunation realized the woman was right next to him.

He opened his eyes and saw a Denarian woman with short blonde hair smiling down at him. "Are you all right?"

"Wh.... who... are you?" Sivtra's voice was rough, his throat dry and raw.

"My name is Durrea," she said. "And we saw what you did to save the people of Axsella."

"What I did?"

A series of images flashed before Sivtra's eyes. He was at the console of a large transporter, jerking the controls at the last second and crashing it into the ocean.

He was boarding the transport with only one thing on his mind: cripple the Denarian military by crashing it into Axsella.

He was standing beside General Hodera. And she was feeding him specific instructions, to die. After everything he did, even after saving her from an assassination attempt, she was telling him to die for her.

Sivtra blinked his eyes several times and looked around. The room he was in was bare, the walls a clean white with no windows. Even the bed he was on didn't have any kind of blanket or sheet.

"Where am I?" Sivtra said.

"That is not important right now," Durrea said. "You are safe. Tornatrax is gone, and Excelsior has gone with him. Our planet has already begun restoring itself, and no matter which god's influence remains over Denab IV, we are working toward planetary harmony between Denarians and Krunations. You are welcome to stay and help us if you wish."

Sivtra took a moment to absorb all of this information, and without any hatred in his heart, he smiled at the Denarian woman.

"Yes. I would like that."

CHAPTER FIFTY-NINE

Arinna and Jason walked back to the Leap of Faith in silence. She asked for permission to send Jason back to Earth by herself so the two could share their thoughts about what happened on the top of Klierra Peak. What Matthew's sacrifice meant for the planet, even the universe. But instead, Jason kept muttering under his breath, "I can't believe it."

Arinna could only nod. She couldn't believe it either, but what could she say? By the time they reached and entered the Leap of Faith, she spent almost the entire trip trying to say something, anything, to comfort him. Considering she could barely bring any comfort to herself, she knew the search was futile.

As they passed through the doorway and walked to the control console, Jason at last had something else to say. "He saved my life."

"He saved all of our lives," Arinna replied, relieved she could finally say something of substance. "While we were on Earth, he spoke of how little confidence he had in his ability to reach the same level of greatness Semminex and

Valertus had before him, and yet tonight, he took himself so far beyond what his predecessors could do."

"That's Matty," Jason said with a nod and a ghostly smile. "He was like that with his comic strip back on Earth. He kept saying he would never be good enough to make it a success, but the quality was always there. I knew he had it in him to make it. And now—"

"And now Matthew became a success beyond any possible estimation."

"But..." Jason's eyes welled up with tears again. "But he won't be here to celebrate it."

Those words struck Arinna, and suddenly she realized what she wanted to say to him. And more importantly, to herself. "But he is here," she said. "With Tornatrax gone and the tether severed between Denab IV and Earth, the clouds and the haze over our atmosphere left with him. Nothing can block his view from above to look down upon us and ensure his wishes come to fruition. You may not know this, but before Matthew and I came to Earth, we were attacked by General Hodera and her soldiers. When we defeated them, he could have destroyed the retreating soldiers, but he did not. He believed there was potential for peace, and because of his wishes, the first steps have been made."

"Wow," Jason said.

Arinna's words continued to spill out, "While he may not be here in person to see all of this happen, I know we will be able to feel his presence each step we make."

"Sounds like a line in a movie I know," Jason said, then put on his best Dr. Leonard McCoy voice. "'He's really not dead, as long as we remember him.'"

"I like that message," Arinna said, smiling at Jason, then turning away to place her hand on the control orb on the console.

"You should take a trip to Earth sometime and stay over. We'll watch it, but we have to watch Part III right after it."

"Why?" Arinna asked. The screen above the console showed she was locked on to planet Earth. "What happens in Part III?"

"Well, not to spoil it, but in Part II, a major character sacrifices his life to save his crew. And in Part III, the crew risks their own lives to bring back their friend."

Arinna turned to face Jason again as the Leap of Faith doorway opened. "Yes, it sounds like something I would like to see. I am certain Matthew would enjoy it as well."

"Oh, yeah," he said with a laugh. "He must have watched those movies dozens of times when he was growing up." Jason felt the gravitational pull coming from the open inter-planetary doorway, and he looked over his shoulder at the deep space beckoning him. "I guess that's my ride," he said to Arinna.

"It is."

"When I get home, I got work to do on the series before we go into production. Gotta come up with a new name for the Lost Islands."

"Please give Becky my highest regards. And tell her–" The words caught in her throat. She took a deep breath. "Please tell her Matthew accomplished his mission. He is at peace."

Jason pulled Arinna close and wrapped his arms around her. She retuned the embrace and gave Matthew's uncle a kiss on his cheek.

"Thank you," Jason whispered in her ear. "For everything you've done for him."

"He did quite a bit for me," Arinna whispered back. Her tears dripped on Jason's shoulder before the two pulled away from each other.

Jason walked to the open doorway, but before he allowed himself to get sucked inside, he looked over his shoulder one more time. "Matthew told me something his father said years back. At the end of the day, no matter if you're rich or poor, everyone is looked at the same way: as an inspiration or a cautionary tale." He smiled at Arinna and said, "Both of you are an inspiration. Never forget that."

"None of us will."

Jason gave one last wave and took one more step toward the Leap of Faith. A gleaming white ball of energy surrounded his body, and it shot out toward the cosmos, escorting Jason home. The doorway slid shut, and Arinna shut down the console, soaking in the stillness of the Leap of Faith chamber. Everything was so quiet. No sudden battles. No Krunation surprise attacks. This would take some getting used to, she thought.

Arinna stepped out of the Leap of Faith chamber and smiled, optimism colliding with her grief. Was this chance for peace with the Krunations really going to be a reality? Could these races put away their animosity and walk into the future together? If so, then Matthew Peters could do what his predecessors Semminex and Valertus failed to accomplish and become the inspiration he always yearned to be.

And if he wouldn't be here to see it himself, she owed it to Matthew to see it for him.

EPILOGUE

In the beginning, there was only an idea. That idea became a reality. And then, it became the planet Denab IV. It wasn't perfect, but it was good, and it was worth fighting for, as were the people for which Excelsior laid down his life.

Night passed into day on the occupied half of Denab IV, and the Denarians and Krunations greeting the morning were rewarded with the neighboring stars twinkling above. They likely rejoiced, maybe praised Excelsior for making it happen, but on Klierra Peak, none of it was heard.

The top of the legendary mountain was seared off, and the residual heat was so intense, it resembled a volcano from Earth. The remnants of Tornatrax's prison had melted into nothing. The smoke from the heat rose into the sky overnight and continued throughout the day. It looked like it would go on forever.

At the very center of the surface, in pristine condition, was Excelsior's sword, the blade buried into the mountain.

The jewel on the handle's end was gleaming, blinking on and off with the rhythm of a heartbeat.

Lying beside the sword was the motionless body of Matthew Peters. His uniform was torn. His helmet was in pieces. A deep gash was on his shoulder, and an even larger wound was on his chest. His eyes were shut, and cuts and scrapes on his face and body complemented his wounds. He had gone through hell, but the expression on his face revealed Matthew was finally at peace. His mission to bring Excelsior home was complete.

If anyone were close enough to touch Matthew, he would feel ice cold. And they would hear the voice of Elder Klierra whispering to him, "You have done well. You have earned your rest. I will remain by your side. I will keep you safe." Those same words, playing over and over within his head. If anyone were close enough to hear it, they would leave knowing all was well on Denab IV.

But if they did walk away, they would miss the voice escaping Matthew's lips.

A voice that was not his own.

"Yesssssss."

To be concluded in

GREATER GLORY:
PART THREE OF THE EXCELSIOR JOURNEY

ACKNOWLEDGEMENTS

They say, no man is an island. And the journey to take "Excelsior" and its first sequel to publication is the ultimate example of this. I couldn't be more thankful for the support of the people listed below, so please allow me to introduce you to all of the people without whom, this book would not be where it is today:

George & Peggy Zur Heide
Wesley & Susan Sirois
George & Viola Sirois
Jeremy Rodden
George Nicolaidis
Kathy & Jimmy Morbit
Jason & Jackie McSheene
Dara K Marsh
Art Horowitz
George Hill
Helene, Henry, John & Annabelle Henkel
Collins Headley
Dave, Liz & Eleanor Havasi
Bill Hald

Steve Gustafson
Chris Ethridge
Mary Ellen & Marty Craig

And, of course, my team...

M.A. Phipps, my amazing cover designer
Jeff Collyer, my ever-patient publisher
JeriAnn Geller, my invaluable story editor and guide
    to Denab IV
Rebecca Jaycox, my awesome content editor

and

Matthew Henkel

Always my hero